MURDER IN THE TEMPLE

SOAR CHRONICES: BOOK ONE

By

MALORY

MALORY

TABLE OF CONTENTS

For Lu,

Arebella had to be based on someone

CHAPTER 1 - BROKEN LEGS AND BAD DEBTS

"Are you fucking kidding me?"

The Bailiff squinted down at the angry man lying on the bed. At least, he assumed the speaker was angry. Considering his line of business, Brona rarely had the opportunity to come across people in a good mood.

"Jana Lowe?" he asked, checking the name on his clipboard.

The man on the bed sat upright, hastily pulling on a bloodstained shirt over the top of an equally stained vest. "Mate, you know who I am. You were in here just last week. Remember? You took away half my furniture, all of my jewellery and most of my shoes."

Brona frowned, trying to recall the last time he'd been in this particularly rundown part of Soar. The problem was all these crappy places tended to look the same, and it was hardly like he was employed for his memory skills. Saying that, there was something vaguely familiar about the door he'd just put his foot through.

And the pissed-off man with all the bruises?

Yes, that did start the old neurons flaring.

Then, it all slotted into place. "Ha! You're the guy without a Class!"

***

Lowe stood, steadying himself against the wall as his head swam. He'd ended up burning all his mana away the night before, and, as always, there was a debt to be paid for such profligacy. Although, whether running dry in order to heal a sucking chest wound was really all that profligate was a question for another day. "That too. I'm also the guy you took twenty gold bars of footwear from to cover a debt of a bar of silver. What could you possibly be back for now?"

Brona raised his clipboard to his nose to better make out the writing. His lips moved as he deciphered it. "Different client this morning, Mr Lowe. This is 'Merk's Tailoring.' You failed to keep up payments on an HP Enhancing suit."

"Fuck's sake!" Lowe crossed to the far corner of his bedroom and picked up a bundle of ripped and damaged clothes. "You mean this shit?"

Brona shrugged. "I'm just here for five gold bars."

Low's face went white. "Five? For fuck's sake, man! It was two gold when new and didn't do as advertised. I should be suing that crook, Merk!"

Brona shrugged again. He tended to find that when you were his size, a casual shrug reminded people about the size of his shoulders. "And I'm sure my company would happily represent you should you file the appropriate paperwork. As you know, our motto is "Can't Pay, We'll Fuck You Up" and satisfaction is guaranteed.

Although, not usually to the people I end up calling on. Speaking of which, five gold bars, please."

Lowe threw the ruined suit back to the floor and put his hands on his hips.

He wasn't by any means a small man, but he doubted he really wanted to get into a fistfight with a Bailiff. Even a Level 14 one, such as Brona, would have access to Skills that would probably further ensure his day continued to be a shitty one. "Look, I don't have five gold bars."

Brona clicked his tongue sympathetically and looked around the room. Now that he thought about it, he did recall being here before. There hadn't been much to take that time either. "Look, I really don't want to have to hurt you again. Are you sure there's nothing you can offer?"

Lowe opened his inventory. To be honest, he had any number of odds and ends that he could probably put up as collateral, but if the Bailiff lacked the Skill to scan his personal storage space, he certainly wasn't going to offer any of them up.

Besides, he was damned if he was going to be held to ransom over some shitty protective equipment that had given up the ghost at the first sign of a swinging battleaxe.

He opened his mouth to share these ruminations with the Bailiff and then quickly closed it when the flat of Brona's hand slapped him on the cheek. The force of the blow took him off his feet and left him sprawled on his bed.

"Dude! What the fuck?"

Brona opened his hands in a 'what am I supposed to do?' gesture. "Standard operating procedure, Mr Lowe. However, on the plus side, I am pleased to say you now owe four and three-quarters bars of gold. Mr Merk is clear he will accept payment in the form of the brutalisation of your body, so we can continue on this path if you would prefer. By my calculation, two broken legs would clear the debt in its entirety."

Lowe stood back up again and shook the stars from his vision. "Can I remind you that I have no Class? You're basically demanding money with menaces from a guy who would struggle to hold his own against an asthmatic toddler."

"Yeah, I thought that last time. You're a Level 19, right? How did you make it that far without a Class?"

Lowe took a breath. "Would the story of the ruinous nature of my career to date be worth four and three-quarters bars of gold?"

Brona shook his head. "'Fraid not, mate."

"Fine." Lowe sat down on the floor and extended both his legs. "Have at it."

∗∗∗

The soft buzzing of the Sending Stone brought Lowe back to consciousness.

He'd mercifully passed out after the Bailiff had stamped down on his left leg. However, it seemed that was where his good luck had run out. It looked like the hit to his Health Points had been considerable, suggesting the breaks were unlikely to simply heal on their own. He must have been out for a good few hours, though, as there were now a good few drops of mana available to push towards the two fractures.

Lowe pulled a common Ring of Regeneration out of his inventory and slipped it onto the index finger of his right hand. By his reckoning, he had at least a sevenday before the next of his creditors sent the heavies in, so he could afford not to keep all his goodies hidden away for a bit.

The burst of Mana Regen was welcome, and the pounding headache receded for the first time in a few days. Of course, that then gave room for the searing agony of his splintered legs to take precedence.

So, it wasn't all sunlight uplands and frolicking unicorns.

One of the Skills he had been left with after his summary Classtration (was that the official term? Who knew and - more importantly right now - who cared?) was a reasonably uncommon ability to trade his Mana Pool for Health Points at a preferential rate.

Provided he had enough mana available, there were relatively few injuries Lowe was not able to eventually shake off. It was *Roll with the Punches* which had made him one of the more effective of Soar's Investigators. When you were ferreting around in the lives of the great and the good, it helped if you could tank the occasional punishment beating.

Unsurprisingly, this had meant he tended to get assigned the really high-risk, low-reward jobs. Which, of course, led with crushing inevitability to a reasonably spectacular fall from grace when he stepped on the wrong toes.

The buzzing of the Sending Stone was beginning to get on his nerves.

However, the fact it was this which was bothering him, rather than two broken legs, suggested he was feeling a bit better. He stopped filtering all his mana to his injuries and squirted some of it towards the communication device. "What?"

"Lowe?"

The voice of his ex-boss was not exactly at the top of his list of things to hear right now. "Sorry, you have the wrong stone. This is the Happy Egg Escort Service. We're up for a good yolking."

There was a pause during which Lowe imagined the wide-set eyes of Cenorth narrowing in frustration. It was an expression he'd seen often enough over the years. "Jana, I'm really not in the mood for you this morning."

"Oh, excuse me! I'm so sorry for bothering you. Imagine me phoning you up out of the blue and disturbing you on this fine day. What a colossal wankdoodle I am." Lowe pulled the stream of his mana out of the stone and directed it back to his legs. With a snap, both bones suddenly pulled themselves back into shape. He rotated his ankles, easing out some of the stiffness.

The stone started buzzing again.

Lowe ignored it. He had no interest in hearing what Commander Cenorth had to say.

It had been over a year since he had been put on 'gardening leave' from his job in Soar's Security Service, and he felt more than a trace of bitterness at the absence of contact from his previous colleagues.

He stood and made his way out of his bedroom and into the living space of his small apartment, straightening up the chaos as he went. To be fair to the Bailiff, it looked like he hadn't indulged in too much wanton destruction this time. There were a couple of tables tipped over and one or two cupboards ransacked, but nothing too terrible.

Although, if we were at home to Mr Glass Half-Empty, that was probably because anything worth nicking had been appropriated on one of the previous visits by debt collectors.

Soar was an expensive city to live in, particularly if you didn't have a patron god watching your back.

Lowe had been doing his best to make ends meet by acting as a sort of unlicensed private detective. But so far, all he had been able to do was annoy a particular element of the criminal underclass who took great delight in kicking every colour of shit out of him whenever he poked his nose into their business.

It had been a rough year.

A knock came at the door.

Considering it was hanging off its hinges, this suggested a level of courtesy not usually found in his latest visitors.

"Jana? I think your Sending Stone might be playing up."

Lowe moved to the entrance hall - all his pictures had gone, he noticed - and met the eyes of Cenorth.

The tall, thin Level 45 Sentinel of Justice had once been one of his closest friends. He wasn't sure he would have taken a *Fireball* for him. But he'd certainly have warned him one was on the way.

"It's working just fine, Commander. I have it set to filter out the arseholes. Sounds like it's firing on all cylinders."

"Look, I'm sure I'm the last person you want to see right now."

Lowe left the following silence hanging in the air.

His Ring of Regeneration was doing its business, and combined with *Roll with the Punches*, he started to feel a little more chipper. That was until, with a jolt, he remembered the ring had been a reward from Cenorth after the completion of a particularly challenging quest.

Never to be one not to cut off his nose to spite his face, he slipped the ring off and back into his storage.

"Jana, this isn't a social call."

"Imagine my shock and surprise. You being such a fixture around here and all."

Cenorth pressed onwards. "Have you got much on at the moment? I heard you went private?"

"And I heard you were a tosser. Funny the things you can pick up on the grapevine."

"Look, we can talk about what happened, but now's not the time. A case has come up that I think is right up your street. I've been permitted to ask if you will come and give it the once over. On a limited basis, of course."

Despite himself, Lowe felt his stomach swirl with interest. There were only so many kickings you could take from Hoodlums and Wannabe Gangsters before a change would be as good as a rest. "How limited?"

"Private consultation. I'll be your client. To smooth things out, you will receive a temporary reinstatement of your rank. And a good word will be put in when your case finally comes before a tribunal."

Which would be never, Lowe knew. There was no need for the powers that be to take anything further. Without a Class and with all his savings depleted, he'd be dead and gone in a few more months.

Sighing, he turned one of the upturned chairs upright and indicated that Cenorth should sit. "So, spill. What's the deal?"

"Excellent. Okay, so listen up. How much do you know about Gravalk?"

CHAPTER 2 – DEAD ON ARRIVAL

The eighth bell had just tolled when Aintra Weber had left his home in the Quarter of Ash and walked the half-league to the junction of Beldam and Caprice.

It was a walk he had taken for much of the last decade, a path steeped in his family's history. His parents and his grandparents had lived in the same house, their voices echoing through the corridors when they spoke, at length, about the quiet dignity of the area during their youth.

As he stepped around the detritus of the night's activities - and over a few revellers who hadn't quite had the HP to survive whatever mixture of drugs and alcohol they had thrown down their gullets - Aintra reflected that he was pretty glad none of his relatives were still alive to see what had become of the district they had so loved.

As far as Aintra could tell, his family had been proud when he had chosen to follow the family tradition and evolve into a Coal Stirrer.

Not that he'd been inundated with choices, of course.

Not many administrative options were available to you when you were disposed towards the element of fire. Paperwork was essentially the domain of those who frolicked in air or water, but he'd stuck at it, and his persistence had been rewarded. That had been just the beginning of his journey, and he was, if not eager (it didn't do to be too anticipatory in the Quarter of Ash), then at least content to see where it would all lead.

Every morning, he thanked his lucky stars that he'd been fortunate enough to attract Gravalk's warmth towards him and - of course - that on his first day he'd been directed to attach himself to a young, up-and-coming meteor who was destined to blaze an unlikely trail through the lower floors of the Temple.

That young firebrand had been Gianna d'Avec and she was now the High Priestess of Gravalk. As her secretary, he had made a decent living. Not good enough to escape his parent's home, to be sure. But when they'd died, having no other issue, he found himself a property owner in a part of the city described by those foul creatures who fell into the trade of Estate Agents as 'vibrant'.

As a gut wound.

Sure, a Level 32 Coal Stirrer was hardly going to set the world alight - a little fire-based humour there - but if he kept his head down and ground out those last eight levels, he'd have any number of possibilities open for him at his Level 40 threshold.

At least, that had been the plan.

But then, last night, the High Priestess called him to her chamber in the Temple and informed him that his service would not be required when she ascended from the third to the second floor of the Celestial Temple.

He had stood, stunned for a moment. He was sure he must have misheard.

But those blue eyes had stared, implacably, back at him. No, there had been no mistake. After ten years of diligent, capable service, he was being "let go".

"I am sure you understand, Aintra."

He hadn't and had said so.

"You couldn't honestly have thought you would join me on the Second Floor?"

He had. But there did not seem to be much point arguing.

There rarely was with the High Priestess.

She had gone on to explain that it had been explained to her that it would be beneath her dignity to have her major-domo be sub-Level 40. "I'm told there are standards, you understand? I did my best to plead your case. If I thought you had it in you to blitz those last eight levels, I'd be more than willing to boost you. But I think we both know how unlikely that prospect would be."

Aintra had thought that a little harsh. Sure, he had not kept up with his mistress's prolific pace of levelling over the past decade, but, then again, neither did his role in maintaining her diary and ensuring she was where she was supposed to be, open that many avenues to gather XP.

On the other hand, her habit of incinerating anyone who irritated her had given her any number of free levels.

It had never occurred to him that the growing gap between them would be a matter of shame for her. Or to Gravalk, who he presumed had made the final decision on his demotion. Heat blossomed in his cheeks as he walked, remembering how the interview had concluded.

"If you could ensure your notes are left in good order for your successor, I would appreciate it." And then she had turned from him as if dismissing him from her mind.

In a way, he imagined she had done just that. Gianna d'Avec was nothing if not relentlessly focused.

Aintra's usual route to the Celestial Temple was to cross Beldam and make use of the portal that stood by the Fountain of Youth. There were more convenient transportation hubs available to him, but the short walk from his house to this spot had been as much part of his routine as anything else these past few years.

He rested his hand on the lip of the portal, ignoring the queue that immediately started to build up behind him. It appeared that a large number of people were making their 'shamble of shame' back to their own, more salubrious, parts of Soar.

Eight levels until Level 40 was not insurmountable, of course.

There was no prospect of him reaching that standard before, if rumour was true, the High Priestess displaced Mdamic of Yolgorth on the Second Floor at the end of the season.

However, given time and focus, he would have been able to make that journey. Of course, he had not put any of his Progress Points into Skills which would lend themselves to the speedy gathering of XP. Coal Stirrers were, by their nature, somewhat passive folk. The Skills he did possess were focused on recall, writing and the manipulation of data.

It was not a skillset that would attract many recruiters to his door . . .

Neither, he had to acknowledge, was he likely to be much use in any of the Dungeons beneath the city. He hadn't been to those parts of the Lower City in years but was fairly sure Raiding Parties were not crying out for admin support.

He supposed he could always book a month-long place in a Level 20 Dungeon and just grind out the required XP that way, but he doubted he had that sort of single-minded dedication.

If he did, he wouldn't have become a Coal Stirrer in the first place.

"Will you fucking shit or get off the pot!" a voice came from behind him.

Aintra half-turned and saw a growing queue of hungover - and worse - people behind him.

"My apologies. Wool gathering."

"Gather it fucking somewhere else."

Quite. He triggered the portal.

***

The Third Floor of the Celestial Temple was deserted at this time of morning; its massive open space lit by the slowly rising sun.

The giant stained-glass windows in the reception areas bathed the floors in a kaleidoscope of light which, on a typical day, he found quite lovely. Today, he was struck by how gaudy it all was.

Oddly, there was a strange mistiness in the air as if something damp had been left in the laundry for too long.

He pushed out a soft breeze of hot air to remove the scent of mould and connected with all the locks to the various chambers that spanned off this central space.

Aintra had been very proud of the *Secret Keeper* Skill he had been gifted by Gravalk when he reached Level 30. It allowed him to add up to thirty different lock patterns to a template and then unlock them all with a thought.

He was unsure what use such a talent would be in the brave new world of his impending unemployment. Perhaps a life of crime beckoned? But, somehow, he did not quite see it.

He noted that Gianna's chamber was one of those that he had unlocked and frowned.

He could not remember the last time he had arrived in the building before her.

Of course, it was spectacularly unusual for a High Priestess to choose to reside in a place other than in the Temple itself. Still, having made that unusual choice, d'Avec was never less than fastidious of being at work before Aintra arrived each morning.

Aintra was just crossing to light the candles that covered the walls and ceiling when the Sending Stone on his desk began to pulse. That was also exceptionally unusual.

What a morning he was having.

He moved to sit behind his desk and then directed a stream of mana to the stone, causing a rather hysterical elderly woman's face to hover before him.

"It's Mylaf speaking. I'm the High Priestess's housekeeper."

Aintra grimaced, feeling his irritation rise.

He had spent many unprofitable hours liaising with this woman. Mylaf was of the opinion nothing mattered more than her mistress being fed and watered at the appropriate moment.

He had yet to find a way to convince her such concerns were lower down Gravalk's priorities than she apparently thought. That would be one of his tasks he would not miss with his . . . replacement.

"Yes, Mylaf. It's Aintra Weber. Have you forgotten to activate the reciprocal image again?

There was a pause, and then the eyes of the woman focused on him. "Oh, Mr Weber. I'm so glad to reach you. Is our mistress there?"

Aintra's irritation increased to being really quite cross indeed. This, for him, was close to a berserker's fury. He was a reasonably calm soul, especially for someone touched by fire, but he thought it something of a stretch for a Drudge to seek kinship with him with the choice of the word 'our'.

Mylaf's Class would never allow her to rise above Level 15, no matter how diligently she ran the High Priestess's household.

But, then again, neither would she ever be summarily dismissed, a treacherous voice whispered in the back of his head. He quickly pushed that thought away.

"No, Mylaf. I'm the only person here."

The levels of worry in the Drudge's face increased. "But she's not here, Mr Weber. She never came home last night."

"I'm sure this is not uncommon, Mylaf. It is not clear to me why you felt the need to call."

Mylaf was almost wailing. "She would never have not come home without telling me! That's not happened once for as long as I've known her. And I was with her parents for years before . . . well, all the nastiness. I looked after her from then on. And she was always home before midnight for all those years. I've just checked her bed. It's not been slept in."

Aintra sighed. Gravalk save him from anxious women. "I can assure you, she isn't here, Mylaf. The portal was secured when I arrived, and her chamber door was locked. But bear with me; I will just go and check."

He waved his hand at the Sending Stone and pulled out his mana. No sense in wasting energy while he went on this damned fool quest.

He stood and crossed to d'Avec's receiving chamber and as expected, found the secondary tamper lock engaged. He activated *Secret Keeper* again, enjoying the moment of pressure as the security measure tried to resist him. But, as always, it popped open, and he was able to swing the heavy double doors ajar.

Then he stopped for a moment, his air stolen from him.

What he saw in the chamber was so alien that he stood gawking for several seconds before the images started to make sense.

The windows at the back of the chamber were flung open, and the floor was covered in water, which was already pretty remarkable. If there was one thing everyone knew about the High Priestess of Gravalk, it was that water should not be brought into her presence.

But then, Aintra reflected, looking at the dismembered corpse of his very ex-mistress, he imagined being a little damp was the least of her worries right now.

Aintra moved forward, trying to make sense of the sight before him. Gianna's torso was occupying the Scarlet Throne that dominated the centre of the room, but all her extremities had been detached from her body and spread across the chamber.

Trails of blood ran the length of the floor, from limb to body, giving them the impression of strings being connected to a puppet. It took Aintra a moment to locate d'Avec's head, but looking up, he saw it resting amongst the candles of the chandelier.

Then, remembering himself - somehow - he quickly crossed to close the windows, locking them, and exited through the double doors. He engaged *Secret Keeper* and then returned to the Sending Stone. "Everything is fine, Mylaf. The High Priestess is just very busy this morning. She'll be in touch shortly."

He cleared the stone with a wave before the Drudge could respond.

What was he to do? In less than a bell, all manner of priests and acolytes would flood this floor. What was he supposed to tell them?

His hand wavered over the Sending Stone for a moment. He needed to alert . . . someone as to what had happened. By her very fiery nature, Gianna d'Avec had few people who would mourn her passing.

Much less would be inclined to seek to avenge it.

Then, a thought spiralled clear of his fog of confusion. There had been all that unpleasantness in the Manufacturing District a few years back, hadn't there? Some prominent industrialists had lost his head, and the Security Services had pounced to clear it up with little fanfare and even littler press.

What was the name of that strange man who had led that investigation?

Perfect Recall snapped into being, and a face and a name swam into focus.

Aintra reactivated the Sending Stone and pulsed out a message to Cuckoo House, the home of Soar's Security Service.

"Calling Inspector Lowe? Inspector Lowe, please."

CHAPTER 3 – BLOOD ON THE MARBLE

A shower, a shave and a change of clothes later, Lowe arrived with little fanfare at the Celestial Temple.

Indeed, such was the volume of people milling around its ground floor that he doubted anyone would have noticed should he have been carrying a banner with the words 'Murder Investigator' emblazoned on it.

The giant lobby-cum-reception area of the Temple was open at all sides, with waves upon waves of humanity surging in and out.

Any semblance of order Lowe might have hoped to maintain around the crime scene had long since been shattered. It seemed as if the entire population of Soar had seized the opportunity to trample across the Temple's pristine marble floor. Which, considering the infamous neediness of most of the gods here, was probably true.

Morning prayers hit a little different when the deity you were worshipping kept scrupulous records as to who had bothered to be in touch that day.

And meted out the smitings accordingly.

Pushing and shoving his way through the crowds, Lowe finally ended up at the portal he had been told would take him to the Third Floor. However, as he raised his hand to activate it, he cursed at seeing it glowing red.

Unavailable.

"Inspector Lowe?"

His eyes turned to the giant guard standing to the portal's left. Lowe found himself cricking his neck to look upwards. A Temple Warder who clearly not only never missed leg day but also had his Level expressed as 'PP'.

Of course, that might just mean his bosses were masking a comparatively low level so the Warder could go about his business without being seen as a soft target. However, it was much more likely Lowe had found himself in the presence of a monstrously heavy hitter.

"That's me. And you are?"

"Warder Latham. I have been assigned to you whilst you investigate what has occurred on Temple grounds."

They shook hands. It was not Lowe's first rodeo, so he avoided any attempt to demonstrate his virility by squeezing the Warder's hand. He liked his bones just fine where they were.

"'Assigned' as in you will throw yourself, selflessly, in the way of any attempts on my life?"

The giant man grinned wolfishly. "Might be worth rationalising your expectations a touch there, little man. My role is to rip you in two if the Council deem your investigation may become a threat to their interests."

"Ah," Lowe stood awkwardly for a moment. "Can we come to some sort of deal whereby you give me a quick heads-up if you think I'm flirting with doing anything that might trigger that response?"

The Warder's smile did not so much a quiver. "Probably not, to be honest."

"Excellent. Glad I know where I stand with you. Would be great if that wasn't in a potentially giant pool of my own viscera without appreciating why. But I appreciate your candour."

"It won't be personal."

"Good stuff. I'll keep that in mind." Lowe nodded towards the portal. "I presume as I was woken up and ordered along here, I wouldn't be crossing any unseen lines by requesting access to the Third Floor?"

Latham touched the portal, which immediately shimmered green. "That would be telling. Why don't you step through and find out?"

"Awesome. I can already tell we're going to be great friends."

With hardly a wince - well, not much of one anyway - Lowe walked forward and vanished.

***

Lowe hated portals.

There were all sorts of Skills that could be taken to make the dematerialisation and reconstruction that took place when using one more comfortable. However, most of those were only accessible to those over Level 20, and the few that weren't were so prohibitively expensive that they were the sole purview of the more affluent members of the aristocracy.

"I'm no expert - no, hang on, I am. I have the qualifications and everything - but is vomiting all over the crime scene absolute textbook behaviour?"

Lowe wiped his mouth and looked over at Cenorth. "Fuck you very much."

"If you're quite finished?" Cenorth stepped over the pool of Lowe's hastily consumed breakfast and beckoned for him to follow. "She's in the receiving chamber at the far end. I should warn you, though, it's not a pretty sight."

"Don't worry. I'm strictly a one-boak-a-day guy."

Cenorth looked back at him with an expression of someone starting to regret his recent life choices. "Are you sure you are up for this, Jana?"

Lowe ignored him. "If she's such a mess, are we sure about identification? Seems pretty unlikely that anyone could mess with a High Priestess in her own chamber. Maybe it's someone else?"

"Don't worry about that. It's definitely her." Cenorth picked imaginary fluff off the shoulder of his long, black coat. In response, Lowe self-consciously tried to shake out the worst of the creases in his jacket. He always felt like Cenorth's penniless cousin from the arse-end of nowhere when they stood next to each other. "There's enough of her left to make that pretty undeniable."

"Who found her?"

"Her secretary, a minor-Classed called Aintra Weber. Does something with spreadsheets if you can credit that? Who knows what a High Priestess needed with that, but he seems competent enough. He's the only one on the floor who has access to the portal and each of the chambers. The Temple Warders locked the portal down sharply after we made them aware of what had happened. Incidentally . . ."

"I have a shadow?"

17

"I mean, sure, if it makes you feel better describing him as such. You do you. I'd probably be tempted to view him as an assassin with a knife already drawn. But, you know, sure. A shadow. Nice metaphor."

"Awesome. Cheers for that. So, ignoring my impending death, the only person - outside of the Temple Warders - that knows what's in that chamber is this . . . Aintra?"

"For the moment. But if any of the other avatars decide to poke their esteemed noses in, I doubt that will stay the case for long." Cenorth glanced at his watch. "Look, Jana, I don't want to shine you on here. This is the hospital pass to beat all other hospital passes. Whoever murdered a Level 67 High Priestess is going to be well above the capacity of the Security Services to bring to justice. If you ask me - and I have made my opinion on the matter plain to the Council - this will be a matter of gods settling scores. You're on this because I have no one else that's . . . "

"Expendable?"

"That's the spirit. Knew I could count on you."

"Fuck's sake."

"Look, I know how you feel."

"Really? You've done much investigating under threat of summary slaughter, have you, mate?"

Cenorth's face hardened. "Inspector Lowe. You have the opportunity here to repair your reputation. There are those who have always whispered that your clearance rate had more to do with your Class than any natural talent for detective work. What better way to shut them up than to clear up the murder of an avatar whilst Classless and using nothing more than your wits and instincts? Now, you can go back home and play Private Detective - a role that my sources suggest you are curiously unsuited to - or you can do your best to clear up this potentially dangerous case."

"And I'm back in the Service if I solve it?"

"Not at all. But if you are still in one piece when this is all over, I'll go to bat for you with First Desk at Cuckoo House."

Lowe bit back his initial, harsh response. Cenorth didn't owe him any favors. In fact, his friend had helped Lowe's career in more than one way over the years. The scandal that brought him down was entirely of his own making, and nothing his boss could have done could possibly have mitigated it.

"Okay. I need a list of everyone who had access to this floor from yesterday morning to when the Temple Warders shut it down. I also need a plan of any and all places that are linked to this portal."

"I can do that for you."

During their little contretemps, they had reached the door to the receiving chamber. Without another word, Lowe pushed it open and slipped inside.

The scene on the other side was unlike anything Lowe had ever seen before.

He had spent long enough in the Soar Security Services to be no shrinking violet around violent death. In a world entirely governed by how quickly you could gather XP, regular and shocking predations of the strong upon the weak were basically an occupational hazard of life.

Sure, the Mayor did what he could to ensure there were other, less homicidal routes to advancement - Dungeons, Raids, Quests and suchlike - but when it came down to it if you were on the cusp of reaching your next Level and a squishy bag of points shambled next to you, the chances were, an 'accident' was going to occur.

But even within that context, the remains of the High Priest . . . Bloody hellfire on a stick.

The first thing that struck Lowe was that this wasn't a common-or-garden massacre. Just looking at the dismembered corpse told him that.

If the victim was a Level 5 nonentity, then this was the sort of aftermath that could be pretty common.

Very moveable object meets fucking irresistible force.

"The High Priestess was Level 67?" Lowe asked Cenorth quietly.

"Indeed."

"And we're sure of that? She wasn't somehow, I don't know, spoofing a higher Level and was actually as squishy as a marshmallow?"

"We're sure."

"Well, fuck me. This would suggest a reasonably small pool of suspects." Lowe looked around at the devastation. "I mean, is there even anyone that falls under our jurisdiction capable of doing this?"

"Looks can be deceiving. You, of all people, should know that." Cenorth was backing away now that he could leave the case in someone else's hands. "It goes without saying that there will be a lot of eyes on this, so be sure to let me know if there are any resources I can push your way. I mean, no one is willing to work with you - the words 'avoiding the splash zone' have been used - but if there is any technical support you require, give me a shout."

With that, the Commander vanished towards the portal, leaving Lowe alone with a dead body and a Temple Warder who may - or may not - be about to kill him at any moment.

Having no other ideas, Lowe crossed to the dismembered torso on the Scarlet Throne.

Sprays of arterial blood spread out from it, decorating the whole space. Due to the astonishing healing properties of someone of the High Priestess' Level, there were pints upon pints of the stuff sloshing around.

"I'll state the obvious," Lowe said, speaking to himself as much as to the Temple Warder, "I'm going to presume the head was the last body part to be removed. I doubt even a Level 67 can heal their way through decapitation."

There was no reply from his giant shadow, not that Lowe expected one. "So, we've got an assailant capable of inflicting catastrophic damage whilst at the same time able to subdue our victim so that she was unable to fight back."

"How do you know she didn't resist?" The question was a low rumble from the corner of the room.

Lowe waved to the space around them. "No fire damage. I'd be pretty damn certain that if she was even nearly in possession of her faculties, this place would be a melted ground zero."

He was aware of Latham moving behind him, but he did his best not to shiver. "So, what, someone knocked her out and chopped her up?"

Lowe shrugged. "Could be. If she were a lower Level, I could imagine the attacker could have suppressed her aura. Maybe prevented her casting? Bigger dogs eat smaller dogs all the time. I've seen that more times than I can count. But Level 67? I mean, the sort of mana that would require would be . . ."

The Temple Warder glanced upwards. "Arkola?"

Lowe kept his face exceptionally still. "Could be," he said neutrally. If anyone was going to accuse the Supreme Being at the very top of the Celestial Temple of merking a subordinate, it certainly wasn't going to be him who did it first.

Cenorth might be willing to put in a good word for him, but even a Commander of the Security Services wouldn't put his head in that particular monster's mouth.

"Could be a gang of pissed-off worshippers with a very specialised set of skills who just got phenomenally lucky?"

"Lucky. Hmmm." Latham seemed distinctly unimpressed. "So, what next?"

Lowe shrugged again. He sensed he would be making that gesture a lot in this case. "I guess we speak to the secretary and then to anyone who might not have been a fan of the High Priestess."

Latham laughed. "That, my little friend, will be quite a list."

CHAPTER 4 – BURNT OFFERINGS AND BITTER TRUTH

It turned out the Temple Warden was not exaggerating.

"Would it be easier if you just gave me a list of people *without* a reason to want this blasted woman dead?"

"With great power comes great potential to piss people off." Latham's face was expressionless as he placed another stack of scrolls on the floor next to the exasperated Inspector.

Lowe returned the first crate of material delivered to him and looked around the receiving chamber again. The smell of blood was beginning to get to him, and he was eager to get back to . . . where?

His ransacked apartment was hardly the sort of place he wanted to spend any more time than he had to. He could retire back to one of the local pubs, but he sensed this was the sort of thing Cenorth would look askance at.

Perhaps Arebella could be persuaded to put him up for a few nights?

He locked that thought away at the back of his mind.

"We will need to open this floor up again shortly, little man," Latham boomed out. "The business of the great Fire-Demon Gravalk does not cease just because his High Priestess had an accident. Is there anything else you need out of here before we release the body to the Deathcaller?"

Lowe wasn't wild that the nickname 'little man' appeared to be sticking but figured now was not the time to make a big deal of it. "Give me a few more minutes to fix the scene in my mind."

As he spoke, Lowe triggered *Grid View*, one of the other Skills he had retained when his Class had been removed.

He slowly turned his head to the left and then to the right, up and then down, ensuring his eyes swept over every corner of the chamber. It was a Skill that was exceptionally heavy on the mana, but it did mean he would have instant recall of all aspects of the crime scene whenever he wished to review them.

Using it left him pretty vulnerable to getting his arse handed to him without *Roll with the Punches* kicking in to save the day. However, if he wasn't going to use it for this case, what was the point in possessing it?

Unbidden, frozen images from cases long ago swam forward in his mind. *Grid View* gave him perfect recall for anything he saw when the Skill was active, and the memory never faded, no matter how much time passed. If he closed his eyes, he was transported back to the scene in question and could interact with what he saw as if he were really there.

He had long ago learned that the Skill was both a blessing and a curse. There was satisfaction in remembering cases that his diligence had brought to a successful conclusion, but there was the flipside, too. He would have liked to have the chance to forget some of his failures.

During some long, dark nights of the soul, he often found himself returning to some especially brutal crime scenes, exploring evidence, and picking at the detritus of murder, as if he might stumble upon a golden nugget that would finally allow him to put the investigation behind him.

More often than not, though, such explorations just made him hate himself a little bit more.

Lowe gritted his teeth and focused back on his latest crime scene.

The Throne that the torso was wedged into was, as its title suggested, already Scarlet long before Gianna had leaked all over it. Intricately carved imagery of flames and fire marked the seat and the armrests with a giant depiction of Gravalk on the whole back.

Rumour had it that when the High Priestess channelled her power, the eyes of the Fire Demon would open to add its own power to her casting.

"It's interesting the Throne did not help her in a struggle for her life. I would have expected this to be the last place someone would try to take her. If she'd been aware she was under threat, I doubt there'd be many beings who could survive an encounter with her in here. Interesting."

The Temple Warden remained silent yet surreptitiously tapped his watch in a way that suggested that if Lowe didn't hurry up, there'd be significant violence soon.

It was quite an expressive gesture.

Lowe ensured his Skill captured the other pieces of furniture in the chamber. There were a few interesting scrolls on the large mahogany desk that sat in the corner of the room. They appeared to all be addressed to "The Bitch" and were a series of screeds about the High Priestess, suggesting various and creative ways in which she could seek to lethally procreate with herself.

Lowe was no stranger to the odd poison pen letter himself, but these missives had an unusual level of venom.

"Do you know anything about these?"

Latham scanned through them and then passed them back. "The Warders were aware that Gravalk's High Priestess was being threatened on and off for much of the last three or four years. We encouraged her secretary to destroy the scrolls when they were received. Obviously, though - for whatever reason - he felt the need to keep passing them on."

"These are pretty vicious. And fairly specific." Lowe picked one of the threats at random. "Were you not concerned that whoever wrote these might seek to follow through with the threats?"

Latham's face remained stony. "The High Priestess was one of the great powers of Soar. If she was not concerned by the content, then it was not for the Warders to gainsay her." Lowe went to interrupt, but the Warder pressed onwards. "I do not know if you are familiar with those who exist at the higher levels of the Celestial Temple, little man, but they are not like the rest of us. These avatars are within touching distance of being gods themselves. Gianna d'Avec was, perhaps, a week or so from moving to the Second Floor. What would anyone possibly write that would bother her?"

Lowe's eyes very deliberately rose to look at the High Priestess's head that remained lodged within the chandelier. "I don't know, mate. But something managed to get under her skin."

***

There were three people waiting in the meeting chamber when Lowe finished his initial exploration of the scene. He hadn't found anything particularly noteworthy at this stage, but neither had he expected to.

Murders broadly fell into two categories.

There were ones when you arrived to find one dead body and one extremely chatty person eager to clarify how what had happened was an accident / not their fault / entirely what the deceased deserved. These were extremely common in Soar - XP gains, remember? - and it often took longer to complete the paperwork than they did to solve.

On the other hand, there were the ones Lowe was beginning to worry the case of Gianna d'Avec was likely to be. He was going to need to work very hard indeed—and have a huge amount of luck—to get anywhere at all.

At present, all he really knew was that the High Priestess hadn't died of natural causes but that pretty much everything else remained in play. Particularly as Gianna d'Avec had been receiving pretty dramatic and vivid death threats for a few years, and Latham was giving him the impression that the cartloads of potential suspects he'd so far seen were being lowballed somewhat.

All in all, Lowe did not feel much more informed right now than he did when he arrived at the Temple. And now he was preparing to be face-to-face with the three people who worked most closely with the High Priestess, and he was not wholly sure where to take things.

Of the three, it was only the Coal Stirrer who was remotely upset about the death. While not exactly bawling his eyes out, he at least was having the good grace to keep a downcast expression.

The other two, both Priests, seemed cock-a-hoop rather than distraught. They were both short and round, with the higher Level one, Hiwalk, being - according to the text above his head - something called a Hell Raiser whilst the other one - Setort was a Blazing Candle.

Not for the first time, Lowe found himself somewhat baffled by the sheer range and complexity of Classes. It was a language that - now that he was outside of its reach - felt like it was curiously beyond him.

An exclusive club from which he was recently denied entrance.

Having no other real idea of how to begin, Lowe decided to direct his first questions to the only person in the room who seemed to give a damn. "Mr Weber, I understand you found the body?"

The older man nodded, his long grey hair falling over his eyes, needing him to sweep it backwards with both hands. "Indeed. I've never seen anything like it before in my life."

"The dismembered corpse of an avatar? I'd hope not." Hiwalk snorted.

23

Lowe decided to ignore the Hell Raiser for now. "And it was your usual procedure to open all the chambers when you arrived at work in the morning? You must have been a trusted advisor?"

Hiwalk snorted again. Lowe wondered if he had a sinus condition that could be eased by a punch on the nose. "Hardly! But someone in the Order needed to hold *Secret Keeper*, and I doubt anyone else wanted to waste the Skill slot." The Hell Raiser glanced at the text above Lowe's head with interest. "Although I imagine you don't know very much about that, do you? You're that Classless Inspector that was recently in the press."

Lowe favoured Hiwalk with a brief smile. He'd have rather told him to 'go fuck himself', but - at least in the opening hours of an investigation - he had learned to try to keep relations cordial.

Nevertheless, he slipped his Ring of Regeneration back on and added a Torc of Shielding to his left arm. Between *Roll with the Punches* and the Uncommon armour, he probably wouldn't be one-shotted by a pissed-off priest.

And sometimes that's the rainbow on a dreary day.

"I have had some small successes on behalf of the Security Service. Not all in Soar have the luck to be Classed."

The other priest tilted his head. "But I'm sure I read in one of the daily rags that you were Classed, were you not? Wasn't there some sort of scandal last year around . . ."

Lowe turned back to Aintra. "Your usual procedure in the morning, sir?"

The Coal Stirrer seemed oblivious to the two priests who had suddenly become very interested in the investigator before them. "I do not think I had ever been in the Temple before the High Priestess until this morning."

"So, you did not usually open the door to her receiving chamber?"

"No, sir. There was never any need. Although she did not live here - as would have been her right - she was always here very early."

Lowe wanted to explore that further, but Hiwalk was interrupting again. "Didn't you say, Weber, that the door was locked when you arrived? That means whoever killed her locked the door behind them when they went."

"How many people in the High Priestess's service would be able to lock that door?"

It was Setort who answered. "To her personal chamber? Hardly anyone, I'd imagine. Aintra has the *Secret Keeper* Skill, of course. Beyond that, only those Gianna trusted implicitly would have access."

"Either of you?" Lowe asked neutrally.

Both shook their heads. "The High Priestess was not especially free with her favour," Hiwalk said through very, very thin lips.

Latham was suddenly at his shoulder, whispering in such a way that everyone in the room - and probably the building - made out what he said. "We have finally been able to persuade the High Priestess's Drudge to reveal the whereabouts of the d'Avec home. I suggest you visit there as soon as possible before the press beats you to it."

Lowe had heard more subtle dismissals in his time, but he currently had little else to go on. And if he had to look at Hiwalk's face much longer, he was likely to make things . . . complicated.

"That's fine. I presume someone has informed the household about d'Avec's demise?"

"Oh, no," Latham said with a smile. "We thought it would be much better coming from you."

CHAPTER 5 – THE HOUSE OF SECRETS

If Lowe thought there was anything strange about a Level 67 High Priestess residing in a thoroughly disreputable part of the undercity, he did not feel it was really his place to comment.

After all, considering his own current accommodation, there was a whole aphorism concerning people-in-glass-houses-not-raining-down-meteorites thing going on.

Indeed, compared to the place he'd called home for the past year, Gianna d'Avec's residence was a veritable palace.

The priests, Hiwalk and Setort, were not shy about expressing their disapproval of Gianna d'Avec's decision to live outside the Temple. Whether it was due to the perceived disrespect towards Gravalk or their own inability to locate her house, Lowe couldn't be certain. But he suspected it was a healthy dose of both.

Even he was finding it somewhat difficult to reconcile the sheer power that the woman had at her fingertips with the sad street down which he now walked. If you could literally cause the world to quake with the force of your displeasure, it seemed pretty unlikely you'd feel living in this place was an appropriate environment.

Lowe stopped before an emerald green door and looked up at the three stories of d'Avec's home. Sure, it was in a better state of repair than most of its neighbours, but there was absolutely nothing about this place to suggest, until that morning, its occupant was poised to become the second most powerful being in the whole of Soar.

Interestingly, though, the moment he had exited the portal onto this part of the street, he had felt the push of at least a dozen passive dissuasion Skills focus in on him. At least one was strong enough to immediately bring him out in hives, and if he hadn't spent his entire professional life being told to 'fuck off' by professionals, he could imagine it would have been difficult to force his way to the front door.

The High Priestess had taken her privacy seriously and done what she could to convince people not to take too much interest in the place that she called home.

Lowe admired the subtlety she had shown in this. He doubted anyone would have made an issue of it if she had gone for more . . . permanent solutions to prying eyes. For example, he knew of one minor celebrity who had set up a nasty version of *Acid Bath* to explode over anyone who so much as pressed her doorbell. Although, the cynic in Lowe thought that this was probably less about privacy and more about seeking a way to upgrade from 'minor' to 'major' starlet.

Nevertheless, whatever this house might lack in grandeur, it certainly was making up for it in 'nothing to see here, move right along' energy.

Considering why he was here, Lowe found that pretty interesting.

He was about to rap his knuckles on the door when it opened of its own accord and an elderly, moist-eyed woman was looking out at him.

"Yes?" The woman - Lowe glanced upwards and read the woman's name and Class - peered suspiciously at time. "We don't trade at the door here. Piss off before the *Anti-Hawker* Skills really kick in." She moved to close the door in his face,

"Mylaf, is it? I'm Inspector Lowe from the Security Service. Could I step inside for a moment, please?"

The woman raised her hands to her mouth, and tears poured from her eyes. "I knew it. I just knew it. Something's happened, hasn't it?"

Lowe felt the intensity of the dissuasion Skills kick up another notch as if in response to Mylaf's distress. He had a tricky little ring in his possession that would make him utterly immune to any such effects, but he didn't like to use it over much. In his experience, there were advantages to be found in people underestimating him - particularly when dealing with the highly Leveled Classed - and he only flashed his more exotic treasures around when the chips were really down.

You never knew who was watching.

"Perhaps we should talk inside?"

Mylaf stepped aside and let Lowe slip past her. The almost overwhelming pressure of a palpable sense of doom receded as soon as the door was shut behind them. Lowe almost gasped in pleasure when the weight of it lifted off him. Those were some expensive passive charms on this building. That was much more in keeping with what he expected from someone of d'Avec's standing.

"Is there anybody in the house, Mylaf? Do you mind if I call you by your first name?" Lowe said as he moved, as indicated by the housekeeper, through to a large, well-lit sitting room.

"No to both questions, sir. My mistress did not have anyone. Not since her parents . . . died. And I've never been one to stand on ceremony. She's dead, isn't she?"

Lowe sat down in a ridiculously comfortable armchair and regarded the woman steadily. "What makes you think that?"

"She didn't come home last night!" He was somewhat taken aback by the intensity of the woman's wail. Her hands went to her head in an almost hysterical gesture. And then, as if a switch were flicked, she was immediately calm, and an odd glow entered her eyes. "Can I offer you refreshments, Inspector?"

Lowe was reasonably familiar with the Drudge Class and wasn't surprised that a woman on the edge of completely losing her shit had chosen to retreat into the rational embrace of her Skills. He assumed she had activated *Hostess with the Mostess*, which was a standard part of any good Drudge build. Considering who this woman served, he thought this would likely be a Rare version of the Skill, maybe even in the Epic tier if d'Avec had thought particularly well of her.

"I would very much appreciate that, Mylaf. Please produce the most appropriate beverage and sweet confectionary you believe would be suitable for me."

Mylaf nodded, almost mechanically, and a table with a cup of steaming tea and a plate with a slice of Victoria sponge upon it appeared next to Lowe. He motioned for the Drudge to sit herself down.

The moment Mylaf was off her feet, the glow vanished from her eyes, and she began crying again. But softer and more under control than before.

"Mylaf, I am sorry to tell you that it would appear your mistress has been murdered. I wish I had better news to share with you."

"I knew it," the Drudge whispered over and over again. "Oh, that poor girl."

Lowe waited to see if Mylaf would say anything else, but when she didn't, he pressed onwards. "Can you remember when you last saw the High Priestess?"

"First thing yesterday morning. She always left the house very early, so it was my practice to be up no later than the fifth bell to ensure I could help her with anything she required."

"It is unusual that the High Priestess chose to reside here, isn't it? Most avatars live within the Celestial Temple itself."

"This is her parents' house." The way Mylaf gave that answer suggested there was no more that needed to be said. To Lowe's mind, there were any number of follow-up questions. But, perhaps, now was not the time.

"And did the High Priestess need anything from you yesterday morning?"

"Not yesterday, sir. I have . . . do you understand the nature of my Class?" Mylaf was looking above his head where the absence of his own Class was loud and clear.

Lowe smiled. "I have had some experience with Drudges."

Mylaf nodded as if gratified a difficult and potentially awkward explanation had been avoided. "Well, my mistress was quite particular about her food. She had grown up in relative poverty and, I think, saw it as an essential aspect of how changed her life had become that she had access to finer meals."

Lowe nodded along, not quite sure where this was going but happy to let the woman talk. Mylaf saw the confusion in his eyes and smiled, jutting her chin towards the tea and cake at his side.

"Perhaps if you tried my food, you would understand what I'm getting at."

Feeling increasingly nonplussed, Lowe picked up his cup of tea and sipped carefully at the hot beverage. It was a lightly spiced green tea with a bitter taste that he instantly loved. However, the appearance of a notification in the centre of his vision instantly dragged his attention away from his tastebuds.

It was fortunate he was already sitting down.

You have consumed "Spiced Jasmine Ambrosia," a Legendary tea brewed by Mylaf. This drink provides the "Echoes of the Ancients" bonus.
Duration: *47 bells and 59 minutes*
Cooldown: *Once per lunar cycle.*
Effects:
1. ***Ancestral Wisdom:*** *You gain a significant boost to Intellect and Wisdom, enhancing spell accuracy, magical defence, and problem-solving abilities. This manifests as a +10% increase in Wisdom and Intelligence.*
2. ***Phantom Aid:*** *During battle, spectral ancestors momentarily appear to assist in your attacks and defence. This results in a 20% chance that any attack you make is automatically supported by a spectral force, adding an additional 50% damage or reduction for that instance.*
3. ***Temporal Insight:*** *You gain the ability to see a few seconds into the near future. This foresight manifests in combat and negotiation, allowing you to anticipate an opponent's next move, providing a significant advantage in both avoiding damage and exploiting weaknesses.*
4. ***Legacy's Burden:*** *As a balancing factor, you will feel the weight of your ancestors' unfulfilled quests and ambitions, compelling you to pursue challenging objectives or face*

internal conflicts about your destiny and legacy. This will drive you to seek out new quests or moral dilemmas that align with the themes of duty and legacy.

Consumption Warning: *Due to its potent nature, consuming another dose of 'Spiced Jasmine Ambrosia' before a complete lunar cycle diminishes the positive effects and could induce adverse effects, such as "Ancestor's Disfavour," where you will find yourself haunted by critical failures at crucial moments as your ancestors express their displeasure.*

Lowe almost spat out the liquid in shock but considering the potency of the tea he had been provided with, he carefully swallowed it and looked, with alarm, towards Mylaf.

What he had just been granted was an insane boost from a consumable a Level 15 Drudge could apparently manifest at will.

She smiled at his stunned expression and nodded towards the Victoria sponge.

"You can have both a drink bonus and a food one. Please, take a bite. You look like you will need it."

Cautiously, Lowe picked up the cake and took a bite.

Funnily enough, it wasn't the nicest thing he had ever tasted in his life, but that paled into significance compared to the resulting notification.

*You have consumed "Feywild Frosting Delight," a Legendary cake baked by Mylaf. This food provides the **"Mirth of the Fey"** bonus.*

Duration: *11 bells and 59 minutes*

Cooldown: *Once a fourteenday.*

Effects:

1. ***Euphoric Agility:*** *You experience a surge in physical agility and dexterity, granting you enhanced reflexes and acrobatic skills. This manifests as a +3% increase to Dexterity, improving your ability to dodge attacks, perform intricate manoeuvres, or engage in tasks requiring fine motor skills.*

2. ***Charm of the Wild:*** *The cake's magic makes you irresistibly charming, enhancing your charisma in all interactions. This results in a +4% bonus to Charisma, allowing you to sway crowds, negotiate more effectively, or pacify hostile entities with your enchanting presence.*

3. ***Fey Camouflage:*** *Borrowing from the tricks of the Fey, you gain the ability to blend into natural surroundings almost invisibly, enhancing stealth capabilities. This effect allows you to move unseen through forests, fields, and even dimly lit streets, providing an advantage in both evasion and surprise attacks.*

4. ***Laughter's Echo:*** *Whenever you laugh, the sound carries an enchanting echo that momentarily disorients all who hear it. This can be used strategically to interrupt enemy spellcasting, cause momentary confusion in ranks, or simply to escape tight situations.*

Consumption Warning: *Overindulging in Feywild Frosting Delight more than once per fourteendays will lead to "Fey Whimsy," where you may find yourself subject to sudden bursts of laughter or dancing, potentially at inopportune moments, as the wild magic of the Fey overtakes your senses.*

This time, Lowe couldn't stop himself from choking out a mouthful of crumbs. Mylaf waved her hand, and the offending food vanished before it even hit the carpet.

CHAPTER 6 – TEA, CAKE AND A CORPSE

It turned out Lowe needed more than just a moment for his head to stop swimming—and only part of that discombobulation was due to the unexpected boost Mylaf's consumables had given him.

Ever since losing his Class last year, Lowe had - by necessity - had to become familiar with how to exist with much lower stats than had previously been the case. In fact, the whole experience had been so devastating that he actually couldn't remember the last time he had so much as opened his Core Sheet, much less carefully read it.

However, with the incentive of checking out the impact of Mylaf's concoctions, he managed to swallow down his pride and look at it.

Name: Jana Lowe
Level: 19
Class: ***Removed***
Primary Attributes
- Strength: 70
- **Dexterity:** 65 → 69 (+5% Mirth of the Fey)
- **Intelligence:** 85 → 94 (+10% from Echoes of the Ancients)
- **Wisdom:** 78 → 86 (+10% from Echoes of the Ancients)
- **Charisma:** 60 → 66 (+10% from Mirth of the Fey)
- Constitution: 75

Secondary Attributes:
- Perception: 80
- Willpower: 74
- Luck: 58

Health Points (HP): 1150
- **Regeneration Rate:** 2 HP/min (natural); 15 HP/sec (via Roll with the Punches)

Mana Points (MP): 400
- **Regeneration Rate:** 1 MP/min (natural); increased to 2 MP/min when Mana falls below 10%

Stamina Points (SP): 550
- Regeneration Rate: 5 SP/min

Skills

1. **Roll with the Punches** (Passive) Rare - Level 23
Converts 10 MP to heal 15 HP per second. Activation depletes 5% of the maximum mana pool.

Cooldown: None.

2. **Grid View** (Active) Rare - Level 14

Records up to 30 minutes of footage for perfect recall of details.

Cooldown: 1 hour.

Mana Cost: 50% of total MP.

3. **Slugger** (Active) Rare - Level 18

Next melee attack deals triple damage.

Cooldown: 10 minutes.

Mana Cost: 30 MP.

*** Skill slots 4 and upwards are blocked as per Council decree ***

Although he had steeled himself against the familiar burn of shame at seeing such low numbers, what he read still hurt.

Even with the uptick following the consumption of Mylaf's food and drink, he was still utterly tragic. What was worse was knowing that those flat % increases she had provided him with would be utterly game-changing for someone with anything approaching decent numbers, but for him . . . it was all just a complete waste.

He fought down the self-loathing and plastered on a smile for the Drudge. It was not her fault that he was clearly the weakest person who had ever sat in this room.

"Well, I have to say you have quite the ability there, Mylaf!"

She dipped her head in thanks. "I have been - had been, I guess - with the mistress for a very long time. I worked for her parents, of course, and she had known me for her entire life. As she became more and more successful, she was pleased to upgrade my Skills to the Legendary tier and then to spend the gold to ensure they levelled up regularly."

Lowe whistled. Well, that would explain the insane buffs a cup of tea and a mediocre bit of cake prepared by a Level 15 could offer.

As he considered the implications of this, he found himself - entirely unwillingly - transported back to Mr Clariy's classroom when he had been a boy. In this memory, the Professor was droning on and on about one of his favourite topics: Levels and Skills.

"Of course, ladies and gentlemen, you will all understand that Skills level up through use. No surprise there, even for those of you on the back row. Just as most of you will find the wherewithal to move your way up through the levels by acquiring XP, your attendant skills will constantly develop. However, where people and their techniques differ is that, at the time they are acquired, each Skill has a tier linked to the effectiveness of that ability. And why is that interesting, Mr Lowe?"

Lowe remembered thinking it was not nearly as interesting as trying to look down Griselda Byron's almost see-through tunic, but he'd wisely refrained from sharing that with the Professor.

"I don't know, sir."

"You don't know . . ." Clariy sighed, then determining he was slightly more interested in the sound of his own voice than berating a sixteen-year-old boy, continued unabashed. "Every single Skill you possess will level up with use. It will get incrementally more powerful with each Level it acquires. So far, so good. However, and it is crucial that you appreciate this, there is a hard ceiling for how good each Skill can possibly become. A common Skill at Level 200 will not be nearly as impactful as an Epic Skill at Level 5, for example. A Threshold Bonus Skill you acquire via godly patronage at Level 30 will be infinitely better - even at its earliest stage of development - than any Skill you have had since Level 5."

The memory faded, and Lowe found himself back in Mylaf's quiet, calm company. In theory, you could upgrade any Skill - move it from Common to Uncommon and thus increase its effectiveness - but it was a prohibitively expensive endeavour, either in terms of gold or Progression Points.

For most people, waiting to see the broader tier of abilities offered to them as they progressed through their Class was much more cost-effective than upgrading any early Common Skills they may have. Indeed, as most patron gods were reasonably free with rewards at various thresholds, it was not uncommon for even those with minor Classes to end up with a Rare or even an Epic Skill.

However, since becoming Classless and having all of his Skills above Common locked by the Council, Lowe has been left in a pretty difficult situation. With no patron god and no prospect of acquiring any more Skills, he had needed to make a difficult choice and had chosen to pour all of his time, energy, and money into getting the Skills he had as high as they could go. Even then, the best he'd been able to do was round all three of his abilities off at Rare.

At times like this, he wondered why he had bothered.

He could not even begin to calculate how much gold Gianna d'Avec had sunk into her Drudge's Skills to raise them to the Legendary tier. He doubted he would earn enough money to do that to one of his Skills even if he survived for a couple more centuries.

How the other half lived.

"I'm going to assume it was your habit to ensure the High Priestess left in the morning with her various cooldowns refreshed?"

"Indeed. However, yesterday morning, she informed me that she had partaken of the consumables she required the night before and had no need for fresh food or drink." Mylaf tilted her head, "You will be aware that, due to the power of Legendary consumables, there can be an adverse effect should you try to make use of them within their cooldowns?"

Lowe had read the warnings on the tea and cake he had just eaten and was not remotely interested in risking the adverse reactions. He assumed the High Priestess had felt the same!

"Do you know what she had eaten?"

Mylaf shrugged. "It was my mistress's habit to store food within her inventory. I could not possibly know what she had eaten unless I had asked her. Which I didn't."

Lowe took a moment before asking his next question, doing everything he could to avoid requesting a doggy bag to take the tea and cake home with him. "What did you think had happened when your mistress did not return last evening?"

The Drudge began crying again. "If I am honest, sir, I knew something must have been terribly wrong. I just could not bring myself to admit it before this morning. When I contacted Mr Weber at the Temple, I was hopeful there may have been some emergency that had delayed her overnight."

Lowe shuffled in the very comfortable seat, painfully aware that he was feeling better than he had in a year and, for a change, had mana to burn. It was odd to be so upbeat when interviewing a grieving woman, and he was finding the experience extremely distasteful.

"What will happen to me now?" Mylaf's voice brought him out of his brooding.

"How do you mean?"

"The mistress. Without her, what do I do?"

Lowe grimaced, wishing he had taken the time to learn a little more about the situation before allowing himself to be bundled out of the Celestial Temple by Latham. He would usually have familiarised himself with any number of things before visiting a murder victim's home, and he found himself cursing the Temple Warder for putting him in this position. Honesty, however, seemed like the best policy. "I am afraid I do not know, Mylaf. This is right at the beginning of the investigation, and I do not have access to the sort of answers I would usually like. For example, do you know if the High Priestess had any relatives?"

"She had no one, sir," Mylaf was dabbing away tears with a handkerchief that was constantly cleaning itself. Lowe had to force himself not to stare. That Skill, as well as the one she had used to clear up the expelled crumbs when he had choked, suggested *Hostess with the Mostess* was not the only Legendary Skill the Drudge possessed. He doubted even the Mayor of Soar himself had staff with such outrageously overpowered abilities. "Her parents . . . passed away when she was younger. What a terrible time that was. And then, well, the mistress was not one to easily make friends. I would doubt if there was anyone in her life at the Temple with whom she would take freely. Oh, there was a young gentleman she was seeing discretely, but that all ended a few weeks ago. I never met him, and I do not think the mistress was taking it too seriously."

"Do you have a name?"

"I do not. As I say, I think we would have been formally introduced should the mistress have taken the relationship seriously."

"So, who do you think she would have spoken to if she were in - I don't know - in trouble of some kind?"

Mylaf blew her nose loudly on the self-cleaning handkerchief. "That would be me, sir."

Lowe tried to keep his expression kind. "I do not mean any disrespect, Mylaf, but are you really suggesting a Level 67 avatar would confide her fears in her housekeeper?"

Mylaf smiled back, and Lowe found himself struck by the sincerity of her whole demeanour. "I know it is difficult to understand, sir, but the mistress truly had nothing other than Gravalk in her life. We spoke, at great length, each evening about her hopes and dreams for the future. After what happened to her parents, there was simply no more important thing for her to do than to reach the summit of the Temple. She was so . . . focused that there was no time for anything else."

Lowe stood surreptitiously, taking another sip of tea and a bite of cake to refresh the cooldowns. There would be more questions for Mylaf but now was not the time. He was making his way to the door when he became aware of the tumult of noise rolling around the street outside.

It seemed like Soar's press corps had finally caught up with events at the Celestial Temple. And, more importantly, they had located the High Priestess' home. He wondered how that somewhat confidential bit of information had found its way into the public domain . . .

Something for Cenorth to look into, Lowe thought. He was amused to see that some of the younger, less experienced Journalists were struggling under the impact of the dissuasion aura the building was generating. It appeared he got away quite lightly just with just a bad case of hives.

"Oh, my," Mylaf was at his shoulder and was distressed at the noise. "What on earth am I supposed to do now?"

Blatant self-interest fought with chivalry for a moment in Lowe's soul. He wasn't too sure which won out when he next found himself speaking. "It might be sensible for you to relocate for the time being, whilst all this initial interest blows over. I might know of a little apartment that would be absolutely perfect for a Drudge looking to stay busy whilst keeping her head down . . ."

CHAPTER 7 - MURDER AND MISDIRECTION

"You've employed your chief suspect!"

Cenorth's voice projecting out of the Sending Stone was in danger of reaching a pitch and intensity that would attract the local bat population. As most of the species that inhabited Soar were of the thirsty, vampiric variety, Lowe mused aloud that it might be sensible to 'calm the fuck down.'

Oddly, this did little to lower temperatures. "Do you have any idea how unethical that is!?"

Lowe kept his voice at a tone he considered to be his best 'who, me Guv?' level. "Firstly, let us remember that Mylaf is not anyone's 'chief suspect'. She's a Level 15 Drudge who, if she could as much as crease the High Priestess's trousers, deserves a medal for services to laundry for so comprehensively outperforming expectations. Secondly," he barrelled on before Cenorth could interrupt, "there are enough high-level security Skills focused on that house that there is simply no way anyone could leave - even via a Portal Stone - without appearing on any number of logs. I am satisfied Mylaf did not exit the d'Avec home from the moment the High Priestess arrived at the Temple the previous day until I arrived yesterday afternoon to break the bad news."

Lowe paused then to allow his boss to weigh in. He took it as a very good sign that the only thing that greeted him was an expectant silence.

He was probably not going to get fired over this.

Then he remembered that, to all intents and purposes, he had already been fired and, what was more, didn't really care what Cenorth thought of him any longer.

"Thirdly, and it would be good for you to remember this, I have not 'employed Mylaf.' I am merely offering her sanctuary from the attentions of the thousands of Journalists currently camped outside her door. A situation that has presumably come about because someone in your office - I'm betting on Jenert, by the way - leaked the news of the d'Avec murder for cookies."

Cenorth made a non-committal noise, which may or may not indicate that a certain overweight Press Officer has already felt the edge of the Commander's tongue this morning. "But that aside, the fact that she possesses a Legendary version of *Hostess with the Mostess* has nothing to do with it. I suppose!"

"Of course not," Lowe said, ostentatiously taking a bite out of a Red Velvet cupcake which boosted his constitution by a flat 200 - he didn't think he'd ever had it that high, even when he was Classed and under some significant Security Service buffs. It was - and, obviously, this was all a bit relative in the joy/despair continuum - pretty disappointing that he could only benefit from two of Mylaf's consumable bonuses at one time, with one of the buffs having to be from food, and the other from drink.

Since using the High Priestess's Portal Stone to return to his apartment complex - again, the money d'Avec had spent on the single most discrete stone Lowe had ever seen, with more privacy settings than the average spy network, was noted; this was not an avatar who wanted anyone tracking her movements - Lowe had been surprised by how quickly the Drudge had adapted to her new surroundings.

After making sure she was happy with the arrangement, he had left her to make herself comfortable whilst he returned to the Temple and tried to work his way through the list of names Latham had provided that both might wish the Priestess harm and had access to the Third Floor.

He had returned that evening somewhat jaded by the experience.

The length of the list of possible murder suspects - and those just within Gravalk's priesthood - was astonishing, and he'd only been able to speak to those who were willing to have their day interrupted by a Classless investigator of dubious authority. So far, he'd avoided asking Latham to weigh in and force the issue with the others, mostly because he wasn't sure the Temple Warder would come through for him.

Thus, during a wholly unprofitable afternoon's questioning, all he'd been able to determine was that most people who worked for Gianna d'Avec thought she was, in the words of one particularly charming priest, 'a bitch who deserved what happened to her.'

This was not an uncommon sentiment.

It was thus gratifying when he returned late last evening to step through his door and apparently enter an entirely different world—one where alien concepts such as dusting, washing, and baking were very much in evidence. Then he reminded himself that he was putting her up because it was the right thing to do, not because he was hoping she'd tidy up behind him.

However, Mylaf had confessed to him that she had not had so much fun in years. "I loved looking after the mistress. I'd been with her since before she could walk, and I'd have never left her service in any other circumstance. But -" and with this, she looked around the small apartment she now shared with Lowe - "well, a Drudge needs to work to feel valuable, and there is far more for me to achieve here than I ever needed to do for the High Priestess."

That was clearly undeniable.

Lowe's two-bedroom flat - well, one bedroom and one room of unclear purpose that, until the arrival of Mylaf, had simply been the 'room where belongings go to die' - was already wholly unrecognisable.

The floors were clean, the curtains washed, the cushions . . . well, he had some now.

And that was before encountering the smell of baking goods that greeted him as he arrived after a somewhat taxing day of talking to people delighted their boss had been murdered. The scent was of a depth and quality he had never experienced in his life.

He might even have shed a little tear.

After ensuring he had everything he needed, Mylaf had then retired to bed - humming happily to herself as she went - leaving Lowe to ponder both the nature of the case and his conflicted feelings about using the Drudge in such a way.

Lowe understood that the 'cruel' thing to do in this circumstance would be to ban Mylaf from doing further work in his flat. For someone whose entire Class was built around service, that would be the equivalent of giving a Winter Spearmen an enforced summer holiday at the beach. Just because Lowe didn't want to do any of the things Mylaf had been up to that day didn't mean they didn't give her immense pleasure.

But whichever way you looked at it, one human being 'serving' another in such a way was a touch distasteful. Unlike the beef and mustard sandwich he had just finished demolishing with great joy.

With a sigh, he'd parked the idea of being able to solve the inequality of Class distribution for the night and - before going to bed - pulled open Grid View.

When on a case, it was his custom to spend some time at the crime scene as a prelude to going to sleep. More than once, he'd been amazed at how his subconscious could unpick details that his conscious mind had missed.

The evening light was casting a soft, murky glow through his freshly laundered curtains as the haunting tableau of Gianna d'Avec's receiving chamber swam into focus in Lowe's mind.

The first thing that struck him was that the High Priestess had been dismembered with a brutality that belied the studied elegance of her surroundings. His eyes were inevitably drawn to her torso, still upright on the Scarlet Throne in a macabre parody of a regal poise. From there, it was hard not to obsess about the limbs strewn about with ghastly randomness, each severed messily as if ripped clear with great force and no precision whatsoever.

There had been no blade involved, that much was clear.

Her right arm lay beneath the grand window; fingers curled as if in a final plea for mercy. The left was draped over the ornate writing desk, almost an afterthought. Her legs, one under the Throne and the other splayed near the chamber's entrance, created a disjointed path through the crimson-stained water that soaked the polished marble floor.

Blood had mingled with the water, forming a viscous, dark liquid that lapped against the base of the Throne and the scattered furniture.

It was an unusual detail, Lowe thought, the water.

Its presence was such an anomaly in a place dedicated to Gravalk, the Fire Demon. Had that been intended to be purification, or rather desecration?

Pondering that momentarily, Lowe breathed in, seeking to recapture something that had tickled his notice when he had been there in reality. The air was, of course, heavy with the metallic tang of blood. But there was the faintest scent of something acrid, like burnt copper. Or some flavour of incense? It felt a touch out of place.

Above, Gianna's head was gruesomely perched on the chandelier, swaying gently with each draft that slipped through the cracked window. Her eyes, lifeless yet wide open, seemed to stare accusingly at the chamber below. But, Lowe thought, that was probably just his standard background paranoia and guilt, giving a texture that was not there.

Nevertheless, the chandelier's once-gleaming crystals were now drenched in blood, casting a ghastly red light that danced across the ceiling and walls.

Dragging his focus away from the corpse's remains, Lowe began meticulously cataloguing the scene, his eyes drifting over the details he would not have previously taken on board.

There, on the edge of the writing desk, a single, damp footprint—the shape of a boot, not Gianna's bared foot—pointed towards the window. Likewise, the windowsill bore scratches, as if someone - or something - had clambered in or out with haste.

Near the Throne, a series of gouges in the floor suggested a struggle; the heavy seat dragged forcefully around, perhaps? Or the High Priestess' death throes?

Looking over towards the corner of the room, beside the scattered death threats on the desk, was a tiny, half-burnt candle, the wick still smouldering. Again, like the odd smell in the air, it seemed out of place amidst the chaos.

Lowe wondered if it was a remnant of an interrupted ritual or an extinguished signal. A closer look revealed a thin strand of seaweed entwined with the wax—an odd relic in a fire-worshipping sanctum.

Grid View had then faded as Lowe's mana bottomed out. He briefly considered waking up Mylaf to see what she had in the way of snacks that might help with that. But, on second thoughts, he'd see that this would be crossing a line between awkwardly accepting the support of a person who liked to help and becoming a needy mooch.

Having quite a bit to think about, he'd retired to bed.

And, amongst fresh, clean sheets for the first in a grotesquely long time, dreamt about a piece of seaweed.

*

"I'm going to be going out shortly," Lowe said once Cenorth's furious voice had faded away, slipping on a clean jacket from which - as if by magic - various stains of unknown origin had removed themselves. "I need to speak further to Aintra Weber this morning as to whether he noticed anything unusual when he found the body."

Mylaf's eyes had filled with tears, and he cursed his bluntness. The previous day, he had spent so long speaking to people who were glad d'Avec was dead that he had forgotten there was at least one person who mourned her. "Are you any further to uncovering what occurred?"

Lowe shook his head. "It's early days yet. We're still trying to gather as much information as we can. I'm hopeful Mr. Weber will have something useful for me, though."

Mylaf nodded and returned to directing various cleaning tools and implements to their work around the kitchen. Lowe had done his best to dissuade her but— without all that much encouragement—had relented.

"I will see you this evening, sir," she had said with a smile, pretty much shooing him away.

Lowe made his way, thoughtfully, through his front door and then attacked the steps down to the ground floor of his building with a confidence he did not truly feel.

He was beginning to suspect no one really wanted this case solved.

Quite apart from him being the only investigator in the whole of Soar who had been put on it, the absence of a bereaved family pressurising the Mayor was going to be an issue.

And then there was the fact that despite Gianna's exalted rank, not even the Temple was pushing for answers. If this Level 67 avatar could vanish and never be heard of again, it felt like everybody would prefer that.

Feeling more than a little sorry for Gianna d'Avec, Lowe approached the Portal Stone that would return him to the Temple.

CHAPTER 8 – ONE LAST PUNCH

The air was cool at this time of the morning, and Lowe turned up the collar of his jacket against the biting wind.

As he was enjoying a much higher Health Pool and significantly raised Mana Regen courtesy of Mylaf's French toast and freshly squeezed orange juice, he actually didn't need the extra protection.

This was going to take some getting used to.

Likewise, the temporary rise in his physical stats meant he was making the journey across the broad avenue of Captivation far quicker than usual. Not that the hundreds of commuters dragging their way towards this district's Portal Stone—heading for jobs that singularly failed to put a spring in anyone's step—noticed Lowe pretty much bounding past them.

He was lost in his thoughts of the case - that someone else had been in the room and had, presumably, entered and exited through the window, was playing on his mind - which charitably might explain how he managed to miss that the street was suddenly completely devoid of other people.

Indeed, the first he knew of the somewhat ominous change in his circumstances was that the only sound he could hear was his heels clicking on the cobbled streets.

He spent a moment in complete disorientation. Captivation was one of the busiest streets in this part of Soar, and the idea that there was suddenly no one about during the morning rush hour was . . . just plain silly.

And then there was a second, unwelcome change to Lowe's surroundings.

A bunch of other very heavy footprints were suddenly behind his own, and he found himself being grabbed roughly from behind and driven forward to grab a mouthful of brick.

"This him, boss?" a low rumble asked

"I don't know, Zurro. Why don't you make an enquiry of this fine young man and find out whether he is the man we have been asked to meet?"

Lowe was spun around to receive a crunch of fist against jaw, which rocked Lowe backwards and back into the wall behind him. *Roll with the Punches* triggered, and he pushed himself blindly forward at his attacker, just in time to catch a second punch to connect on the other side of his face.

This threw him, again, back into the wall - fracturing his skull - at which stage discretion seemed the better part of valour, and he stayed where he was.

Splattered against the brick like a beetle.

"Ha! Man's like a fucking Weeble. He wobbles, but he don't fall down!"

Not for the first time, Lowe wondered whether the Skill he had worked so hard to level up was really worth it. The healing was nice, of course, but it did tend to encourage people to come on a bit stronger than was truly necessary.

He sometimes felt he was treated like a particularly novel punching bag.

Lowe's mana plummeted downwards as the injuries were repaired, and he found himself very glad for the Skill of his new housekeeper. If he was going to survive whatever this confrontation turned out to be, then having access to a deeper Mana Pool and increased Mana Regen was likely to be a pretty key reason.

"Guys, trust me, I'm not resisting. If there's a message you have for me, I'm listening. There's no need for any more unpleasantness."

Strong hands grabbed his jacket and drove upwards against the wall, tearing skin as it did so. He was lifted - far too easily - upwards so that his feet dangled about a foot off the floor. His jaw itched as a bunch of new teeth popped through his gums, displacing those shattered by that second punch.

"You're going to be told this once, do you understand?" The second voice, presumably the boss of the strategically shaved Ogre accosting him, came from slightly to his left. Lowe tried to launch Grid View from his peripheral vision, but he couldn't quite make out the face of the second speaker, so he dropped the Skill before wasting any more mana.

He was probably going to need every last drop to keep him alive.

"Absolutely. I'm all ears!"

"Do you know what, Zurro? I'm not wholly sure Mr. Lowe is taking this situation as seriously as could be hoped. Let us see if we can concentrate his mind a little more. Please relieve him of one of his ears."

One of the hands at Lowe's throat let go, and then there was a rather stomach-churning ripping noise followed by a blinding pain down the left-hand side of his face.

It didn't take a detective of his renowned ability to realise what happened.

"Fucking hell, boss! Look at that! It grows right back!"

"Interesting," the second voice was closer now, "that must be very helpful in your professional sphere. I wonder how much mana it requires to work?"

"Too much," Lowe managed, very aware that he would not be able to continue to receive too much of this sort of punishment before bottoming out. Indeed, without all the buffs that Mylaf's breakfast was giving him, he sensed he might already be dead.

Or, at the least, permanently earless.

"So be it. Never let it be said I am not a merciful guy."

Lowe held his tongue, not wanting to risk making a bad situation worse.

"Gianna d'Avec. You are to let it go."

"No worries. It's done."

There was a pause. "I must confess I am a touch disappointed to hear that. What? Is there to be no pledge of 'duty' to the city? No tearful follow-up questions about why we are making you abandon a case? I had heard such good things about you, Mr. Lowe. Why, I had even briefed Zurro that we would have to be at the very top of our game to warn you off this case. What a waste of an early get-up."

"Mate, you've just had your goon tear off my ear. Whoever you are, you've got enough clout to clear a fucking street at rush hour just to kick the shit out of me. Maybe, once upon a time, it would have been different, but if you know anything about me since I became Classless, you'd know I'm all about self-preservation."

"Oh, Mr. Lowe! Have you truly become so craven?"

The thing was, he really wasn't.

And the part of his brain that still believed he held a Class was very much not at home to this sort of intimidation and wanted to do something about it. And that part of Lowe was aware he had enough mana left - providing the light torture section of this morning's activities had now passed - to do something injudicious, should he be so inclined.

Of course, the smart play was to do precisely what the second voice was telling him: to let Cenorth know the case was a bust and then return to a life of quiet desperation and failure, where the kickings tended to stop just short of actual murder.

Hey, please don't knock it until you've tried it.

On the other hand - and that was the hand that was trying to get his attention - if he could just keep these guys talking for a bit longer, his consumable-boosted Mana Regen should give him just enough juice to be able to trigger his third and final Skill.

He'd needed to argue long and hard to retain *Slugger* when his Class was removed.

Traditionally, the Classless only had two Skill slots, and whether it was appropriate for him to hold the third was a matter of some debate by the Council. Eventually, though, when the impact of his low Mana Pool was highlighted, it was decided it was all a somewhat moot point.

One ex-colleague was even heard to describe him as 'One Punch Man.'

The fucking wag.

"Mr. Lowe. I asked you a question. It is considered rude in most cultures to ignore such things. Perhaps you need some re-education."

The boss had obviously indicated it was time for some further roughing up as the goon holding him aloft took a moment to re-adjust his grip and pulled his fist back for what, at the very least, would be a reasonably devastating blow.

At that precise moment—and had he any belief left that the gods of Soar gave him any thought whatsoever he may have thanked them— Lowe felt his only offensive Skill become available.

A year of frustrations boiled to the surface.

He had thought he had made his peace with what had happened, but . . . well, apparently not.

Before he knew it, his mana had dropped to zero, a headache the size of a small continent threatened to split his brain in two, and—perhaps most significantly—his right fist felt very heavy indeed.

He couldn't remember the last time he had used this Skill in anger.

The beauty of *Slugger*, and the reason he had chosen it as his Level 15 reward from a god who hadn't bothered to answer his prayers for more than a few years, was that it was almost entirely undetectable. Unlike flashier skills, it didn't make his hand glow. There was no accompanying choral music. And he didn't need to say anything trite to trigger it.

He didn't even need a backswing.

With no further ado - he couldn't hold the energy in his fist indefinitely without risking an explosion - he flashed a punch forward towards the centre mass of the Ogre.

Interestingly, one of the other useful things about *Slugger* is that it did not need the person using it to have any noticeable talent for hitting things. This was quite lucky, as Lowe really sucked at using his fists. It wasn't that he didn't have plenty of fighting experience, it was just that - certainly of late - he had become more used to leading with his face.

Right here, right now, though, he felt it was time to roll the clock back to another, more vengeance-minded version of himself.

Lowe's fist - and then his entire arm - passed straight through the chest of the Ogre holding him, displacing skin, ribs and - and this was pretty gross - a fairly sizeable heart out through the back in an explosion of viscera.

A wash of XP hit Lowe, surprisingly pushing him into Level 20 - he had been miles and miles away - but that was an issue for a later time where hopefully he would still be alive to consider it.

He was dropped to the floor as the lifeless corpse holding him up crashed to the cobblestone ground.

"Oh, Mr. Lowe. You are really going to regret doing that." The boss' soft voice was above him.

To be fair, Lowe would've agreed even before looking up into the eyes of a very irritated man holding a ball of lightning. Mana exhaustion was no picnic, and without anything left to fuel *Roll with the Punches*, he was feeling pretty exposed.

In fact, there was a part of him which actually welcomed the oblivion coming his way.

The boss pulled his arm back and released his missile.

CHAPTER 9 – THE LONG FIGHT BACK

"Admit it, you're feeling pretty good about yourself right now, aren't you?"

Silence.

"After all, it can't be every day that someone in your position gets to do the right thing. I mean, think about it. You'll actually be able to sleep the sleep of the righteous tonight, knowing you made a difference."

Silence.

"All your little Temple Warders will be so proud. You can go home and tell them that Daddy had a difficult choice to make today, and he chose appalling yet entirely justified violence. "

"Little man, will you please shut the fuck up?"

Lowe glanced at his saviour's face and wisely closed his mouth. He was still not entirely clear on the series of events that had manifested Latham directly behind the guy about to blow a fairly giant hole in his torso with some sort of ball-lightning Skill, but he wasn't going to complain.

Although now he had the chance to think properly about it, presumably the Warder had also been there when the Ogre Lowe himself had killed had been breaking jaws and tearing off ears, so it wasn't all gratitude pie right now.

Speaking of pie . . .

Lowe pulled one of Mylaf's cookies out of his inventory. He knew he could only have one food and one drink-based boost running, and he currently had a 25% increase in overall HP running, thanks to his delightful breakfast. For obvious reasons, that was not a buff he'd be anxious to swap out by eating something new. However, he'd used up all his Mana with *Slugger,* and he had a history of long and painful experiences of being glad he had enough of the blue stuff sloshing around for *Roll with the Punches* to kick in when shit got real.

As his go-to move was, most usually, to accept a pasting - sometimes survival trumped dignity - he needed a speedy Mana boost.

According to Mylaf, the cookie he was holding would instantly refresh the HP and Mana of whoever ate it back to 100%. Using such a prize with his current pathetic stats hardly seemed worth it. Potions that could do the same thing were currently far outside his price range, but at least they were actually purchasable for a handful of gold.

The cost of a consumable which - regardless of Level - would restore you to peak fighting weight...

Well, that was insane.

Being in possession of Mylaf's baked goods was the closest thing to guaranteed immortality a person could achieve. At least without spending close to the GDP of a medium-sized Petty Kingdom in some prestigious, high-end Merchant.

The image of Gianna D'Avec's shredded corpse popped into his head.

It appeared, regardless of buffs, there was always a bigger fish.

He had one last examination of it before munching down.

Item Name: Starlight Solace Cookie
Tier: Legendary
Description: This ethereal cookie is imbued with the radiant essence of starlight, captured during the rare celestial alignment of five moons. Its delicate, shimmering surface pulses with a soft, comforting glow, casting faint shadows that dance in rhythm to unknown cosmic melodies.
Effects:
Complete Restoration: Instantly refreshes all Health Pools (HP) and Mana Pools (MP) to full, regardless of the consumer's Level or condition.
Celestial Blessing: Grants a temporary aura that increases damage resistance and mana regeneration by 20% for 1 hour after consumption.
Usage Restrictions:
One-Time Use: Once consumed, the cookie crumbles into stardust, leaving behind a faint scent of vanilla and cosmos. This will also remove any currently running consumable buffs.
Sacred Rarity: Due to its powerful properties and the difficulty of its creation, only one Starlight Solace Cookie can exist at a time in the universe.

Yeah, using this at his Level and with his stats was complete overkill. However, if he didn't eat it, Mylaf couldn't make another one, and she obviously enjoyed doing that. So, he was probably honour-bound to eat it, wasn't he?

Even he couldn't look himself in the face after that bit of selective moral reasoning.

Nevertheless, Lowe crunched down on it, instantly feeling like he could take on the world. It had been so long since he'd truly been able to forget what Mana exhaustion felt like that, for a moment, he could ignore the two corpses lying at his feet.

But only for a moment.

"Any idea who these guys were?" Lowe asked the Temple Warder between bites of cookie.

Latham wiped the blood-red blade of his massive sword on the back of the smaller of the two bodies. "Standard hired muscle. Nothing worth worrying about."

Lowe thought that was pretty rich, considering how the encounter had been going before the Warder bothered to intervene. "I don't know, mate. They were giving me plenty to think about. I don't think I'd be telling tales out of school to say I was having more than a few moments of worry about what was occurring."

"I had your back."

"They tore my fucking ear off!"

"And it grew right back. Stop your whining. Oh, and you're glowing, by the way."

Lowe bit down his rising indignation at Latham's insouciance over his loss of body parts. That was right, wasn't it? He'd levelled up with that punch, hadn't he?

"I didn't think I was that close to my next threshold. What Level was the big guy who was brutalising me whilst my buddy stood and watched?"

Latham prodded the larger corpse with his foot. "No one mentioned you were such a whiner. He was a Greater Hoodlum, Level 46."

Lowe coughed out his final bite of cookie. "Level 46!!!"

"Yup!"

"I shouldn't have been able to cut his hair, much less punch his heart out of his chest."

"True."

"So, what the fuck happened?!"

"Well, you're in my aura, aren't you? What else would you expect?"

Lowe flapped his mouth like a goldfish that had been given a particularly challenging algebra problem. His brain quickly tried to make sense of what Latham had said.

It was a fairly open secret that the various guards employed around Soar received significant bonuses when operating within the city limits. The Temple Warders, Justiciars, Dungeon Keepers, and the rest of them were charged with keeping order in a world where the entire population had access to an almost unlimited range of powers.

It had not taken too many incidents before the Mayor had needed to take action, and my word, action he had taken.

Overnight, all those directly employed in the city's defence became no longer bound by their individual Levels. Whilst they were going about the lawful business, they had the equivalent of Level 99s.

Surprisingly, crime levels dropped reasonably quickly after that.

"So, just to check. I'm a Level 99 now?"

"Don't be fucking stupid," Latham was pulling the bodies into a suitably dark alley off the main road, carrying one in each hand as if they were bags of flour, "when you're under my aura, you will have an *Equaliser* bonus which will allow you to fight on a relatively equal level with your opponents."

"That sounds pretty cool!" Lowe was already thinking of the advantages such a buff would give him. Presumably, what had just happened would merely be the first of many such visits from people who would rather he did not properly investigate the death of Gianna d'Avec.

He might get quite a lot of use from *Slugger* . . .

"Don't get too excited, little man. You're Classless, so anyone of a reasonably high Level you find yourself in a confrontation with will have any number of Skill advantages." Latham casually tossed the body of the Greater Hoodlum away. "Trash like this? He hadn't even raised a basic shield. If he had, your punch would have just bounced right off him."

Lowe let that sink in. "So, basically, unless I'm being massively disrespected, there's going to be no benefit to having your aura on me?"

"Think on the bright side. Anyone who looks at you or knows anything about you will assume you're a bottom feeder. Disrespect is going to be your superpower. You'll probably get lucky again a few more times."

"Cheers for the pep talk."

"You're welcome."

*****

The bodies sufficiently hidden, they continued on their way towards the Temple. As they walked, Lowe tried to decide what to do with his new Progression Points.

Typically, when a citizen of Soar hit Level 20, their patron God would give them an opportunity to evolve their Class. Unfortunately, possessing neither a patron nor a Class meant crossing that threshold was rather more underwhelming for Lowe.

He was actually surprised by how much that fact stung. He assumed he had made peace with what had happened the preceding year.

But Level 20 was when most people moved from being considered background noise to being worthy of notice. It was oddly painful not to be able to count himself amongst them.

Nevertheless, as he kept telling himself, in many ways, Lowe was himself reasonably extraordinary in having reached Level 20 with no Class Skills whatsoever.

His three Skill slots had undoubtedly helped with that, but even then, he should not have been able to continue to function in a world where might was very much right.

"Are you going to do anything with your Progression Points? The flashing light is giving me a migraine.

Lowe ignored Latham's snark and continued exploring his limited options.

The centre of his core was, obviously, a blank space where his Class should sit. It was a solid grey in his mind, and he could do nothing with it.

Nestled around that hard, unyielding centre, were his three Skills: *Roll with the Punches*, *Grid View*, and *Slugger*. All three were softly glowing blue, indicating their Rare status.

Should he wish, it looked like he could use his Level-up bonus to push one of those Skills into the Epic tiers. That was probably the way he was going to go.

He'd once enquired of a Merchant, long before he lost his Class, how much gold it would take to do that with *Roll with the Punches* and he had laughed at the answer, assuming it was a joke.

Not so much.

So that was a rather attractive place to put his new Progression Points. In fact, it was an absolute no-brainer.

It was sometimes challenging to work out how a Skill would change in moving from Rare to Epic - such information was carefully, some may say, obsessionally, guarded in Soar - but it would hardly make him more squishy, would it?

Lowe selected *Roll with the Punches* and was about to evolve it when Latham grabbed his arm and twisted it.

"What the fuck!"

"That would be a real waste."

Lowe tried to pull his arm free, but the Temple Warder's fingers dug into the flesh of his bicep.

"Mate, it's not like I'm overburdened with options!"

"Open your Core Sheet."

Unsure what Latham was getting at, Lowe pressed down on the hard grey of his core to access his statistics. As always, the pain of their paucity hit him anew. Without all the bonuses which come with possessing a Class, there was something pathetic about the sight.

Character Name: Inspector Jana Lowe
Level: 20
Class: None
Unused Progression Points: (5) plus (10) Threshold bonus

Primary Attributes:
- Strength: 70
- Dexterity: 65
- Intelligence: 85
- Wisdom: 78
- Charisma: 40
- Constitution: 75

Secondary Attributes:
- Perception: 80
- Willpower: 74
- Luck: 43

Health Points (HP): 1150
- **Regeneration Rate:** 2 HP/min (natural); 15 HP/sec (via Roll with the Punches)

Mana Points (MP): 400
- **Regeneration Rate:** 1 MP/min (natural); increased to 2 MP/min when Mana falls below 10%

Stamina Points (SP): 550
- Regeneration Rate: 5 SP/min

"Stick it all in Intelligence." Lathan still hadn't let go of his arm, and Lowe was having to actively push Mana into *Roll with the Punches* to repair the damage.

"What's the point? A Level 8 with the lowest Waste Management Class will still have more than me. It's got to be better to have an Epic Skill."

Latham let him go and spun him round to face him. "Classes are overrated."

Lowe opened his mouth to protest that, for sure, when you were a Temple Warder, it was easy to look down on a game you'd already won, but the expression on the man's face gave him pause. "Go on."

"Classes rely on someone else: a god, the Council, a benevolent master. We talk about evolving Classes, but all we mean is that someone more powerful than us chooses who we are allowed to become. There's a reason the number of Classes is infinite and growing. Because those in charge are endlessly capricious. The only way to fight that system is to use your Progression Points on your core stats. That way, no one can ever take them away from you. You can spend the rest of your life being a human punching bag - and making *Roll with the Punches* Epic will help with that, or you can stick two fingers up to them all and take control of your own stats."

"You want me to dump all 15 points in Intelligence?"

"Little man, I couldn't care less. I'm just telling you what I'd do in your shoes."

Lowe paused momentarily, then stuck everything into where Latham had suggested.

The effect was ... interesting.

CHAPTER 10 – BEHIND THE SCARLET DOOR

Anything to do with being clever.

Which was not true.

At least, not in the context of Core stats.

For those who had no background in Build Management, there was a crushing disappointment to be experienced when they piled Progression Points into that stat and remained as moronic as they had previously been.

For those who had a bit more about them - or more to the point, had the support of a loving family, professional body or grizzled, grumpy mentor with a complex backstory - there was a better appreciation that Intelligence was an overarching stat that was predominantly linked to the Mana Pool and, perhaps more importantly, to the efficiency of mana usage.

A higher Intelligence stat meant more mana at Jana's disposal and, potentially, more potent Skills.

Likewise, Intelligence also contributed to a person's resistance against magical attacks and their ability to counteract or dispel the effects of Skills, enhancing survivability in encounters with arcane adversaries.

Considering most of the commonly available bits of gear for those with a minor Class would be inscribed with enchantments to do much the same thing, it was generally seen as somewhat of a waste of a resource to directly put Progression Points into that particular stat.

Indeed, any fiddling with the Core stat sheet had long been written off by those in the know in Soar as undesirable min/maxing. One that enough gold spent on enough gear could easily replicate.

The boosts available through evolving your Class and the rewards you could purchase once you caught a patron god's eyes were so numerous that the only sensible use of the points gained through moving through levels was to develop the rarity of your Skills.

Before everything went spectacularly wrong, Lowe had followed the received opinion.

That was why, in his Classtrated state, his Core stats were in such an abject state. Each of his Progression Points from Level 1 to 19 - including his Level 10 and Level 15 bonuses - had been spent on pushing up the rarity of his Skills. That the best of those Skills had been torn away from him was the least of Lowe's complaints about his treatment at the hands of the Council, but - without a Class or a god looking after him - it did mean he was fairly damn fragile.

"This is all a bit stable door, horse bolted, isn't it? " he asked Latham, confirming he wished to raise his Intelligence to 100. "Most people my Level will be well on their way past 500 with their Class bonuses, won't they?"

It didn't look like Latham planned to answer, but then he took a deep breath and turned to look straight into Lowe's eyes. "What do you know of Essence Transmutation Theory?"

The segue was so unlikely, coming from a Temple Warder in the middle of a suspiciously quiet high street, that Lowe nearly got conversational whiplash. "I'm sorry, what?"

"Essence Transmutation Theory. Have you heard of it?"

Lowe started shaking his head and then paused. There had been something at college, hadn't there? "Isn't it to do with, I can't quite . . . purity of stat points?"

Lathan gave a half-nod. "Okay. This will be easier then. Consider my Strength stat." A number hovered over the Temple Warder's head. Lowe took an instinctive step back.

"Fucking hell, mate. Do you have to be careful not to rip your cock off when you piss?"

Lathan didn't laugh. Lowe was beginning to suspect the big man did not find him either witty or charming. "Now, most of that comes with my Class and pretty much every Temple Warder will have broadly similar numbers. If I mock out what my Core sheet looks like without my Class bonus . . ."

The numbers he projected above his head dropped by two-thirds but were still astonishingly high. "I still have all sorts of gear and equipment that boost me up. But if I switch those off for a moment . . ."

The number plummeted again, reaching a more crushingly regular 134.

Lowe felt himself shrugging. "Still more than enough to kick my sorry arse."

"But that's the point, little man. Essence Transmutation Theory teaches us that the only true measure of our worth is not what is given to us by others but what we can develop for ourselves. Should I displease my superiors and be stripped of my Class and gear - a fate of which you are intimately familiar with - where would I be? Have you any idea how much XP I need at my Level to rank up again?"

"I'd assume a lot."

"You'd be right." Latham suddenly looked around him surreptitiously. "Look, there are lots of people who think you were screwed over, little man. The thing is, because of your relatively low level, you've actually got time to put it right. If you make a start right now. Being sub-Level 20 is critical. It means you have a chance to actually progress. Essence Transmutation Theory. Read up on it. And don't waste your Progression Points."

Then, as if a switch had been flicked, the conspiratorial tone in Latham's voice vanished. He was striding ahead down the street, and Lowe needed to run to keep up.

He was just about to draw level when the boost to Intelligence caught up with his brain.

***

By any reasonable measure in Soar, 100 in Intelligence was a paltry amount.

There were amulets - the city had once loaned Lowe one for a particularly difficult case - that added 250 in one go. However, having spent much of the last year coping with 80-odd, suddenly having his Mana Pool surge in volume was a headrush.

Intelligence also impacted upon several of the hidden secondary stats that Lowe had never really been interested enough in mapping out: concentration, nerve, memory, et al. So, as that hard-coded Core stat rose, his view of the world somewhat shifted and crystallised around him, causing him to stumble.

Latham's arm moved in a blur and caught him before he fell.

It was somewhat disconcerting to be handled like a ragdoll, but Lowe managed to let his pride accept the hit. It was hardly the most humiliating thing that had happened to him in the past week.

"Thank you," he mumbled, "my vision is just taking some time to settle down."

Latham did not say anything.

Lowe was trying to find a way to get the Temple Warder to open up about Essence Transmutation Theory some more when they reached the portal stone.

With barely a backward glance, Latham had activated it, and - in moments - the two were stood on the Third Floor of the Celestial Temple.

Lowe immediately headed to the small room that functioned as the Coal Stirrer's office. He had hoped that d'Avec's secretary would be more at his ease answering questions in his own environment, but it quickly became apparent that was not going to be the case.

The old man's eyes held a hunted look, and his face in the morning light was completely drained of any life. In theory, Aintra should be able to fill in any number of blanks about the night before the High Priestess's murder.

Whether he had the inclination to do so was another thing.

They had been speaking for a little over a bell, during which time Lowe had learned nothing new about the crime but far more than he ever needed to know about the inner workings of the backroom staff of a god's avatar.

Any thoughts he had that this was a remotely glamorous life had long since been dispelled.

Stifling a yawn, he tried to move things towards a conclusion. "Is there anything else you can think of adding to your initial statement, Mr. Weber?"

"I doubt it, sir. I have tried to be as forthcoming as possible."

Lowe went to stand and then paused and resettled himself in the patchy leather chair that had farted every time he had moved during the interview.

"Sorry, just one more thing. Did you like the High Priestess?"

It was possible that Aintra's face went even paler than it already was. "Like her, sir?"

"Yes. As a person. Did you, for example, find her to be pleasant company? Did you enjoy working with her? Was she a delight to be around? It would seem to me that you served her for a very long time, and I would appreciate getting your insight into her character."

"The best part of ten years," the Coal Stirrer murmured.

"You entered the Temple at the same time, I understand?"

Aintra nodded back. "Gravalk spoke to us at much the same moment."

"She must have been very grateful to have someone at her side who knew her little wants and needs. After all that time, I imagine you had become fairly central to the working of this cult. Especially as she was preparing to move to the Second Floor?"

A blush entered Aintra's cheeks. He cleared his throat as if making to speak, then hesitated. Lowe waited. It appeared to him that the Coal Stirrer had something he needed to get off his chest. In his experience, letting people talk in their own time was always wise.

He doubted Aintra was about to confess to murder- with the Skills the High Priestess had in her possession, he thought it unlikely that the old man could have inflicted so much as a papercut - but you never know.

He'd known stranger things to happen. Though not many.

After the silence had continued for longer than Lowe would have expected, Aintra seemed to come to a resolution. "I'm sure you would have found this out yourself, anyway. Temple gossip being what it is. The High Priestess had let me go."

Lowe was careful not to react, nodding for the secretary to continue.

"She'd asked to see me before I left that evening. Apparently, at Level 32, it would not be appropriate for me to serve her on the Second Floor."

"That must have been hard for you to hear."

"It is what it is, sir. And what it is is pretty awful. But I was probably due for a change after so long in one role. In eight levels, it would seem sensible to evolve my Class anyway. I would probably have looked to leave my lady's service at that point in any event."

Lowe let the lie sit there between, like a particularly pungent turd. Aintra shuffled about in his chair but didn't take the opportunity to add anything to his story.

Eventually, Lowe decided to prod things onward. "Interesting. We may need to come back to that. For now, though, can you tell me if the High Priestess often remained in her receiving chamber after you all had left for the evening?"

Aintra almost sighed with relief when being able to move on to routine matters. "It was not especially uncommon, sir. You will be aware that she made prodigious progress up the floors of the Temple, and that sort of growth does not happen merely through meeting business hours. I often would lock up the rest of the floor, leaving the High Priestess in situ."

"And yet her door was locked when you arrived on the morning you discovered her body?"

The Coal Stirrer paused as if he had not considered that before. Lowe did not like the pantomime the man was presenting here. Unless he was a moron - and Aintra Weber was certainly not that - he'd obviously come to the same conclusion, and pretending this was the first time he'd considered it was not convincing.

"Yes, that is strange, is it not?"

"Yes. It is. And you did not accidentally lock her in when you left?"

Despite the tense atmosphere in the small room, Weber smiled at that. "Hardly, sir. One did not make such errors around the High Priestess. At least, not twice."

"So, for clarity. The High Priestess was alive when you left shortly before the tenth evening bell. You did not lock her door. When you arrived the following morning, the door was locked, and Gianna d'Avec was butchered behind that closed and secured door. "

"Those are the facts as I understand them, sir."

Lowe did not miss the rather formal language used there. In his experience, when people retreated behind formality, it was because they had practised what they were saying, which was interesting.

He looked anew at Aintra Weber and let the silence develop.

Aintra cleared his throat several times before Lowe put him out of his misery. "So, and this will be my final question, you contend that only you and the High

Priestess could lock and unlock that door. No one else in the service of Gravalk could do so?"

Aintra's face took on a pained expression. "I may not be the most powerful being on this floor, sir, but I can be sure of that. If it was not I who locked that door, then only the High Priestess or our Lord Gravalk himself could have done it."

Lowe smiled and looked back at Latham. The Temple Warder had spent the interview looming, impressively, in the doorway.

"Well, Mr. Warder. It sounds like we need a meeting with a god, doesn't it?!"

CHAPTER 11 – A FLOOR TOO HIGH

"I am, under no circumstances, accompanying you on a visit to a god."

"Go on, live a little. What's the worst that can happen?"

"Says the man without a Class!"

"Exactly. How is Gravalk going to make my life worse?"

"I think 'life' is the operative word there, little man. And even if he doesn't evaporate you entirely, spending the rest of your existence with third-degree burns is probably going to be a touch sub-optimal."

"Your concern for my wellbeing is touching, Temple Warder."

"Fuck that! I'm responsible for keeping you in one piece until you come up with a theory of what happened to the High Priestess. At that stage, fuck your well-being. But until then, I'm going to do my best to keep you away from walking on any landmines. Like prodding a Fire Demon who is likely feeling a little touchy after his avatar was murdered in her own chamber. Besides, I like my Class just fine."

"What? Do you mean to say that you've not been taking your own advice over Essence Transmutation Theory? You shock me to my very core. Imagine that? An extremely powerful Higher Classed not following some abstract theory of build development. Hypocritical much?"

The blow Latham struck Lowe splatted him – no metaphor here - against the wall. *Roll with the Punches* kicked in whilst the investigator was still flying through the air, taking advantage of the increased availability of mana, and quickly repaired the fractured skull and reversed the significant brain damage. Even then, Lowe was left with only 10% of his pool.

Latham strode forward to loom over the crumpled man. "Do not mistake my tolerance for friendship. I have been charged with keeping you alive until it is determined that your status is no longer desirable. Be under no illusions; I will follow any orders I am given regarding you. If I have offered you advice about your build, it is because I feel some pity for your situation. There but the grace of the gods and all that. You should not presume that gives you any right to discuss my own Progress Point choices. Do you understand?"

"Dude, I'm going to suggest that was a slight overreaction to some low-level banter. I was joking."

Lowe was a touch alarmed to hear significant slurring in his words. He pushed his remaining mana into *Roll with the Punches*. Sometimes, the passive nature of the Skill only concerned itself with immediate risk to life, and he needed to manually mop up any less critical damage.

His understanding was that ranking it up to Epic would have smoothed that out a little, but since taking Latham's advice, it would be many more levels - or an insane amount of gold - until he had the resources to have that option again.

Lowe decided not to point out the irony. He couldn't afford another slapping from a giant with absolutely no sense of humour.

Latham, for his part, simply glowered back at him. If he felt any remorse for the attempted murder, he was hiding the guilt very well. "It is not your place to question how I spend my Points."

"Fuck me, Latham! Most people would consider a quiet 'no comment' sufficient to steer the conversation to calmer waters. Grievous bodily harm feels a touch forceful in the circumstances. How do you deal with arguments with your friends? Gladiatorial death matches?"

A mix of complicated emotions swan over Latham's face, and then he stuck out a hand to help Lowe get to his feet. "My apologies. I am not used to interacting with people who are so . . . vulnerable."

"Mate, I think you can probably work on your approach to conflict resolution." As he spoke, Lowe slipped back on his Ring of Regeneration and was about to switch his consumable bonus to help with his Mana Regen via a nice bit of Battenberg, but something stopped him.

He suddenly was not so keen on Latham knowing everything about him nor what resources he had to call upon. Although, he didn't really want to be wandering around Soar with less than 50% of his Mana available.

The two men regarded each other for a moment. Lowe was damned if he was going to break the silence.

Finally, Latham cleared his throat and then threw the Inspector a flask of some sort of golden liquid.

Lowe caught it and quickly examined what he had been given. Only a tiny part of him expected it to explode. "A Potion of Restoration? Mate, I've had worse make-up gifts."

"I said I was sorry, little man. I will endeavour to control my temper in the future, but you should know that some topics should be considered taboo."

"So, you can get all up in my business about where to put my Progress Points, but if I so much as touch on your own build choices, I get my arse kicked, with some expensive shiny coming my way to make amends? I'm not going to lie, mate, that feels a touch like we're in an abusive domestic relationship."

The look Latham gave suggested that levels of abuse remained hitherto to be explored.

***

Few of the buildings that stretched for the sky in Soar were quite as imposing as the Celestial Temple.

It probably goes without saying that when you have the literal power of life and death over the little beings below, you tend to end up with highly motivated craftspeople. But as the avatars within the Temple made that point loudly and often - usually concurrent with vaporising whatever mason, plumber or carpenter that had displeased them - it is going to be said anyway.

If it seemed to the citizens of Soar that regardless of famine, flood or financial crisis, the Celestial Temple continued to grow more and more glorious as their own circumstances cratered into the mud, then they were to be congratulated on their perspicacity.

The Mayor of Soar had not reached his station in life by pissing off immortal beings, no sirree, Bob.

The Celestial Temple occupied the very centre of the city, with tens of streets running off it. It was often mentioned that the various thoroughfares lined with shops, houses, and industrial facilities that led to and from the giant tower were like the spokes of some enormous wheel with the Temple at its heart.

To which the Mayor would reply, whilst seeking to stand just outside the inevitable splash zone, "Too damn right. Have you seen the size of some of those thunderbolts?"

It was visible for leagues around, with its roof's vast black stone edifice shining with a, if not an entirely holy, then certainly intimidating glow.

The current resident of the Second Floor, Mdamic Lavall. watched the city hustle by beneath him with all the self-satisfaction of someone who never needed to commute to work again. It wasn't that he did not like the 'little people' below; it was just . . . No, that was entirely fair.

He didn't like them at all.

Fuck those guys. And the donkey they were riding around on.

If there was one thing that Soar gave you, it was opportunity.

You could be born as the lowest of the low, but that did not, in any way, put a ceiling on how high you could rise. Providing, of course, you put your nose to the grindstone, pulled yourself up by your bootstraps and . . . some other meaningless cliche that he was too giddy to verbalise properly right now.

That bubbling excitement just below the surface momentarily took hold of him, and an arching bolt of *Righteous Judgement* blazed from his eyes to incinerate one of the passing ants below. That this gave him an unusually high burst of XP suggested that he must have accidentally targeted someone above Level 40.

Mdamic opened a quick mental channel to his PA. "Szana? Can you look into who was recently moved beyond this vale of tears on the corner of -" he checked his geography - "Sorrow and Fortitude. Send the family my regards and make the usual apologies."

"The ineffable nature of Yolgorth?"

"Whatever eases their pain. You're good at this sort of thing. Of course, if it turns out it was a deserved smiting, please present the usual invoice." He cut off the communication and turned to his unwelcome visitor.

"You know," Khaled Sahil, the Chosen of Oh, mused aloud, "some people might consider it distasteful to celebrate the death of a peer quite so openly."

"Fuck those people. Bring them here right now, and I'll do it for you. With a glaive. The grasping fire bitch is dead. What's not to like? I'm even considering declaring today a Holy Moment of celebration."

"Far be it from me to offer advice to an avatar of your power and station," Khaled said, "but you might want to dial down the glee ever so slightly. To my understanding, at this very moment, the Security Services are running their mucky little paws over what I believe in the vernacular is described as 'the crime scene.' I assume someone will be stopping by shortly to discuss your relationship with her."

Mdamic's eyes flashed with barely restrained thunderbolts. "My relationship? Those ground apes better have more sense than to bother me with their mewlings. Yolgorth will not take kindly to his important business being disturbed by nonsense."

Khaled's eyes scanned over the Archdeacon's desk, noting the half-eaten breakfast, completed crossword and a pad full of doodles. It did not truly seem that the 'important business' of Yolgorth was truly taking everything this avatar had got.

"I would caution you to reconsider that viewpoint. I'm told that the powers that be are actually taking Gianna's death more seriously than might have been expected."

Mdamic dialed down his frustration a touch. "Where are you hearing that?"

"What Oh's adherents might lack in raw power, we tend to more than makeup with 'ear to the ground' attentiveness."

"Ha! I guess that's something snakes are good at, eh?"

Khaled laughed dutifully, but his smile did not quite reach his eyes.

In truth, he was growing distinctly unimpressed with his role as a punching bag for an ex-Barbarian who got lucky in god-bingo. "Maybe. I guess that depends on what you might have to trade for the information."

Mdamic's huge, scarred hands smashed down and through his desk, reducing it to kindling. It was reasonably unusual for an Archdeacon to possess quite such an imposing physique as the Speaker of Yolgorth retained. The muscles - and the swords. And the battle-axes. And the temper - had undoubtedly added to his success in reaching the heady position of Level 72. "You will tell me, or you will die!"

Khaled didn't blink at the primitive show of strength. As one of the key gifts that Oh had bestowed on him when he passed the Level 60 threshold was the Legendary skill, *Never Surprised*, he was capable of glimpsing what the next few moments would bring.

This was both extremely helpful to his long-term survivability in circumstances such as these and also an absolute buzzkill in more social settings. Indeed, it had put such a dent to his love life that he had made no effort, as of yet, to level it up to increase the amount of time he could anticipate.

Who wanted to know how an evening's seduction would end before you even made your move?

"You know how this works, dear heart. There are no freebies at our level."

Unlike Yolgorth, who was best known as the god most likely to absolutely fuck you up if you spilt his beer, Khaled's patron - Oh - had no shortage of alliances he sought to maintain. There was literally no limit to the amount of arse his avatar would be ordered to kiss to bring his plans to fruition.

Whilst Khaled was at present bumming around on the eighth Floor of the Temple, plans were afoot to help him rise.

And, right now, he was in possession of information about the fate of a certain Fire Demon's avatar that was quite tasty.

"What do you want?" The Archdeacon's eyes blazed with barely repressed fury. More than one avatar of a lesser deity had come a cropper in this chamber. Regardless of his Legendary skill, Khaled cautioned himself that he would do well to remember that Mdamic hadn't reached Level 72 without being an absolute monster.

"Very little, I assure you. The games of we poor souls on the eighth Floor can matter nothing to someone like yourself."

"I grow bored of this. Ask."

"The Great and Bounteous Oh recently lost control of a Starter Area north of the Terreto Province. A rather distasteful business involving Orcs, Kobolds, and a Princess of questionable virtue I won't bore you with. It would be extremely beneficial should that area suddenly experience . . . I don't know . . . a catastrophic thunderstorm?"

"How catastrophic?" Khaled saw the glint in Mdamic's eye and knew he had him.

"I think Oh was hoping for anything north of wholly apocalyptic. Her precise words were, 'Let the ungrateful buggers burn.'"

"And for that . . . service, you will share what you know about the investigation?"

"Indeed."

Mdamic's eyes changed to the colour of spilt blood for a heartbeat and then switched back to their usual blue. "Done. I assume all XP gains - such as they are - are mine to claim?"

"Why, of course. Oh would never dream of suggesting otherwise."

Mdamic licked his lips. Even such a colossal span of destruction - he sensed there was every chance Terreto Province would drop into the sea - would do nothing for his level. Nevertheless, it was always enjoyable to have the XP wash in. "Now, tell me."

Khaled was somewhat baffled that someone who would obviously be very much in the crosshairs of the Security Service was acting in such a careless way. Did he not realise that the whole reason why d'Avec was boosted so quickly to the Third Floor was that there was quite some dissatisfaction with the performance of Yolgorth's chosen on the Second?

Those worries were not simply going to have gone away with her death. Indeed, from the whispers his subordinates had picked up, notice had been taken of the dramatic effectiveness of the more ... direct approach to removing obstacles.

When he replied, Khaled did his best to keep any sense of this out of his voice. "There are a number of pressures being brought to bear to ensure that the wrongdoers are brought to justice. I hear Arkola has become personally involved."

Mdamic glanced upwards instinctively. "Seriously? Arkola is taking an interest?"

"No one likes to think that those on the higher levels of the Celestial Temple are vulnerable to base butchery. You, more enlightened beings, are supposed to be above all that."

There was an awkward silence whilst Mdamic assimilated the subtext in his friend's words. "I assume you have come with some advice for me?"

Khaled smiled. "I always have thoughts for Yolgorth's chosen, should he be interested in commentary from a far less illustrious figure."

Mdamic surreptitiously activated *Clear Sky Thinking*, an often-overlooked Skill available to those who had Yolgorth as a patron.

As soon as the calm rationality of the Skill washed over him, he saw precisely what Khaled was doing. Had he not been under the influence of the Skill, he would have been turning the sneaky sucker into a pile of ash quick smart.

As it was, he could see there was probably merit in letting the relationship continue. So his 'friend' thought he was that easy to manipulate, did he? Well, two could play at that game.

Mdamic smiled. "And I am always happy to hear your commentary. However, it would be good to understand the price before sampling the product."

"Oh, nothing very much. For this information, Oh is happy to have a favour to call on in the future. One she promises will not inconvenience the Great Yolgorth."

"An unspecified favour?"

"One without strings, I assure you."

Mdamic reached over the table and grasped Khaled's hand, pulsing an unnecessary level of lightning into the man opposite to seal the deal. "We have a compact. And Yolgorth will respond directly to Oh should the terms turn out to be unacceptable. Or if, indeed, there are some hidden 'strings' hanging around. Now, give me your advice."

Khaled paused to allow the pain in his hand to fade.

He truly was coming to despise this avatar. "My advice would be that it would be sensible to show an element of concern and worry about the events on the Third Floor. Should the Security Services choose to speak with you, demonstrate that d'Avec's death is an unspeakable tragedy. Offer any help that is required and, under no circumstances, give the impression you are happy with what has occurred. I assume you have an alibi?"

Mdamic raised an eyebrow. "Surely, I am not going to need to account for my movements. I am Yolgorth's chosen!"

"And a Level 67 has been massacred. I would assume the suspect pool for such a crime is going to be vanishingly small. It would be sensible for you to ensure your name is not on it." Khaled let the silence stretch out a little before speaking again. "I hesitate to prompt the memory of one such as yourself, but you do remember that we ate together that night?"

Mdamic's face clouded. "Something about that rings a bell . . . "

"I will ensure that all the details are supplied to your P.A in short order. Merely to refresh your memory of the event. The dinner will already be on your calendar, of course."

"Of course."

They shared a few more pleasantries before Khaled made his excuses and returned to his own more mundane level.

Mdamic sat in silence for a while, replaying the conversation in his head. He'd let *Clear Sky Thinking* drop off - it tended to make his teeth itch if he had it on for too long - which probably accounted for him missing one particular, important issue in the deal he had just made.

It wasn't just that Khaled was giving *him* an alibi, but he'd provided the Chosen of Oh with one, too.

CHAPTER 12 – THE COFFEE WAS COLD, BUT THE GRAVE WAS FRESH

On the morning after the abrupt conclusion of the meteoric rise of Gianna d'Avec, a group of mercenaries more or less wholly - some would say 'obsessively' - dedicated to her death met for their usual breakfast bap.

Anyone watching this small collective—four women and two men—would have thought them unlikely terrorists.

Indeed, it was difficult to rationalise their white-hot hatred for the High Priestess alongside mundane things such as their prodigious consumption of bacon, sausage, and strong white tea.

It would be tempting to assume that the threat from this rundown cafe was so insignificant that Gravalk's avatar should never have had a moment's concern.

Tempting, but very, very wrong.

Whilst a quick scan of the pinched, tired faces mechanically chewing on their morning repast would find nothing more sinister than the usual rundown residents of this district of the city, a more thorough glance would reveal something far more alarming.

For example, not one of these early morning snackers was below Level 40.

Sure, in and of itself, this was not especially unusual. Live long enough, pray to the right god, and be reasonably lucky and most people - whilst not exactly *likely* to cross that threshold - could reasonably expect to have a shot at it.

For example, a particularly diligent Accountant would feel they'd missed out if they retired without at least being within touching distance of that level.

No, it wasn't their levels themselves which marked this little group out for special attention, but rather the significantly combative nature of their Classes.

Which meant the atmosphere in Crazy Xim's cafe was somewhat strained this morning.

"She was definitely on the Scarlet Throne by the eighth bell," a short, dark-haired woman with the rather ominous sounding Class of Nightmare Reaver. It should be noted, though, that the possible intimidation factor of her doom-laden Class was somewhat undercut by the spreading ketchup stain on her tunic that she was brushing at, ineffectually, with one hand, whilst trying to consume the rest of her roll with the other.

"That was her schedule for the last year, Tenia," the taller of the two men replied, slurping his tea. "I think we can take it as fucking read that she was on her throne at that time."

The woman blinked somewhat owlishly and then narrowed her eyes at the man who had spoken.

Once upon a time, she'd liked him. There'd been something between them besides a shared interest in the complete and brutal destruction of a certain red-haired High Priestess.

But familiarity had bred contempt. And what could be more familiar than a daily contact stuck forever in the raking over the coals of sorrow and anger.

Impotence of revenge led to its own sorrow.

"Some of us took our role in this endeavour seriously, Charl," she almost spat at him. "Since we uncovered that the bitch didn't actually stay in the Temple overnight - which I worked out, you will remember? - my job was to track her whereabouts. Which I did, without error, for nearly five years. It is hardly my fault that the rest of you couldn't organise an assassination in a charnel house."

As always happened when the two clashed, Charl found himself on his feet - body inflating to ridiculous proportions as anger triggered the main Skill of his Berserker Balloon Class.

The second man, a squat wiry figure with a beard that made him look, to his mind, like a pirate and in everyone else's like he had spent a long, hard winter sleeping rough, tutted. He had made that noise countless times over the years when this confrontation had played itself out.

As an Empath Nullifier it was entirely within his skillset to put a nice thick coating of calm over proceedings and, for the first couple of years, he had given enough of a damn to do so.

Then he had realised that neither Tenia nor Charl were really going to do anything to each other and that he was simply wasting mana.

Maybe one of these days, the big guy would lose his shit and tear the snidey mare's head off. Then wouldn't he feel silly? But he doubted it.

He flicked his eyes to their erstwhile leader, sitting silently in the middle of her two sisters, watching the daily drama playing out precisely as it had the day before. Although, considering the news they had just received, probably wouldn't tomorrow . . .

The blonde woman caught him looking.

"You have something to add, Irek?"

"Not me," the bearded man returned his focus to his breakfast. "This ain't my circus and those two-" he jerked a thumb at the Reaver and the Berserker -"sure ain't my monkeys."

***

Against her better judgement, this made Hel smile, but the frustration of the situation quickly stole away any sense of humour. "Charl, cool your jets. You don't know when you'll need that mana. And Tenia? Leave him be."

Neither of those addressed acknowledged her words, but she knew they would now settle down—they always did. These daily meetings had progressed almost like clockwork—if the particular clock was designed by a madman stuck in a time loop, relentlessly masturbating over an image of his pet turtle.

First, Tenia would outline the High Priestess' arrival at the Temple. Realising she did this, rather than stayed overnight on the Temple's Third Floor, sadly, had represented the only significant development they'd achieved in about a year. That they didn't know where d'Avec went - or why. Or how – was an area of significant tension. What were they, a highly trained elite, covert intelligence squad well used to operating behind enemy lines? Ahem.

59

Secondly, Charl would get all pissy he already knew this and then Tenia would bite back at which stage it would all go def-con 1 as her fucking <Empath Nullifier> was in too much of a funk to keep a lid on everyone's rage.

Hel rubbed a hand over her face, reached for her own bacon roll, and wondered what they were going to do now the focus of their rage had been taken off the table.

It had all been so much simpler, way back then. When the clean, hard burn of it was at the very centre of their existence. Such drive ensured that they tolerated each other's . . . foibles. But the relentless grind of the years and the constant, undeniable fact that, regardless of how many promises they made, plans set in motion, nor death threats sent, they were approaching their fifth year into this mission and if they had caused Gianna d'Avec as much as a head cold, then there was not a shred of evidence for it.

And now someone had killed her.

Hel snorted, causing the rest of her team to glance towards her in concern. As a <Wind Tyrant>, she could do some fairly destructive things with a sneeze and none of them wanted to be the focus of that particular storm. She ignored them. She'd gotten used to doing that too.

Here they sat in the same cafe, having the same conversations, arguments, and snarks as they had done many times over the years.

It was enough to make Hel weep.

Hel did her best not to glance at her silent sisters sitting on either side of her. Arwel and Erwell were all that remained of her own family, and neither had spoken for their entire lives. Seeing your parents cooked from the inside out would do that, apparently. That they had both become Wraiths was hardly a surprise. That Hel had sufficiently subverted their death wishes to keep them with her to accomplish this task was more of one.

But there were some things you didn't want to dwell on at the eighth bell in a busy working man's cafe. Not when there was bacon to eat.

It had all been so simple. All they needed to do was waylay Gianna d'Avec as she entered or exited the Temple each day. The fact she did that, despite being able to reside in there permanently, had seemed such a gift when Tenia brought it to them.

They had the firepower, the Skills, and the kamikaze indifference to their own survival to ensure that they had every chance of overcoming the Level disparity. Dungeon delvers did such things, daily, and as a matter of course. And they had an expectation - nay, a desirable necessity - of coming out of their encounters alive.

And yet, for all their advantages, they had not been able to make it happen.

And now someone else had done it for them.

The funny thing was, despite the fact that an event they had long dedicated themselves to bring about was coming to pass, nobody was actually feeling remotely happy. Nor, it turned out, did they have anything to talk about which wasn't concerned with planning the violent death of a certain High Priestess.

Irek met Hel's eyes and raised his eyebrows again. She gave a little shake of her head in response. It turned out that she didn't have many better ideas than he did.

Well, wasn't that wonderful. He felt a wobble in the emotional state of one of the two Wraiths - he could never tell them apart- and pressed down more firmly with his Skill.

It was like pouring water into a desert.

"What the fuck are we still doing here?" They all turned to Tenia who, to be fair, was pretty high on their list of most likely to lose her shit first.

"We've met here every day for the last five years. I kind of think it would look pretty damn suspicious if, the morning after a brutal murder, a bunch of Level 40s with rather destructive classes suddenly stopped meeting for breakfast. What do you think?" Hel's voice was tight, and each of them surreptitiously refreshed their defensive Skills.

"What do you think happened?" asked Charl for the sixth time since they sat down.

Arwel and Erwal gave a strange screaming noise in reply that caused silence to fall amongst the rest of the patrons. Hel glanced towards Irek and indicated he needed to do his fucking job and ramp up the levels of chill. The last thing they needed was her sisters freaking out and stripping flesh from bones.

"Look, I'm just going to come out and say it. It wasn't me." Tenia crossed her arms over her chest and sat back, glaring at the others.

Charl nodded. "Me neither."

Irek opened his arms wide. "Goes without saying."

Hel was aware they were all looking at her and her sisters. "It's not quite that simple."

That hardly smoothed out the growing tension.

"I could be wrong," the Nightmare Reaver began, "but it's a pretty fucking binary position. Did you guys kill the High Priestess?"

"Well, first of all, why don't we all keep our fucking voices down. I hear the Security Service are pretty damn motivated to close this case."

"Fair enough, Hel, but what do you mean 'it's not that simple?'" It took a lot to get Charl's goat going, but there were signs that particular ruminant was off and running downhill.

"And stop fucking messing with our emotions!" Tenia pushed out a quick screech of *Banshee* towards Irek, which made the Wraith sisters' little outburst earlier seem like a minor giggle, knocking him to the floor.

Hel flicked a gust of wind towards Tenia, lifting her—and holding her—into the air while simultaneously catching Irek and putting him back on the righted chair.

"Let's all settle the fuck down."

If the group's antics near the window disturbed the rest of the patrons, they didn't show it. To be fair, a little light mayhem was hardly the sort of thing to cause comment in this particular establishment. Nevertheless, the charged scent of personal shields being raised wafted through the air.

Charl snarled and began to increase in size. Hel sucked all the oxygen out of his lungs and quickly returned him to his normal size, spluttering as he did so. She wagged her finger back and forth. "Stop it!"

There was a moment of tense silence.

Tenia gave up struggling and hung sulkily, letting her power bleed from her hands. Irek dropped *Good Cheer* and began channelling *Conciliation* whilst Charl struggled to breathe, going increasingly red as his lungs refused to inflate. The Wraiths sat impassively, staring up at the Temple through the window.

"Do you want me to explain, or do you want to be dicks?"

"To be honest," Irek said, increasing his output and taking yet another Mana potion, "it'd be great if we could do both."

"Well, boo-fucking-hoo." Hel released Charl's lungs and let Tenia fall, unceremoniously, back to the ground. "Let's try to remember who we are — or at least used to be - and keep the total fucking shambles to a minimum."

"For the one of us who appears to need to explain how she might have killed our target without mentioning it to the rest of us, you're being pretty punchy this morning." Tenia glowered.

"Look, as I said, it's not that simple." She glanced at her sisters who continued to sit staring up at the Temple. "It was just before the tenth bell. I was locking up for the night as usual and-" she paused, flashing back to her blind panic of the night before- "well, I realised neither Arwel nor Erwel were in the house."

They all turned to look at the Wraiths, their silhouettes blurring and fading under the intense observation. "And that's unusual?" Irek asked.

"Is it unusual for me to lose track of two beings who have the ability to drain the life force out of anyone they make physical contact with? Who I have had to give my personal assurance to the Council will not take another life in this city? Yeah, pretty fucking unusual."

Irek pushed down on his active Skill a little more. As usual, though, he found that Hel was curiously resistant. In theory, someone of a similar level couldn't be able to push back in this way. However, he couldn't ever remember being able to affect her overmuch.

"So, what happened?" Charl had caught his breath and didn't seem to be holding any grudges over his brief suffocation.

"Well, I knew there was only going to be one place they could have gone. I mean," she jutted her chin towards them, "look at them!"

Her two sisters were staring idly out of the window, their eyes locked on the Third Floor of the Celestial Temple. "It's all they live for. And I use 'live' in the broadest of all possible senses."

"So, you're saying they killed her?" Tenia's voice dripped with skepticism.

Hel's eyes darkened, tempests swirling in their pupils. "I'm not sure at what stage in our relationship you decided you could speak to me in such a way. I would urge you to reconsider the advisability of your tone."

There was a brief moment when Irek could feel Tenia preparing to make an issue of it, and he switched to his most powerful Skill, *Mood Killer*, which, in theory, should take the heat out of any situation.

"Tell your pet manipulator that if he doesn't get out of my head, I'm going to be visiting his dreams tonight, and then we will be having some fun." Tenia's eyes were fixed on Hel.

"Irek. Please." Hel's voice was soft, and with reluctance, he released his Skill. "Now, are we going to play nice, or do I need to remind you the difference between being a monster when asleep versus actually being a real and present one right here."

"To be fair, Hel, it sounds like it's you that's saying you fucked up," Charl chipped in. "Just tell us what happened."

Perhaps realising that when a Berserker Balloon was the voice of reason, you'd probably strayed a little too far away from the reservation, Hel let some of the Skills she was holding drain away.

When the atmosphere calmed slightly, she continued, the hard-edge vanishing from her voice. "It wasn't hard to work out where the two of them had gone and I caught up with them just after they'd entered the Temple. "

"And the Temple Warders?" Irek asked

"At that time of night, it was a skeleton staff, and, well, we all know how good my sisters are at getting in places they shouldn't. Anyway, they'd somehow baffled the Portal Stone and were slipping through to the Third Floor. I caught them both, but I was dragged through alongside them."

"And?" Tenia seemed to have forgotten her previous antagonism and was leaning forward in interest."

"She was still in there. I could hear her arguing with someone within her chamber."

As she spoke, Hel was transported back to the night before, Anwel and Erwel straining against the leashes of air she had placed around them. She'd never truly struggled to control them before, but now - so close to their quarry - they were almost insane with fury. Hel had needed to pop a bubble of oxygen around them all to deaden the noise their snarling and wailing was causing.

She remembered that the light coming from beneath the High Priestess's door had cast a sinister glow around the rest of the floor, and the shadows cast by the Wraiths clawing attempts to break free and assault the door to the receiving chamber were monstrous.

For a moment, Hel had considered letting them loose and adding her own power to the assault. This was an opportunity that surely would not occur again. In all their years of dogging d'Avec's steps, she had never stayed inside the Temple this late after the close of business. It was what had made it so impossible for her to waylay. For a glorious moment, she could see the end of their long vigil.

But then reality kicked in.

They'd planned this so carefully for a reason. Without Charl, Irek or Tenia, there would have been no realistic possibility of success. Even all working together, she put their chances at 50/50, but with only half the team, they were just going to be free XP.

"I have given you my answer," the voice of the High Priestess exploded out from behind the door. Hel could not make out to whom she was speaking and quickly pulled back on her sisters, dragging them back towards the Portal Stone.

"And you just left without doing anything?"

Hel ignored Tenia's scorn. She was suddenly struck by something she hadn't registered at the time. There had been a dampness to the air on the Third Floor, which was wholly unusual around the High Priestess.

Had there been ... water coming from under her chamber door?

"What happened next, Hel?" Charl was leaning forward, the table creaking under his weight.

Hel put that thought away. "We got out of there as fast as we could. But I can tell you, Gianna d'Avec was hale and hearty just past the tenth bell."

CHAPTER 13 - WATER IN HER BLOOD

"I can assure you, there can be little doubt about the time of death. Despite the . . . damage caused to the body, enough of it remained intact for me to note that life finally extinguished no later than the seventh bell."

Lowe had never liked this Deathcaller. There was something about a person who had dedicated every aspect of his Class to focus on dealing with the dead which was . . . weird. It didn't help, of course, that Penarth Lant was, by any measure, a creepy motherfucker.

He was short, barely five foot tall, and was that curious mix of both skinny and fat: his arms and legs being stick-thin, but with an enormous pot belly that he massaged as if soothing a kicking baby. Adding to his unattractive vibe, he was also completely hairless – in a naked mole rat kind of way - and had incongruously thick glasses perched on the end of his giant nose. To Lowe's certain knowledge, Lant had no need for any vision correction and wore them merely to give himself an excuse to press his face into the personal space of pretty young Mortuary Assistants.

Creepy. Motherfucker.

"You seem unusually confident in that assertion, Penarth."

Despite his desire to call on Gravalk, Lowe had recognised that a little bridge-building was required with Latham first. The Temple Warder had saved his life this morning (of course, he'd then absolutely kicked his arse a few moments later), and he'd probably earned a little bit more consideration than Lowe had shown him thus far.

He'd therefore agreed with Latham's suggestion that before bothering a Fire Demon or even interviewing any further suspects, it would be sensible to give the Deathcaller a visit and see how the land lay.

"Mr. Lowe . . ."

"Inspector," Lowe corrected.

Penarth blinked, then ran the word around his mouth as if it were a peculiarly unpleasant piece of fruit. "Inspector. To my certain understanding, after the unpleasantness of last year, you had been stripped of rank, Skills and your position. Has there been a reversal of that . . . calamity?"

Lowe chose to ignore that the emphasis on that final word sounded uncommonly like 'joyous and much celebrated circumstance.' "I have been re-activated to investigate the demise of the High Priestess."

"No other sucker wanted the job, I presume?" Penarth cackled.

Lowe shrugged. "Perhaps. But I'm more interested in a time of death right now. You have no doubt, no doubt whatsoever, that Gianna d'Avec was a dead body by the seventh bell? You understand this is likely to be reasonably important?"

Penarth gazed owlishly back. "No. This is, after all, my first day on the job, and I am, of course, profoundly stupid. We have discussed - many times, if I recall correctly, Mr. Lowe - that Deathcalling is not an exact science. My apologies,

Temporarily Reactivated Inspector Lowe. However, on this occasion, there is enough evidence that the High Priestess was beyond this vale of tears by the time I have indicated for me to make that statement with confidence."

"And that evidence is?" Lowe was doing an impressive job of keeping his temper under control. Penarth sighed and reached for a scroll lying on his messy desk. He pushed his glasses to the top of his bald head and peered at his crabbed handwriting.

"There is no evidence of residual mana in any of the subject's channels. You will know, with all your years of experience in the business, of course, what that signifies?"

"Assume I have not been keeping up with my reading of 'Mortuary Monthly'."

Penarth's voice took on - if possible - an even more supercilious tone. "It has been determined that Mana usage has a half-life of three-quarters of a bell, with it becoming untraceable within ten hours. At that stage, channels go through a process called 'lamination' for the next three bells. Gianna d'Avec's channels contain no mana and only minor lamination. This would indicate that the last time that the High Priestess used her mana was, at most, thirteen bells ago. As I am sure you will agree, it is unlikely a Pyromancer of her talent would not have used her mana in her defence, then it stands to reason she fought - and died - no later than the seventh bell."

Latham clicked his tongue, and Penarth pulled down his glasses to peer at the corner of the room. "Do you have a comment Temple Warder?"

"Only that it sounds to me like you have identified the last time the High Priestess used her mana, not when she died."

"Your point being?"

"Only that you seem rather certain the two events are linked."

Penarth cackled his high-pitched laugh. "It would, of course, be easier to determine a time of death should the Temple Warders have been, oh, what is the word? Ah, yes. 'Warding'? Tell me, I presume you have conducted your own investigation into these events. How was someone able to gain access to the Priestess's floor without crossing your esteemed compatriots? Moreover, it is my understanding that this particular avatar was rarely to be found within the Temple after the sixth bell. Has there been any explanation for why she was working out of hours?"

Lowe took a step backwards to be outside splatter range should Latham take umbrage at the Deathcaller's words. He was unsure what defences the Level 39 had, but he severely doubted, if Latham made an issue as things, he had much to keep that ugly dome intact.

Oddly, though, Latham's reaction was more shamefaced than Lowe would have expected. "We are looking into the failings of our systems, as you would expect. But that has no bearing on whether you are accurately noting the High Priestess's time of death."

Penarth pushed his glasses up onto his forehead again. "For clarity," his voice had taken on the hectoring tone again, "I can say with certainty that Gianna D'Avec did not use her mana after the seventh bell. If you want to argue that she died after that - without any use of her Skills in her defence - then that is entirely up to you. In the absence of a witness to argue differently, I will confidently sign the Death Certificate to that effect."

"Even if you make my life more difficult?"

"My dear Temporarily Reinstated Much-Maligned Inspector, the only way I could care less about your life would be if you turned up on my table."

"Well, fuck you too. Is there anything useful you have to add besides a somewhat questionable time of death?"

Penarth went to snap back an answer, then paused as if reconsidering. "Okay. Being as how you have been such a joy, why don't you have a look at her?"

He waddled over to the table in the centre of his room, holding his belly in a protective cradle. Lowe had been doing his best to ignore its presence, as well as what was presumably lying under the blanket that rested on top of it.

With little ceremony, the Deathcaller whipped the covering back, exposing the body that lay beneath. Despite having seen the corpse in situ, there was something more impactful about seeing Gianna d'Avec like this. Someone, presumably Penarth, had reconstituted the body, sewing each of the detached parts back together. The effect was to bring home the humanity of the victim in a way that seeing the blood-soaked chamber had not.

Lowe found himself looking upon the face of a woman much younger than he had anticipated. Without the drama of the Third Floor setting, with the aftermath of violence exacerbating everything, he realised Gianna d'Avec had been barely into her twenties.

Thinking back to Aintra Weber describing serving her for the last ten years and Mylaf's stories of years working for her, he had expected her to be much older. It occurred that the High Priestess had entered the Temple as little more than a child.

He was about to ask Latham how common that was when he realised, he'd missed what Penarth was saying.

" - which I am finding hard to explain."

"Sorry, Deathcaller, I did not catch that. What was the point you were making?"

Penarth made much of sighing and rolling his eyes at the Inspector. "I will repeat myself once more for those in the cheap seats, at which stage I will ask you to remove yourself from my mortuary and await my report like every other member of the Security Services."

The strange little man paused and cleared his throat for effect. "It is somewhat interesting, considering the element with which the High Priestess was most familiarly associated, that the level of water within her blood is exceptionally high."

Lowe thought back to the water that covered the floor of the High Priestess' chamber. He had assumed something was leaking - a burst pipe, perhaps - but now he was not so sure.

"When you say 'exceptionally high' . . ."

"A level that, for a normal being, would have demonstrated an incompatibility with life. I am, though, happy to note that this particular victim is the highest level that has ever made an appearance on my table. I have made enquiries of my peers across the continent as to whether it is normal to see such a phenomenon in those approaching the upper threshold, and there has been little consensus. The only true thing that can be said is that everything and anything is possible."

Lowe found himself looking at the stitching at the neck and at the sockets of her arms and legs. This had been a brutal death. "So, to summarise, you have identified that the last time Gianna d'Avec accessed her mana was shortly before the seventh bell. On top of this, you note that there is an unusual concentration of water - an element which is the antithesis of her fire mana - within her blood. I guess I need to ask, do you think those two factors are connected?"

Penarth's head was nodding like a child's toy. "I have no idea."

Latham chimed in. "Do you think it is likely that the two are connected? "

"I couldn't possibly comment. There is such a lack of information available about those post-65 that I would simply be guessing."

Lowe ran his hands through his hair. "Just thinking aloud, here. If we assume that it was not normal for the High Priestess to have an overbearance of water in her blood, and we further consider that the reason she was unable to make use of her mana was this particular condition, how could this state of being come to pass?"

Penarth threw his hands up in the air. "I am not in the business of blind guessing! That is, I may suggest, what you are supposed to be doing."

"Gravalk," Latham said with certainty. "The Fire Demon must have forsaken her."

Lowe nodded. "I'm afraid, mate, I rather think we're going to need to make that call on a god after all."

CHAPTER 14 – ASHES IN THE CHANDELIER

It turned out it was much easier to make an appointment to see a god than might have been initially assumed.

"You're kidding me?" Lowe said, sure Latham was shining him on.

"Not at all. It is, after all, one of the founding principles of Soar that the gods are available to speak to any citizen that wishes an audience."

"And there's no downside?"

"Of course, there's a fucking downside. Why do you think no one does it? Should the god find your petition to be frivolous, irritating or - as is most often the case - just wants to be a dick, you'll lose your Class, half your levels and, if you're even slightly unlucky, your life too."

"That doesn't seem that they're really that committed to those founding principles after all, does it?"

Latham stopped striding down the corridor in the basement of the Temple and allowed Lowe the chance to catch up. "Little man, what do you expect? They're gods. They have more enjoyable ways of spending their time than being questioned by the likes of you."

"So, what do I do? Just close my eyes and pray?"

Latham looked at Lowe with such disgust that Lowe felt actively ashamed of himself. "No. You don't 'just close your eyes and pray'!" He raised a meaty hand and tapped the sign above the door they had halted outside: it read 'Contact Booth. "You step inside one of these bad boys, then you close your eyes and pray."

Lowe pushed open the door and looked around inside. It was a strangely nondescript space, considering this was supposed to facilitate contact with one of the almighty. There was a chair, and next to it was a side table with a jug of water and a glass on top of it. The only other thing in there was a massive series of pigeonholes dominating one wall. Inside each of them was a huge packet of incense sticks.

"Come on, get on with it. I don't want to be down here any longer than I have to be." Latham pointed to a chalkboard sign that read '0 days since our last Smiting.' "Bad shit goes on down here."

Lowe had a moment reflecting on whether he should be so gung-ho for something that was so freaking out a Temple Warder. However, despite how much he'd rather die than admit it to anyone, he had felt more like himself in the last day than he had for as long as he could remember.

Of course, he'd spent much of the last year trying to forget how much he enjoyed the cut and thrust of an actual investigation. Even his testy back and forth with Penarth had the comforting familiarity of long experience. His time trying to make enough gold to get by as a PI hadn't had anything like the same buzz.

Murder had its own gravitational pull.

But, as well as that sense of doing something that mattered again, there was also something about the unlined face of this particular victim lying on the Deathcaller's table that had lit a fire under him. Even more so than the attack on him in the alley, that was spurring him towards uncovering the truth about what happened.

Random beatings were part and parcel of being in the Security Service - there was even a whole expenses form dedicated to claiming back medical expenses associated with 'Punishment Kickings' - but it was rare to feel something of a connection with the victim.

The humbleness of the High Priestess's accommodation and her unexpected youth were making him pretty motivated to get to the bottom of what had occurred.

And if that meant speaking to a god, then so be it.

"So, what do I do?" he asked Lathan, stepping into the booth.

The Temple Warder sighed and followed him into the room, locking the door to the Contact Booth behind them. "It's not that complicated, little man. Find your god, light the offering, then sit down and wait." He painted towards the pigeonholes.

Lowe walked over and was immediately overwhelmed by the number of names before him. There appeared to be no apparent order, and he didn't recognise many of them. "This is chaos!"

"This is Soar. We have more gods than there are citizens."

Lowe kept scanning up and down the wall. "Help a fellow out. Where's Gravalk?"

Latham sighed and walked to the rows of pigeonholes. He pointed to one towards the lower left-hand corner. "You better believe that I'm not touching anything in here. This is a fool's errand, and I'm not risking a connection with a fucking fire demon that just lost its avatar. "

Lowe reached into the small wooden cupboard and removed a packet of incense. He removed one stick and carefully put the others back. The packet instantly filled up again.

"Now what?"

"You cannot seriously be this fucking helpless! Weren't you supposed to be some sort of shit-hot Investigator?"

"I like to think my particular set of skills were somewhat more ... specialist." Latham's expression suggested he had limited confidence this was the case. "What do I do know about praying to the gods?"

"Okay. This is a one-time crash course. Take a seat, light the prayer candle and hope whichever god you are bothering is in the mood for triviality."

Lowe sat down, holding up the incense stick. "Do you have a light?"

"For fuck's sake. You know, there are babes in arms out there that can light their own birthday candles, little man?"

"Good for them. I, on the other hand, possess no such skill."

Latham's eyes flicked to the right, and a somewhat unnecessarily large flame burst into being on the top of the incense, burning half of it away instantly. "Get on with it."

Lowe settled down in the chair and poured himself a glass of water, holding the incense, which smelt distinctly of the aftermath of a forest fire. "So, I just pray?"

"You know how to pray, don't you, little man? Just close your eyes and beg."

Ignoring the jibe, Lowe closed his eyes. He couldn't remember the last time he had prayed; it was certainly long before he became classless. A more suspicious man might think the two events were somehow linked.

But a long-term citizen of Soar understood how little that was likely to be the case. The gods did not care for them.

Feeling foolish, he reached out with his mind, breathing in the forest fire smell to help him focus. "Erm, Gravalk? Could you spare a moment?"

There was no sudden moment of epiphany. Bushes did not burn. Tablets were not handed clown. And there was no sudden realisation of oneness with the universe.

Instead, Lowe became aware of a low growling sound just at the edge of his hearing. As if he'd stumbled into the presence of an especially malign guard dog.

For whatever reason, the temperature in the Contact Booth felt like it had gone through the roof. Lowe tried to open his eyes, but his facial muscles were no longer under his control. Sweat sprung out on his forehead and began to run down his cheeks, pooling at the collar of his shirt. The smell of burning wood suddenly became deeply sulphuric, and Lowe's sinuses felt like they were being scoured from the inside out.

When they came, the words were less in a language Lowe understood and more on a fundamental soul level: "What do you want?"

Lowe wished he was able to lick his lips, but his head was frozen in place. "My name is Jana Lowe. I am Investigating the murder of ..."

"Bored now."

The temperature increased exponentially, the sweat on his skin evaporating, his eyebrows and hair beginning to char.

"Your High Priestess. Gianna d'Avec. I want to catch whoever killed her," Lowe sent desperately. The heat surrounding Lowe stopped increasing, holding at an unbearable level. "Why?"

Lowe was not certain how to respond. He was, he was sure, literally, metaphorically and spiritually melting in the presence of the Fire Demon. What answer was likely to get a positive response?

His mind flashed back to sitting on his mother's knee. "The thing you must remember about the gods, Jana, is if all else fails, flatter them." Even at the time, he had known there was something distasteful about omnipotent beings who cared more for their feelings than anything so mundane as 'the truth'. Right now, though? Fuck it.

"The disrespect. It is wrong that anyone could seek to displace your avatar. They need to be brought to justice."

It might have just been his fever talking, but he could swear the temperature lowered a degree or two.

"Disrespect? I have been disrespected?"

Lowe tried to project every possible version of 'Don't let them do you like that, bro,' he'd ever witnessed. "Someone killed your High Priestess. I would think you'd want them caught. And, you know, burned alive or something."

"Will have new High Priest, soon. Quick lived things. Fragile."

The heat was rising again and Lowe thought desperately for another approach. "But that should be to your timetable, shouldn't it? You are a god. You should be able to choose when to end the lives of your avatar. But that was stolen from you. By a murderer."

"Stolen?"

Lowe shared the image of the dead High Priestess on the despoiled floor of the temple. Of the water spilt across the floor. "Someone went against your will. Can you help me find out who?"

The heat in the Contact Booth dropped through the floor and then, just as quickly, became hotter than the inside of a forge. In the middle of the Sun. On a particularly hot day. As it did so, a cavalcade of images hit him. Gianna arguing with various figures - some Lowe had met, some he didn't recognise. Then the High Priestess was alone, holding her head, tears streaming from her eyes. But they weren't tears, were they? The water was exploding from her like a waterfall - just pushing its way through her pores.

The pressure of the water caused the explosion of her left leg from her body first. Then her right. Both in a shower of blood, gore and water.

It was a horrific sight, ending when her head exploded straight up to land in the middle of the chandelier. In the corner of the vision, a shadowy, hooded figure slipped out of the chamber and locked the door behind them.

Then the heat vanished, and he could move his face again. Lowe opened his eyes and fell to his knees, screaming in relief. Latham was helping him up, pouring the jug of water over his head. "What happened? Did Gravalk answer?"

Lowe shook his head, trying to clear the noise of Gravalk shouting out the same words over and over again. "How dare they! How dare they! Burn them. Burn them all!"

CHAPTER 15 – SHADOWS IN THE MARBLE

If Latham thought there was anything odd about what had happened, he didn't mention it.

The Temple Warder had dusted Lowe down and marched him out of the long corridor of the Contact Booths and back up the stairs to the ground floor of the Temple proper.

His brief contact with Gravalk had given Lowe much to think about. He now had an explanation for the unusual nature of d'Avec's death and confirmation that whoever had been present at her . . . demise had been able to lock the chamber door behind them.

Lowe had learned enough about him to activate *Grid View* during his vision, and he was looking forward - if they were the right words - to properly examining what he had captured. But that would have to wait as Latham almost carried him across the floor and out of the Celestial Temple. He had an appointment with the High Priestess's lawyer.

As Lowe approached the large, domed building, he reflected that the Tower of Law was not quite as impressive as the Celestial Temple. Because if there was one thing lawyers understood, it was that there was a significant percentage in letting your most prestigious—not to say homicidal—clients take the lead in architectural brilliance.

Instead of the towering majesty of the gods' home, the Tower of Law had an understated grandeur. It sat on the edge of the financial district and, as opposed to the many entranced Temple, had just one heavily guarded door.

In his prelapsarian existence, Lowe had spent many long hours in this building. Most of the time, of course, it was in trying to persuade reluctant Advocates to get off their arses and seek to prosecute the criminals he had nearly killed himself - sometimes literally - to get into a dungeon.

Oh, that he had been, for want of a better word, 'dating' one of the lawyers that worked there may, perhaps, have also been a good reason for him spending so long within its walls.

However, as Lowe approached the entranceway to the Tower, he realised he hadn't been there in over a year.

On either side of the heavily barred iron door stood two Justiciars, neither of whom he recognised. They were watching him suspiciously. But no, Lowe realised, it wasn't him they were giving colossal stink-eye to. It was Latham.

When they were a couple of feet away, the two guards clashed their massive halberds together, barring the way with an imposing metallic X.

"The Tower is closed today."

"I have an appointment." Lowe had absolutely no time for territorial dick-waving. "Open up, there's a good gate monkey."

The guard to the left, Kaith, a Level ?? Justicar jutted his chin at Latham. "There's no chance of the likes of him getting in here."

Latham didn't say anything; he just unsheathed his massive sword from its scabbard on his back and rolled his shoulders. That was pretty damn loquacious as introductions went.

The second Justiciar, Ganorth, also a Level ??, put a fairly unattractive sneer on his face. "Mate, put the pigsticker away. I wouldn't swagger into your fucking Temple expecting a warm welcome. You don't try on that shit here. Toddle on back to the god-botherers."

It seemed like Lowe would have to be the person to calm everything down. He looked up at the Temple Warder and put on his best 'it's going to be okay' smile. Funnily enough, he did not get to use that expression very much. "Look, I know people in here, and they're expecting me. I'm going to be okay."

Latham didn't take his eyes off the two guards. "My orders are unequivocal: I will not let you out of my sight during this investigation."

"No one's going to kill me in the fucking Tower of Law!"

Latham paused and then spoke in a tone that suggested he was addressing a particularly slow child. "I know you are labouring under the misconception that I am following you around for your safety, but – as I keep trying to make it clear—my job is straightforward. I am to be at your shoulder throughout this investigation in case it needs to be terminated."

Lowe tried to determine how much truth there was in those words. He thought there was a bit more of a bond between them than that. The Temple Watcher had given him advice about his build, hadn't he? But then again, he'd been pretty free with his hands at other times.

Lowe took a step away from the big man's shadow. "Okay, well, cheers for that. But I need to find out the terms of the High Priestess's will, and it doesn't look like matey boys here will give you access. So, see you later."

Lowe strode towards the crossed halberds, which, much to his surprise, opened to let him pass. He didn't glance back to see what Latham did, but considering the lack of the sound of bedlam, he assumed he hadn't followed. Lowe put his hand on the door and was portalled inside the Tower of Law.

***

It took Lowe a minute for his head to stop spinning. He channelled as much mana as he could to *Roll with the Punches*, but, as usual with portal travel, it seemed travel sickness was not really a physical symptom.

"Jana? What are you doing here?"

Excellent, the hits just kept on coming. Maybe if he kept his eyes closed, it would turn out his ex-girlfriend wouldn't be there when he got control of himself.

He felt a gentle hand rest on his shoulder. "Portal sickness?" Her soft voice was filled with empathy; of course, it fucking was. "Just breathe."

Realising he was probably beginning to draw attention for all the wrong reasons, he opened his eyes and met the gaze of Arebella Telut.

A long-term ... acquaintance.

"Bella. I wasn't expecting to see you here."

The woman standing before him was short, barely five feet tall, and had long blonde hair framing a heart-shaped face. One of the things he had always found difficult about her during their on-again, off-again relationship was the way her dark brown eyes pierced him and held him like a fish on a spear. For someone used to talking himself out of any number of awkward situations, he had always found her calm regard disconcerting.

"Clearly," she took her hand off his shoulder and stood back, smiling at him warmly. "Imagine my surprise when I saw your name on today's visitor list. I'd have thought you might let me know you would be calling in."

Lowe was aware that other people were coming through the portal and starting to push past him. He slipped his hand under Arebella's arm and led her to a side alcove away from the passing traffic.

"It's just on a case. I didn't want to bother you."

"You never bother me by dropping in." There was a momentary pause. "Although it's been a while since you did so."

"Well, you know. Kind of felt that after what had happened, you'd appreciate me keeping my distance."

Arabella tilted her head. "That's silly. You know that sort of thing doesn't matter to me."

The thing is, Lowe did know that. From the moment he'd lost his Class, she couldn't have been more supportive. But enough people had had quiet words in his shell-like that Arebella's bosses were looking askance at her relationship with a figure who had attracted such scandal. So, he'd done what, in his mind, was the decent thing.

He'd ghosted her without any explanation.

Lowe looked at her properly after his vision had cleared of vomit-inducing tears. And his eyes widened.

"You've evolved your Class!"

Arebella blushed slightly and tucked a loose strand of hair behind her ear. "Well, I haven't had much to go on other than my work lately." Those words might have seemed accusative in another person's mouth, but she meant it literally. "And I was fortunate to be assigned a case that carried an unusually high XP reward."

"So, what is a Veritas Assessor when it's at home?"

Her blush deepened. "It sounds grander than it is. I've just gained access to a broader range of techniques focused on parsing statements for inconsistencies."

His face must have betrayed his confusion because she cleared her throat and pressed onward to clarify. "I've specialised in being able to identify lies."

Now, it was Lowe's turn to blush. There was nothing like hearing your . . . was she still his girlfriend if they'd not seen each other in months? Whatever. It felt something like a relatively clear statement of intent when someone you'd been in a relationship with chose to specialise in spotting untruths.

He was feeling pretty judged.

"Well, good for you," he said, anxious to end the conversation now. "It's been nice to see you. I'll call you." No sooner had he said the last sentence, but the sides of her mouth creased downwards slightly. He suspected she had one of her new Skills running whilst they were talking.

"Sure," she said, the smile on her face not reaching her eyes.

They looked at each other for a moment, and Lowe was once again struck that he had lost more than just his Class in the last year.

Then she stepped closer, lowering her voice so she wouldn't be overhead. "My office is on the next floor up. Stop by before you leave. I think I've picked up something about the death of the High Priestess that you need to know."

Arebella pressed a small Portal Stone into his hand, and he caught a trace of her perfume. It was one he'd bought her for her birthday. She'd asked for it, and it had taken him weeks of searching to identify a supplier. His colleagues had been less than kind about what this suggested about his investigatory powers.

He smiled awkwardly at her as he stepped away. "I've got to see a Mr. Velehim about the d'Avec will, but then I'll stop by. If you're sure I won't be taking you away from something better you should be doing?"

Arebella turned and walked away, looking back over her shoulder. "Don't let me down, Jana." She fluttered a wave and then was lost in the crowds of lawyers and their clients.

Lowe stood momentarily, pretending he hadn't heard the unspoken 'again' in her voice as she walked away.

CHAPTER 16 – A COURTESY OF VIOLENCE

It would be fair to say Lowe was not at his best in the immediate aftermath of his meeting with Arebella.

Indeed, he hadn't realised exactly how discombobulated he was until he found himself asking the small, wizened Senior Recorder to repeat himself for the third time.

"Mr. Lowe," the man sighed, speaking from beneath insanely bushy eyebrows, "do you have somewhere else you would rather be?"

"Yes. I mean, no. I'm sorry, I've been distracted, haven't I? My apologies."

Cadi Verahalim sat back and folded his arms, dislodging an avalanche of dandruff off his shoulders as he did so. "I hope you realise, Mr. Lowe, that I bill for my time by the second. I am doing you a considerable favour by blocking out my calendar to assist the Security Service in its enquiries. My patience is not, however, infinite."

Lowe bit back a response, reflecting that the old lawyer was justified for being a touch narked at his lack of attention. "Once again, sir, I am sorry for my behaviour. Please do continue."

Somewhat mollified, the Senior Recorder sat forward and smoothed out the document he had been referring to. "Fair enough. Never let it be said that I wasn't a man to accept a grovelling apology when it was offered. As I was saying, the High Priestess was of the habit of altering her Will."

"Is that unusual?" Lowe didn't think he'd updated his Will since Cenorth had forced him to write one the second – or was it the third? – time he'd bled out on the job.

Verahalim gave a little shrug. "Avatars are not like the rest of us, Mr. Lowe. I have often had cause to reflect that the closer my clients are to the gods, the more likely they are to have their eyes on their own demise."

"That's a fair comment."

Verahalim's face suggested that, at his Level, it was somewhat pointless – indeed, spectacularly rude – to suggest otherwise. "Quite. Where, perhaps, the High Priestess was unusual is that she had no one really to leave her considerable wealth to. Her updates were to add various charities to the list of beneficiaries."

"Charities?"

"I have said." The Senior Recorder was clearly reaching the very outer limits of his patience.

"Pardon me for casting aspersions, but it is somewhat against what would be seen as her public persona. Even her colleagues have been somewhat reticent in their praise for her personality. I am a touch surprised to hear that she would choose to dispose of all her estate in that way. Are you sure there is no particular person that would benefit in the event of her death?"

Verahalim scowled back. "It has been a point of principle to me over the years not to be overly concerned with my client's personality."

"So, all of her assets are, essentially, to be given away?"

The lawyer glanced over the Will. "Well, there is a consistent provision of a relatively small sum for her Drudge. I hesitate to tell you your business, but I have my doubts that two hundred and fifty pieces of gold would be sufficient to encourage an attempt in the life of a Level 67. Particularly by a glorified dustpan and brush."

Lowe had investigated cases of murder where the sums involved were far less than two hundred and fifty, but he took Verahalim's point. He made a mental note to let Mylaf know that she had been remembered by d'Avec – albeit in fairly minor terms.

"Is there anything particularly noteworthy about the charities?"

Verahalim looked like he had been asked to investigate a bucket of cat sick. "They are charities, Mr. Lowe. Orphans. War Veterans. Young Carers. With each level-up, the High Priestess was in the habit of adding another one to the list."

"And did any of them lose out because of the addition of another recipient?" Lowe was unsure whether he could see a crack squad of chuggers hunting down the High Priestess for the snub of leaving them slightly less money.

"No, Mr. Lowe. To be clear, Gianna d'Avec only came to see me to log a new Will when her wealth increased. She seemed curiously determined to ensure all of her money was allocated. It occurred . . ." the little man's face scrunched up in discontent. The effect, Lowe assumed of nearly giving an opinion away for free.

"What occurred, Mr. Verahalim?"

The Senior Recorder steepled his fingers at his lips, considering. His whole body gave a little shrug as if casting off his reluctance. "It had occurred to me that she found something distasteful about her money. I wondered whether she was seeking to dispose of her wealth in this manner because she felt she had something to make up for."

"But you never asked her?"

Verahalim paused. "I did ask her, not at this latest Will change, I would have you know, but some years back. Her answer has stayed with me."

"Which was?"

"'When you have so much blood on your hands, every bit of mercy helps.'"

***

There wasn't really much more for the two of them to discuss after that, and shortly later, Lowe made his excuses to leave. He'd scanned the last five of d'Avec's Wills into *Grid View*, but he wasn't sure what benefit that would be. It was basically just a list of worthy institutions, increasing in number with each new iteration.

Lowe paused outside the closed door and stared off into the distance. He didn't know what to make of that. In his experience of murder cases, you followed the money and that led you to where you needed to be. But, unless Mylaf had lost her mind for a few months' salary, there was literally no evidence of anyone killing the High Priestess over money.

And what the fuck was a High Priestess of Gravalk doing giving away all her money to charity?

77

Without realising it, he was spinning Arebella's portal stone between the knuckles of his left hand. The sensible thing to do was to let her get on with her life. She was clearly making impressive progress, and the Tower of Law being what it was, a connection to a washed-up Classless with all sorts of scandals connected to them was hardly the sort of thing to enhance her career.

And yet. And yet. And yet.

He was so distracted by his thoughts that Lowe didn't notice the approaching fist until it caught him on the jaw.

The impact spun him to his left, catching his knee a painful blow against the wall. The portal stone he was holding spun away down the corridor. Oddly, that irritated him more than anything else. He activated *Slugger* and flashed out a return punch — interrupting *Roll with the Punches* as his Mana drained away. Fortunately, those excellent points he'd dropped into Intelligence gave him a bit more of a buffer than he'd been used to: that and Mylaf's goodies.

This turned out to be particularly pertinent as, when his swinging fist made contact with the stomach of his attacker, it stopped dead, and the bones of his hand shattered into quite a number of constituent parts. Unfortunately, the good luck didn't end there. The power of *Slugger*, finding itself unable to transfer itself into the intended victim, stopped, then travelled back up Lowe's arm, turning his radius and ulna into – literal – dust.

This stung a bit.

But not as much as the follow-up punch to the other side of his head, which briefly knocked him out.

***

As he came round, staring at the ceiling, his woes were added to by the all-too-familiar feeling of Mana exhaustion throbbing into a massive headache and *Roll with the Punches* spluttering off.

"Mr. Lowe? No, please do not speak. I'm sure you're not feeling at your best right now. For future reference, do remember that when you are not within the aura of your bodyguard, it is unwise to assault your betters. Are you still with me, sir? Blink twice if you are."

Lowe tried to blink, but only his left eye responded. If by 'responded' you meant 'filled with blood'.

"I imagine that will have to do. Now, for the point of this little confrontation. No one needs the death of Gianna d'Avec to be solved. Trust me on this. Surely you recognise that the whole reason you have been put in charge of this case is that failure is assured? No, no, don't try to get up. I'm not sure you will survive me tapping you again. Instead, please do listen to the sincerity of my message. All that is required of you in this little performance is that you stumble around in your trademark, shambolic manner and, perhaps this time next week, come to the conclusion that you are defeated in the absence of any new leads. Groan, if you are following the logic of my argument."

Lowe made a half-hearted gurgle.

"Excellent. It appears we are having a meeting of the minds here. Now, it is disappointing that you have needed to hear this message twice. However, I understand professional pride and the undoubted bravado caused by having a Temple Warder at your side. This, of course, was what induced you to be somewhat resistant to the request of my more junior colleagues. It is though," and the voice drew closer to him, though the speaker's face remained outside his vision, "important you recognise there will be no third discussion of this matter."

Lowe felt pressure on his ankle and assumed his assailant was standing on it. To be fair, there were so many other demands on his pain receptors that he kind of considered this unnecessary effort. "One week, Mr. Lowe. At which stage you will shrug your shoulders, report this as unsolvable and vanish back into obscurity."

The pressure on his ankle continued to increase, the bone creaking. "Should it come to my employer's attention that you do not comply with this request, there will be consequences." Lowe's ankle shattered, adding some further joy and happiness to his day.

"And let me be clear," the voice was just next to his ear now and became a whisper. "I understand you may be tempted to damn the repercussions and accept whatever punishment I can deal out to you. Your reputation precedes you in this. However, please consider how many of your – I hesitate to say 'friends', perhaps 'acquaintances?' – your decision may impact upon. Should you disappoint me next week, you will live – however briefly – to regret it. It has been a pleasure, Mr. Lowe."

All that remained to be heard was the soft sound of footsteps moving away down the corridor.

CHAPTER 17 – THE SMOKE NEVER LIES

Lowe's suspicion that he had been somewhat set up was not disproved by the absence of anyone stumbling upon his broken body. For a building as busy as the Tower of Law, it was unlikely that he could lie undisturbed for quite so long.

His attacker had not only been able to smack him about as if he were a newborn kitten - suggesting a Level of at least 40 - but also had enough clout, or at least his employer did, to clear the floor. Lowe remembered back to the avenue earlier when something eerily similar had happened. Whoever was responsible for these two beatings had some significant pull . . .

As he waited for his Mana to come back - one of the key frustrations that he had with *Roll with the Punches* was that it sucked out his Mana immediately, meaning his current healing process was basically the equivalent of throwing a cupful of water on a towering inferno - Lowe reflected that he'd be wise not to jump too far in assuming whoever was focused upon kicking his arse had anything to do with the death of the High Priestess. The temptation was there, certainly, but the nature of Soar and the complexity of favours and backscratching meant that his most recent tormentor might be six, seven steps removed from the actual perpetrator of the crime he was investigating.

There was every chance he was taking a kicking because of something he'd done years before, and his current case was simply an excuse to get the expense of hiring muscle past some crime boss's Accountant.

Taking tiny little breaths so as not to disturb the fragility of his healing bones, Lowe accessed his inventory but quickly found he couldn't summon the requisite concentration to pull anything out. The throbbing pain was really quite distracting.

There was simply nothing to be done but lie in the corridor, helpless, until he'd healed up sufficiently to be able to grab one of Mylaf's creations.

Lowe was not overly disposed towards self-pity, but it was times like this where he found himself bitterly remembering those first few moments after his Class was stripped from him. He remembered being overwhelmed by helplessness that, until that second, had been quite alien to his life. Of course, it had since become his daily experience. At times like this - and this precise situation had played out far too often over the last year for the good of his mental health - he tended to pretend that he'd died at that moment and that a new, different, reduced Lowe had been born from the ashes.

In truth, it was the only way he could cope with the waves of shame and disgust that threatened to drown him as he lay, utterly powerless, waiting to be able to move again.

"Jana?"

And the hits just kept on coming.

"Jana, what's wrong?" There was a flurry of footsteps, and then Arebella's face appeared in his vision. "What happened to you? Are you okay?"

Lowe didn't trust himself to answer without sobbing. His jaw was in far too many pieces. Then, a Health Potion was pressed to his lips, and a minor portion of his agony receded. He moved his lips experimentally and found he could form the word "Mana".

As soon as the blue liquid sloshed down his open throat, *Roll with the Punches* sprang into action and started to reconfigure his shattered frame. It was an odd quirk of the Skill that it was far more efficient for him to be fed Mana potions than taking five or six of the equivalent red Health potions.

Even so, it took three more vials of Mana before the confounding agony receded sufficiently for Lowe to be able to pull a flask of Mylaf's breakfast smoothie out of his inventory. The +400 HP snapped, quite literally, everything back into place. Which was quite the vibe.

"Let's get you to my office, and then you can tell me what is happening."

Lowe barely had a chance to warn her about the likely undesirable outcome of using a portal right now before she pressed the stone she had retrieved from further down the corridor into his hand, and they both vanished.

    *

With *Roll with the Punches* now having enough Mana to work with, Lowe was feeling a bit more like himself. If, of course, he could ignore the fact he'd recently redecorated Arebella's very nicely appointed office with the remains of a banana, orange and apple smoothie.

"Sorry about that," he managed as her Personal Assistant appeared and cast a cleaning Skill on the rug. And the bookcase. And the curtains. And, after a moment of hesitation, Lowe himself.

"It's fine," Arebella said, filling a glass of water and passing it to him. And the most painful thing was that he knew, in her mind, it was. That was the biggest problem he found with dealing with her. She was absolutely the nicest and kindest person in the entirety of Soar. "I should have remembered a portal would have that effect on you. Especially without your Class."

The Personal Assistant exited, giving Lowe the sort of look he assumed was the last thing a bag full of puppies saw before being lobbed into the river. It actually made him feel a touch more normal. Genifer had fucking hated his guts long before the scandal. In fact, it made him feel almost at home, being the recipient of her white-hot scorn.

Once she was sure he wouldn't drop the glass, Arebella perched opposite him, curling her legs beneath her in the chair. He knew she did this because, being so short, the alternative was that her legs would dangle about half a foot from the floor. "How are you feeling?"

Lowe shrugged. He wasn't in any physical pain anymore, and his mana exhaustion had passed, but the echoes of his beating lingered on. "You get used to it," he said with more bravado than he felt.

But the truth was, you didn't.

"And you have no idea who attacked you?"

He'd never liked to lie to Arebella, even before she'd gained a Skill that highlighted untruths. "It probably has something to do with the case I'm on."

She smiled. "Probably?"

"Well, in between arse kickings, he directed me to let it go. I'm just putting two and two together like the talented investigator I am."

Arebella stared at him for a moment as if weighing him up and deciding whether he was robust enough to share something. With a little nod, she appeared to make up her mind, stood, and crossed to the other side of her desk. She placed her hand on one of the drawers—there was a quick flash of light—and the drawer slid open.

Lowe raised his eyebrows at that. Arebella had another new Skill, apparently. Her threshold options must have been unusually rewarding.

With no further ado, she dipped her hand into the open drawer and withdrew a manila folder. "This was pushed through the door of my apartment this morning."

With just a touch of hesitation, she passed it over to him.

Lowe flipped it open, already having a pretty good idea of what he would find. As threats went, he could appreciate the simplicity. The folder contained a bunch of detailed images of Arebella in and around Soar - was she on a date in one of them? - and also a handwritten note: 'Lowe will abandon his case.'

No 'otherwise'. There didn't need to be.

This was about as classic an intimidation technique as existed. It wasn't even the first time one of the criminal underclass had tried it on with the pair of them. Of course, back then, he had a Class to rely on to keep her safe . . .

"What are you thinking?" Arebella was watching him carefully, her face set.

"That it's disappointing the High Priestess's killer will never be brought to justice."

She scrunched up her nose in distaste at that. "Jana, I can take care of myself."

"Who's worrying about you?! Did you not see the state I was left in?"

"I'm not even going to waste the Mana checking whether that was a lie. You're not going to drop your investigation because someone has threatened your ex-girlfriend."

Somehow, the 'ex' hurt more than anything that had happened since he'd entered the Tower of Law. Nevertheless, Lowe slapped a grin on his face and held up a picture of Arebella enjoying a candlelit meal with some long drink of water in an expensively tailored suit. "I'm sure he wouldn't be delighted to know I was putting you in danger. I've got enough troubles without your latest beau coming calling to teach me the lesson I so richly deserve."

"That's Petra from the gym. We're friends."

"Sure. Tell that to the look in his eye." Lowe tapped the picture, "Bloke's pretty confident he's on a promise in this shot."

Arebella took a deep breath, even as her face hardened. "Jana, I know what you're doing. You want a row because it makes it easier on you if I lose my temper and throw you out of here. And how do I recognise this? Because we've played out a hundred versions of this scene. I'm not sleeping with Petra. Not least because that would come as something of an unwelcome surprise to his husband of ten years."

That brightened Lowe's day a touch. Although the look in Arebella's eye as she continued dampened that slightly.

"I am, despite it all, grateful that you care for my wellbeing, but I am done being used as an excuse for you doing something that pisses you off. It's not me who decided I didn't want to be in a relationship with a Classless. It wasn't me who asked you to move out to the arse-end of nowhere and not be in touch for the best part of a year. And it's not going to be me who makes you step away from a case that, if you solve it, gives you a chance of getting back into the Security Service. I showed you these pictures because I thought they would be helpful to your investigation."

Arebella put a hand on her hip - oh dear, did he recognise that particular bit of body language - and stared him down. "So, put your ego away and look properly."

Grasping at anything that would allow him to break eye contact, Lowe looked down at the pictures. On a truly fundamental level, he recognised that he'd spent their entire relationship seeking to sabotage it before she had the opportunity to hurt him. That they were both perfectly aware of this did little to mitigate the drama.

He noted that there were eight images in all, and Arebella looked awesome in each. As for the restaurant scene—and yes, now he looked carefully, he could make out the wedding ring on her dinner companion's finger—she had been captured leaving work for the day and also returning. Out with a small group of friends - all of whom Lowe knew for a fact despised everything about him. One of her at the very desk from which she was now glowering at him. One in a small local market purchasing ingredients for a meal - just enough for one, he saw and was surprised how a tightness in his stomach released. And the last one was of her asleep in her bedroom, her hair spilling around her on the pillow like a halo.

It was a pretty damn intimidating 'we can get you whenever we want' message.

He leaned forward to pass them back to her, for Arebella to growl at him. "No, look properly!"

"Did you just bare your teeth at me?!"

"If you can't see it, that's the least I'll do to you."

Lowe looked back at the pictures. Presumably, there was something Arebella had seen that he was missing. He pushed his various, complicated feelings about the subject of the images away and looked at them with his investigator's eyes.

It took Lowe longer to realise what she had been getting at than he would have liked: he blamed his recent traumatic head wounds. Once he knew what he was looking for, he flicked quickly through them a few more times, making sure what he'd realised was the case in each of them.

Satisfied, he nodded and glanced up at her. "These are all taken in Skill dead zones."

Due to the occasionally homicidal instincts of the more powerful beings in Soar, the Mayor had decreed the construction - largely in the more well-to-do districts - of small areas where Skills could not be triggered. Of course, they weren't foolproof and were only as good as whoever had generated any particular 'dead zone', but it was pretty unlikely the protection would have failed in all eight images.

"So?" Arebella was smiling now.

Lowe's mind raced. If you assumed any remote image capture Skill would be difficult to activate in a dead zone—not impossible, but certainly a challenge—then the only guaranteed way to achieve these pictures was . . .

"A spotter. In order to anchor the image capture Skill, there would have to be someone near you, within the zone generating Mana. Did you happen to notice . . ."

"Pictures three, five and seven."

Lowe pulled out these images and studied them. Arebella came to stand behind him and seemed about to help. He shushed her good-naturedly. "Leave me my pride, Bella."

And there it was—the same hooded figure on the edge of the frame, the tell-tale glow of an active anchor Skill around his hands. And what was more, it was someone Lowe recognised.

MALORY

The Blazing Candle, Setort.

CHAPTER 18 – THE SHADOW WORE RED

This time, it was the Temple Warder who had to sprint to keep up with Lowe. "How did it go, little man?"

"Oh, you know how these legal types are—lots of dull chit-chat which will doubtless cost the city a fortune."

"You know your shirt is drenched in blood and . . . is that vomit?"

"What can I say? Some of the conversation got a bit lively."

"I sense I'm missing something here. Can we slow down a minute?"

Lowe eased off on his pace, drawing to a reluctant halt outside one of the many coffee shops that had grown up around the Tower of Law. Of course, everyone understood that these places provided their clients with a very different substance to coffee, but - oddly enough - the owners were curiously well-defended if ever a case came to court.

Lowe had bounded out of Arebella's office so quickly, he wasn't even sure he'd said a proper 'goodbye'. It wasn't quite that he had had a fairy light moment, but some things had started to click into place, and he wanted to strike while the iron was hot. He was sure she would understand his hasty exit: it was hardly the worst thing he'd done during their relationship.

However, in the cold light of day, he wasn't quite sure what his next steps would be. Once upon a time, he might have had the moxy to rip a Priest of Gravalk a new one for being involved with threatening the wellbeing of his . . . friend(?), but those days were long since gone.

And it went a bit bigger than just the threat against Arebella, didn't it?

He had been, specifically, warned off solving Gianna d'Avec's murder. That it now seemed that one of her priests – the Blazing Candle - was involved in that? Well, that only began to make sense to him in a few very specific circumstances. And none of them were good.

As they were standing in the middle of the walkway, Lowe's abrupt stop and Latham's considerable girth were causing something of a traffic jam for the other commuters. With a nod of his head, Lowe indicated they should partake in whatever legal refreshment the owner of 'Drink U Like' was able to scare up.

As it took the Junior Server quite some time to understand they wanted a beverage rather than . . . something more stimulating, it seemed wise for them to grab a table in the corner while they waited. As the shop had emptied rather abruptly at the appearance of a Temple Warder and a member of the Security Service, there was no shortage of room.

Once they were settled around the small walnut table, Lowe decided it was time to take the plunge with the big man. "Latham, can I trust you?"

The Temple Warder screwed up his face in disgust. "I made the parameters of our working relationship clear when we met. I am to shadow you and keep the Council appraised about the nature of your progress."

"I think that is what I'm getting at. Is it your sense that the Council wants the murder solved? I mean, I have no illusions as to my current standing with those in the halls of power. It hardly seems Soar is giving everything it's got by pulling me off the bench to run the investigation."

"Are you suggesting there is a political desire for you to fail?"

Their coffee arrived. It appeared to be so unusual for someone to actually order a drink in this place that the server almost shook the liquid free from the cups as he crossed from the counter to place them before them.

Avoiding the expectant eyes of a waiter oddly committed to the quality of his coffee, Lowe filled Latham in on his experiences within the Tower of Law— including the threats that had been made to Arebella and what he'd subsequently uncovered about the priest called Setort.

When he finished, Latham stroked his chin thoughtfully. Noticing he had not yet touched his coffee, the Junior Server stepped forward. "I say, Temple Watcher, do you have . . ."

"Fuck off!" The sheer malevolent pressure from Latham's aura created a wide circle around the table at which they were sitting, which no one was especially interested in crossing.

"So, the Justicars just let someone kick the shit out of you?"

Lowe was a touch alarmed by the effervescent anger fizzing around the big man. "Well, it wasn't like they were standing there holding his towel. I'm fine, by the way."

"Of course you are. You're a fucking cockroach." Latham's reply was almost absent-minded. There was a pause whilst the Temple Warder appeared to be conducting some sort of internal debate. By the look on his face, he wasn't enjoying the discussion. Eventually, it seemed one side won. "Little man, I can assure you that the Council is very focused on having the death of the High Priestess cleared up."

"How do you know?"

"Because I am not given pointless assignments. They want you free and safe to work."

Lowe added that to his mental list of things to explore further. "Well, aside from your contention that you are too important to be wasted having a bum's back aside, what else have you got?"

"No one gets to kill avatars." Latham's furious anger was back. "It doesn't matter whether they agree with a god's views or not, the Council is not going to idly sit by and allow the casual slaughter of a Level 67 High Priestess go unavenged. Do you have any idea how important the gods are to the economy of Soar?"

Lowe thought the question was rhetorical until he realised Latham was staring at him expectantly. "Um, a lot?"

"They are the basis of the entire system of government!"

"Okay . . ."

Latham's voice was loud enough to be heard outside the shop now; people were doing their best not to stop and stare. "No, seriously. The range and variety of Class upgrades available through the patronage of gods dwarf anything any of the other cities' experience. You can track a direct relationship between the significance of Soar on the world stage and the growth of the Celestial Temple. The Council - for fuck's sake, even the Mayor himself - cannot countenance this death remaining unsolved. It cannot become known that Soar is not a safe place for avatars. Should the gods choose to explore other options, that would be a disaster on an unimaginable scale."

"Okay. Sold. No worries, I believe you. You can lower your voice slightly." Lowe took a sip of his coffee, which was rancid. He wasn't sure if this was because the Junior Server had no idea what they were doing or if Mylaf had ruined him for all future drinks. It seemed likely it was a little of both. "But that doesn't answer the question as to why it's me that's been put in the field. I have to say, my attacker's spiel of 'no one gives a fuck, so they've put you on it' rings a lot more true than 'this is the most important event in modern history, let's put the washout on it and cross our fingers.'"

Latham took a sip of his own drink, winced and put it down. "The Council's memories are longer than a year-old scandal. You may have lost your Class, but you are the best investigator in the history of Soar. Even without the majority of your Skills, there was never anyone else that they wanted on this."

Lowe's head whirled. He opened his mouth to speak, but Latham hushed him with a look. "Little man, I am the last person in the world to blow smoke up your arse. But I've been told to keep you alive and ensure you are able to complete your work. Some powerful people have faith that you're the one to unravel this. And it must be unravelled. No one gets to kill avatars."

"Okay. Fine. Well, I'm off to speak to a priest who appears to be stalking my ex. Do you think you can keep him from cooking me alive?"

Latham smiled wolfishly. "It would be a pleasure."

They both stood to leave and reached the door before Latham stopped and slapped his forehead. "Oh, hang on one moment, little man."

The Temple Warder turned towards the Junior Server and waggled a finger at him. "Just as a head's up, trying to poison a member of the Security Services, let alone a Temple Warder, is a really, really silly thing to do."

Lowe looked over at the cup of brown liquid from which he had only taken a few sips. "The drink was poisoned?"

"Oh, yes. Quite a nasty one, too. Fast acting. The sort that closes down all your vital organs. If you haven't already, I'd be making sure you purge pretty much everything out of your system. Your clothes are fucked anyway, so it's not like they can be ruined further."

Taking the Temple Warder on trust, Lowe pushed *Roll with the Punches* to expel all toxins from his system. He chose to believe that the thick, noxious black sludge that emerged from his pores - all of them - was whatever poison he had been slipped. Rather than just . . . well, his lifestyle of late.

Latham gagged a little at the sight of what was oozing out of Lowe but then returned to glaring at the quailing man. "Just so we're clear on your immediate future, I am absolutely going to kill you. However, if you want to let me know who put you up to it, I will put in a good word with whichever god you worship. Which is?"

"Felent," the Junior Server whispered.

"Fair enough. Let me know who paid you to do something this monumentally stupid, and I will get a message to Felent about where she can locate your soul. If she so wishes. Although, I doubt she'd be too wild that one of her followers just tried to kill a Temple Warder, but you never know. So spill."

The young man shook his head. "I can't, they'll kill my family."

Latham shrugged. "Your call."

Lowe was not sure of the Skill that the Temple Warder summoned to vaporise the Junior Server, but he was absolutely sure it was not one that he would want to see used again.

It took far longer for the screaming to stop, considering the writhing body had vanished sometime before.

"I mean, I have some notes if you're interested? Purely from an investigatory point of view, of course."

Latham turned to face him. "What? He tried to kill me! He got off pretty lightly."

Lowe shook his head and moved for the door. "Yes, well done you. However, there are a couple of questions which it might have been useful to explore."

"Such as?"

"Well, just off the top of my head. Number one, how did he know we would be coming in here? It was almost by random choice that we stopped here. Were we unlucky that we happened to stumble upon someone who had been paid to kill us? That feels pretty unlikely. So, what, are all the shops around here briefed to poison us on spec? Or was someone following us and taking the opportunity to slip into the kitchens to offer a bit of bribery to spice up our drinks a bit? If so, who was it? And why? I've just been warned off fairly comprehensively - if they wanted me dead, that was the time to get the job done. So, assuming the dude in the Tower of Law isn't behind this, who the fuck made the poison attempt?"

"Those are all good questions, little man."

"Yep. Shame the guy who could have answered them isn't with us anymore. But at least you got to show what a big bad man you were, hey?"

CHAPTER 19 – NO GODS, NO JUSTICE

After seeing him turn the Junior Server into soup, the crowds on the street outside were significantly less interested in Latham than they had been when he was inside the coffee shop.

Of course, the sight and smells of Lowe were also fairly inhibitive to people seemingly wishing to be too close to them.

As they tried to make their way across the city, the situation had become so dire that, even though they were still a few crossings away from the Celestial Temple and Lowe felt time was of the essence, they felt compelled to halt at a Dry Cleaner's. It was time for Lowe to clean up and sort out his clothes.

"Do I even want to know what the poison was?" Lowe asked, doing his best to scrub the thick, black substance off his skin.

Latham was guarding the outside of the washroom - although, at this stage, he was more protecting the public from the stench rather than ensuring there were no further attempts on Lowe's life. "You won't have heard of it. Pretty exotic and very expensive. Safe to say, whoever slipped it into the coffee meant business."

Ever since his beating, Lowe had felt a solid ball of rage building up inside him, which he was doing his best to keep under wraps. Finding out that Arebella had been threatened had encouraged it to grow, and if the poison attempt was in danger of causing it to explode, then having to throw away his best shirt because it was soaked in a variety of his own body fluids was hardly helping . . .

He emerged from the washroom and crossed, bare-chested, to the shop's counter. "Look, I understand you can't clean it, but have you at least got one similar in my size that I can replace it with?"

The Commercial Assistant at the Dry Cleaners could not have looked less interested if he had tried. "You see the sign, mate? We clean shit, we don't sell it."

Lowe pointed at one of many white shirts hanging up behind the Level 6 teenager. "Just give me one of those, and I'll make it worth your while."

"Fuck off, grandad." The boy's eyes flicked upwards, reading the investigator's Classless state. "I need this job for the XP. I let you take someone else's stuff, and I'll end up in a worse situation than you. No offence, but there isn't enough gold in the world."

Doing his best not to see whether *Slugger* could punch this little twat through the wall, Lowe took a deep breath and placed one of Mylaf's cookies on the counter. "Who said anything about money? Forty-eight-hour Charisma boost. +25%. I imagine a likely lad such as yourself could be quite a hit with the ladies with this bad boy."

The Commercial Assistant narrowed his eyes. "Bullshit."

Lowe shrugged but kept his finger on the cookie. "Look, as you can tell by the state of my clothes. I'm having something of a morning. I've met with a lawyer, been beaten up and then someone tried to poison me. And there's a chance I made a fool out of myself in front of my ex. I'm just taking a moment out here before I go and relieve some of my frustrations on someone who may or may not deserve it. At the moment, I'm not looking to make your day any harder than it needs to be. However, I can happily add you to my shit list if you want?"

"Grandad, I've been threatened by bigger swinging cocks than you just in the last hour. Dry Cleaning's cut-throat, man. Besides," and his eyes darted upwards again, "I ain't sure you've got enough lead in your pencil to fuck with me."

Latham cleared his throat from his position by the washroom. "Okay, as entertaining as this has been, I'm now bored. Give him the shirt, take the cookie, and we'll say no more about it. On the other hand, you can see how fast your retail career progresses with one arm wedged up your arse. And trust me, if you are wondering whether I'd do it, my pencil is all fucking lead."

***

The proud owner of a crisp, white shirt and a brand-new suit that the Commercial Assistant managed to put his hands on when Latham growled in just the right way, Lowe was feeling a million times better as he approached one of the many doors to the Celestial Temple.

He hadn't quite decided how he wanted to play it with Setort, but almost for the first time since Cenorth had gotten him out of bed to look into the case, he actually felt like he was getting somewhere.

In his mind, he could feel a theory developing that a disgruntled priest looking to remove a problematic boss got involved with powers that could quickly get out of control. It didn't quite fit in with Gravalk seemingly being quite pissed off with what had happened - it felt like somewhat of a promotion-limiting move to piss off your god - nor with water being the murder weapon. However, right now, it was the best he had got to go on.

Even as he thought that, though, for some reason, *Grid View* kept trying to pull his attention back to a candle with a piece of seaweed in it, but if he tried to think too hard about it, the idea drifted away.

Well, it would come. Or it wouldn't.

Certainly one of the two.

Lowe's temporary good mood lasted right up until he reached the entrance to the Temple, and a Temple Warder moved forward to block his path. "No entry, I'm afraid, sir."

Lowe tried to step nimbly around him, but the big woman moved to intercept him. And she was *big*. Lowe's tastes went for the petite and feminine. An image of Arebella flashed, unbidden, into his mind, which he dismissed as quickly as possible.

"I cannot let you pass, sir."

"You don't understand. I'm on a case. My name is Inspector Lowe."

The Warder smiled, not unkindly. "Be that as it may, sir, but you are not going to be able to access the Temple."

"I'm so not in the mood for this. The Security Services are seeking to uncover the perpetrator of a crime committed under your noses. All I have had today is shit from people who do not want me to do my job, and now you, someone who should be anxious for me to find you a criminal to execute summarily, are making my life harder. If I were you, I'd be anxious to help me!"

"Lowe . . ."

"It's alright, Latham. I've got this." He met the woman's eyes, cricking his neck looking up. "In just the last few days, I've taken too many beatings, had my friends threatened, been poisoned and had a god melt the skin off my fucking bones. If none of that has put me off, no Bodybuilding Brenda on a power trip will keep me from going about my business."

"Little man, perhaps we should . . ."

"Dude, chill out. So, what about it? Are you going to stand here and stop me? Are you? Are you really?"

The Temple Warder, with a strange smile on her face, stepped to one side and waved him through. "Be my guest, sir. I hope you have a simply lovely day."

With a satisfied glance back at Latham, Lowe marched towards the open door and -

The next thing he knew, he found himself lying on the ground ten feet from the door, looking back at the two Temple Warders gazing down at him without sympathy on any of their faces.

"What the fuck!"

The female Warder shrugged her massive shoulders. "I did try to tell you, sir. The Celestial Temple has been temporarily closed to all below Level 25. Due to your insistence on being allowed to breach the protection field, I'm afraid you have just triggered the Repulsor Shield."

Latham clapped the woman on the back - Lowe noted that the bone-shattering impact barely made her wobble - and then moved to help the wholly dazed Lowe find his feet. "Orders from one the higher Floors, apparently. Not unusual, but certainly not common. Of course, the timing and the specifics of the level cap are somewhat suggestive."

"No shit. So, let me get this straight. I finally uncover a lead which might get the case somewhere, and - what do you know - I'm suddenly unable to access the crime scene, question witnesses or even, gods forbid, speak to my only suspect! What the fuck am I supposed to do now?"

Latham led him a little distance away from the Temple and lowered his voice. "Look, I can put in a complaint, but I'd imagine whoever made this happen will have all sorts of coverage for their actions. There's no way Arkola has actually ordered this, but by the time anyone actually looks it over, we could be a week down the road and . . ."

"Fuck's sake. Everything's working against me here! And the thing is, not everyone fucking with me could actually have killed her! This case is fucked."

"Not necessarily, little man. You can't get into the Temple as a Level 20. Ergo, we just do something to change that."

"I don't understand."

Latham grinned and flexed his own shoulders - which, Lowe noted, were quite some advance on the female Warder's. "No reason why you should. Tell me, little man, what experience do you have of Dungeon Delving?"

CHAPTER 20 – LEVELS, LIES, AND LOCKOUTS

"Are you sure about this?" Lowe asked dubiously.

The closest Dungeon to the Celestial Temple was surprisingly near where Latham had outlined his plan. It was easy to forget when going about your normal business in Soar that - within walking distance - were these giant infrastructures just beneath your feet.

It had been a short stroll to the stone staircase that led to the undercity and then a slightly longer walk to reach the staging area.

"If you know a better way to put on levels, I'm happy to hear it. Legally, of course. I'm assuming you'd look askance at me just beating people 99% to death and letting you make the finishing blow."

"I'm just going to throw that out there, shouldn't *you* be looking askance at that?"

Latham shrugged. "If you think I reached my illustrious level without making questionable moral choices, you're kidding yourself. I doubt anyone above Level 40 in the city hasn't needed to treat 'right' and 'wrong' with an element of pragmatism. If you'd like, I can call in a few favours in the cells. There's all sorts of high-level fuckers down there no one would miss."

Lowe wasn't sure if Latham was joking, but looking at the man's severe and broad face, he decided he probably wasn't. "So, just as a standing order of business, shall we take murder off the table?"

"Suit yourself. Well, that does kind of leave us with limited options to help you quickly jump five levels. This being the most obvious one."

Lowe looked at the console pillar in front of him. It stood about four feet high, its chipped stonework revealing its age. The inscriptions that ran up and around its base may have said anything: if you squinted just right, you might make out the words "Abandon All Hope" or maybe "Beware of Dog"—Lowe thought it was hard to tell, really.

At the top of the pillar, a gemstone, the size of a dragon's egg, sat nestled in a cradle of bronze. Every few seconds, it emitted a half-hearted glow as if unsure whether it wanted to light up or return to bed.

The pillar's control panel itself was a testimony to overengineering: a series of levers, buttons, and dials covered its front, with one particularly ominous button labelled "Do Not Press." The lever next to it was stuck in a position that could have been "Open Sesame" or "Release the Kraken."

Quite a queue was building up behind Lowe as he took all this in, but - hardly surprisingly -no one was that anxious to give a Temple Warder the hurry up. "So, what do I do?"

Latham reached forward as if to touch the gemstone, then hesitated. "I better not touch it. I'm good, but there is no way I will be able to power-level you through a dungeon that is appropriate to me. Put your hands on either side of the stone and clear your mind."

"Fuck's sake, noob. Get a move on!"

Latham turned around and glared at a Level 58 who was almost bouncing up and down in frustration. "I so much as hear you breathe again, and the only place you will be going is the Medical Tower. In pieces."

The moaner flushed red. As a Paladin, and a highish level one at that, he probably wasn't used to being spoken to like that. Pride warred with self-preservation, and he took a half-step back.

Hoping to avoid conflict - Lowe assumed Latham could take the guy, but the fallout was likely to squash the lesser beings in the queue flat - he put both hands on the console and cleared his mind.

Dungeon Delving had never really appealed to him. Even in a profession that was solitary by its very nature, he had been considered a loner in the Security Services. Success within a Dungeon needed you to make nice within a team, and that had never been his preferred approach to things.

In fact, his lost Class had given him all sorts of crunchy benefits for operating alone. Besides, joining a random pick-up group to grind out some XP had just had no draw.

"Welcome, Jana Lowe," a screen popped into being above the gemstone, filling the centre of his vision. "Please select your chosen difficulty."

A large number of greyed-out options appeared before him. The only one he could seemingly select was 0-5.

"Fuck's sake." Latham was reading the screen over his shoulder. "Have you seriously never done any of these?"

"I told you I hadn't. So, what do I do?"

Latham gave a weary sigh. Lowe was starting to get used to hearing him make this noise around him. "No choice, really. Just pick it. We might be able to get some sort of bonus if we're quick about it."

Lowe chose the option, and a further three screens appeared.

Castle of Otrantly

Swamp of Melum

Forest of T'Keth

"Shit, I forgot about all this crap. Little man, you are a fucking disgrace. My niece has done these three and she plans to be a Dressmaker. Fucking hell. We're going to be here all day. Just choose the Castle."

Lowe did so, wisely biting back any snark. From what he understood, what Latham was proposing was the sort of deal only the highest of high spenders had access to. Letting a veritable, certified monster boost you through dungeons for the XP was frowned upon, but it was one of the easiest ways those of an insanely high level could generate gold for the gear they needed. For example, Latham could have hired himself out - for one boosted run - to that Level 58 Paladin for several years' salary as a Temple Warder.

Once Lowe had selected the Castle, there was a short countdown, and then he felt the same way he did when operating a portal stone. His eyes streamed with tears, and—when they cleared—he stood in the middle of a medieval Castle's courtyard.

Latham was next to him, a look of profound disgust on his face. "Do you know how long it's been since I had to come to this fucking place? Shit, let's get this over with."

"What do you want me to do?"

Latham strode to the door in the corner of the room and kicked it open. "Just try to keep up."

***

It took three minutes for the Temple Warder to complete the dungeon, and that was only because he got lost at one stage and had to bring down an entire section of the wall in order to get back on track.

Lowe was intellectually aware that the colossal number of casualties that were racked up was not 'real' in any way that made sense to him, but he still found the level of slaughter distressing.

The Dungeons that dotted the continent had been uncovered centuries past and had been a mainstay for those seeking XP ever since. For a small fee, people could be transported to an instance of another location - and a different time - and work their way through a series of mini-bosses before ultimately battling a boss who would drop level-appropriate loot.

The residents of these Dungeons were, for all intents and purposes, 'alive', but no matter how many times the individual Dungeons were completed, the set-up remained the same.

"Who are these all?" Lowe said, looking - although not too closely - at the defeated boss. He had been an eight-foot tall Knight Templar. Or he had used to be. Latham had chopped him into two, even, four-foot sections with one swing.

"Who cares?" Latham's eyes unfocused for a second in a way Lowe recognised meant he was checking out his stat sheet. "Fucking hell. I got more XP for my last bowel movement."

The Castle vanished, and the two were stood back at the console pillar.

"Go on, time's a wasting. Let's get cracking."

"You're not doing a second? For fuck's sake, you know the rules Temple Warder. It's one and done. Everyone knows that." The Paladin had managed to find both his balls and also failed to read Latham's level of frustration.

Sensing some real-world violence was imminent, Lowe chose the Swamp and triggered the console.

***

It took most of the rest of the day before they reached the Dungeon Latham had initially planned to power-level Lowe through. The queue behind them had become disgruntled, then irritated and then, finally, vocally pissed off. So much so that, at one stage, they'd returned from burning the fleet of a Pirate King to ashes to find a Dungeon Keeper waiting for them.

Like Latham, she was a Level ?? and did not look like she was delighted to make the pair's acquaintance. The Paladin was almost effervescent with joy at this turn of events. "Warder Latham, am I to understand you are hogging this console?"

The woman's voice was oddly raspy as if she had spent her life on smokers. Compared to Latham, she was ridiculously delicate in size - was she some sort of gnome? - but obviously had the power to bounce Lowe around the staging area without using a single Skill.

He briefly wondered if he'd enjoy it, but one glance at her expression cleared that up nicely.

"Keeper Rosaline, long time no see."

The small woman glanced at the console and then turned and spat on the floor in disdain. "Power-levelling, Latham? I never thought I'd see the day." She then glanced at Lowe and then up above his head. "And a Classless at that?"

"A guy's got to do what he needs to do to make it through the day. Especially when a certain Keeper refuses any of his attempts to go for a drink."

"So, it's because I stood you up that you're causing a ruckus at my work? Smooth. What would you do if I fucked your mate? Level this place?"

Lowe enjoyed the moment of awkwardness. Although he was growing to appreciate Latham's protection, the whole omnipotent, insufferable thing got old.

"Look, I know this has taken a while. Trust me, it was never part of the plan. But he's never so much as stepped in one of these places before, so I've had to put in more groundwork than expected."

A little burst of air exploded upwards to move a stray strand of hair from the Keeper's forehead, followed by a little puff of mist over her face. Lowe took another step back. He seriously doubted he wanted to be too close to a Level ?? Kineticist if she decided to get into it with Latham.

"I'm hearing a lot of 'your problems', but I am unclear how they became mine?"

"Look, I just need to run him through 'Ambush at Iraklion' one time. We've unlocked it now. Just one more run. Please?"

If the Dungeon Keeper had been pissed off before, the look she gave Lowe now could have curdled not only milk but the entire herd of cows.

"Fucking hell. The gods save us from noobs."

"Tell me about it. Just one more run. No need to be a fey bitch about it, Ros."

"Don't call me that." There was a pause during which Lowe was sure the Paladin was close to ejaculating in anticipation of their arse-whooping. "Okay. You get one more run."

The groan from behind them stopped the moment Rosaline glanced backwards. The pulse of fire that whipped over their heads probably had something to do with their new-found respect too . . .

"Thank you, Keeper. One run, and we'll be out of your hair." Latham motioned for Lowe to access the console and to be quick about it.

Needing no further encouragement, he leaned forward and selected the 20-30 option for Dungeons, which was no longer greyed out. He was about to choose 'Ambush at Iraklion' when the Keeper leant forward and tapped it for him.

The words changed colour, taking on a deep, glowing red, and two skulls appeared on either end of the phrase.

"Ros, that's not going to work for us. Dude's Classless!"

"Tell it to someone who cares. You've blocked this console for the last few hours, and - what's worse - you've caused me to need to get out of bed on my day off. I have no fucks left to give if your little payday doesn't come through. Truly, my fucks have run dry as far as you are concerned."

Latham looked at Lowe, grimacing. "We can come back tomorrow, little man?"

Rosaline shook her head. "Nope. I'm locking you out for the week. Need to show that Temple Warders don't get any special treatment."

There was a reasonably comical moment where the vast man and the tiny woman squared up. Mainly because the pretty gnome clearly got the better of the hulking giant in the face-off.

"Shit," Latham sighed. "You win. Come on, let's go. We can find a different way to do it."

Lowe paused, hands hovering over the console pillar.

Truth be told, he'd made out like a bandit during the day's Dungeon runs. Not so much in terms of XP, Latham was too insanely over levelled for that, but in terms of coins and gear, the gains had been insane. By the time he'd flogged all the stuff he'd accumulated to the nearest Merchant, he reckoned he'd be close to bringing one of his skills to the Epic tier.

But the point of this exercise hadn't been about money or Skill upgrades. It'd had been to get him access to the Celestial Temple. For that, apparently, they needed this last run.

How hard could it really be? Lowe triggered the instance before Latham had the chance to clear that one up for him . . .

CHAPTER 21 – DEATH'S SAFE ZONE

"Oh, for crying out loud! Whatever you do, don't move a muscle."

"Why?"

"Because as long as we don't move, the Dungeon won't start. And if the Dungeon doesn't start, you get to live a little while longer."

Lowe thought Latham was laying it on a little thick. As far as he could tell, the only thing that had stopped the big man from instantly finishing the Dungeons they had breezed through thus far were the laws of physics. The Temple Warder literally could not have moved any faster.

Latham, though, carried on cursing a blue streak under his breath—and over it—while Lowe tried to orient himself to the new setting.

They appeared to be in the middle of a forest clearing, sitting near a blazing campfire with five or six NPCs alongside them. The fire was frozen in place, and their new companions were captured, motionless, in the middle of a meal. To his inexperienced eye, Lowe couldn't see there was all that much difference in this than in the thirteen Dungeons they'd completed thus far.

"You're being a touch dramatic here, aren't you? This is a Level 20-30 instance. Sure, I'm going to be woefully underpowered for what's about to happen, but it's not going to be one-shot kill territory, is it?"

"Yeah, that was going to be Plan A. But Ros . . . Dungeon Keeper Rosaline used her discretion to make it into a Heroic Dungeon."

"So? I'm feeling pretty damn heroic right now."

"Fuck's sake." Latham's teeth were gritted into a snarl. "Five years back, the Mayor agreed that a new method of XP collection should be opened to allow a second version of familiar existing Dungeons to be released. I imagine you remember there had been a bit of an uptick in unexplained 'accidents' occurring which were strangely connected to those on the threshold of their next level?"

Now he thought about it. Lowe did indeed remember that period a few years back when it was like those on the edge of thresholds completely lost their minds. The Summer of Suckers, one wag had called it. Lowe didn't remember finding it all that funny.

Latham carried on. "Thus, the Heroic Dungeons were born. An opportunity for those who had completed the more mundane versions to be able to gather XP without - crucially - murdering citizens. How do you not know this?"

"Dungeon Delving, isn't it? Never took any interest, to be honest. So, I guess what you are saying is that this might be a bit harder than what we've done so far?"

"No. I'm saying this is going to be a fucking nightmare."

***

97

There are more effective ways to assimilate vital information than being frozen in place in the middle of a wood, but Lowe did his best to take on board what Lowe was drilling into him.

The Heroic version of 'Ambush at Iraklion' followed much of the same storyline as the 'normal' version that they had intended to complete - basically, a standard 'capture the flag' mission. They'd done a couple of those earlier in the day and had perfected the ideal tactic.

Lowe stood stock still while Latham fucked up everything and anyone who moved before taking the opposition's flag from their cold, dead hands.

Apparently, though, this strategy would not be available to them here.

"The moment we move, these fuckers are going to attack. I reckon I can get three of them in one go, but you're going to have to take on one and avoid the other before I can help out."

Without turning his head, Lowe tried to get a read on their adversaries. They were all Level 30s and of the Outlaw Class. "Any advice for me?"

"Sure. Let me think. Yep, this feels pretty fucking pertinent. Don't enter a Heroic Dungeon without a team of twenty to back you up."

"Excellent. Thank you for that. Anything other than 'I told you so' to offer before we begin?"

Latham growled back. "The guy on the far left of their group -the one with the bow? - go after him. Chances are, if he doesn't one-shot you, your *Slugger* Skill, enhanced by my aura, will significantly fuck up his day."

"And you'll get the others?"

"I'll do my best, little man. But, and you need to listen to me now, the second the last of them drops, a timer will kick in. We'll have that long to get the flag before we fail this Dungeon."

"And that would be bad, right?"

"Terminally so, yes."

"Fucking hell. And people do this for fun?"

"Screw fun. People do this for the XP." There was a pause, and then Latham started to speak, obviously thinking aloud. "The thing is, I can't just leave you here while I run and claim it. There's going to be waves of attacks here as well." The Warder's eyes flicked upwards at the enormous red flag that was hovering above the fire.

"So, what's our plan?"

"You mean other than entering a Heroic Dungeon with just the two of us and you being as much use as a eunuch in a brothel?"

"Shall we take that as read?"

"Look, as soon as these guys are down, grab the flag and stick as close to me as you can. If I didn't think I was going to need both of my hands, I'd fucking carry you, but we'll make do the best we can. You have any better gear than that?"

Lowe nearly shook his head, then remembered the dire necessity to stand very still. "What you see is what you get, I'm afraid. I've got some decent rings and torcs and the like. But they don't have any particularly helpful stats for combat."

Lowe could be wrong, but he was sure Latham muttered 'fucking noob' under his breath. "Shit, I haven't got anything in my inventory low enough you can wear." He cursed again. "Look, just keep an eye out for anything that drops in here. Equip anything you come across. At least, with this being Heroic, the chances are it will be infinitely better than the crap you are wearing. You never know; we might actually get lucky. The loot table, in this sort of instance, can be pretty tasty. Makes the chance of almost certain death more palatable. You ready?"

Lowe absolutely wasn't, but as this was his fault, it did not really feel like his place to comment. All this just so he would be able to enter the building in which sat a priest he needed to interrogate about stalking his ex.

His life had become quite odd of late.

"Go on the count of three. Give me a chance to prepare *Slugger*."

"Remember, take the archer down and then kite whichever of these others homes in on you."

"Kite?"

"Fucking hell. Run away from in a faintly tactical manner."

"Cheers."

"Then loot, equip anything decent, grab the flag and then get behind me." Latham's voice became a hair more sombre. "Keep your Mana stores high; this ain't going to be pretty. If all else fails, try to take non-immediately lethal injuries. Gut wounds, rather than headshots, if you can. Give yourself a chance to heal."

Lowe thought he'd heard more rousing pre-battle speeches, but before he could make that point, Latham was counting down, and there were suddenly more pressing concerns.

***

On three, Lowe turned and threw a *Slugger* punch at the man holding a bow with a quiver full of arrows on his back. As he did so, in the corner of his eye, he saw Latham instantly eviscerate a man with an axe across his lap before spinning to decapitate an unarmed man standing to his other side.

He would have liked to watch how the Temple Warder dealt with the last of his opponents, but things at his end had all become intense. Because the Outlaw archer had dodged his punch and was preparing to launch an arrow into his chest.

Lowe just had time to turn to the side, catching the projectile in his shoulder, the impact flinging him yards backwards. *Roll with the Punches* kicked in, the sudden healing forcing out the arrow. Alarmingly, between that and *Slugger*, most of his Mana was already gone.

Lowe was just getting himself back to his feet when a second arrow hit him, this time in the stomach - *look at me*, Lowe thought, *I managed to take a gut shot. Good to see that part of the plan working out just peachy* - and then Latham was there, all flashing blade and chiselled jaw, and the clearing was very quiet.

"Come on, remember the plan. Loot, equip, flag and fucking shift." The Warder looked down at the arrow and pulled it out with a quick jerk. "Well done. You remembered."

"Yeah, that's me. All about the details."

There was nothing particularly noteworthy about the loot - should he survive, the eight gold would doubtless be put to good use. But the Cape of Wrath he picked off the archer added +15 armour to the +5 from the suit he was wearing and, as Latham snorted: 'every little helps.'

As he passed Lowe the flag, he asked, "You see the timer, right?"

99

Lowe thought it would be hard not to see the giant crimson number counting down at the right of his vision, and he nodded rapidly. "We have until then to get the flag?"

"And to protect ours. So let's go."

It was about all Lowe could do to keep up with the bigger man, who moved with appalling grace and speed, leaving a trail of devastation in his wake. Lowe was struck, over and over again, at the size of the gap that existed between the highly Classed and mortal beings. And it wasn't just the Level disparity, Latham appeared to have a Skill that allowed him to increase his movement to an astonishing degree - if Lowe had to put money on it, he would have said it was a Legendary version of *Blur* - and it seemed to charge up each time Latham took an injury.

And my word, did Latham take a pasting on the journey through the woods. As a connoisseur of a good kicking, Lowe always prided himself on his ability to get hit and keep moving forward. Latham, though, made him look like a whingy child unwilling to prance through a field of stinging nettles and bear traps.

Time and time again, the Temple Warder was hit by arrows, blades, clubs and axes - many of the blows intended for Lowe - and he did nothing less than give complete and utter death in return.

"You see the golden glow?" Latham pointed to a light shining a little way to the left, turning the gesture to a punch that caved in an attacker's skull.

"Sure."

"Safe zone. We get there, we can take stock, and the timer will stop."

A crossbow bolt took Lowe in the knee, and he found himself stumbling forward. Without missing a step, Latham stooped, snatched the falling man around the waist and hurled him towards the Safe Zone.

Lowe crashed through a bunch of trees, adding a broken collarbone to the shattered kneecap on the list of his woes.

He shuddered to a halt in the middle of a glowing circle, briefly losing consciousness as *Roll with the Punches* took a deep breath and plugged up various holes and fractures. Lowe came to just as Latham appeared through the trees with a ridiculous smile on his face. "Well, this has been fun, hasn't it?"

CHAPTER 22 – EVERY COIN HAS ITS PRICE

"How went the looting?"

Lowe scowled at the Temple Warder. "No idea, mate. I was doing all I could to keep up with you. I just left auto-loot running as I was . . . you know, *running*."

"Well, have a look. You've got to have picked up something better there than what you currently have on. Once we leave here, the next bit is going to be a touch spicy, so it would be helpful if you could be a touch more . . . solid."

Lowe glanced at his inventory, and quite beyond the pages of gear, he was staggered at the increase of his gold. "If I'd known Dungeons were this lucrative, I'd have rethought my career path."

Latham snorted. "This a touch unusual. This place is rated for a twenty-man, Level 30 team. There are supposed to be a lot more noses in the loot trough."

That made sense to Lowe. There was a staggering volume of gear, materials and potions washing about in his inventory. "Are you sure you don't want a cut of this?"

The Temple Warder's good humour immediately vanished. "I have no financial need, little man. All my Skills are Legendary, my Level is maxed out, and I am as highly evolved as my patron wishes me to be. What could I possibly spend it all on?"

Even so, Lowe knew he was looking at a not-inconsiderable fortune, and it didn't seem right that it was coming his way when he'd had so little to do with its generation. "I can't accept all this, Latham."

"Look, think about it this way. That was the most fun I've had in months. I'd happily pay twice the amount you've probably gathered for such an experience. Having a helpless duckling along for the ride added massively to the jeopardy."

Lowe wasn't all that delighted to be considered a handicap in this particular encounter, but it was nice to be able to put a price on his own uselessness. For once.

"How does the gear look, little man? Anything good?" said Latham, adjusting his own armour, which Lowe couldn't help but notice was repairing itself as he did so. Perhaps the big man was right; he really didn't need the money if he was already kitted out with Legendary stuff.

"There's mountains of it. It's hard to tell. I've got, literally, pages of grey stuff."

"No worries. Set anything sub-Epic to auto sell and go see the Merchant."

It was as if the tubby man in the flowing green robes appeared in the corner of the Safe Zone the moment Latham mentioned him. There was a glassy expression on his face, which suggested he was an N.P.C.

Lowe walked up to the man, unclear on the protocol. The Merchant came to life as soon as he drew near. But it was not 'life'—nothing like it. In fact, Lowe thought, there was something profoundly creepy about this simulacrum of reality, and he found himself instinctively recoiling back.

"How can I help you, sir?"

Trying to hide his distaste - it wasn't this thing's fault he was what he was, was it? - Lowe did his best to keep it civil.

"Can you clear my inventory, please?"

The pages of newly acquired gear vanished in a blink, and it seemed like his financial good fortune had doubled. He was left with just one item. And, for the life of him, Lowe had no idea what the item was.

"Ah," Latham said, "I didn't like to get your hopes up, but I was counting on that showing up."

Lowe turned the small brass coin over in his hand. "I don't think I've ever seen anything like it before. It's a Token of Reset?"

"Indeed. Not a top-tier item, of course. It's only usable by those who are sub-30, and, honestly, it's pretty rare for anyone at that Level to want it. Let me tell you, though, if it were appropriate for my Level, we'd be having quite the discussion right now."

Lowe was sure this wouldn't have been a chat he'd have enjoyed.

"I don't think I understand. What does it do?"

"Well, that rather depends on whether you followed my advice and read up on Essence Transmutation Theory, doesn't it?"

***

Lowe had dipped in and out of a few scrolls that covered Latham's weird progression ideas and had spent more than a few frustrating hours trying to understand what E.T.T. - as it was described in the various scrolls he'd accessed - actually was.

"Let's say I have a working knowledge."

"Excellent. Well, a Token of Reset will effectively allow you to test it out."

Lowe let the coin run across his knuckles. "You want me to pull out all my Progression Points and stick them in Intelligence?"

"Little man, I don't give a flying fuck what you do with your build. But if I had my time again - which is what this token gives you - I'd do it like a shot."

Lowe continued to run the coin backwards and forwards. "But if I pull them all out, my Skills will go back to Common. That will make me more of a helpless duckling than I was before, wouldn't it?"

Latham nodded. "True, but you'll have control over your stats. And, right now, you've got the cash to rank your Skills back up the rich person way."

"Why are you pushing this? I mean, what's in it for you?"

There was a pause as the Temple Warder frowned and seemed to consider how he wanted to answer. "Look, I have many regrets in my life. I like to think that if I had someone to push me in the right direction, I might have been able to end up in a different place. Listen or don't listen, but don't ignore some hard-won experience."

"Mate, you're the tankiest Tank that ever tanked some tank. I'm finding it pretty hard to hear how you fucked up your life when you've just soloed a Heroic Dungeon."

Latham walked away and sat down on an upturned log. "Little man, things are not always the way they seem. Do what you want with that token, but this is going to be your best - and probably your last - chance to do something about how your life is going. We've got a couple of bells before the Safe Zone will destabilise; let me know when you're ready to move on."

And then, to all appearances, the Temple Warder went to sleep.

Lowe watched him for a moment, and then, once the snoring started, he moved over towards the Merchant again.

"How can I help you, sir?"

"I have the Token of Reset. How much is it worth?"

"A Token of Reset has no intrinsic value. This Token is soul-bound to you, sir. I will not be able to offer you anything for it."

"How do I use it?"

"I do not understand your question, sir."

So much for the helpfulness of N.P.C.'s.

Lowe closed his eyes and tried to sense the token. As soon as he did so, a new screen opened. And one he had not seen before

Do you wish to reset your Progress Points? Answering 'Yes' will consume your Token of Reset. This action is irreversible. Any breaks to Builds are entirely at the user's own risk.

Well, that didn't sound too fucking doom-laden or anything.

"How many Progress Points will this give me back?"

Calculating *appeared in Lowe's vision. Soon to be replaced by:*
Locked Skills = 100 Points
Available Skills = 55 Points
Threshold Bonus = 45 Points
Allocated Progress Points = 15 (these are unavailable for redeployment)
Total available Progress Points = 165 Progress Points
Do you wish to proceed?

Lowe's mouth was open in shock. He had made use of 200 Progress Points? That was such an insane number that, at first, he couldn't believe it. But then, thinking about things a little more clearly, it did make sense. A handful of Points every few years, maybe a bonus here and there, he could see that number could be accurate.

The question blinked incessantly. Did he want to proceed?

Adding 200 Progress Points in Intelligence would be . . . interesting. That wouldn't be a million miles away from what he possessed when he was still Classed, which felt crazy.

Do you wish to Proceed?

Why wouldn't he? It could hardly make his life any worse, could it?

Lowe accepted the prompt and felt his knees go weak as his Progress Points were sucked out of him. He felt *Roll with the Punches, Slugger,* and *Grid View* return to Common, as well as the myriad of Skills that had been locked away during his Classtration.

Interested, Lowe opened up his stats and, trying not to think too hard about it, dumped every single Point into Intelligence.

The 100 number started shooting upward as if it were a possessed counter. As soon as the number hit 200, though, it screeched to a halt, and another screen appeared.

Allocated Progress Points have reached the maximum. Do you wish to rank Intelligence up?

"Erm, Latham?" The Temple Warder continued snoring. It felt like waking a sleeping Latham was likely to be one of those life-limiting things it would be sensible to avoid. "Well, in for a bronze, in for a gold," he said, answering with a hesitant 'yes'.

At first, Lowe did not think anything had happened. And then the text around *Intelligence - 200* went gold and then blasted upwards to reach 265.

As soon as that message faded, another one replaced it.

Bonus +50 PP for bringing first Core Attribute to Level 2. Please note that these P.P. must be allocated to a Level 1 Core Attribute

Without quite knowing why, Lowe split these bonus points in half and dropped half into Wisdom and the other into Strength.

He couldn't quite believe his own stat sheet.

Primary Attributes:
- **Strength:** *95 (Increased from 70)*
- **Dexterity:** *65*
- **Intelligence:** *265 (Increased from 100)*
- **Wisdom:** *103 (Increased from 78)*
- **Charisma:** *60*
- **Constitution:** *75*

It had been so long since he had felt even remotely like himself that tears welled up slightly in his eyes. Of course, there was the proportional loss of power to *Roll with the Punches, Slugger* and *Grid View*, which was a bummer, but he had a sneaky idea he might be able to do something about that.

The Merchant was staring at him, his unblinking gaze really freaking Lowe out. "What?"

"I notice that you have several Skills, sir, that are rated as Common. I will be able to upgrade those for you for a small fee."

Lowe grinned. "It seems rude not to, doesn't it? Show me what you've got."

CHAPTER 23 -GLASS JAWS AND GOLDEN FISTS

"Come on, sleepyhead. Places to go. Ambushes to defeat."

Latham's eyes snapped open and took in a somewhat more confident Lowe than before his snooze. "You're looking spunky."

"I took some advice."

"Did you indeed, little man? And how did it work out for you?" Latham asked, his voice laced with a hint of curiosity and more than a touch of amusement.

Lowe paused, not sure how to answer. His Mana Pool was pretty much at the level it had been before he had lost his Class, which was an extraordinary feeling after so long. But there was something different about Rank 2 Intelligence. It had made his Mana . . . richer, somehow. He found himself wishing he'd spent a bit longer studying that Essence Transmutation Theory scroll. Mindful of conserving his available resources, he hadn't committed it to *Grid View*, which he realised - with a smile - was not something he'd need to worry about so much moving forward.

"It's fair to say I'm glad to have a chance to test the theory."

Especially so since he'd been able to offload all his looted coin on the Merchant to bring his three Skills back up to Rare. This had been a *very* profitable Dungeon for him. So much so that he was already wondering what it would take to convince Latham to boost him through a couple more.

When the case was resolved, of course.

"Don't even consider it," the Temple Warder said, his tone firm. "This is a one-time favour to get you to Level 25. I don't make a habit of Power levelling the Unclassed. There are names for those who make a living from this sort of thing, and I have a reputation to uphold."

Despite the momentary pang of disappointment, Lowe could understand that. What had been done for him was already far ahead of anything he could have hoped for. And, with five more Levels, with the threshold bonuses, he could plan to plugin even more Progression Points.

"Fair enough. So, what's next?"

Latham stood and stretched. "From memory, there should just be one more stage. We've got the Raid Boss to take down, for which I hope you're no longer so squishy that I need to focus on protecting you rather than taking him out." The Temple Warder suddenly looked at the ground as if shy. "Did it work out like I thought? Were you able to reclaim your Progress Points? Even from the Skills taken from you when you lost your Class?"

Lowe shared his Core Stats screen with Latham, causing the big man to frown. "What does Rank 2 next to your Intelligence mean?"

"No idea. I kind of hoped you would be able to tell me."

Latham shook his head. "It's not anything I've read about. When did it happen?"

"When I hit 200 Progress Points in Intelligence."

Latham shook his head again. "That's not something of which I'm aware. But then again, I don't know of anyone who would *only* have had Progress Points in a particular attribute. All the examples of those who have tried this I've heard of were seeking to supplement their Class advantages. I've not come across anything in the literature of the Unclassed trying it."

"We are pretty rare." Lowe's smile was brittle.

"Rank 2? The text's even a snazzy gold colour. Fancy. Does it feel any different?"

"It does, and it doesn't." Lowe pushed some mana into *Slugger*, feeling his hand fill up with the comforting heaviness. "It's working like before, but . . . " he raised his hand, noticing an odd shimmer across the surface of his fist. "Did you see that?"

"Try it out."

"On what?"

"Hit me."

Lowe raised his eyebrows. "Yeah, sure. And then I'm going to solo a Level 50 Dungeon and fuck the Mayoress as an encore."

"I mean it. It's not like you're going to hurt me. And it would be good to know what sort of heat you're packing before we move on."

"Mate, this kind of feels like one of those situations where you lure me into doing something foolish and then kick my arse to teach me a lesson."

"You say that like it's happened more than once."

"Once was enough."

"Suck it up, buttercup and hit me. What do I need to do? Insult your dress sense?"

With a sigh, Lowe half-heartedly raised his fists into a pugilistic posture. "Seriously, mate, if you've got some sort of exotic Skill that makes my pants catch fire when I try this, I'm going to be pissed." With that, Lowe unloaded *Slugger* onto the side of Latham's jaw.

The outcome was somewhat unexpected.

The jab didn't drop Latham to his knees - that would have been insane. The Temple Warder's Level was so far above Lowe that it was surprising that the big man did not regularly cripple his companion just by breathing near him. Likewise, by the very nature of his build and Class, Latham had the sort of passive defensive Skills more usually found on bank vaults. Thus, some significant expectation management was required when Lowe's fist made contact with his face.

In other circumstances, a split lip might have been underwhelming. Right here, right now, however, the two men reacted as if they had just discovered a method of turning water into Stamina potions.

"Motherfucker!" Latham spat a tiny globule of blood to the floor, his massive grin splitting the already healed wound.

Lowe, for his part, was staring at his fist with a look of profound wonder. "What the fuck!"

"So, it is all true!" Latham's voice was almost breathless with joy. "Progress Points *are* more pure than Class-generated ones. Little man, do you know what this means?"

Lowe did not answer, still looking at his hand. Latham grabbed him by the shoulders and shook him, rattling his teeth as he did so. "Do you understand, Jana? You've got some game!"

"I barely broke your skin," Lowe protested half-heartedly.

"Little man, your fist should have vapourised before it even made contact with me." Latham waved away Lowe's outraged expression. "Chill, I have Health potions. You would have been fine. The key point is that there's absolutely no way in Soar that you should have been able to hurt me in the normal run of things." His eyes were suddenly unfocused as he checked his damage log, whistling at what he found. "Yep, you are now a certifiable baller. I'd have expected a Level 40 with some sort of Skill like *Pugilist* to be able to do that. Okay," he said, cracking his knuckles. "Let's see if it works in reverse."

Lowe enjoyed the next round of experiments considerably less.

***

On the plus side, *Roll with the Punches* apparently experienced a similar upgrade to *Slugger*. Whatever Rank 2 Intelligence did to Lowe's mana, it also meant that his healing ability was equally as beefy as his offensive one.

It was pretty hard though, to hold on to the half-full glass while it was being systematically brutalised to tiny shards. The beating from Latham seemed to go on forever but was probably over in less than twenty seconds, with the Inspector returning to consciousness shortly afterwards.

The first thing he saw was Latham's smiling face looming over him. "Glad someone was having fun," Lowe croaked.

The Temple Warder held out a hand and hauled him to his feet. "Where's your childlike sense of wonder? This is simply amazing!"

Lowe looked down at yet another shirt ruined by an epic bloodstain. "Glad to be of service."

"Your passive Skill gives you the sort of survivability of someone twice your level. I actually had to put a bit of weight behind the last punch to overwhelm your healing factor. Do you understand what that means?"

"That you're a sadistic son of a bitch?"

Latham put his hand on Lowe's shoulder. The Investigator winced instinctively but then realised the impact hadn't hurt for once. "You are showing all the signs of being a Level 40. And that's at Level 20 and, crucially, without having a Class. There's not even a Class I've heard of that can breach that sort of gap. You could eat Mylaf's food for a year and a day and still not have the numbers needed to pull that off."

"Okay . . ." Lowe could understand that this was remarkable, but Latham acted like it was a seriously big deal.

"No, it's more than 'okay'. This suggests that when you reach Rank 2, whatever the fuck that is, you *double* the effective worth of your statistic." Latham was almost hopping with excitement. "You're living proof that Essence Transmutation Theory isn't just pie in the sky. You prove that you don't need a Class to be competitive. That we don't need to find a patron god to survive. That we can get by on your own without any of that!"

Lowe wasn't wild about the fanatical gleam in the Temple Warder's eye. He had come across a lot of people in his previous career who looked like that. Usually right before they started slaughtering people who didn't share their view of the world. "Mate, let's chill things a little. All of that sounds simply lovely. But shall we keep

107

that sort of chat on the inside? I can think of at least half a dozen gods who would see what you've just said as heresy. And I'd kind of miss having you around."

Latham took a deep breath and nodded, but Lowe could tell his words of caution had fallen on deaf ears. There was no zealot like a convert, he thought. "Latham, I mean it. As the only one of us who has had to experience being stripped of his Class and most of his Skills being blocked, I can tell you it's no picnic. There's a reason I was offered execution as an alternative. As a 'mercy' due to my years of service."

But Latham wasn't really listening. Lowe watched as he made a conscious effort to drag his mind back to the here and now, but the glow of possibility did not fade from his expression. "Okay. I hear you. However, in light of developments, I think we should try to mix things up a little. Moving forward."

Lowe felt a sinking feeling settle in his stomach. "Mix things up, how?"

"How do you feel about soloing a Level 30 Heroic Boss?"

CHAPTER 24 – A FLAG, A DAGGER, AND NO TIME TO DIE

"Do you really think there's any answer to that question which isn't me laughing hysterically?"

"Little man, you have an offensive and a defensive Skill equivalent to being a Level 40. This Dungeon is rated for 20-30. What's your worry?"

"My worry!" Lowe's voice trembled with a hint of hysteria. "This is a Heroic Raid Dungeon. I'm a Classless Level 20. Does any part of that sound like I'm remotely prepared to face a Boss alone?"

"Faint heart never won, fair lady."

"We're throwing aphorisms around now, are we? What about many hands make light work?"

"Too many cooks spoil the broth."

"How about the Temple Warder can go fuck himself with a pole wrapped in barbed wire? I always like that one. Apt."

They glared at each other for a few moments, and then Latham grinned. Lowe didn't think that smile boded well for his immediate future. "Here's how this is going to go, Little man. By my calculations, you should just about hit Level 24 when we get out of here. I miscalculated the XP penalty for having me in your party, so you're not going to reach the necessary level to access the Temple. No Level 25. No Setort. No answers as to what is going on."

"Fine. So we come back tomorrow and run another one."

Latham shook his head. "Nope. I burned bridges getting access today. There's no chance any Dungeon Keeper, let alone Ros, will let us anywhere near a console for at least a week. However, if you solo this Boss, you will absolutely cross the necessary threshold. So, that's the situation. Your move."

"Well, isn't that convenient? Almost sounds like you might be lying."

"Your deductive powers are truly a wonder to behold. The killer of Gianna d'Avec should be quaking in their boots."

"Cute."

"Funnily enough, I don't hear that very often."

"Can't imagine why, you smug fucker."

Lowe ran his hands through his hair. The whole point of this Dungeon Dive was so that he could get his hands around Setort's throat. His mind flashed again to those pictures of Arebella; the Priest stood just at the edge of the image, providing the necessary anchor power for . . . someone to overcome the dead zone and take the picture. There were layers here, and the key to being able to start unwrapping them would be putting that Burning Candle against the wall and asking him some fairly searching questions.

"Seriously. This is the only way?"

Latham nodded. "If it is worth anything, I didn't mean for it to happen this way. Honestly, this isn't a big conspiracy. Maths just isn't really my thing."

"Okay, so I need to take the Boss down on my own. And you'll step in when, inevitably, I start getting stomped?"

"Ah, about that." Latham was avoiding Lowe's eyes again. "I'm going to need to stay away from the final fight. To cross over Level 25, you'll need all the XP from the Boss. Me being here will just split the rewards."

"Awesome. So it's going to be me against a Heroic Raid Boss and no safety net?"

"See, and there was me thinking you were not going to get into the spirit of things."

***

To give Lowe any chance at all, the moment they stepped outside of the Safe Zone, Latham took care of any and all other combatants in the Dungeon. It appeared the big man might have been holding back on bringing the thunder.

As the last Outlaw fell, Latham gave an ironic salute and exited the Dungeon. The forest of Iraklion suddenly sounded very quiet indeed.

Shouldering the red flag, Lowe made his way down the road, which very much screamed 'this way to your sudden and inevitable death.' The timer in the corner of his vision continued to countdown, but he didn't pay it very much attention.

Either the final surviving bad guy in the woods would shortly be dead, or he would be. There really wasn't any other way that this would play out.

Lowe tried to channel some of Latham's confidence in him. If Rank 2 doubled the effectiveness of his Intelligence, then his Skills would have the equivalent power of being Level 40. Awesome. That should make all this a walk in the park, taking candy from a baby while not sweating at all. But he couldn't shake the feeling he was a Classless Level 20 in a Heroic Raid Dungeon.

He was fucked.

The first arrow took him in the shoulder, the second hitting just millimetres to the right. Fortunately, *Roll with the Punches* passively kicked in faster than Lowe's reaction time. Which was helpful. Especially as the third arrow took him in the throat.

"All alone, is it?" a jolly voice boomed from the woods with an oddly musical accent. "That's not going to work out too well for you, boyo."

The arrows popped free from Lowe's wounds as he rolled for cover. He had *Grid View* running and quickly tried to determine where the attack had come from. His extra mana meant he didn't need to worry about rationing its use any longer, and it gave him the equivalent of an eidetic memory, even for the things he didn't consciously see.

There. All three shots came from a patch of shadows just a little down the path.

"Don't suppose you fancy doing this in melee range, do you?"

The answer was another arrow, this one hitting him in his right hip. It came from about three feet closer. The Boss was closing in on him, trying to get the best angle for a killing shot.

"You may well be able to tank a headshot," Latham had told him when they'd been planning this attack, "but I wouldn't want to bet the house on it."

"'Fraid not, boyo. Way I figure it, a Level 20 stupid enough to try to solo me must have some sort of wild trump card, eh? No. I'm happy wearing you down from range."

Lowe briefly felt satisfied that despite the agony the hits were causing, his health points were holding steady. Not entirely trusting Latham's fervour, he'd also loaded up on Mylaf's finest HP food and drink, but - so far - it did not seem like he needed the boost. He was shaking off the damage from the arrows, but that didn't mean he wanted to keep getting shot.

"I'd heard this was an honourable Dungeon. Do you really want me telling people I needed to flush you out of the forest like a bitch?"

There was a bright flash, and then a giant arrow careened out from the trees in a golden streak to hit him right between the eyes.

Good news? Lowe *could* apparently take a headshot.

Bad news? Half of his HP had vanished, and something called *Skill Suppression* was now active on him.

He lay, flat on his back, arms stretched out in a crucifix position. Without *Roll with the Punches* functioning, there was no active healing running nor any repairs taking place to push the arrowhead lodged in his forehead out. He didn't appear to be taking any further ongoing damage, but without active skills, that was probably a moot point.

"That looks nasty, boyo."

A friendly-looking face appeared above him, grinning mischievously. The Boss's suntan was topped and tailed by short brown hair and a snazzy goatee. He was wearing green camouflage, with a few branches tucked into the cap on his head.

"*Skill Suppression* is a pain in the arse, isn't it? Well," the Boss continued, "a pain in the head, I imagine. You can call me the Hood."

Lowe tried to speak, but the words wouldn't come. Arrow to the prefrontal cortex was a deal, apparently.

"Not that you're going to be saying anything for long, I imagine, boyo. I don't know what you had planned or who put you up to trying to solo me, but it's fair to say it's all gone a bit wrong."

Lowe couldn't disagree. He was completely paralysed. Cheers, Latham. Another fine mess you've got me into.

The Hood vanished from his vision for a second and then reappeared holding a dagger. "Well, it's been emotional. Catch you on the flip side."

Lowe tried to push at both *Roll with the Punches* and *Slugger*, but whatever skill the Hood had landed on him resisted. He pushed harder as the dagger swept down towards his eye.

It was as if time slowed down as his end approached. But instead of seeing his life flash before him, it was just the legend *Skill Suppression* that dominated. As soon as the dagger made contact with him, that would be that.

He pushed again at his Skills. No joy. Although, did those words wobble slightly?

Having no other options, he threw everything he had at his Skills, trying to break the block. The words were definitely wobbling. The dagger was less than an inch from his eye now.

Unbidden, Arebella's face appeared. She'd be safe if he died, wouldn't she? They'd have no reason to hurt her if he wasn't around to solve the case. But then the realistic part of his mind kicked in. She knew about the threat. She wouldn't let it lie. She'd keep asking questions, and whoever visited him in the Tower of Law would doubtless find his way to her office.

If he died here, he was pretty much committing her to the same fate.

And then the words *Skill Suppression* weren't wobbling anymore; they were fracturing into tiny little pieces and the Hood's dagger was buried through his right eyeball to the hilt.

***

The Boss stood and dusted himself down. Odd chap, he thought. Fancy trying to solo him as a Level 20! He'd never heard anything like it. At the least, you needed eight men, including a tank and an off tank, to avoid a wipe.

Something pinged into his shoulder. The Hood looked down at a bloodied arrowhead. That was odd. He turned around just in time for the appalling sight of a man with blood flowing from a terminal knife wound to his face, driving a red flag straight into his chest.

There were no more words. There was no more time. As Hood's eyes rolled back in his head and the Dungeon reset, he just had time to think you learned something new every Dive.

The Dungeon collapsed around him.

CHAPTER 25 – CUT LOOSE FROM THE SKY

"I can't help but think it might have been nice to mention *Skill Suppression*."

"I didn't want to worry you."

"Ah, bless your heart. It was much nicer to find out about it when he shot me in the face. Glad you didn't rob me of the surprise."

"You're doing a helluva a lot of bitching for someone who's just been power levelled to Level 25."

"I know. It's almost like I was tricked into a fight for my life without having access to all the necessary info."

"Little man, you were always going to be able to power through anything the Hood could hit you with. Technically, you insanely outlevelled him. You should have been able to shrug it off without a thought."

Lowe stopped dead in the corridor outside the entrance for the Dungeon and turned to glare at the Temple Warder. "Technically! I was this close—" he held his thumb and forefinger apart in front of Latham— "to wearing a dagger as a conversational piece eyepatch for the rest of my life. So don't come at me with this 'technically' bullshit."

"But you didn't. You smoked a Level 30 Heroic Raid Boss. You've got to be feeling pretty good about that."

To be fair, Lowe was feeling pretty damn epic right now. He'd dropped the 15 Progress Points (5 standard plus 10 Threshold Bonus) into Wisdom and was enjoying the upgrade 115 Points there had on his regen. So much so that he would have to think about which of Mylaf's goodies he would have as his 'go-to' snack. With all the extra mana, regen, and then the impact of his enhanced *Roll with the Punches*, he wasn't clear about where he'd get his best value. He would need to spend an evening with a calculator and a stats spreadsheet.

And that was before talking about his gear reward . . .

"Can I see it again?" Latham asked eagerly.

"Dude, if you want your own Bracelet of Accuracy, you can spend a few seconds soloing that Dungeon yourself," Lowe said, touching the leather vambrace he'd looted from the Hood's corpse. Its stats were reasonably unremarkable, especially for a Legendary piece, but the active Skill was cool. It guaranteed a critical hit, regardless of any defensive mitigations.

"Don't be that guy. I couldn't equip it anyway - it's sub-35."

"Well, boo-fucking-hoo to the high Levelled tosser."

"You know, I don't do this job for the admiration or the undying thanks of those I help, but you could try a little harder on the old 'you're the whole reason I'm still alive, oh and by the way, thanks for the life-changing information that let me double my fucking level' thing."

"Feel better now you've got that off your chest?"

"Not as much as you would think."

They carried on walking and reached the stone staircase leading up to the city of Soar proper. Lowe put his hand on the banister and turned to Latham. "You know I'm grateful, right? For everything."

Latham winked back at him. "Don't get mushy on me, little man."

And they made their way upwards.

***

It was the same Temple Warder who was waiting at the entrance to their destination. "Look, I've told you this already. You're not high enough -"

Lowe gave her the finger as he walked past, breaching the Level 25 barrier and moving into the Temple proper. He located the portal stone to the third floor and was frustrated to see it was showing as 'unavailable'.

"Don't worry, I've got you." Latham reached forward and activated the portal. "But, for political reasons, I'm going to wait down here. I'm not sure how Gravalk will view you strong-arming one of his priests, and it might be prudent for me to have some distance if he orders your immediate execution. I can probably slow down aid getting there, too, if it comes to that."

Lowe nodded. "Do you have any advice?"

Latham's face was impassive. "Dude's a Level 30 Burning Candle. By my reckoning, you have the equivalent of twenty Levels on him - not that he will know it - and he's put your girl in danger. The best advice I can give you is to remember to leave enough of him alive so he can talk."

"Good thinking." And Lowe stepped through the portal.

Interestingly, it appeared that having that second rank in Intelligence reduced his portal nausea a bit when he reconstituted. Aintra Weber was directly in front of him, looking confused.

"Mr. Lowe, we weren't expecting you."

"No one expects me. I'm mysterious like that. Like a particularly virulent virus. Is Priest Setort about?"

There was a moment when the Coal Stirrer eyes flicked to a chamber on the left of the hallway, and then he was looking Lowe in the eye and was smiling broadly. "I'm afraid Priest Setort has already left for the day. Since the death of the High Priestess, it has been difficult to keep some of the younger priests to normal office hours."

Lowe pushed past the older man, not feeling especially good about the discourtesy, but he hoped Aintra would understand. Eventually. He crossed to the chamber the Coal Stirrer had glanced at and tried the door. It was locked.

"Mr. Weber, please open this door for me."

Aintra shook his head. "No sir, I will not. You have no right to be here. None at all."

"Fine. Be like that." Lowe channelled *Slugger* and drove his closed fist into the door.

Nothing happened.

Aintra coughed discretely. "Obviously, it goes without saying that the doors on the third floor of the Celestial Temple are proof against any number of physical, magical and telepathic attacks. Whilst I applaud the spirit of . . . erm . . . hitting it very hard, I'm afraid that approach will not be successful."

Lowe felt the burn of embarrassment on his cheeks. He was not too proud to admit it, but his recent success in the Dungeon, as well as the impact of resetting his Progress Points, had left him feeling somewhat invincible. He'd even been able to forget, however briefly, that he no longer held his Class.

And now he'd been brought down to earth with a bump. By a door.

Oh, well. Back to the drawing board.

"Mr. Weber, it is essential that I speak with Priest Setort. This is a matter of urgency. I believe he is in possession of information connected to the murder of Gianna d'Avec. I must speak to him immediately."

"What's all this?"

The other priest Lowe had spoken to in the immediate aftermath of the slaying of the High Priestess - Hiwalk - came out from his own chamber, a furious look on his face. There were small birds flying around his head. Made of flame, Lowe was somewhat surprised to see.

"My apologies you have been disturbed, Priest Hiwalk. I was just explaining to this gentleman that I cannot possibly allow him access to the chamber of Priest Setort in his absence."

Hiwalk's eyes blazed fire - Lowe wondered what a Hell Raiser actually had as a Skillset - and he whirled on the inspector. "Have we not been bothered enough? Is it not sufficient to you that we have lost our High Priestess? That our entire cult will now be dismissed from this floor and back down to the very base of the Temple? That our god will shortly be removed from the Council? Is that not enough for you!"

The man's voice increased in volume until he was bellowing out his final words, the birds circling his head screeching out their own anger.

Lowe took an instinctive step backwards before reminding himself that - even if just in theory - he had a whole host of levels on the priest. Oddly, it was hard to remember that in the face of such white-hot rage.

There was a moment of silence, and then Aintra filled the void. "It is not that we do not wish to be helpful, Mr. Lowe. Rather, that it is not appropriate to breach a chamber door in the absence of its priest. There is a way that these things are done, you will understand."

"Oh, don't be tiresome, Weber. Setort's in there." Hiwalk seemed to have settled down remarkably quickly. "Just open the damned door, and then the good inspector can do his business and leave."

Aintra looked disconcerted. "But, sir, the chamber is locked. The priest has left for the day."

"And I tell you, he has not. We have . . . dinner plans. We discussed leaving together just this morning. Patronising he may be, but Setort is reliable to a fault. He will be in there. Probably asleep. Just open the damned door."

Pursing his lips, Aintra activated *Secret Keeper*, and the door swung open.

The first thing that struck Lowe was he was always surprised by how much blood the average human body kept inside.

No, that was not quite right. The very first thing that hit Lowe, along with Aintra and Hiwalk, was a violent gust of wind that knocked them off their feet. The rumination about blood was the next thing that entered Lowe's head as he tumbled, head over foot, to rest against the wall.

But he was up and on his feet in no time - thank you, *Roll with the Punches* - and running back into Setort's room. He crossed to the window - ignoring the shredded corpse that no amount of health potions was going to coax back into the land of the living - and made a grab for the figure jumping out into the air beyond.

The assassin flung some sort of nasty Skill his way, shearing off at the elbow the arm that was gripping their hooded cloak. Some sort of Wind Mage, Lowe assumed. He made sure *Grid View* captured the exposed and startled face of the woman who dropped towards the ground, her descent slowing before - as a tiny dot - landing safely and running off into the milling crowds.

"Mr. Lowe, your arm!" Weber was looking at him in horror.

"Oh, not to worry," he shrugged, although less than successful than he would previously have done before losing a limb. "It'll grow back soon. Unlike, I fear, Priest Setort."

They each turned to look at the body, blood still leaking from what looked like hundreds of wounds.

Whatever Setort might have to say about his stalking of Arebella, someone had managed to silence him in the very nick of time.

CHAPTER 26 – WIND-WHIPPED ALIBIS

The moment Hel's feet hit the pavement, she was off and running.

To have been within the Celestial Temple at the time of one Priest of Gravalk's death was unfortunate; to have been seen at the discovery of a second was the beginning of a somewhat unhealthy habit.

It was the sort of thing that might be thought to invite comment.

And who had been the man she had hit with *Wind Blade*? That had been unfortunate. All she had wanted to do was to free her cloak so that she could slip away through the open window. But panic had taken over, and she'd overpowered the attack. Sloppy.

As the poor guy had been only a Level 25, she'd probably one-shotted him totally by accident.

"Fucking hell," she said to no one in particular. "What a complete and utter disaster."

What in Soar had she been thinking? Well, that was the point, wasn't it? She hadn't been. From the moment she'd noticed Arwel was missing a glove, she'd known the only place it was likely to be was in the High Priestess's chamber. Hard-won experience - over many, many years - had taught her that if any given situation had the potential to be fucked up beyond all recognition, then assume that was what was about to happen. Of course, her sister's glove would have been left at a crime scene. Where else would she possibly find it?

It had been, oddly, relatively little challenge to get access to the Third Floor. Really, if she came through this in one piece, she would be writing a very stiff letter to the Temple Warders to express her outrage at the ease with which security at the holiest site in the city could be circumvented. If she and her little team had known it was this easy to pay house calls, then their little vendetta could have been sorted years back.

That thought put a hitch into Hel's step. But that was the point, wasn't it? The Celestial Temple was incredibly tricky to gain access to. She'd managed not once but twice in a couple of days. Now, Hel had a very healthy appreciation for her talents and abilities - it would have been hard to have come through what she had without a substantial dollop of self-regard - but even she thought it was stretching credibility to believe she'd got in and out, scot-free, twice.

Had someone smoothed her entry? And if so, who?

"Or, more pertinently, why?" Hel asked a very started Darkling Assistant who was just crossing her path, walking the opposite way down the cramped street.

He started to smile, but then, noticing her Class and Level, he blanched and, head down, scurried away.

Hel barely noticed - he was hardly the first moderately attractive man to turn tail and run when they got a look at her stats - but slowed her walk down to an amble, deep in thought.

Any number of people in Soar wanted the High Priestess dead. Many of them were highly enough placed in society to know of Hel's reputation. And a couple of them were even powerful enough to be privy to the confidential intel about why she and her little gang might be motivated to do something about it. However, even with all the resources these 'clients' had to bring to bear, they had never got close - not once - to accessing d'Avec's floor of the Temple.

Twice in as many days? Both times following a murder?

Someone was up to shenanigans.

Although, Hel thought, it hardly helped that tonight she'd managed to break into the wrong room . . .

That was hardly her fault, though, she told herself. Hel couldn't fly, per se; rather she was able to drive herself upwards on spiralling tunnels of air. It looked pretty impressive and certainly was the simulacrum of flight, but it gave her much less specific control than may be assumed. It was actually a very disorientating experience if she did not keep her wits about her, and this - apparently - was one of those occasions where her focus had failed.

So she'd ended up outside a different chamber on the Third Floor than she had intended. No harm. No foul. Apart from the fact that she'd found herself, once again, in the presence of a slaughtered worshipper of the Fire Demon.

Violent death had never bothered her - hardly surprising considering her line of work - but Hel preferred her murders to be clean and clear. What had been done to that priest was overkill. And in every sense of the word. Indeed, in her experience, that sort of sloppy mess only usually occurred when several pressing questions had been posed, and the answers had been less than satisfactory.

Hel suddenly stopped and looked around her. She had no idea where she should be going. If the Temple Warders had not known about her presence in the High Priestess's chamber on the night of her murder, then they couldn't help but have her scent now. The last thing she was willing to do was to lead them back home. Whilst Wraiths were not outlawed as of yet, she could already see the narrative developing where both she and her sisters were likely to have an 'accident' when being questioned over recent events.

"Fuck it up, down, left and right. And right back again. After everything, what a bloody trite way for it to end."

Hel pressed her back against a shop window, earning an angry shout from someone inside. Without opening her eyes, she rearranged the rude man's neatly arranged clothes rails with a small, yet intensely motivated, localised *Cyclone*. He seemed to mind her resting against his window less after that.

Irek would put her and her sisters up, she was sure of that. Tenia could be relied upon to help her out if the chips were really down. Even Charl would be happy to have them as guests. Although he'd tell everyone who'd listen they were there . . . But she couldn't do that to any of them. Temple Warders didn't fuck about when the security of the Celestial Temple was concerned.

That train of thought reinforced the fact that it kind of made the slackness of those giant guards over the last couple of days even more noteworthy. She was being set up, wasn't she?

"Shit. Shit. Shit." Hel banged her head against the glass. If the manager of the shop was irritated at all the knocking, he was too busy trying to escape a vengeful twister focused on royally devastating his stock to mention it.

And the thing was, even if she was able, by some miracle, to skate from the charges over the priests, they had her bang to rights on the slaying of the man who'd grabbed her. Hel replayed that moment in her mind. Who had that been?

He wasn't a priest; she was sure of that. Tenia was very good at collecting all necessary information around a target, and she knew the names of all the Priests of Gravalk. So, who was it she had killed?

Hel had no useful memory Skill - it was hard to opt for one of them over an extra offensive skill that was likely to get much more use - but she had always been good with faces. It was frowned upon in her line of work to pick off the wrong target, so she'd relied on that natural gift more than once in a pinch.

That man had been familiar, hadn't he? Like he was someone - not famous - but known. Like she'd read something about him. A minor celebrity? Hardly. What would one of the movers and shakers of Soar's entertainment scene be doing on a closed floor of the Celestial Temple? No. If he wasn't a priest, he had to have a reason to be there. A member of the Security Services? That'd explain his reaction to seek to restrain her once she broke into the room.

Excellent, she thought. I killed an investigator. That sort of thing always went down well. Commander Cenorth was famously sanguine about the deaths of his officers. She was actually amazed the whole quarter wasn't already sealed off.

In fact . . . that was a good point, wasn't it?

Hel pressed off the window - shattering it with a hastily cast Wind Blade behind her. No one ever got poorer betting on Hel holding a grudge - and began to walk briskly away, risking a quick glance over her shoulder back at the towering sight of the Celestial Temple.

No fuss at all.

They hadn't even started to close off the entrance. It simply wasn't credible the dogs of war had not yet been released.

She thought back to the man from whom she had detached an arm. Why would she be familiar with the face of a low-Level member of the Security Services? They jealously guarded their privacy. You only ever heard anything about them when one of them fucked up enough to be dismissed, and the Press Officer threw them to the wolves . . .

Hel suddenly slapped herself on the head. "The fucking Classless!" A few people looked around due to the force of her shout, and she stared them out. "You want to make something of it?"

Surprisingly, no one did.

Hel started running. The funny thing about newspaper reports into such things is that they tended to overshare the details, didn't they? It shouldn't be hard to find an address. And if, as she was coming to suspect, the man had survived - hadn't there been something about him having an unusual healing Skill? - then there might be an opportunity to have a further conversation.

It felt like there were a number of things she needed to explain.

CHAPTER 27 – QUESTIONS AT THE EDGE OF A BLADE

""I do not wish to cast aspersions here, Jana, but it is kind of the point to speak to the witnesses *before* they are murdered."

"Really, sir? My mistake. I thought it might take the challenge out of things too much if people had the chance to share vital information with me. I'm like a mushroom, you see. I simply thrive being in the dark and having shit thrown at me."

"And this is the man you suspected of stalking Arebella?"

"Yeah, no doubt on that one. I have him in the damned image."

Cenorth cleared his throat tactfully. "Quite. Quite. And, in those very limited circumstances, if you had chosen to express your dissatisfaction in forceful terms, then that is the sort of thing we are entirely capable of overlooking. If you get my meaning?"

Lowe did. It was one of the features of life in Soar's Security Service that had never sat well with him. He understood that when you were responsible for keeping order in a city where even the boy who shined your shoes in the morning was capable of significant carnage, a certain latitude was given as to how you managed that.

Indeed, the Mayor was fond of saying he didn't much mind the various organised gangs that preyed on the Lower City. Not when he had the biggest, most violent gang on his side.

Lowe's unwillingness to quietly ignore the more brutal excesses of his co-workers had not stood him in good stead during his fall from grace. Surprisingly, when people did not feel you had their back, they were highly motivated to put a knife in yours when the time came.

To be fair, since his elevation to Commander, Cenorth had done his best to curb the more arbitrarily psychotic members of the force, but his question demonstrated how little had actually changed.

Lowe looked at the shredded corpse of Setort. The man had not died easily: he doubted there was a drop of blood left, or a bone unbroken, in that corpse. And his boss would let it slide if it turned out Lowe had extracted a little vigilante justice for taking pictures of his girlfriend?

Sometimes, Lowe found life in Soar rather grim.

"I didn't touch him, Commander. The door opened, the body was there, and his killer was leaping through the window."

Cenorth raised his eyebrows. "It doesn't need to be a case of 'the big boy did it and ran away'. Say the word and . . ."

Lowe gestured at his bare arm, where his suit and shirt had been lopped off at the elbow, and blood splattered all over his front. "They cut off my fucking arm, sir, as they escaped. I appreciate you looking out for me, but I didn't kill this guy."

"Fair enough. Shame, though. The paperwork on a second murder, on the same floor of the Celestial Temple . . . The Temple Warders are not coming out of this looking especially good. I even heard a rumour that the Mayor wants the Justicars to take over. Arkola is reportedly hopping mad."

Both of them surreptitiously glanced upwards towards the First Floor—the idea of that supreme being hopping brought a quick smile to Lowe's face.

"I'm glad you find my pain amusing, Jana. Arebella's okay, by the way?"

Lowe nodded. "As good as ever she was."

"Good. Good. I always liked that girl. Far too good for you, I can tell you that now."

"Goes without saying, sir. Was there anything else you wanted? I'd like to pop home and change." Lowe indicated the severed remains of his jacket. "I worry someone's going to think this is the latest fashion trend, and I'll never get anything done once I go viral."

"Quite. Before you go, I assume you have a theory as to what has happened here?"

Lowe shrugged. "Someone didn't want me speaking to Setort and resorted to playing silly buggers. Did you see they raised the cap to be able to enter the Temple?"

Cenorth nodded. "To a point suggestively higher than your level. Or," he glanced upwards," at least it was this morning."

"I ate my greens. Well, no sooner had I overcome that barrier and was on my way here, but the man I needed to speak to was cut into tiny pieces."

"And you think the two things are related?"

"Sir, someone knew I'd be speaking to Setort about the package Arebella has received, and they shut him up before he could talk. That's obvious. The problem is, I'm not sure whether that and the death of the High Priestess are connected."

"Two priests killed on the same floor within two days of each other. Surely whoever attacked you - and presumably killed Setort - is also responsible for the death of d'Avec?"

"Maybe. Maybe not. I haven't formed an opinion on that yet. Been a bit busy, regrowing my arm and all. I'd just say, in my experience, if you have a felon with a talent for one element, it would be pretty odd for them to use another. Whoever attacked me was handy with Air. The High Priestess was taken down by Water."

"Indeed. Well, I hope it goes without saying if you could try to get to the bottom of this before we run out of Priests of Gravalk, that would be wonderful. Council meetings are getting a touch . . . fiery, is my understanding."

"I'll do my best, sir. Now, if you could excuse me, I'm going to go and get appropriately dressed again." Lowe moved towards the portal stone. "Oh, and if Deathcaller Lant comes up with anything more interesting than 'he was tortured to death', can you let me know?"

"Surely, Jana."

***

Cenorth watched until Lowe's blood-soaked figure vanished into the portal's swirling mists. Then, he took a sending stone out of his pocket. He shook it to clear any residue mana and channelled a considerable amount in as a replacement. It took several heartbeats, but - with a snap - it connected to a paired stone he never enjoyed reaching.

121

As always, there was no sound from the person at the other end, so Cenorth spoke into the void. "It is as you suspected. We may need to consider moving to Plan B."

***

"He's busy."

Lowe squinted up at the Temple Warder with a clipboard who appeared to be in charge of what was developing in the reception area of the Temple. Everywhere Lowe looked, he could see massive, lumbering Warders suiting up for what he assumed was about to be a pretty intensive search operation in the Celestial Temple.

"Can you let him know I'm going home now?"

"Absolutely. I have nothing better to do right now than be your personal social secretary. Can I get you a cup of coffee while you wait?"

"That would be lovely, thank you."

Temple Warder Gricken looked down at Lowe and snorted air out of his nostrils. The effect was not unlike a very angry bull preparing to charge. "Look, Inspector, if I see Latham, I'll tell him know you were here. But I can tell you, there's no way he'll be allowed out of the Temple tonight. It's all hands-on deck until we determine what's going on with the security protocols."

Lowe was somewhat disconcerted that Latham was not able to accompany him back to his apartment. Of course, he understood that the Temple was in chaos after the second murder in the week, but he still felt oddly vulnerable without the thought of the big man at his side.

Sensing that was the best he would get from the Warder, Lowe slunk away. Even reminding himself that he had, just that afternoon, been able to solo a Heroic Dungeon didn't make his journey home any less stressful. It was hard to forget the feeling of helplessness in the Tower of Law when that hidden presence had battered him down.

But, in the still, evening air of Soar, it was impossible to be too worried about such things, and in no time, he was pushing through the door of his home with a smile on his face.

Certainly, since Mylaf arrived at his door, returning to his apartment had become a more attractive option. Where he had become used to his rooms having a gloomy atmosphere, with a sad, musty smell in the air, now there was a cheerful brightness spilling outwards into the corridor outside, undercut by the constant scent of baking.

In fact, the place pretty much gleamed under the attention of the Drudge, which made the muddy footprints on the doormat even more noticeable.

"Mylaf?" Lowe called, pushing as much fake unconcern into his voice as possible whilst simultaneously filling both hands with *Slugger*. "I'm just grabbing some fresh clothes, and then I'll head straight back out. I'm afraid my second-best suit has taken another significant downgrade."

Lowe shrugged off his jacket so that it puddled on the floor and paused, listening for any sign of life. "Oh, and I'm afraid I may well be needing a new shirt. Blood again. Not my fault this time."

The Drudge still didn't answer, and Lowe crept around towards the back wall, eyes roving the doors that ran off the hall to try to sense from which direction the danger might come.

"Mylaf? Are you still up?"

"Mr. Lowe," the Drudge's voice was a study in neutrality. "I am afraid I may need your assistance in here."

Lowe followed the sound and pushed open the door to the kitchen. Mylaf was sitting perfectly still behind the table, a knife floating at her throat.

Lowe winked at her and looked around, spotting, in the far corner of the room, a hooded figure he'd last seen diving through a window, having chopped off his arm.

"Inspector Lowe. Please drop whatever the hell overpowered Skill you're currently channelling. I'd like to talk to you about the death of a certain High Priestess."

CHAPTER 28 – 'BOSOM BUDDIES'

"You okay, Mylaf?"

"Perfectly so, Mr. Lowe. Occupational hazard of working for the High Priestess. This is not my first steer of the hostage rodeo."

Lowe's gaze shifted from the Drudge to the woman holding her captive. Intriguingly, her name, Level and Class were shrouded in darkly glittering smoke trails. In the *Grid View*, when he had been observing the assassin, this had not been the case, a detail that was not lost on him.

"This seems to be a tad excessive. If anything," he indicated his bare arm, "I should be the one hunting you down."

"I just want to talk."

"Obviously. That's why you've broken into my home, attacked my friend and disguised your name and various attributes. All my favourite conversations start that way. I'm sure we'll be going shopping together and braiding each other's hair before long. I cannot tell you how often dead priests, desperate escape attempts and slicing off my limbs were simply awesome icebreakers."

"I didn't kill the priest. Or the High Priestess."

"Sure."

"I'm telling you the truth!"

"Absolutely. And I have no available context to cause me to see you as someone with anything less than scrupulous, unblemished integrity. The knife to Mylaf's throat is simply a decorative piece."

"The truth is the truth."

"Funny thing is, that is not my experience. For example, in this situation, there's your truth, Mylaf's truth and then whatever truth I tell my boss after the eight security officers outside finish stomping you into dust."

The woman's eyes flicked to the door behind Lowe, not long enough for him to do anything, but he was pleased to see the momentary lack of attention. He might be able to work with that. "There's no one out there. You had no idea I was here."

Lowe shrugged. "Believe what you like. As I said, there's truth, and then there's *truth*."

The woman shifted her weight from foot to foot, uncertain. "You do realise I could kill you both in a second?"

"Go for it. Nothing is more convincing for someone seeking to prove their innocence of murder to - you know - kill an innocent bystander. Textbook persuasive technique. Hat-tip."

"I'm willing to bet every piece of gold I own that you get beaten up an awful lot, don't you?"

"More than average, I'd guess."

There was an awkward pause during which it became clear that Mylaf was the most chilled person in the room. Then the woman made a gesture, and the knife flew away to stick, point down, into the chopping board. The smoke hiding her details dissipated, revealing her name, Level and Class.

Lowe whistled. "So, you're quite the nasty customer then?"

Hel sat down at the table, running her hands through her hair. "You have no idea."

***

Mylaf had served up a cup of hot chocolate that eased the tension in the room. It apparently did something to their feelings of aggression, which was pretty interesting. It suggested the Drudge could produce consumables which did something to emotions, not just boost stats. He'd have to explore that at another time: perhaps when not in conversation with a fucking Wind Tyrant.

"You said you wanted to talk. So talk."

Hel took another sip of her steaming drink. "I was in that room tonight because I wanted to retrieve something."

"Which was?"

"My . . . an associate of mine left something behind on the Third Floor on the night the High Priestess was murdered."

"As you can imagine, I have a number of follow up questions."

"They didn't have anything to do with d'Avec's death. We.." she winced and looked at the chocolate accusingly. "Look, I don't misspeak. Is there something in this?"

Lowe raised his eyebrows at Mylaf, who smiled as she answered. "It's not a truth serum if that's what you're worried about. It has simply - temporarily, I assure you - increased your affinity for each other. I call it *Bosom Buddies*. You both just feel comfortable speaking plainly around each other. I thought after, you know - " she jutted her chin at the blade in the chopping board - "it would be wise to smooth out relations a touch."

Hel paused for a moment, then obviously decided she had very little to lose. "I was there too. That night."

"As you can imagine, my questions are breeding like rabbits."

"Look, just let me talk for a bit. On the night of the murder, I lost track of both of my sisters. There are some very specific and bloody reasons why that is a bad thing. Fortunately, I quickly tracked them to the Celestial Temple and caught up with them outside the High Priestess's room."

"And I'm sure she was delighted to see you all. Was there dancing and moonlight and love and romance?"

"I'm not really sure she cared too much. Being dead and all."

"Oh, right. 'It was like that when I got here.' Glad we're sticking to the truth here."

"Fuck off." Little spinning tempest appeared in her pupils. "She'd been dead a while by the time we got there. We arrived, freaked out at the carnage, and left as soon as we could. But my sister had dropped her glove. I was there tonight trying to retrieve it before someone put two and two together and got the necessity for summary execution out of it."

"That's quite a risk you took. Breaking into the Celestial Temple."

125

"My sister is important to me. As is loyalty."

"And you ended up walking into another murder scene?"

"I said I was loyal, not lucky."

Lowe took another gulp of his hot chocolate and regarded Hel over its rim. She was definitely not telling him the whole truth, but he didn't think that was about either of the murders. Neither she nor her sister had been involved in those. But something else she said was bothering him.

"A glove?"

"What?"

"You said your sister left a glove at the crime scene?"

"Yes." Hel hesitated for a second and then pressed on. "Look, my sister is a Wraith. Both of them are. You are familiar with that Class?"

Lowe nodded slowly. "I am. I had not realised there were any in Soar at the moment."

Although he kept his voice neutral, his mind was racing. Wraiths were an unusual Class that could not level up: not that it mattered as they were already colossally powerful by their very nature. It had been suggested that gaining this Class was an involuntary response to trauma. There had been a few days following his Classtration when he had felt a significant pull in that direction. He resisted, mainly because there was a strict 'behead-first-ask-questions-later' policy in place when it came to a Wraith. If he had wanted to take the dying option as a way out, he'd have taken it when it was offered.

"They are being allowed to fly under the radar at the moment. As long as they are under my control."

Lowe felt his respect for the woman opposite him go up a few notches. Keeping Wraiths from going tonto was a deal. They were such a violent, unpredictable Class that it was usually only a few days before the Security Services zeroed in on their location. Although, as they pretty much decimated everything around them, it didn't really take spectacular investigatory powers. You just followed the screams.

Lowe thought back to the smoke hiding Hel's Class. That would help, he supposed, but Wraiths were extraordinary looking beings . . .

"Hence the glove," he said aloud.

"What?"

"You have them all bundled up, don't you? Big, shapeless gear, hidden Class, never letting them out of your sight." Lowe nodded appreciatively. "Lots of effort. Lots of stress."

"It's nothing."

Lowe noted the worry lines at the corner of Hel's eyes and chose not to comment. "Until you lose track of them, they slaughter the High Priestess and then leave some evidence behind." Okay. He chose to comment a little.

Hel let out a low sigh, and the room shuddered under the force of the emerging gale. "I'm telling you, they had nothing to do with the murder."

"Okay. Okay. Let's not lose the sense of comradely accord we've built up. How about you explain to me why you are so certain?"

Hel tossed back her hair where it had fallen before her eyes and fixed him with a frank expression. "Because we've been planning to kill the bitch for years, and they wouldn't rob me of the satisfaction of being there when she finally fucked off and died."

***

Mylaf had produced some beef and mustard sandwiches, which, in addition to tasting delicious, doubled Lowe's Perception. "I thought, Mr. Lowe, that it would help if you could both see things as clearly as possible," she said, leaving them alone in the kitchen.

"I'm going to level with you," Lowe said between bites of the food, "'I'm innocent because this wasn't the way we were going to smoke the victim' isn't exactly the cast-iron defence statement you seem to think it is."

Hel shrugged. "You wanted the truth. I wasn't saying it was pretty."

"What did she do to you?"

Hel looked as if she would refuse to answer, but a resigned look came over her face. "Fine. I guess I owe you that. For the arm and all. There's four of us - I'm not giving you any other names - who were involved in . . . overseas activities for Soar. The sort of thing that's not exactly off the books, but neither did we have a parade every time we returned with mission accomplished. You know what I'm getting at?"

Lowe did. There'd been a time he'd flirted with joining one of the 'Out of Bounds' squads, as they were called, but his talents had always been better used in unpicking puzzles rather than causing them in other cities. He looked at Hel with a new appreciation: she wasn't just a talented assassin. The woman was a Council-endorsed one.

"You're using the past tense. I'm assuming something went awry?"

"You could say that. We'd been tasked with hitting a bank in . . . no, you don't need to know that. All went fine - we were a good unit - until it came time to exfiltrate. There was some sort of fuck-up, nothing that hadn't happened a million times, but we ended up having to fight our way out. We - " she paused, eyes unfocusing as if she were back on the job - "were pretty punchy and might have caused more casualties than was considered ideal."

Lowe nodded understandingly. This was a tune he knew rather intimately. "The Council disavowed you?"

"Of course. That was standard, and we knew that would be the deal the moment the bodies started falling. What we didn't anticipate was that they'd be cleaning house before we even got home. Apparently, a newly appointed Council member argued furiously that the only way to make amends for the civilian casualties was a similar blood-letting in Soar. None of the rest cared either way - it was hardly the first time such a thing had happened - but this newbie seemed to have a bee in her bonnet about all the collateral damage. They appeared to be taking it very personally. As she was an up-and-coming avatar, they let her have her head. We were just a day out from returning to the city when it happened. They killed everyone. All our friends. All our families. Anyone we'd so much as nodded at in the street. Everyone just went up in flames. We came back to our lives - quite literally - ablaze.

"Gianna d'Avec?"

"Gianna fucking d'Avec. She was so hung up on the deaths of a bunch of lower-classed nobodies in the arse end of nowhere that she personally incinerated everyone I loved."

"Sounds like you'd be pretty motivated to kill her."

"Damn straight. Now, think how pissed off I am that someone beat me to it?"

CHAPTER 29 - ALL QUIET IN THE NIGHT

Hel's story made sense. It was exactly how Lowe had heard this sort of thing worked out. The 'Out of Bounds' squads were rockstars; right up until the moment, they very much were not. Hel's team wouldn't be the first team to be royally fucked over by the Council and wouldn't be the first to seek bloody retribution.

"I guess you've been sending her death threats?"

"Absolutely. As often as we could get access to her post."

Lowe finished off his share of the sandwiches and sat back. "You had Wraiths in your squad?"

"No." Hel dropped her eyes. "It turns out the High Priestess was more focused on spectacle than thoroughness. My baby sisters survived the fire. Physically, at least."

There wasn't much more to say about it than that.

With a nagging feeling he was missing something, Lowe tried to put the events at the Celestial Temple together. One of Hel's sisters, or both of them, had slipped away from her notice and sought out d'Avec. That fitted with what he knew about Wraiths - they were nothing if not single-minded.

After hours, they'd have a chance of breaching security - particularly if Hel had managed to exercise some kind of control over their Skill choices. The issue with most Wraiths was that their uncontrollable rage was as unfocused as it was destructive. If their big sister had convinced them to select something like *Infiltration* or *Sneak Thief*, then, in the absence of Temple Warders at a time the High Priestess would usually have vacated her chamber, he could see how they could have got in.

The fact that the High Priestess did not stay in the Celestial Temple overnight made the Third Floor unusually vulnerable.

Lowe thought about the vision Gravalk had given him. Although he could imagine a set of circumstances in which a pair of Wraiths would have a chance to tear a Level 67 to pieces, that wasn't what had happened here, was it? There had been no Wraiths bringing their own brand of chaos and destruction to d'Avec's chamber in what Gravalk had shown.

So, he could see them arriving after she had died - with the Temple Warders not having their usual measures in place to keep them out - dropping one of their gloves when Big Sis arrived to get them out of there. And he could see the woman sitting opposite him risking a second break-in to get rid of the evidence they'd left behind that they had been there.

Likewise, if there was any suggestion of Wraith involvement in the death of the High Priestess, he could see why the powers that be would want things closed up tightly.

No one needed that sort of panic on the streets of Soar.

Against that, no vision from the Fire Demon - a god about to make a fast descent down the hierarchy of the Celestial Temple - was going to be believed. Wraiths had a special place in the collective moral panic consciousness.

"What are you thinking?" Hel asked, leaning forward over the table.

"That - and it might be the sandwiches talking - I think you're on the level."

"So, what next?"

But something was bothering Lowe—a little itch on the edge of his thinking. "Hang on. You say one of your sisters dropped a glove. Do you mean whilst they were in the High Priestess' chamber?"

"Yes. So, they tell me. If you have experience with Wraiths, you will know they don't have the imagination to lie. They're both clear that it was left behind when I pulled them out."

Lowe pulled up *Grid View*. He'd repeatedly examined the crime scene over the last few days and had never seen a glove anywhere. No, there was nothing there. It was as he'd thought.

"Hel, there was no glove there when I arrived."

"That makes no sense. Why would someone remove evidence? Particularly if it could be used to point the guilt to someone other than themselves?"

Lowe had no answer to that.

***

The two of them talked into the early hours.

By the time Hel let herself out, Lowe was certain that no one in her little group had anything to do with either of the murders. The psychology was all wrong: with a bond that strong, it was all for one, one for all.

And the use of water to explode d'Avec . . . no. That didn't seem like the sort of satisfying conclusion to things that the wronged 'Out of Bounds' squad would be looking for.

Or, as Hel had put it, "we wanted to watch the bitch die slowly."

"Are you sure you are okay?" Lowe asked Mylaf as she swooped in to clean up the used crockery.

The Drudge smiled as, with a clash of porcelain, the dishes washed themselves and then were directed back to their place in the cupboard. "Honestly, Mr. Lowe, I was quite missing the experience of being violently assaulted by an intruder. It was truly a regular occurrence in the service of the mistress."

"Seriously?"

Mylaf nodded. "She was a good mistress, but I understand she was a difficult person outside the house."

"To the extent people would regularly break into her home and attack you?"

"May I sit, sir?"

"Of course. I'm not all about the whole 'yes, sir', 'no, sir' thing. Can we find a way to keep the pastries coming and the cleaning happening but ramp up the informality?"

Mylaf tilted her head to one side. "You are an unusual man."

"It's been mentioned."

"Well, sir - sorry, what would you like me to call you?"

129

"Jana's fine."

"Well . . . *Jana.* The mistress was exceptionally driven. After losing both of her parents so young - "

"You mentioned that before. Do you know what happened to them?"

"I do. It's just - " Mylaf paused - "I assume you will treat all this discretion?"

"Mylaf, I had my arm cut off a few hours ago, and the only person who seemed remotely bothered was the high-level assassin who did it. I could be the least discrete person in the whole of Soar, and I'd still have no one to gossip with."

"Fair enough. It is not like this is entirely confidential, anyway. The official story, to my understanding, is that they were killed in an explosion on their way back from work. As Flame Wardens, they had been contracted to one of the bigger energy companies."

"Flame Wardens were killed in an explosion? What happened? Did a sun go supernova?" Lowe's brain caught up with his words. "She killed them?"

"Wholly accidentally. It appears that Gravalk identified her at birth as a future High Priestess. Unsurprisingly, she found herself with more power than she could handle for most of her youth."

Lowe tried to imagine carrying the weight of murdering your parents, regardless of how accidental the conflagration was. "Is that why she stayed in the family home rather than living in the Temple?"

"I think so. Certainly, she never showed any inclination to move to better premises despite the rise in her status."

"What about what Hel said? Do you think d'Avec would have slaughtered their families?"

Mylaf took a moment to respond. "I think, if her god had asked her to do something, there is very little the mistress would not have done. Besides, if the Council determined something needed to be done, I well imagine she would have put herself forward to enact it. She was singularly driven to raise herself up the ranks of the Temple."

"Why?"

"I guess to make it all worthwhile."

Lowe could see that making a sort of sense to Gianna d'Avec. There were acts he had undertaken in his first few years with a Class that would not stand scrutiny so many years down the line. He'd never massacred anyone's family, but he was self-aware enough to know that in the wrong circumstances and with the right pressure, a younger him would have made a poor decision.

He thought back to the High Priestess's last will. "Would it surprise you to know," he asked Mylaf, "that d'Avec was leaving the majority of her money to charity?"

"Not at all," Mylaf's smile was sincere. "She always said she wanted to do more for those in the undercity. Her efforts there were the main reason unhappy people kept coming to the house. Her altruism in that regard was not appreciated by those who preyed in the shadows of those streets."

Lowe thought on that. "Do you have a theory as to what happened to her?"

"I think," Mylaf began and then stopped. "I'm sorry, sir, it is not my place to give you advice."

"I wouldn't have asked if I wasn't interested, Mylaf. Of everyone I've spoken to, you are the only one who has a good word to say about her. I think your opinion on this matter is pretty important!"

The Drudge tapped her fingers on the kitchen table in an odd beat. "No, I suppose you wouldn't. All I can say is that the mistress had something on her mind the week before her death. She was working much later each night and seemed out of sorts when she was home. There was very little that she would not share with me, Jana, but those last few days were different. She was remote. Distant. I think whatever was keeping her at the Temple for all hours had something to do with her murder. That's what I think. And now I should go to bed."

Lowe was left alone as she abruptly vacated the kitchen.

He sat there silently for a few minutes. He couldn't help but think he had enough of the pieces of the puzzle now to begin to see the shape of things, but the image refused to swim into focus.

With a growl of frustration, he flicked off the light and took himself to his own bed.

***

Hel waited in the shadows outside of the apartment complex.

It hadn't needed her years of experience to identify the eyes in the darkness watching the building Jana Lowe called home.

She'd liked the man. Liked his directness, which was rather refreshing in her line of work. He seemed to have believed her story, which was true enough in its own way. Certainly, true enough to escape detection by whatever buff that Drudge had been able to put into her food.

And there was no judgment when he heard about her sisters.

There were four watchers, she decided. All were in their low to mid-30s, and none of them had a particularly threatening class. Doubtless, they were there to ensure Lowe didn't further his investigation.

Being dead was a pretty effective break on such things.

They'd become pretty animated when the light in the kitchen switched off, but she waited until they made their move towards the Inspector's door before she acted. Just to be fair.

They didn't get within four feet.

***

A series of low thumps disturbed Lowe's sleep, but after listening for a few seconds, he rolled over and was back snoring in no time.

131

CHAPTER 30 – STORMS ON EVERY FLOOR

Lowe was awoken by a frantic Temple Warder hammering at his door. "What the fuck, Latham?" he said, pulling the door open.

The big man pushed past him, scanning the apartment as he did so. "You okay, Jana?"

Lowe trailed after him, trying to ruffle some awake into his face. "Sure. Why?"

"Nothing happened here last night?"

In response to the noise, Mylaf appeared at the door of her own room. She was immaculately dressed, as usual, Lowe noted. Did the Drudge sleep fully clothed in preparation for a moment when she was needed to spring into action and provide sustenance? "Warder Latham. Mr. Lowe. Would either of you care for some tea?"

"I think he'd better," Lowe said, closing the door. "Perhaps with something that enhances his chill."

***

Lowe eventually got the story from Latham as to why he was so discombobulated this morning. It turned out someone had done their very best to keep the Temple Warder extremely busy from the moment Lowe had gone through the portal to find Setort's body: a series of random chores and unnecessarily complicated administrative tasks had lasted until just a few minutes earlier.

"At first, I thought it was just the usual Temple bullshit. Even I'm not above being occasionally fucked over by the rota. However, there are only so many times you can be sent out to patrol an empty floor before you get suspicious. Then one of the others joked about you having a 'bad night', and I put two and two together. From what I hear, you should be a bag of broken bones right now."

Lowe shrugged, "Slept like a baby."

It took Latham around half a bell to satisfy himself that no lurking hoodlums were hidden in Lowe's closet. After that, he sat himself down and tucked into a grotesquely overfilled plate of eggs and bacon.

Lowe watched him eat with fascination. It made sense that someone of the Warder's size would need to consume a sizeable number of calories, but - as Latham moved on to plate two - he hoped Mylaf could produce some sort of statin potion.

Lowe sipped his own tea - a rejuvenating Peppermint that gave him a +10% stamina boost for two bells - and tried to get a word from Latham between munches. "I have to say, mate, I'm flattered to know you cared. I got my arse handed to me in the Tower of Law, and you didn't bat an eyelid."

"Let's say, since you were able to demonstrate that Essence Transmutation Theory has merit, you've gone up a little on my list of people I'd rather were kept alive."

"Honestly?" Lowe thought that sounded a little cold.

Latham chuckled and punched him gently on the arm, making the Inspector very glad for both his tea and the extra mana he had to heal the fractures immediately. "Nah, just joking. You've grown on me. Like a haircut, I wasn't sure about, but others thought was fly. But seriously, I was pissed someone was playing silly buggers."

Latham's face suddenly became serious, and he put his heaped fork back on the plate. "Little man, it seems some serious people are coming for you. I've been charged with keeping you alive until . . . well, until you piss off the Council enough for them to tell me to kill you. And someone still had the juice to give me the run around last night. That takes balls. You were supposed to come a cropper last night, and whoever arranged it was comfortable in acting against the Council."

"Or it was the Council?" Lowe suggested.

The two of them looked at each other for a few moments, considering.

"Well," Latham whistled, "that's a lovely thought. That means I'm on their shit list too. Cheers for that."

"Just sharing the love, mate."

They both sipped their tea in silence. Mylaf appeared and swapped out Latham's plate again. This time, it was piled high with pancakes and syrup.

"Well, it might just be the tea talking, but I figure there's not much point brooding," Lowe said. "There's just under a week before the deadline from the dude in the Tower of Law runs out. But I cannot see any random fuckers being sent to kick the shit out of me coming from that source."

"How come?"

"Dude who battered me didn't strike me as someone lacking in confidence. He made his point, he threatened Arebella, and he gave me a sevenday to wrap it up. I can't see him sending goons - especially ones that never actually turned up - a day later. What would be the point?"

"Fair enough," Latham conceded. "So, we've got Mr. Law as a principal antagonist. . . What?"

Lowe was smirking. "That's just a significantly fancy word for a guy who looks like his forehead could bench press twice my body weight."

"Fuck you very much," Latham continued. "So, we've got Mr. Law. And you think we can assume he's not the same person who gave me the run around last night and scnt some missing-in-action muscle to your place?"

"I don't see any percentage in him being involved. I figure you nccd to look closer to home for that."

Latham tilted his head, considering. "To be honest, we could be talking about anyone from the Eighth Floor upwards. That's where the movers and the shakers tend to reside. They're the avatars the Temple Warders tend to take notice of. Any of them would have the pull to mess with the rota. And they'd have the power to arrange some goons."

"Goons who never showed up . . ."

"True. So we're probably not looking at an Arkola masterplan here. Although, I doubt they'd bother with intermediaries. The fact all your particles are still in place suggests you've not yet sufficiently irritated them for your death to be desired."

"They just haven't had enough time to get to know me. And you're sure the Council hasn't turned turtle on the investigation? It could have been them?"

"Nope. My standing orders are the same. You're to be kept alive until you make your report. In any event, if they wanted you rubbed out, they'd just have me do it. No point sub-contracting when I'm within neck-snap range."

Lowe would have liked to think the Temple Warder was joking again, but he feared he might not be. "So not Mr. Law, not Arkola and not the Council. But we reckon it must be someone within the Temple itself?"

"Only thing that makes sense."

Lowe leaned back in his chair. "Don't you think this is all over elaborate? Mr. Law is connected to Setort via the threat to Arebella, and someone from the Temple - but not Mr. Law - is trying to warn me off, too. And then there's whoever tried to poison us in the Coffee Shop. Where does that come in?"

Latham swept the last of the pancakes around the syrup and popped it into his mouth. "Mr. Law is either a Big Bad with tentacles that reach into the Temple, or he works for someone who fits that description. He or his boss just want the investigation to stop. On the other hand - shall we call them Mr. Temple? - they are highly enough placed to be able to mess around with the Temple Warder rota, but not powerful enough to have access to hired guns who, you know, actually turn up. But - and trust me, the rumour mill was clear on this - Mr. Temple absolutely wants you dead."

"Dead? You said I was supposed to have been turned into a bag of broken bones."

"I didn't want you to worry."

"Oh, cheers for that. Much better for it to come out casually in conversation. Informally, like. Right, so Mr. Temple is behind the poisoning too?"

"Seems on brand."

"So Mr. Temple is more likely to be involved in d'Avec's death? Whoever it is wants me off the case. Permanently. Mr. Law just wants the whole thing dropped in a week. That feels pragmatic rather than an act of guilt."

Latham coughed discretely. "Not necessarily. I say this with all love, but Mr. Law might just be confident in your reputation as a fuck-up. He might be chilled for you to stumble about impotently for a week."

"Nice. And I made sure you had a nice breakfast, too."

"Just calling it how I see it. But where does the assassin who cut your arm off last night fit in? Mr. Law cleaning house?"

Lowe filled him in on his evening visitor, ending with, "But I don't think she had anything to do with the High Priestess dying. Or with Setort. I mean, she was clear she wished she had done and was pretty pissed to have missed out on the opportunity."

"And it was her little group that was sending the death threats?"

"That's what she said."

"Fucking hell. Give me a clean armed robbery any day. You know where you stand when a bunch of guys in masks try to storm the Temple."

"I'm with you on that one. So, we have three interested parties that we know of. Mr. Law, Mr. Temple and Mrs. Tyrant."

"Who's your favourite for d'Avec's murder? And how the fuck does Setort fit in?" Latham asked, brow furrowed.

Lowe finished his tea and pushed the cup away. "I have no fucking idea."

***

"You used my fucking name!" Khaled stormed through the open door of Mdamic's office, his face flushed with anger. "Are you out of your mind?"

Mdamic let the scroll he was reading roll up and vanish back into his inventory. Slowly, he raised a finger to point at the Chosen of Oh. "You, sir, are being impertinent."

"There's four missing Security Squires. With my fucking name against their requisition. How long do you think it will be before someone comes asking questions?!"

"Questions to which you have no answers."

"As if that's going to satisfy them! What possessed you, Mdamic?" Fortunately for Khaled, *Never Surprised* kicked in, letting him dive to the floor before a flash of lightning took him in the chest. He rolled left and right, narrowly avoiding follow-up explosions as Mdamic stood and stalked forward.

"Do not forget your place, Khaled. I have more than enough mana to keep this up all day. Certainly longer than your little pre-cog ability will be active. I will accept your apology now."

Still rolling away from Mdamic's lightning attacks, Khaled shouted, "I'm sorry for babbling. I was momentarily overwhelmed by unreasonable irritation."

Mdamic paused in the act of flinging thunderbolts and smiled, the dark clouds over Soar vanishing and the sun breaking through. "Grovel accepted. Now, shall we discuss things in a calm and rational manner?"

He indicated a chair and walked back to the other side of his desk, where he steepled his fingers in a gesture Khaled was coming to despise.

"Now, did I direct some Temple resources to take the investigator into d'Avec's murder off the table? Yes, I did. Did I use your authority to do so? Yes. It seemed prudent to cover my tracks. Do I feel bad about doing so? Not at all."

"But to what possible end? My sources tell me that the Security Service has put their least respected man on the job. A Classless, no less. What did you hope to achieve by this stunt?"

Mdamic's smile broadened. "And I thought you were the brains in our little partnership. Had not Oh whispered to you about the identity of this Classless? Yolgorth has certainly made his feelings clear to me."

Khaled shook his head. "I have heard nothing that causes me concern."

"Then you need to listen harder. There is a concern, and Yolgorth is not the only god to hold this opinion that someone is taking advantage of d'Avec's death to cause trouble. This investigator - this Lowe - has a reputation for following tracks further than desired. We all have things in play that it would not do to have too many eyes upon. Especially," and he pointed towards the floor above, "one particular set of eyes."

Khaled nodded reluctantly. "But using my name . . ."

Mdamic waved away the protest. "You will be questioned and answer honestly that you have no idea what occurred. The more pressing issue - and I would encourage you to discuss this with your god - is how a Classless investigator was able to kill and then dispose of the bodies of four Security Squires without anyone noticing. I had his Temple Warder running errands all night, and yet it seems Lowe is still hale and hearty this morning. My attempt may have failed, but it has confirmed Yolgorth's suspicions."

"Which are?"

"Investigator Lowe is going to cause a lot of trouble. That is, unless we find a way for him to quickly and quietly stop being an issue.

Khaled stood. "I will commune with Oh over this matter as a matter of urgency."

Mdamic watched him go, letting a flurry of lightning bolts play at his fingertips.

CHAPTER 31 – JUSTICE BURNS AT BOTH ENDS

With Mylaf's words about the High Priestess's unusual behaviour before her demise fresh in his mind, Lowe embarked on a journey to the Middle Court. "You're sure this was the last case she heard before her death?" he asked the Temple Warder as they crossed the busy street.

Latham's eyes darted around, their gaze shifting from one shadow to another, glaring at anyone who dared to approach Lowe. "It was Gravalk's sevenday for assuming the role of the Deity of Justice. However, this was the only case that would have warranted the High Priestess's personal attention. The other priests had handled the less significant matters, but the Ulton case was different. It carried the weight of a death penalty."

"And who did she execute?"

"A minor Earth Mage. To be honest, even though it was a murder, we were all a bit surprised she actually chose to appear herself. In theory, avatars should attend when it is their god's sevenday, but it's the sort of thing she could have passed off without any comment. But, no, she was there for the whole thing. A mate of mine had tried to organise the security detail, but she insisted on portalling in and out herself."

"And he was guilty? The Mage she executed?"

"The High Priestess found him so, and Gravalk's fire was certainly hot that day."

"That was definitely an answer to a question. I'm not sure it was actually the one I asked, though."

Latham blew out air from his cheeks. "I guess it was somewhat of a surprise. The High Priestess, though, was so certain of his guilt that she cut off the defence case short. Wholly within her remit, of course. But that sort of thing is a touch unusual."

Which was why they were calling on Ortel Maybourne, the Defence Counsel concerned.

The short, stocky man with his golden sash was waiting for them outside the gates of the Middle Court. He was pacing up and down, obviously nervous about something. As soon as he identified the two men walking towards him, he hurried towards them.

"Ah, Inspector Lowe. Warder Latham. I've been expecting you."

"Counsel Maybourne, thank you for making the time. We have some questions about..."

"Yes, yes, yes." Ortel started literally dragging them away from the court entrance. He had limited success moving Latham an inch.

"Is there a problem?" asked Lowe.

Ortel looked over his shoulder in the least surreptitious glance Lowe had ever seen. It was a good job that Maybourne had made a decent living in the law; he certainly was never going to have much of a career as a spy. It did not take Lowe's years of experience to determine something had the tubby Druid spooked.

"Please!" Ortel was, literally, wringing his hands. "I have been told, under no circumstances, should I speak to you."

Lowe began gesticulating wildly and angrily as if he were in an argument with Maybourne. "That's fine. We'll go and wait in the pub just around the corner. You know the one? Good, come and see us anytime in the next two bells." He punctuated the final word by rudely poking Ortel in the chest and spinning on his heels. Latham lumbered after him.

***

"Someone got to Ortel?" Latham said, carrying two pints of ale to the table in one hand and four packets of crisps to accompany them in another.

"Cheers. But how are you still hungry, mate? I mean, do you have hollow legs or something?"

"I've not slept in three days, little man. I have a Skill that can burn calories to replenish Stamina, but it's a bugger to keep fuelled. Anyway, I've dropped it all on expenses. After being jerked around all night, I'm not feeling especially loyal to the Temple hierarchy right now." He tore each packet open and tipped the contents down his throat one after another. "Ortel. Who do you think got to him? Mr. Law, Mr. Temple or A.N. Other?"

Lowe sipped his ale, wincing at the odd flavour. Mindful of recent experiences, he pulled a charcoal macaron out of his inventory - Mylaf had produced a batch this morning for just this purpose - and bit into it. Latham raised an eyebrow, so he explained. "The ale tasted funny."

The Temple Warder gulped his own and shrugged his shoulders. "Nah, I think you're getting paranoid in your old age. But if you don't want it . . . " Latham swallowed Lowe's pint in two huge gulps.

"This is truly like sharing a space with a bottomless pit."

"The lawyer?" Latham prompted.

"My money would be on Mr. Law," Lowe said. "He seems to be the one dealing in threats, whereas Mr. Temple appears to be all about the instant murder attempts."

"And yet you're not convinced he had d'Avec killed?"

Lowe looked mournfully at the empty pint glass before him. He started worrying that Mylaf's consumables might have ruined 'normal' food and drink for him. That was going to be a bit of a bugger when this case ended, and she wanted to find other employment. Pulling a face, he turned his mind back to Latham's question. "Let us say the jury's out on that one. Which," he added, noting the appearance of a red-faced little man in the doorway of the pub, "was not an option Trellen Ulton was given."

Ortel spotted them and hurried over to them, taking the third untouched pint and downing it in one. He gave a discrete little burp, produced a *Totem of Silence*, and banged it in the centre of the table.

"Dearie, dearie, dearie me. Never in all my years with the Sash have I encountered such a palaver. No, sir. No sir. Not at all."

Lowe nodded to Latham to go collect another few drinks.

"Counsel Maybourne, thank you for coming to speak to us."

"No, no. Thank you for being the first unexpected visitor I've had in the last day to show some decorum. Dearie me, it's warm in here." He added a *Totem of Air* to the table, emanating a soft breeze.

"Can I take from your comments that we were not the first visitors you have had of late who wished to discuss Gianna d'Avec?"

Latham had returned, and Ortel relieved him of one of the drinks he was carrying, draining it dry. The second pint of ale seemed to settle the Druid, whose level of anxiety suddenly appeared to be under control. He gave a little laugh.

"Who knew I was so popular? You, sir, are the fifth such caller I have had since the death of the High Priestess." He directed the following sentence at Latham. "And not one of your predecessors offered me a drink." The Temple Warder returned to the bar, muttering under his breath.

"Can you tell me what you remember of your visitors?"

Ortel waved his hand and refreshed his *Totem of Silence*. "The first was just some snidey little Street Rat who I doubt knew why he had been paid to ask the question. I sent him packing in short order. Unfortunately, the two men who returned were less easy to dismiss."

"They threatened you?"

"They certainly tried, sir. It never ceases to amaze me how many of the Undercity have not encountered a Druid before."

Lowe winced. "Did you leave much of them behind to be identified?"

"Of course," Ortel sounded offended. "I am not an animal. At least, not most of the time and certainly not on that occasion." He gave an oddly high-pitched giggle. "Little Druid humour there. Ah, the waiter is back. Good show, sir."

Latham sat down, carrying a tray with four drinks, and slammed it down with very little grace.

"So," Lowe felt it politic to continue, "a Street Rat, then a couple of hired muscle. Who else?"

"Ah," and then the short man became, if possible, a little smaller. "Then things became much less pleasant. I was accosted on my walk home by a rather insistent fellow who was clear that my speaking to you would significantly impact my well-being."

"That was yesterday morning?" Lowe thought it was instructive that Mr. Law - if it was him - was warning off potential witnesses. It made him being the one to cut Setort up into little pieces feel a touch unlikely.

"Indeed, sir. He had . . . a number of compromising images to supplement his threats."

"And yet here you are, willing to talk."

Ortel fixed Lowe with watery eyes. "I have been a lawyer for many years, sir. Once upon a time, I considered myself quite the dashing figure. I may no longer expect to progress further in my profession, but I have never allowed myself to be intimidated."

"And your fourth visitor?" Latham had polished off another pint.

"Ah, now she was intimidating. However, she was less anxious about stopping me from speaking to you and more about seeking information. Not unlike yourself, sir." Ortel added shrewdly.

"Let me guess. No Class and no Level on display. Handy with a gust of wind?"

Ortel's eyes twinkled. "I see we share an acquaintance."

"Tell us what you told her, please."

"I can do better than that, sir. After all your hospitality, I'll go so far as telling you the truth."

***

"Trellen Ulton was utterly innocent of the charges against him. You just had to look at him. He was incapable of speaking a mistruth, even when it would have been to his advantage. I came perilously close to being professionally embarrassed in my attempts to direct his statements, but he refused to budge. Earth Mages can be difficult like that. However, poor Trellen was obsessed with the idea someone else had slain his master due to his uncovering of Soar-wide corruption. You could barely get two words out of him without some conspiracy theory spilling from his lips." Ortel took another gulp of ale. "But do you know what's worse, sir?"

"What?" Lowe thought he knew what was coming. Things were just starting to snap into place in his mind.

"I think he was telling the truth. Whoever killed his master, Lord Falyn, did so in such a way that any questions about his business died with him. And then Trellen followed him to the grave in short order, stopping any questions about his brother's activities."

"His brother?" Latham finished the other drinks and had moved on to licking the empty packets of crisps. Lowe retrieved a Victoria Sponge from his inventory and passed it over. The cake did something to Stamina regeneration, which he hoped might forestall some of the epic gluttony he thought would otherwise form a significant part of their future.

"Yes, indeed. Markian Ulton was, to my mind, a far more appropriate suspect than Trellen. However, I never had the opportunity to present that alternative theory to an understanding audience."

"Because the High Priestess incinerated your client?"

"Indeed, but that was hardly surprising, considering."

"Considering what?"

Ortel smiled, the booze adding a sloppy side to his expression. He looked towards the expired *Totem of Silence*, then shrugged. "Well, sir. Considering Markian Ulton was the lover of the High Priestess, it might have been a little awkward had he been accused of murder in her court."

Yes, Lowe thought. It certainly would.

CHAPTER 32 – A GENTLEMAN'S DEFENCE

Lowe had not spent much time in the Jewel District of Soar.
It wasn't that the denizens of those giant mansions did not commit crimes—no, not at all. Rather, he reflected, it was that those in a certain income bracket were dealt with differently.

In fact, he could probably count on the fingers of one dick the number of times members of the Security Services had crossed through the wrought iron gates that separated 'Jewel Town' - as it was known locally - from the plebs who pressed up against them, hoping for a glimpse of a better life.

There was a rumour that a whole department at Cuckoo House - as the headquarters of Commander Cenorth's city-wide force was known - was dedicated to rooting out corruption in the rich. If that was true, Lowe assumed it had access to all the resources of a particularly untrusted paper boy.

"How the other half live, eh?" Latham said, having successfully bullied the Senior Gate Guard to let them through. Lowe felt he'd got to know the big man fairly well over the last few days, but even his pulse quickened when the Temple Warder raised his voice to a particular volume. All things considered, he was pretty impressed the spotty Level 24 managed only to urinate down himself. Twice.

"Half?" Lowe said, gazing at the first house on their left. He lost count of windows somewhere between 'fuckloads' and a 'shite tonne'. "I think we're in the presence of the top 0.5%."

After ensuring Ortel had enough ale to help his way to oblivion, it had been evident that their next stop needed to be Markian Ulton.

Even taking into account the fact coincidences happened all the time in Soar - the goddess Fortuna lived for that shit - there were certainly questions to ask about the circumstances surrounding Lord Falyn's death and the subsequent execution of Ulton's brother by the woman Markian was - reportedly - fucking. That the High Priestess herself turned up dead a little way later did not make this any less suggestive.

"Do you find it kind of odd that absolutely no one we've spoken to seemed to know that the High Priestess was performing the horizontal tango with this Markian?" Latham rumbled as they passed a veritable army of gardeners, ensuring the lush lawns were cut just so.

A maverick part of Lowe had wanted to ignore the 'Do not step on the Grass' signs, but he didn't want to make these guys' days any harder. From their expressions, being a servant in Jewel Town was hardly 'living the dream'.

"Horizontal tango? What are you, twelve?"

"You don't have to swear all the time, you know. We have a vibrant and engaging language from which to draw."

Lowe gawped a little at that. "Have you had a recent blow to the head?"

"No. But one can be arranged for you if you would like." The Temple Warder glanced down at the piece of paper on which Ortel had scribbled an address. "Should be right up here on the right."

If possible, the 'house' they arrived at was even more imposing than any they had previously seen. It dominated the corner of the street, rising five floors into the sky. From what Lowe could see, there were more chimney stacks than he himself owned spoons.

"How the fuck does a middling Earth Mage afford this?"

Latham clicked his tongue. "There's 'afford' and then there's 'afford'. I have always thought that those with the right connections have access to different credit streams than the rest of us."

"And what connections does this dude have?"

"Other than doing the upside-down canary with the High Priestess of Gravalk?"

"You made that up, right?"

"Maybe."

"Tell me, is there a Mrs. - or Mr. - Temple Warder? I'm sensing some sexual frustration. Perhaps you should call the Gnome with the attitude from the Dungeon. You know, blow off some of this steam."

There followed one of those silences where Lowe could understand why the Senior Gate Guard had lost control of his faculties. "Okay. So, moving right along . . . I've not seen anything suggesting d'Avec was bank-rolling this guy. She lived in the family home in the fucking Ash District and left all her money to charity. She wasn't anyone's Sugar Momma."

"You'd be surprised the value certain people put on contacts. I can imagine a set of circumstances where cleaning the High Priestess' pipes would carry a certain cache."

They approached what Lowe was determined to call a 'door' in the absence of a more illustrious word. With a little more iron, it could have pulled off being a portcullis.

"How are we going to play this?" Latham said, the Temple Warder pounding on the wood. "There's every chance this guy is behind Mr. Law - or at least is in the same food chain around him. I'm not anxious for you to be your charming, normal self on his own turf. A wrong word here could have some significant repercussions."

"What are you suggesting?" There was the sound of hesitantly approaching footsteps. "You don't think you can handle a little heat?"

Latham turned to glare at him. "Little man, I'm pretty much fire-proof. It's your flammable arse I'm worried about."

Before Lowe had a chance to answer, with some effort, the door was wrenched open by a stooped old man in what appeared to coat and tails. His name was Jeeves, and he was a Level 43 Butler.

"You've got to be shitting me!"

"And to think I suggested you might not be able to control yourself," Latham muttered.

"Can I help you, sirs?" Even the man's voice seemed to be straight from central casting. "Although it is lovely to greet new visitors, I do not believe we are expecting callers on this fine day."

Lowe decided to take charge. It was a Butler one heavy cream tea away from pulling a hernia. How hard could he be? "We need to speak to Markian Ulton." And then, because he wasn't a dick. "If you please, Jeeves."

If possible, the Butler's expression channelled even more polite disgust towards the Inspector. "I am afraid the master is not receiving guests at the moment. Nevertheless, I would be happy to make you an appointment for an appropriate moment?" Jeeves's eyes were unfocused, and a calendar was suddenly projected outwards in front of them. Lowe could not help but notice the first available slot was in little more than a year's time.

"No. That's not going to work for us, I'm afraid. Security Service business, don't you know. Thanks for the offer, Jeevo, but this is a bit more urgent than that. I think it best we just drop in on him now." With that, Lowe moved to push past the little old man.

This proved to be a mistake.

Although it was certainly one of the more archaic of the servant Classes, Butler was still very much in demand in the households of the more well-to-do. Or, rather, those known as the more-to-lose. Whilst the phenomenally wealthy wanted to feel safe, they did not really want to have a large number of guards cluttering up the place, making the antique furniture untidy and accidentally shooting the corgis.

Therefore, the answer to that particular conundrum was that it was far more elegant to have all your security needs packaged up in one well-spoken homicidal maniac with a fetish for silver polishing.

By the time Latham was able to move to intervene, even considering Lowe's recent upgrades, the Inspector had barely enough HP left to survive an especially stern frown.

"You okay, little man?" Latham called over his shoulder, trying - with limited success - to hold aloft the little ball of frenzied death that was Jeeves, at the end of an arm that was already cut to the bone. The Temple Warder crashed the Butler into the wall a few times, but this did little to calm him. "Fuck's sake!" he swore as Jeeves tore off a strip of flesh with his teeth and then spat it back right into his face.

Lowe blinked as his body tried to deal with the colossal damage it had just received. *Roll with the Punches* was doing its best to keep him alive, but it didn't really know where to start: Jeeves had absolutely bodied him. He could sense his mana exchanging for health at a frightening rate, which made him realise that if he had found this lead a day earlier, before this Dungeon experience, there was no question he would be dead.

"Jeeves, I think I can accommodate these gentlemen. Feel free to stand down."

The voice from down the end of the impossibly long corridor, with various doors leading off it, had the sort of aristocratic smoothness that usually would have wound Lowe up. However, as he was doing his best to climb up from the drain he was rapidly circling; he was willing to let it slide on this occasion.

Especially if the voice was able to call off the rabid wolverine that was gouging chunks out of a Temple Warder.

Fortunately, the moment he heard the voice, Jeeves suddenly became instantly subdued back to his stooped, deferential demeanour. "Of course, sir," he said, hanging limply from Latham's bloodied grasp, "would your guests care for tea?"

CHAPTER 33 – THE BUTLER DIDN'T DO IT. BUT HE TRIED.

The man sitting opposite Lowe triggered every single one of his class prejudices.

And it wasn't just the house that did it. Nor the Butler. Not even Markian's voice or ostentatious clothing were wholly responsible for rubbing the Inspector up the wrong way.

Although - to be clear - they certainly helped develop the sizeable chip on his shoulder.

No, what was especially getting Lowe's goat was Markian Ulton's attitude of supreme self-confidence. There was a particular way of sitting that thoroughly pissed Lowe off, and the man in front of him was utterly embodying it. Oh, and that emotion was exacerbated by Lowe having to accept a new shirt from the man to replace yet another one that hadn't survived being covered in his own blood.

"You know," Latham stage whispered as the tea was served by Jeeves, "it might save time if you just started the day bare-chested. Easier to wipe clean, you know what I'm saying?"

"Or, you know, my fucking bodyguard could have faster reactions than a ninety-year-old man."

"Little man, you tried to forcibly enter the property of a house guarded by a Butler. Even I couldn't foresee that particular moment of madness coming down the mountain. You're lucky I got there as fast as I did!"

"Wanker."

"Tosser."

"Prick."

"Far be it for me interrupt your little . . . tiff, but I assume there is a reason why you have called upon me this afternoon?"

Lowe turned his attention back to Markian. He was, even he had to admit, a startlingly handsome man. Tall, dark and with the sort of chiselled features that made the Inspector want to take better care of himself. Maybe get a whole night's sleep occasionally. Drink water. Say 'hello' to a vegetable once in a while. Perhaps stop getting repeatedly punched in the face.

"Yes, Mr. Ulton. I am investigating the death of Gianna d'Avec, the High Priestess of Gravalk." Lowe waited, wondering if that would cause a reaction.

Markian's face did not move any of its impressive muscles.

"During the course of this investigation, your name has been provided as someone we should seek to speak with. I wondered if you would have any comment on that?"

"Gianna d'Avec executed my brother."

Lowe held Ulton's gaze for an uncomfortable few moments.

Latham coughed, reaching for the plate of biscuits Jeeves had thoughtfully left behind. "We've come quite a long way if that was your only question, little man. I assumed you had any number of invasive and irritating questions. Would you like to check your notes?"

Lowe ignored him. "How did you feel about the death of your brother?"

"Are you asking if the High Priestess's actions might have given me a, how do you say, 'motive' for her murder?" Ulton said the word in much the same way as others might emphasise the phrase, 'child rapist'.

"Actually, I'm looking at things the other way around. Rather than you being all cut up about your brother's death and angry enough with the High Priestess to off her, I'm thinking that she helped you out and removed an obstacle in your way. I hear rumours you would have been implicated in Lord Falyn's death and that Trellen was going to share his thoughts there if the court case had gone on much longer. Seems d'Avec did you a favour when she burned him alive."

Markian smiled thinly. "Meaningless scuttlebutt, Inspector. Had my brother had any evidence to back up his ludicrous claims, he would doubtless have sought to produce it at his trial."

"I'm sure he planned to. Obviously, your friend - the High Priestess - turned up the heat somewhat, and that quietened him right down."

"Perhaps. But we have no way of knowing that for certain, do we? Trellen is dead; what he may - or may not - have planned to say during his trial is wholly conjecture on your part. And, I might add, it was rather unprofessional of Mr. Maybourne to share all of that with you. I wonder what his superiors would make of him breaking the duty he owed my brother's client confidence."

"I never mentioned where I received my information."

"No, you didn't. Funny that. I would suggest you ask the High Priestess to account for her own actions - rather than putting it on me - but she has rather lost her head as of late. Hasn't she?"

"I appreciate this is getting heated, but perhaps we should all speak of a fallen High Priestess with appropriate respect."

Lowe was surprised by Latham's comment and turned to look at the big man. Thus far, he had shown no inclination towards propriety regarding d'Avec. He'd joked repeatedly about her and the manner of her death. What was making him so po faced now? Nevertheless, it was the impact of the Temple Warders words on Ulton that was even more surprising.

"Quite right, Temple Warder. I am sorry for speaking out of turn." Markian picked at a piece of imaginary fluff on his crossed legs as he spoke, clearly disconcerted to have been upbraided.

That was interesting. Lowe decided to press on, using the impetus Latham's intervention had caused. "Did you have anything to do with Lord Falyn's death?"

There was a tense silence, during which time Jeeves reappeared in the giant drawing room, carrying a tray of crumpets. Markian watched the Butler put them down in the middle of the occasional table, removing the empty biscuit plate that Latham had pretty much inhaled. The slow speed at which the old man was moving made somewhat of a mockery of the pincushion he had turned Lowe into, using nothing more than his fingernails and a can-do attitude.

"Do you really expect me to answer that question?"

"I don't know, mate. In my experience, most people like to clear it up sharpish that they had nothing to do with murder. Those who get all 'no comment' about it tend to have something to hide. But you do you."

Markian was not finding Lowe's approach charming. "Inspector, I have a long history of supporting the Security Services. Why, just the other day, I was saying to Commander Cenorth during our regular round of golf that I was always happy to add my financial backing to any hardship funds that might exist. Do you play golf? Well, I was thinking that arrangements should be made for those who, from no fault of their own, find themselves Classless, for example. Would such a bursary be of interest to you, perhaps?"

"Putting that unsubtle attempt at both intimidation and bribery to one side, I'm still not hearing an unequivocal, 'No. I had nothing to do with the murder of Lord Falyn.'"

Lowe bit into one of the crumpets, dripping butter down the new shirt Markian had just arranged for him. By the look on the Earth Mage's face, there probably was not going to be a second offer.

"Was there anything else, Inspector? It turns out I have a prior appointment after all. Jeeves, please show these gentlemen out." Markian stood and was making his way out of the room.

Jeeves moved to intercept Lowe, who followed, firing questions. "Did you have Lord Falyn killed, blame it on your brother and then have your lover cover it up? Were you in a relationship with the High Priestess?"

Markian whirled around; his handsome face now twisted into something more like a sneer. "A gentleman never kisses and tells, Mr. Lowe. Doubly so when the lady in question is no longer around to protect her own reputation. I would have thought someone of your scruples would respond to that instinct. I am sure your young lady friend - Arebella, is it? - appreciates your discretion in such matters. Particularly since your fall from grace. Such a shame, Mr. Lowe. Such a promising career thrown away on a point of principle. Tut, tut, Mr. Lowe."

Lowe was dimly aware that Latham was wrestling with Jeeves again. However, all his focus was on his white-hot rage towards this smug man. It was like his vision had narrowed to a pinprick of anger.

"Are you threatening my friend, Mr. Ulton?"

"I do not deal in threats, Inspector. I have people for that. Now, if there is nothing else . . ."

Fuck it, thought Lowe.

"Mr. Ulton, it is my duty to inform you that you are currently a person of interest in the matter of the death of Gianna d'Avec. I am unsatisfied with your answers concerning the murder of Lord Falyn, and I have concerns as to how you are currently funding your lavish lifestyle. What is more, I suspect you may be involved in attempts to thwart a lawful investigation - namely, with organising various assaults upon my person and threats made against those close to me. I also don't like your face."

Power swelled around Lowe as he activated the Skill that he had missed the most when stripped of his Class. To be scrupulously honest, he thought, it was not *his* Skill per se, but rather one that was connected with his job - no matter how temporarily reactivated - in the Security Services.

"I am placing you under an immediate Restriction Order."

With an explosion of choral music, the text above Markian's head went a bright red as the Restriction Order took hold. The man literally sagged to the floor as the weight of the restriction landed on him.

Lowe strode forward until he stood over him, leaning forward to whisper into the stricken man's ear. "I trust you will be more forthcoming when next we speak. Oh, and 'no'. I don't fucking play golf."

With no further ado, Lowe snatched another crumpet, turned and left the building. Latham extricated himself from this battle with Jeeves and hurried to follow after him, doing his best to keep the goofy grin off his face.

CHAPTER 34 – THE RED LINE

"Have you completely lost your mind?"

Lowe thought it wise not to answer.

"I could not have been clearer that you were on a temporary reinstatement *with limited powers* beyond the immediate investigation into the murder of Gianna d'Avec. Do you remember her? The fucking High Priestess of Gravalk who was killed a few days ago? I was sort of hoping that might have been at the forefront of your mind, especially considering a *second* priest of Gravalk was also murdered yesterday! Some people might think that - bearing in mind that particular god is a FIRE DEMON - you would be putting your all into clearing those two little snafus. Just good sense, really. But no, not Jana fucking Lowe. What's he been doing? Well, let me tell you. This chaotic pinball of an investigator is running up to Jewel Town and acting like he's got jurisdiction to put Markian Ulton - yes, *that* Markian Ulton - under a Red Notice!"

Lowe let this slide by, too. You didn't need to swing for the fences at every ball.

"Oh, but not just any old Red Notice. No, you went big on it! Not only did you imply he was responsible for killing the High Priestess. No, you really wanted to shine today. You decided to really fucking piss on my chips. You suggested he was involved in a shadowy conspiracy around the death of Lord Falyn - a crime that the city has already found someone guilty of and had them executed - and that he is living a criminal lifestyle on illegal earnings. And -" Cenorth had to take a breath here - "you then accused him of funding a series of attacks on a Security Service officer."

"Just a few points of order, if I may?"

Cenorth waved his arms. "Please, I'm dying to hear what you have to say about all this."

"First of all, I didn't imply he'd killed the High Priestess. I outright stated it."

"Lowe..."

"No, no, no. If we're doing this, let's at least be accurate. Neither did I 'suggest' he was involved in the murder of Lord Falyn. The fucker absolutely one hundred per cent did it. He could barely stop himself from admitting it and crowing that I could do nothing about it. Oh, and I do have a witness that his Butler took me out to the woodshed and whacked me with a two-by-four."

"Completely unprovoked?"

"Now you're nit-picking. I guess that largely depends on how stringent we are going to be around the definition of 'breaking and entering.'"

Cenorth slammed his hands down on his desk, scattering scrolls everywhere. "Jana, just stop. I'm not finding you charming right now. Do you have any idea of how badly you have fucked things up?"

Lowe let the echo of his boss's voice fade away before replying. Everyone outside the Commander's office was doubtless enjoying the show.

The fuckers.

"We finished yet, boss?"

Cenorth narrowed his eyes. "No. We absolutely are not finished. Jana, are you trying to make me fire you?"

"Been there, done that, failed to be given any sort of leaving party. I am not sure that's quite the threat you seem to think it is."

"Lowe, you are sailing very close to the line here."

"Look, if I'm going to stand here and take a pasting, can we at least try to make it semantically accurate? I'm either 'sailing close to the wind' or in danger of 'crossing a line.' To do both suggests a familiarity with transport logistics that I'm not sure I have in me."

"Lowe, you have to see why what you have done is inappropriate!"

"Why?" Lowe raised his own voice now. "Are you seriously telling me I am way off base here? It appears to be an open secret that Ulton set his brother up for Falyn's murder. Unless you're suggesting whoever investigated that one is so breathtakingly incompetent, they never stumbled upon the potential lead that, just maybe, the incredibly rich man living in a house the Mayor would respect, without any obvious way of paying for it, just *might* have had something to do with it? Boss, Ulton is shady as fuck! Falyn was murdered because he was about to reveal something scandalous about the business community in Soar. There was no reason in the world for Trellen Ulton to be involved in that. He was fucking helping Falyn investigate! *Markian* Ulton, on the other hand? He's a crime boss who clearly had the High Priestess on his side - oh, and on her back, too. The dude was fucking the High Priestess of Gravalk! At the very least, ignoring everything else, that puts him on the suspect list."

Cenorth tried to interrupt, but Lowe just raised his voice louder.

"Ulton got his lover to wrap up his brother's case as fast as possible. Trellen never even got to offer a defence before she barbecued him. Do you not find that interesting? Noteworthy? Potentially criminal? Oh, and then let's not forget he definitely has tried to have me killed at least once since you gave me the case. You could at least *pretend* to care that someone's taken a hit out on one of your officers. Just for the sake of office morale. Basically, if I rocked back up to Jewel Town and stuck a dagger in his eye, I reckon I'd instantly clear up a shedload of open cases. And you want me to drop the Red Notice? Get the fuck out of here!"

They stared at each other, both breathing heavily. It was the Commander who broke the silence. "Inspector Lowe, I am formally instructing you to declare that Markian Ulton is no longer a person of interest in the death of Gianna d'Avec."

Lowe shook his head. "Nope. No way. He's obviously involved, boss."

"The Council does not concur."

"Since when does the Council direct SSS investigations? They explicitly do not have the oversight. I'm pretty sure there's a whole constitution in a fucking picture frame above the Mayor's desk that makes that abundantly clear."

"Fuck's sake, Lowe! You are not some wide-eyed kid on their first case. Don't pretend you don't understand how this all works. The Council do not wish you to pursue Markian Ulton. Not for Gianna d'Avec's murder. Not for Lord Falyn's. And not for any of the other bollocks you locked into that Red Notice! You will release him from the Restriction Order. Now!"

Lowe stood and carefully pushed his chair under the table. "Sir, I respect that you are in a difficult position here. You've given me a thorough reaming - one of your better ones, I'd say. And we both know I am quite the connoisseur of these things - and I can assure you I am suitably chastened. If it helps, I'll even shed a tear or two when leaving, just so the troops know you have giant cojones."

"Lowe . . ."

"No, I think I've heard quite enough from you now. I am not going to let the Council interfere with an ongoing investigation. I don't have all the answers yet, but I'm telling you something fishy is happening. Look, I'll admit that I could be wrong. Fucking hell, it would hardly be the first time, but putting Markian Ulton on a Red Notice is the right thing to do. I would be failing in my duty if I simply let him slide because he knows the right people's balls to scratch."

Lowe lowered his voice, a note of sincerity creeping in. "I'm doing the right thing here, boss. And do you know what? You're only so immensely pissed off because you know that too, and it's killing you to warn me off. Come on, Yacob. You want to have my back on this. Just give me a few more days, and I'll have it wrapped up for you."

Cenorth stood, not meeting Lowe's eyes. "Inspector Lowe, are you refusing a direct order?"

Lowe's face hardened. "I'm telling you to go fuck yourself. Sir."

Cenorth ground his teeth and dropped his voice to a whisper. "Don't be stupid, Jana. This isn't me coming down hard for no reason. This is the Council telling you to put your dick back in your pants and walk away. Listen to me, you'd earn yourself all sorts of credit in doing so. I hear they'll even look again at your suspension."

"Boss, I've already received one bribe today. That one didn't stick either."

"You're leaving me no choice here. If that Red Notice is not rescinded immediately, that's it. You're done. You will be out - officially this time - and there won't be any coming back. If you thought being Classless was bad, I've been told to inform you that the Council will take special interest in your life moving forward. And it'll be the end of your Temple Warder protection. Think about that for a minute. Some very rich and very powerful people are very pissed with you. You can either make a smart choice and earn a little gratitude, or you can . . . be you and invite a world of hurt."

Cenorth came out from behind his desk and crossed to Lowe, putting a hand on his arm. "As your friend, Jana, I'm telling you to let this go."

Lowe shook his head. "You know I can't do that."

Cenorth paused, then took a deep sigh. "Yes. Yes, I do."

CHAPTER 35 – FANNING THE FLAMES

Latham was waiting outside Cuckoo House, the home of Soar's Security Services, when Lowe came down the stairway. The big man's face was as stern as Lowe had ever seen, which was saying something.

He walked towards Lowe, pointing his finger accusingly. "What the fuck have you done? I've been ordered back to the Temple!"

Lowe shrugged. "Nothing that didn't need doing. And it's not like I haven't been here before."

"They fired you?"

"To be fair, I think telling your boss to 'go fuck yourself' probably counts as a resignation. But I'll let HR figure that one out."

Although he was manfully pulling off a studied insouciance, in truth, Lowe was reeling a little. He had known that making Markian Ulton a person of interest in the case would be putting the wolverine amongst the pigeons. Still, he was a little taken aback at the considerable shitstorm it had started.

And he was more than a little disconcerted by Cenorth's reaction.

When the Commander had suspended him last time, he had been royally pissed off. But he hadn't been worried for him. There had been no 'as your friend' conversation after Lowe had lost his Class.

That the Commander seemed so worried made Lowe think that he'd properly fucked up this time.

Placing someone under a Red Notice was the legal equivalent of pinning a suspect to a display board and getting the microscope - and sometimes the scalpel - out. It meant that all of Markian's logs - financial, communication and geographical - were instantly transferred to a little room in the basement of the building Lowe and Latham were stood in front of. Even now, a team of hyper-focused Forensic Accountants - crucially under no one's jurisdiction whatsoever - would be pulling apart every tiny detail of Markian Ulton's life.

The Forensic Accountants of Soar were actually an interesting anomaly in the Security Services. After a series of corruption scandals, the Mayor had altered the nature of Red Notices so that only the investigator who activated the process could rescind them. The thinking was that this would stop senior officers from unilaterally choking off investigations. The upshot of this was that having refused to cancel the process and then being dismissed, the Forensic Accountants would continue with their work and deliver their report regardless of what Commander Cenorth tried to tell them.

He would have liked to have been there when they, ever so politely, told him to take a running jump.

However, as with so many things the Mayor fiddled with, the theory was much better than the practice. It turned out that linking a Red Notice so firmly to an individual had the unintended consequence of significantly reducing the life expectancy of officers who issued them.

No living investigator. No Red Notice.

Despite this, it meant that Red Notices were kind of a big deal. They were one of the primary reasons most people did their best not to fuck with Soar Investigators. The thinking being that it was infinitely preferable to seek to work with someone who was reasonably bribable than to embroil yourself in a tangle with the administrative equivalent of Stage 6 cancer.

Interestingly, and this was why Lowe assumed the hammer had been brought down on Cenorth quite so strongly, for as long as the Red Notice was active, all of Markian's subsequent actions would be added to the stream of data flowing into that busy little office.

So, for example, any panicked Sending Stone messages sent out since Lowe's visit or, gods forbid, compromising conversations with Council members insisting something was done about the investigator would all be added to the pile.

Lowe could see why that might have somewhat excited the Council, the Temple, and maybe even the Mayor.

Latham was shaking his head. "If Markian was the one who put Mr. Law on you, I sense your sevenday deadline might be about to speed up."

Lowe shrugged again. "Then all the more reason we needed a Red Notice on him. You'd be amazed at the speed at which the guys on that team can go through someone's logs. With any luck whatsoever, we'll have him on the hook for the murders before too long."

Latham drew close, lowering his voice. "Little man, this is a stupid risk. The bodies of four Security Squires - all sliced into little, tiny pieces - have just been found in the park opposite your apartment. Rumour is that they were the ones supposed to be making your acquaintance last night. The Temple is . . . riled up."

"I had nothing to do with that, Latham."

"It ain't going to matter." The Temple Warder turned and punched the wall behind him, putting his fist straight through it. "You've got Mr. Law, you've got Mr. Temple. And now you've got everyone who works with me with enough free time to come down and lynch you for killing some of their own on your case. And that's without adding in Markian Ulton - and whoever is bankrolling him - being pissed off you've opened up their little pandora's box of secrets."

Latham hit the wall again, and Lowe winced. He was beginning to worry about the structural integrity of Cuckoo House. From the looks of the very concerned 'passers-by' who had been lingering around since Lowe had exited, the powers-that-be inside were getting worried, too.

"Even if I were still assigned to you, I'd only give you 50/50 of making it through the night. You are truly and utterly fucked!"

Lowe did his best to plaster on a smile and held out his hand. Latham shook it reluctantly, a look of dismay on his face.

"It's been a pleasure, Temple Warder. We'll always have the Forest of Iraklion."

And, with that, Lowe turned and walked for home.

***

It was hardly the first time Lowe had a clock ticking down on his lifespan, but he'd long ago made his peace with the fact that he needed to go *all in* to do his job properly.

He knew he was pretty unusual in this.

Even before his fall from grace, there was a distance between him and those he worked with at Cuckoo House that had nothing to do with personality. Cenorth had never insisted he worked with a partner - despite that being the norm - for that very reason.

It wasn't just that Lowe wasn't willing to do some of the things his fellows saw as 'the cost of doing business'. It was also that no one else was willing to be around Lowe when he took something . . . personally.

If there was any surprise when he was stripped of his Class, it was only that it had taken so long for the city to get around to it.

So, he understood that everything he had just put in motion was going to come with a cost. And, once again, he realised he was comfortable paying it. Some things just mattered.

If Markian Ulton - or his backers - were responsible for killing the High Priestess, then the Red Notice would reveal that. It would also clarify if Markian were involved in any of the threats against Lowe and Arebella.

Of course, should the Earth Mage turn up at his apartment this evening with an axe, a shovel and a determined expression, that would probably tell its own story, too.

However, Lowe felt there was much more to all this than just one rich, powerful man looking to become even richer.

There was a missing glove. And some seaweed in a candle. And a second murdered priest. And then whoever it was that ordered Security Squires to do him over. And who, in turn, killed them.

There were a whole load of questions he did not think he was much closer to answering than he had been when he first stood on the Third Floor of the Celestial Temple and looked at the body of a murdered woman.

Unfortunately, in his reasonably broad experience, the only way he knew to unstick such a paper jam was to do something big and stupid and wait to see who took exception.

Arebella had often suggested to him that there were easier ways to solve a crime than to wait and see who turned up to kill you. Lowe had explained he just thought of it as cutting to the chase.

Making sure he refreshed every one of his cooldowns from Mylaf's best Perception-enhancing muffins, he approached the foreboding dark alley that cut through the park and to his street.

Every instinct he possessed told him this was the perfect place for an ambush. Anyone who wished him harm had had enough time - while Cenorth chewed him out - to set up something crudely effective in this alley. There were no Observation Hubs active in this part of town, and the chances of any witnesses coming forward - as four Security Squires had found out to their cost - were pretty remote.

This was a part of Soar where bad things happened to good, bad and indifferent people. And no one would care.

Which was just how Lowe liked it.

He knew it was going to be an enormous act of self-harm to walk into the darkness of that alley. At best, he was going to be set upon by someone who wanted to monologue whilst kicking the shit out of him. At worst, they'd just kill him outright.

No quicker way to cancel a Red Notice than to cancel the investigator.

But he was out of ways to move the case on much further.

He would either come out of this experience enlightened, or he wouldn't come out of it at all. Lowe was okay with both.

Which, he realised as he stepped into the darkness, was probably not an especially healthy worldview.

***

A pair of eyes, in which spinning tempests burned, watched—unblinkingly—what occurred next. After the bloodied body of the Inspector was bundled through a portal, those eyes flared, and they, and their owner, quickly vanished.

CHAPTER 36 – TRUTH HURTS, LIES KILL

"You're an unusual man, Mr. Lowe."

Right now, Lowe didn't feel especially unusual. He was hesitant to open his eyes and check out his tormentor - he was fairly sure this was the guy who kicked his arse in the Tower of Law - because every time he had done so thus far, someone had punched him in the face.

Of course, they'd been punching and kicking him for the last few bells, anyway, but by the seventh - or was it the eighth? - time he'd returned to consciousness, he was open to experimentation. Maybe if he couldn't see his tormentors, they weren't really there?

He felt it was worth a shot.

A fist crashed into his stomach, stealing his air - well, so much for that idea. Shame, he'd been pinning a lot on that - and toppling him out of the chair he's been positioned on. Which was actually good news. The fact he'd fallen out of it meant they'd untied the leather straps that had been holding him in place.

Lowe was all about the upside right now.

Two sets of hands picked him up and unceremoniously dropped him back on the chair.

"It's rude not to look at someone who is speaking to you, Mr. Lowe."

He cracked open one eye - the other wasn't too keen on responding right now. *Roll with the Punches* was being quite the little Skill that could, but 20/20 eyesight was so far down the pecking order where his injuries were concerned that he wasn't too surprised. The beating he'd received had been so thorough that his mana stores were utterly depleted - even with all his extra points - and his Skill simply couldn't keep up.

For the first bell or so, they hadn't even asked him any questions.

The man who sat opposite Lowe was almost offensively nondescript. There was no name, Level or Class above his head, which suggested he was in the presence of someone with serious juice. However, to look at him, you would never have guessed it. He was small and dark and had the sort of face that could be studied for half a bell but still would defy an accurate description.

The man was sat cross-legged in the chair opposite Lowe in a spotless cream suit. So, whoever had been slapping him around, it hadn't been this guy in his Sunday best. Although, as soon as he saw Lowe looking at him, the man stood, removed his jacket, popped his cuffs, and rolled up his sleeves. Lowe assumed the hands-free approach was about to change.

"Thank you, Mr. Lowe. Politeness costs nothing."

Four or five quips crossed Lowe's mind, and he considered it a sign of personal growth that he kept them all inside. That or he didn't think his jaw was quite solid enough to move yet.

"As I was saying, you are an unusual man. It may surprise you to know that you are not the first person my employer has required me to question in this manner."

It was an effort, but Lowe controlled his shock and amazement.

After waiting a few moments to see if a reply would be forthcoming, Mr. Law pressed on. "However, you are certainly the first who, at no stage, had asked 'why?' It is almost like you were expecting us to come for you."

Lowe wrinkled his nose in an experimental way to indicate, he hoped, disinterested unconcern. All things being considered, though, that was quite a complex emotion to demonstrate with just a nose wiggle.

Mr. Law looked at him briefly, then glanced over Lowe's shoulder. He had just enough time to realise what was about to happen and brace himself - not that it helped - before a fist crashed into his ear and sent him back to the floor.

He was back in the chair in moments, with Mr. Law's bland, disappointed face watching him.

"This really is all very pointless, Mr. Lowe. I have no interest in causing you unnecessary harm. In fact, it would appear that there is very little permanent damage we can actually do to you - other than kill you, of course." Mr. Law let that hover in the air, regarding Lowe as if he were a fascinating insect sample. "So, how about it? Shall we converse like normal human beings, or do we continue with this unpleasantness?"

He sounded so reasonable, as if they were discussing how best to split the cream and scones in a tea shop. Lowe risked moving his jaw and was pleasantly surprised to see the bigger cracks had fused together. "What do you want to know?"

Lowe would have liked to think that his voice might have carried defiance and courage. He was, therefore, disappointed to hear it bleat out like an especially irritated sheep.

"There we go. I knew we would reach an accord. Now, I do not want us to get off on the wrong foot here. I will not mislead you and pretend there is any prospect of you leaving this room alive. All that remains is for you to decide how unpleasant your final moments will be. I would encourage you to take the path of least resistance. It would be unfortunate if, for example, we needed to collect a certain Veritas Assessor to join you here."

Lowe took a deep breath, feeling his broken ribs protest. "Ask your questions."

"Excellent. I told my employer earlier that you were a reasonable and sensible man who would not wish to involve anyone else in this business. Why don't we start with something straightforward? Who killed Gianna d'Avec?"

It was such an unexpected question that it took Lowe a moment to appreciate what he had heard. He tilted his head, feeling his neck creak in protest. "You did."

Mr. Law sat back, making an odd little tutting noise. He glanced above Lowe's shoulder again, and there was the expected moment of 'unpleasantness'. A helpful hand wiped the blood from his face so that he could be all presentable for his interrogator. "I will ask again, who killed Gianna d'Avec?"

That last beating seemed to have loosened Lowe's tongue somewhat. "Mate, far be it from me to tell you how to hoodlum, but it was only a few days ago you were kicking my arse and telling me to let the whole thing drop. Pick a lane, dude. Pick a fucking lane."

"To be fair, Mr. Lowe, what we know about you made it very unlikely you would follow that advice. Indeed, here you sit, five Levels of progress made and having ruffled all sorts of feathers with your actions. So, I ask you again, who killed Gianna d'Avec?"

Lowe's brain was racing. He had assumed that whoever was holding Mr. Law's leash had been—even tangentially—involved with the death of the High Priestess.

"Why warn me off if you hadn't been involved?"

The nondescript man waggled his finger back and forth. "Now, now, Mr. Lowe. That is not how this works. There is no quid pro quo here. I ask, you answer. Or you will be hurt. Who killed Gianna d'Avec?"

"At the moment, I'm leaning towards Markian Ulton."

"Why?"

"The two were in a relationship. I think the High Priestess interfered with the trial against Trellen Ulton. There are other things I need to explore there, but it wouldn't surprise me to hear that the two had a falling out, and Markian thought it wise to have her silenced before she revealed his guilt in the death of Lord Falyn."

There was a pause. "And for this reason, you put him under a Red Notice?"

Lowe shrugged, pleased to feel that his shoulders seemed to be functioning again. "I was getting nowhere, so figured doing so would cause a reaction." He licked blood away from his split lips. "And I was right on the money. However, if you are not connected to Ulton . . . " Lowe left the question unasked, and Mr. Law did not race to answer it.

Instead, he pressed onward in his polite, even tone. "And you resisted significant pressure to rescind that notice from the Council: accepting being fired and losing your protection detail rather than bow to their demands?"

"What can I say? I react poorly to authority."

"Indeed. Pardon me for pressing the issue, but for clarity, can I report to my employer that Markian Ulton is still under a Red Notice and that his logs are being analysed at Cuckoo House whilst we speak?"

"Sure. Whilst I breathe, I'm not cancelling it. At the very least, that guy needs his finances looking into."

"Interesting." Mr. Law sat back and pressed a finger to his lips as if considering. Then he leant forward again, his eyes almost eager. "I'm going to throw a few names at you. It would be useful if you were to indicate if you have had cause to consider them as suspects in the murder of d'Avec."

Mr. Law proceeded to share a list of the great and the good of Soar, most of whose names hadn't been mentioned by anyone Lowe had spoken to over the case. With every shake of the head, it was like his questioner was becoming more and more frustrated. Lowe sensed this probably did not bode well for his long-term well-being.

"And the priest, Setort. Do you have any ideas about what led to his demise? As you can imagine, operatives able to circumvent Dead Zones are not exactly many and plentiful. I would like to make the acquaintance of whoever killed him. Briefly, at least."

"Best I've got is someone from the Temple. From what I heard, a welcome wagon followed me home from the crime scene. Fits with someone there being responsible."

"Hmm. Well, you certainly do seem to have irritated the Chosen of Oh. You believe that was a follow-up to killing Setort?" Mr. Law's eyes flicked above Lowe again, and the inspector braced himself for another blow. Instead, the bland man gave the hidden presence behind him an instruction. "Can we locate Chosen Khaled, please? I will need to speak to him. As a word of advice, he has a substantially irritating pre-cog Skill that may make collecting him . . . challenging. Carrot rather than stick, perhaps."

Mr. Law's attention returned to Lowe, and with a bead of panic, the inspector recognised that the interrogation was coming to an end. "I have to say, Mr. Lowe, I am regretting pulling you in. It appears you are no further through your investigation than we have been able to get. I had thought, with your actions against Markian Ulton, that you may have uncovered something tangible. Instead, it is rather disappointing to learn that this was just another example of your signature 'spray and pray' approach to detective work. I would caution you to, in the future, be more circumspect in your style, but we both know how this is going to end."

Mr. Law stood and dusted himself down, rolling his sleeves back down and replacing his jacket. He was no longer interested in Lowe and spoke to whoever lurked behind him. "Give it another few bells for the Red Notice to collect everything useful and then dispose of him. I don't want to hear that his body is found."

With that, the dapper man with the unremarkable face left the room, leaving Lowe with a bottomless pain - one that *Roll with the Punches* could do nothing about - settling in the pit of his stomach.

CHAPTER 37 – WIND, BLOOD AND GIRTH

"This is a fucking military compound!"

Hel's face betrayed no frustration at Tenia's tone, but inwardly, she was seething. They'd definitely lost their edge since the last time they were in the field. There was a time when the Nightmare Reaver would never have dared question an order. Even making eye contact with her would have been beyond the small, dark woman. Now, it was bitch, bitch, bitch . . .

To let off some steam, Hel allowed a little hurricane to form in the palm of her hand. "We've taken down worse."

"With all due respect . . ." Tenia noticed the spiralling column of air and managed to actually put some respect into her voice. Fear. Respect. Hel would take what she could get right now. "I mean, what I'm saying is that it's been a while since we were actually active. At least as a team. Do you really think we hit a fucking armed installation as a way of easing ourselves back into the swing of things?"

"Don't you want to know who killed the bitch?"

"Of course I do. But there's got to be an easier way to go about it than tooling up for war!"

"I don't know what you're moaning about, T," came a deep voice behind them. "I'm looking forward to getting back to it. Blow off some of the rust."

Hel wasn't sure whether having Charl on her side was all that helpful. When the brain-damaged team member liked your plan, it was kind of beholden on you to think again.

Tenia obviously thought the same. "Oh, well. If Charl is on board with Operation In Over Our Heads, then I have no worries whatsoever. He's our resident tactician, after all. Awesome. No follow-up questions."

Hel tuned her out.

Following the group that had kidnapped Lowe was no issue at all: they hadn't even bothered to hide their tracks. To start with, Hel assumed they were incredibly sloppy. Then they reached their destination in the euphemistically titled 'Peace' District, and the reason for their nonchalance became clear.

"Why has a group of mercenaries taken you, Mr. Lowe?" she found herself asking over and over again. The guy appeared to be a magnet for trouble.

It was not even a day since she'd disposed of the four oafs from the Temple lurking outside Lowe's apartment. Initially, she'd been tempted to put a scare into them and let them go, but then she'd seen some of the implements they'd brought with them, and it was clear it wasn't just a punishment beating they had planned for the inspector's future.

As far as she was concerned, throats cut by *Wind Blades* was as merciful as she was prepared to get in that situation.

Following that, having little else left to do now plotting the death of a certain High Priestess was no longer on her dance card, Hel had been idly shadowing the inspector as he moved from the Middle Court to - interestingly - Jewel Town, to Cuckoo House and then to his abortive trip home. She assumed something fairly catastrophic had happened at Security Service HQ as after that, Lowe lost his Temple Warder shadow and picked up a whole host of tails.

Hel had dropped Irek a message to drop in on her sisters - the Empath Nullifier was the only person, other than her, who could keep them calm- and let the other two know to catch up with her when they could.

The problem now was that it was just her, Tenia, and Charl, which gave Hel a growing sense of unease that they may be shorthanded for what was to come.

Thinking the same, Tenia made one last effort to talk her boss down. "Hel, I'm all up for a bit of recreational violence - I think my record is clear on that front - but you, me and dumbo - "

"Hey!"

"Like that's not an accurate description. Look, we're good, but that place just screams evil madman's lair. I'm seeing double patrols, nasty surprises lurking in the shadows of those windows, and, if I'm not mistaken, there's the aura of someone well out of league in the basement."

"Nobody's out of my league!" Charl puffed up to twice his normal size, at which Tenia rolled her eyes and went to speak again. Hel got in there first.

"I'm taking all of this into account. But we're still going in." Hel reached out a hand and rested it on Tenia's forearm. "We're not good people, T. We did some terrible things back in the day, and I know I'm not the only one who struggles to sleep at night. Right now, I think we've got an opportunity to pull one back on the right side of things."

"You're willing for us to die getting that guy out of trouble?"

"Of course not." And the hurricane doubled in size in her hand. "But I'm not against a whole bunch of them meeting their god if they get in our way."

***

Shel Murad, Level 31 Sharpshooter, loved her job.

If she occasionally wondered what the targets she was instructed to put an iron-tipped bolt into had done to deserve it, the triple XP she received from hitting them from over 500 yards away helped settle her moral qualms. She and her boyfriend had made plans to get married on the day she crossed her Level 35 threshold. At her current rate of progress, that should be in about a year and a half's time. She'd already spotted the ideal dress and -

"Got another one," Charl whispered - or as much as a twelve-foot tall Berserker Balloon could whisper - as he ripped the sneaky archer in two. It was the third such hidden assassin they'd flushed out as they approached their target building. While 'Hide behind Charl' was not exactly straight from the strategic masterplan handbook, it proved oddly effective.

Unfortunately, what they gained in terms of survivability, they lost in sneak attack potential. Still, you played the hand you were dealt . . .

"Okay - " Hel said, wincing as four bolts struck Charl in the chest, burying halfway into his muscled flesh. Charl had always said he didn't feel any pain when inflated, but he looked like he was taking a fucking pounding - "Tenia, do your thing."

Most people had the wrong idea about Nightmare Reavers. They spoke in hushed tones about how they caused your worst, most profound fears to manifest right before you. Then there was the way that effect lingered well past the initial confrontation - casualties to Nightmare Reaver action had been logged six, seven years after first contact. And, of course, there was the range of 'Quality of Life' Skills the Class had access to - *Life Leach, Slow, Widow's Bite*, to name but three - which made them an absolute ball ache to try to pin down.

And all of that was true.

But no one ever bothered to remark how cool Tenia looked doing her thing.

The screams of various Sharpshooters, Deadshots and Crossbowmen were music to Hel's ears as she flew across toward the building with wind-assisted speed.

This had always been the way they tended to go about things. And she had to admit, a very small - and growing - part of her missed it. Charl would draw everyone's attention, Tenia would add to the panic, Irek would inflame that fear to massive proportions, and Hel would slip in and do what needed to be done. Without the Empath Nullifier, Tenia was required to work a little hard to raise everyone's blood pressure, but she was rising to that challenge like a champ.

"Charl! Door!"

The giant lumbered forward, crushing a buff Door Security under his feet, before shrinking down to the exact size of the barred iron door and crashing through it. "Ha!" he yelled back to Hel, who was standing barely a foot away, "finally hit 45!"

"Good for you!" she yelled back. Charl's hearing seemed to degrade badly when he was in full Berserker mode. Fortunately, he quickly stopped flashing golden, indicating he'd allocated his Progress Points.

Three Lower Henchmen came out from a door down the left-hand side of the corridor they'd exposed, and Hel casually directed the hurricane she'd been pulling behind into their middle. They were instantly torn to shreds: couldn't have been much more than Level 20. "What did you go with?"

Charl smiled, then inflated back to his maximum size, his head and torso crashing through the floor above. "All about the girth, baby!" He levered himself upwards on his forearms and shrank back down to normal size as he vanished through the hole. The crashing noise from above indicated further destruction was taking place.

Hel recalled her hurricane, now stained a deep red, and continued down the hallway. When she reached an open door on the right, she moved her summoned spiral of wind in and around the room beyond, devastating the furniture and causing a number of satisfying screams from whoever was lurking within.

Tenia phased through the wall and came to stand next to her. "I'm not going to lie, these guys are shit." She pulled open another one of the doors and slipped inside - letting off all sorts of nastiness at the cowering guards inside.

Hel had to agree. For all the bravado she'd shown outside, she'd worried that they might be a touch out of practice. Particularly when looking at the sheer range of defences this building appeared to possess. However, the standard of antagonists they'd come up against - at least so far - was rather underwhelming.

With a crash, Charl dropped through the ceiling a little way down, carrying the crushed remains of five Hired Muscle. He dropped them at Hel's feet like a puppy proudly showing off a well-hunted stick. "What's the story, boss? Where are the decent baddies?" There was a pause. "Or are we the baddies? I sometimes can't keep track."

"No Charl. On this occasion, we're not the baddies." Hel said. Although, as that was the moment Tenia returned, covered in blood and licking her fingers clean, she didn't think anyone would be shouting 'all hail the hero saviours' any time soon.

"Any sign of the poor little lamb we're here to save?" Tenia said, teeth stained red like a particularly sloppy vampire.

Hel closed her eyes and reached out with one of her less destructive skills, *Head Trace*. "There's a bunch of heat sources beneath our feet." She paused. "I think this might be where the better talent is."

"And your lost detective?"

"Him too."

Tenia stretched her back out, then opened her arms, letting streaks of malevolent red energy spiral outwards. The answering cries from the rest of the defenders on this floor were, again, not the stuff of the moral high ground. "Well, there's no one left alive up here. What are we waiting for? Unless you've changed your mind?"

Hel shook her head. If whoever had taken Lowe wasn't planning on killing him before they crashed the party, they absolutely would be reconsidering that position right now. "The plan's still the same."

"Fair enough. So we're going down?"

"Yep. Charl, this one is on you. Time to *Get Heavy*."

"It will be my pleasure, boss." He took a massive breath, activated the skill Hel had suggested, and leapt into the air.

<u>CHAPTER 38 – THE TROUBLE WITH HEROES</u>

It took Lowe longer than he might have hoped to realise that something was up in the building where he was being held.

In his defence, he had quite a lot on his mind.

Principally, of course, was his impending death. It was hardly the first time he had been threatened by someone whose path he had crossed - sometimes, it was even to do with cases he was investigating - but he feared Mr. Law was more than his typical opponent.

However, there was nothing he could do about that right now. He scanned the room, searching for a way out. But the walls were bare, and the door was sealed shut. His heart sank a little deeper.

Nevertheless, he was now fully healed and at maximum mana, but - and this was a pretty significant worry right now - he sensed this would just prolong his death. The guys holding him didn't strike Lowe as the sort to give up and go home because the first blow didn't one-shot him.

So, rather than dwell on his imminent, bloody fate, he'd turned all of his attention to the case of Gianna d'Avec. Mr. Law's employer had twice warned Lowe off investigating what had happened in the Temple. But he was confident now that it wasn't because they had anything to do with it.

As far as Lowe could tell, their main concern was that they wanted to identify who was responsible before the Security Services closed in on them.

Which was interesting.

Likewise, although there was obvious, pragmatic glee in having access to all Markian Ulton's logs, he didn't get the impression Mr. Law liked him much for the murder either.

So where did that leave things?

Of course, there was whoever Mr. Temple was. The person who had caused Latham to go missing the night before had to have some juice in that building, but the fact that the attempt on Lowe's life hadn't landed suggested a lack of competence Mr. Law clearly possessed. There was merit in thinking whatever had happened was due to some sort of intestine warfare on the upper floors. Sertor's death likewise fed into that. But . . .

If you wipe out a Level 67 Pyromancer in her own fucking Temple chamber, it felt pretty unlikely you'd fumble an effort on a Classless investigator. His guy told him Mr. Temple was playing their own game - which did not have the High Priestess' death at its heart.

Lowe clicked his teeth. Where did that leave him? He had two separate, powerful entities, both trying to stop an investigation into a murder they - apparently - had nothing to do with. And a third, well-connected, smug and very slappable man is also seemingly in the clear.

In the often-reported words of his dearly departed mother, "What the fuck, Jana?"

And who swiped Hel's sister's glove in between her leaving it and Lowe arriving?

He'd been pondering things for a while when the noise from above finally began to penetrate his mind. Lowe stood and moved to the door - oddly, the sound seemed to deaden when he pressed his ear to it. He stepped back and looked upwards. Yep. It was definitely coming from above.

Was he in a basement?

Then the noise went up a level - hey, let's call it what it was, screaming - and a little kernel of hope started to warm his soul. Had Latham come for him?

There was a series of loud crashes as if someone was tearing down walls, and then a rather ominous silence settled. Had the rescue attempt failed?

Then, there was a bang against the door, nearly removing it from its hinges, and Lowe scuttled backwards to get clear.

A second strike was all it took to free the door from the gap, and a familiar figure stood wreathed in dust and smoke.

***

Mr. Law - whose real name was Leoto Bright - was enjoying his latest assignment.

It wasn't that he found dealing with these people as beneath him . . . no, no, it was exactly that. He had forgotten what an insular little place Soar truly was. Even those who professed to understand the 'big picture' were obsessed with such pointless, little games.

Like that chancer, Markian Ulton. The only time he had smiled in the last few days had been when he'd heard that Red Notice had been slapped on his cocky face. The amount of information Cuckoo House would now have on any number of corrupt officials and petty gangsters had really cheered him up.

However, his employer wanted answers about the death of the High Priestess, and he had only negatives to share. Maybe he should have left Lowe out there as bait for a few more days? See who made a move on him?

Hey, ho. You live and learn. A drive to act precipitately had ever been his primary flaw. That and overconfidence. Because, of course, Leoto Bright had a lot to be confident about.

It was just that overconfidence that had him filter out the chaos above for longer than he really should have done for someone of his experience. His absolute conviction he was the shark in these waters blinded him to the sound of the rest of his shoal being eaten alive.

Only when he searched for a messenger to run to his employer did he notice far fewer minions in the house above him than there should have been. It took him no time for *Threat Assessment* - just one of his Legendary Skills - to identify what had happened and suggest possible counterapproaches. It caused him a moment of concern that "RUN" appeared as a 5% solution in the optimum paths to follow.

What on earth was going on up there?

Refreshing his various bonuses, Bright - more cautiously than he ever liked to truly be - began to make his way up the narrow stairway to the house proper.

***

In the sort of coincidence that suggested at least one god might be taking an interest in what was happening in the increasingly derelict building in the Peace District, Charl smashed his way through to the underground floor at the precise moment Bright made his way upstairs.

Hel lowered herself and Tenia down through the gap on a stiff breeze and quickly moved towards the entrance of a room which screamed 'torture holding cell'. Two figures with the sort of build most usually associated with Prize Fighters stepped to bar her way.

Neither displayed their Class or Level, which cheered the Wind Tyrant up. She had thought they'd left their days of casually slaughtering those ill-equipped to combat her group behind them, and it had been a somewhat dispiriting evening thus far.

So, the appearance of these two had potential.

"Charl, watch our backs. Tenia, the ugly one is yours. I'll take pretty boy."

"'Twas ever thus," the Nightmare Reaver muttered, hitting the shorter of their opponents with a stream of luminous green energy that did little for the poor fellow's attractiveness. Dark red boils burst out on his skin, oozing with a creamy yellow pus. Interestingly, the disfigurement appeared to make little impact, and the man ran forward to tackle Tenia to the ground with a heavy crash.

Hel barely had chance to quip, "T, don't play with your food," before her own foe started to get spicy. There was no art to taking on someone who could hide their attributes. While long enough study could prepare you for anything from a known entity, there was a particular frisson when fighting with an unknown.

Hel threw out a couple of speculative Wind Blades, twisting the air into itself to disguise her own information. To an untrained eye, it might be assumed she was some sort of common-or-garden Rogue. The man before her - and he was damn handsome, she noted - calmly tanked both of her strikes. He did, she was pleased to see, wince when presumably checking his HP after the second one hit. *Yes, that's right, baby. Mama has clout*, she thought, diving to the floor to avoid the man's swinging axe as he blurred towards her and attacked with preternatural Agility.

Interesting, she thought as she rolled left and right, then backwards on a puff of wind as good-looking went to absolute town on the flagstones beneath her. Each strike left some sort of acidic residue behind, further demolishing the hard surface. Hel didn't need all her years of experience to know she did not want any of that on her skin.

A glance told her Tenia had finished off the ugly guard and was now filing her nails with all the studied indifference of someone feeling damned proud of themselves. The body at her feet was revealed to be a Level 53 Man-at-Arms, which, presumably, was what her own dance partner was likely to be. That Class gained multiple bonuses when working in pairs. Bonuses which Hel was confident would have just run out when Tenia separated his mate's head from its shoulders.

Hel took a moment to remind herself about this Class, particularly its unfortunate susceptibility to sudden decompression.

With a flourish, she hardened a shell of wind around the man and sucked the air out in a quick and ultimately bloody explosion.

"I took his mind out when his defensive bonuses were active," Tenia said as if speaking to herself.

"Yes. Well, well done, you."

"Didn't know what his Class was either. Had to go old school on him."

"Yep. You did some solid work there."

"You might say you owe your kill to my efforts . . . "

"Fuck sake, T. You can have the XP." With a flick, Hel directed her gains from the kill over towards the Nightmare Reaver whilst simultaneously summoning a quick *Cyclone Blast* at the torture room's door.

It exploded inwards, and Hel quickly stepped through.

Lowe blinked owlishly back. "Hel? I was expecting someone taller."

Hel smiled and dropped a portal stone on the floor. "Well, you know how it is. Once you pick up a stray, it's hard to watch when they try and put him down."

A shout from outside the room drew both their attention. It was Charl bellowing a war cry, followed by Tenia expressing something like outraged concern.

"We need to go!" Lowe suddenly became very sombre. "Call your people back. They don't know what they're messing with."

Hel didn't need telling twice. She activated the portal stone, throwing the inspector through it and tugging on the emergency threads of air she'd long ago attached to Charl and Tenia for just this eventuality.

Tenia arrived first, throwing everything she had back down the corridor as she was sucked into the room. "Charl!" she screamed as she vanished through the portal.

Then Charl came crashing through the doorframe. Or at least, most of him. Whatever he had been fighting with had removed his forearm and taken a massive chunk out of his belly. He was unconscious - a state Hel didn't think she had ever seen him reduced to.

What the fuck was coming?!

She wasted no time bundling him through the portal, jumping in after him and leaving one of her hurricanes behind to shatter the portal stone into a thousand pieces once she was through.

Unfortunately, this would not turn out to be sufficient.

CHAPTER 39 – A MONSTER LEFT BEHIND

It took Lowe a moment to orientate himself when exiting the portal.

And by 'orientate,' he meant 'vomit profusely. This made for a less than stable footing for the short, dark-haired woman who appeared seconds behind him. The blood-covered figure slipped in Lowe's sick and went sliding into a shop window.

Then, a giant followed, gouts of blood streaming from a plethora of wounds, any of which were clearly mortal. His unconscious - at best - form added its own fluid to proceedings, sliding across the cobblestones on the same track as the woman, crashing into her and through the window.

Lowe stood and moved towards them, but then the portal stone exploded, and Hel sailed through, landing far more elegantly than anyone else had managed thus far this evening. With a wave of her hands, she directed her flight directly to the shop the other two had violated and landed next to the enormous man.

"Fuck a duck, T! What happened to him?"

"Advanced Class," said the dark-haired woman, shaking with pent-up tension. "What the fuck have you got us into, boss?"

Hel turned to look at Lowe, her face expressionless, and then down to her injured friend. "Later. Charl first. Have you got any potions?"

"I've used them all!" the woman's voice was approaching hysteria. "It was a fucking Advanced Class!"

Hel cursed and put her hands on one of the wounds on Charl's stomach, trying to staunch the flow of blood. "How come he's not healing?"

"That guy - he tore out a bunch of organs! - Hel, you don't understand how bad it was. I've never seen someone move so fast. If it wasn't for Charl . . ." Tenia paused and shivered. "I can't remember ever being so underpowered for a scrap."

As Lowe watched, the giant began shrinking as if the air was being released from him. As someone who had become fairly familiar with mortal injuries, he couldn't see how the guy was still alive, let alone that there was any chance of healing him.

Hel looked over at him, her face grim. "We need to move. If whoever that was possessed an Advanced Class, just destroying the corresponding portal stone won't slow him down for long. But we can't move Charl like this. He's bleeding out!"

Lowe put up his hands. "Tell me what you need me to do."

"Can you heal him?"

Lowe shook his head. "My Skill is linked to me. It only kicks in when I'm hurt; I can't direct it outwards."

Tenia's face clouded with scorn. "Fuck's sake!" She squatted down at Charl's side and pulled a belt out of her inventory to tie around his severed arm. Considering the volume of blood now on the shop floor, Lowe couldn't help but think of stable doors and bolting horses.

Hel tilted her head and looked at Lowe strangely. "But you do have something, though, don't you?" she said, stepping forward and touching his chest. "I have a Skill that lets me categorise people. From what you've told me of your Build, you should be flagged as a Tank, but it's not as simple as that."

Hel was staring at him intently, but all Lowe could do was shrug helplessly back. "I don't know what you expect me to do!"

"He's my friend, Mr. Lowe. He came to help me free you because I asked him to. He had no questions and no complaints. He risked his life for you, and it is not right he dies like this. Not after everything else. This is not how his story should end."

"If I could do anything, I would." Lowe's eyes were wide. "I don't have a Class, Hel."

She gently pushed him towards the dying man, and Lowe knelt by his side. The amount of blood was utterly incompatible with survival - and he knew of what he spoke. Hel stood over him, still talking.

"All that means is that you don't have any limits on what you can do. You're not a Tank. You're not tied to any god. You've even got an extra technique slot than you should. I don't think you understand how free you are from the usual bullshit in Soar. Now use all that freedom and heal my fucking friend!"

Hel forced his hands onto Charl's chest, Lowe's fingers slipping deep into one of the wounds. It hardly seemed like a good sign that his prospective patient made no complaint over that invasion. Blood oozed out, but without any real pressure behind it. Lowe assumed the giant's heart had given up. He could hardly blame it.

Lowe pulled up *Roll with the Punches*. It sat dormant as he was, for once, carrying no injuries. There was nothing he could do to trigger it. Well, there was at least something he could do about that. "Hit me," he said to Hel.

It might have been nice if she'd hesitated for even a second, but her fist lashed forward, breaking his nose. His Skill switched on and began channelling mana to his face.

Lowe watched the stream of blood energy as it moved. He'd never really taken the time to do so before. Of course, he was usually more concerned with concentrating on whoever was giving him a shellacking at the time, to be especially bothered about how it kept him alive. With his Intelligence at Rank 2 and with all the extra points in Wisdom, the injury was healed in no time, and it had barely touched his mana pool. His Regen would have it back to full in moments.

"Hit me again. Harder."

This time, the blow fractured his cheekbone as well, a shard of cartilage from his nose sliding back to his brain. There was an awkward pause as *Roll with the Punches* reversed some pretty traumatic brain damage, and then he was able to function again. "Yeah, there's a happy medium between the two. Dial it back a little next time."

Now, however, when the threads of mana spiralled towards his shattered bones, he tried to grasp hold of one of them. He might as well have been seeking to grab trails of smoke. Whilst wearing boxing gloves. Underwater.

He could see them and knew in some sort of fundamental way that they were corporeal and that he should be able to do what he was attempting, but before he could figure it out, the injury had healed.

Lowe growled with frustration and sat back a little. Tenia leant forward, touching Charl's forehead. "He's pretty much gone, boss. It's now or never."

Hel raised her eyebrows at Lowe. "Can you do it or not? We're out of time." She didn't mention that the fragments of portal stone lying down the street were spluttering as if someone was trying to put them back together. The amount of power that would take with a shattered source was astonishing. Given what was coming through, anything Lowe could do to help Charl would probably be academic quite soon anyway.

Lowe shrugged helplessly. "I have an idea, but I'm healing too quickly to try it. Have either of you got a Damage Over Time Skill?"

Tenia perked up. "Absolutely," and she began twirling her fingers.

"One that won't one-shot someone of my level?"

"Ah," there was a pause, then the Nightmare Reaver smiled. "Funnily enough, I actually do."

***

Under less pressing circumstances, Lowe might have objected to willingly having *Body Odour* cast on him. It was a rather unpleasant Skill that said nothing good about the person who had chosen to have it in the technique repertoire. As well as creating a foul stench around the subject—the intention being to force the person under its auspices to become separated from their party—it activated a nasty bacteria on the skin that, essentially, consumed the body from the outside in. Very slowly.

Hel and Tenia had retreated to the far corner of the shop, the Wind Tyrant placing a small tornado between them and Lowe in order to flush the reek up and away from them.

Feeling a touch self-conscious, Lowe put his hands back on Charl's body - he couldn't help but notice the blood wasn't running any more - and looked at the streams of mana flowing from *Roll with the Punches.*

As opposed to the single, powerful stream that repaired Hel's punches, hundreds of smaller tributaries were spreading out to combat Tenia's curse.

However, whereas the damage caused by the punch could be quickly addressed, the constant ticking destruction that *Body Odour* was delivering was much less easily resolved.

"Lowe, get the fuck on with it!" said Hel, raising several feet off the ground and filling her hands with *Wind Blades.* "The portal is about to come back online."

Trying to ignore the sensation of his flesh liquifying, Lowe attempted to grab one of the mana tendrils. At first, he had no luck: his mental movement just passed straight through them. They vanished and reconnected to the constant damage from Tenia's D.o.T. He tried again and again, getting absolutely nowhere.

He was about to tell Tenia to drop her Skill when a final flail dragged some threads along with it. Without any place to go, they quickly diffused into the air, but now Lowe felt he was getting somewhere.

He repeated the gesture, this time making the threads push towards Charl's body.

The attempt failed once. Twice. But on the third time, two or three of the blue threads stuck to the Berserker Balloon's body and began sucking down mana like an alcoholic with the keys to the brewery.

169

"Lowe!"

"It's working. A few more seconds, then he might be stable enough to move," he said with all the confidence of someone who had no fucking idea what he was doing. But, somehow, he knew he wasn't wrong. He could already see the enormous man's chest rising and falling, and some of the more dramatic of the wounds began to flow with blood again. "He's still on his way out, but we've some time now."

He looked up at Tenia. "Can you stop melting me now?"

Body Odour dropped off, and the Nightmare Reaver came forward to help Lowe pick Charl up; one truncated arm over her shoulder whilst Lowe went under the other. Blood was gushing from his injuries now. "Boss, we're good to go!"

Hel tore her attention away from the rapidly opening portal, a flicker of hope interrupting her spiralling dread. But where should they go? The monster forcing his way through a fractured portal could track them pretty much anywhere they went.

But then an idea formed. The gateway at the Tower of Law had significant anti-trace technology, which just might muddy the waters for long enough for them to slip away. "Anyone know anyone in the Tower of Law?"

Lowe was a little slow to respond, mostly because he was still trying to repair the damage Tenia's curse had done to his skin, but also because what skin he did have left was flickering with the gold light of a Level-up. "Erm, sure. I might know someone."

***

Leoto Bright exploded through the remains of the portal stone, his vengeful aura killing all life within a tight four-foot perimeter. He wasn't a madman, after all.

He was momentarily disappointed to see that his quarry had fled and that there was no obvious trail to follow. He sniffed the air but could not seem to get a lock on where they had gone. Which was frustrating.

The shop he was facing exploded into shards of molten rock.

But then, he reflected, they really did not have all that many options left open to them. If Lowe wanted to solve the mystery of Gianna d'Avec's murder - and after their short time together, he felt he knew the inspector intimately well - sooner or later, he would have to return to the Celestial Temple.

Bright set off at a slow saunter. He would wait for the detective there.

CHAPTER 40 – RANK AND RUIN

"When I said, 'drop in any time', I am now wishing that I had added some parameters."

Arebella, her heart pounding, closed the door behind the battered and bleeding little group. She pulled down the blind in her window, a mix of relief and worry etched on her face. Lowe, admiring her dedication to anonymity, couldn't help but feel the puddles of blood Charl had been leaking since they'd portalled to the ground floor of the Tower of Law, slightly giving the game away.

The big man groaned, his head slipping forward as he dropped back into unconsciousness. Tenia sagged under the full weight of her friend. "Lowe, make with the healing." She started to summon Body Odour, but he shook his head emphatically.

"Sorry, Bella," he offered, freeing himself from Charl's arm and stretching out his back. "We had no other place to go."

Either the Skills of the Veritas Assessor confirmed the truthfulness of his statement, or it was the amount of body fluids currently ruining a very attractive rug he remembered them spending a nice afternoon hunting for at the market by her house.

Ignoring that inconveniently nostalgic memory, he settled down next to Charl and put his hands on his chest. Tenia went to cast again, but he shook his head. "No, hang on. Let me try something."

The flashing gold of his skin had given him an idea. He was nowhere near his next Level, so something else must have happened, and he had a notion of what it could be.

He pulled up his status screen and, as he thought, where a fourth technique slot should be was a flashing gold bar. But that wasn't the most interesting thing.

That was that he could select it.

Mentally pressing down on it, he was presented with three options—three new Skills to choose from.

Lowe searched his brain, wondering if he had ever heard of a Classless gaining a new Skill. It didn't take him long to run out of examples. The Classless were a rare enough species in the first place, let alone ones that lived long enough even to have a chance to unlock new powers.

Putting those thoughts away, he concentrated on his options.

Where on earth had they come from? He had no god to offer him choices, and obviously, he didn't have a Class with a whole host of built-in selections to make.

"Lowe, we haven't got a lot of time." Hel's voice interrupted his thinking. "Patch Charl up, and then we need to come up with a plan."

He ignored her.

The first new Skill available to him was called *Masochist*. He didn't need to avail himself of all of his deductive abilities to work out this was likely to be a technique whereby he could hurt himself to gain access to greater power. Unsurprisingly, he did not find this particularly attractive. Sure, it was what he'd been doing with Tenia's curse to get hold of his mana, but he already had a Skill that encouraged people to inflict pain on him. He hadn't especially enjoyed his time in Mr. Law's torture room, and the thought of actively choosing to maim himself on a regular basis - regardless of how much extra power it gave him - wasn't his idea of a good time.

The second available Skill was, potentially, a better shout. With a name like *Circling the Drain*, he presumed it was a last-ditch revive Skill to save the truly fucked. Lowe had been in enough bad situations where a friend or a colleague passed away in lieu of the immediate presence of a healer, and he could see this as a lifesaver. Literally. The thing is, it was such a shock to be able to add another Skill to his repertoire that it seemed a bit of a waste to use it on something he would only be able to use in dire extremes. If he had twenty or thirty Skills, it would be different . . .

So, with a touch of trepidation, he clicked on the third one. And grinned instantly. Unless whatever system labelled Skills was playing with him, then *Medic!* would be precisely the healing Skill he was looking for.

Of course, he assumed - as he hoped it was a pure healing ability - that there would be an initially crappy mana-to-healing rate. Still, if he could use it without stabbing himself or needing the recipient to be moments from death, then it was the sort of utility technique he could get right behind.

Without overthinking it, he selected *Medic!* and felt a massive surge of joy as it transferred to his fourth technique slot.

However, even as he triggered it and started pouring mana into Charl - as he suspected, it appeared for every 500 mana used, there was a return of 250 HP. Not terrible, but hardly an Elixir of Resurrection - a new notification grabbed his attention.

New Title awarded. [Restriction Breaker]. Bonus 100 Progress Points available. Congratulations. You have succeeded in shaking off the bonds of those who would be your betters. Your progress will be followed with interest.

Without even thinking, Lowe pushed all of his points into Wisdom. The number rolled upwards as before, the colour changing again - as with his Intelligence - to gold when it hit 200. A further message appeared.

Bonus +50 PP for bringing a second Core Attribute to Level 2. Please note that these P.P. must be allocated to a Level 1 Core Attribute

Lowe split them into Strength and Dexterity, feeling light-headed as his Mana Regen went through the roof. This allowed him to press out *Medic!* even faster into Charl, who was starting to look much healthier.

A glance at his Primary attributes brought a satisfied smile to his face - particularly the gold colour around Intelligence and Wisdom.

Strength: 120
Dexterity: 90
Intelligence: 265

Wisdom: 218
Charisma: 60
Constitution: 75

Then he realised that no one was speaking. "What?"

Arebella looked at Hel, who looked back at her and then at Tenia. The Nightmare Reaver shrugged and seemed happy to be the spokesman. "You've just done the weirdest Level-up thing."

"How do you mean, 'weirdest'?"

"Flashing lights, choral music, smoke pouring around you. What happened, Jana?" Arebella said, moving to put - he couldn't help but notice - the desk between them.

He was saved from coming up with an explanation by Charl suddenly sitting up, letting out a spectacular fart and looking around blearily.

"Did we win?"

It turned out, despite being in the presence of several pretty beefily levelled mercenaries, not a one of them had a decent cleaning spell. They, therefore, needed to spend a solid bell cleaning up Arebella's office and trying to remove the long streaks of blood that led from the portal stone on her floor directly to her door.

"Okay. I feel it is about time I get an explanation." All things being considered, Arebella had been pretty understanding thus far. Lowe figured he owed her the whole story.

He was just getting to the bit when he chose to lead an unstoppable Advanced Class psychopath straight to her place of work when he realised that everyone was looking at him like he was mad.

"So, all this happened, and you didn't even have anything to tell him?" Hel's expression was dark.

"I prefer to think that I manfully resisted horrific torture and did not share any crucial information."

"Because," Tenia clarified, "you don't know anything."

"I mean, you could look at it that way. I prefer the version where I come across like a hero."

Arebella sat down in the chair next to him. Due to the cramped condition, her arm rested against his. He found it oddly comforting.

Without further interruption, he filled them in about cracking the healing code and then, after a deep breath, explained what he knew about Essence Transmutation Theory.

"Show me your stats," Hel said, "I've never heard of anything like it."

Feeling like he was in a Doctor's office, half-dressed and being asked to bend over, Lowe shared his details with her. She glanced at them and then pushed them out to Tenia and Charl. Both of them whistled.

"This is fucked up," Tenia said.

"How do you mean?"

"You're a Level 25 without a Class," Hel said, taking over, "You're basically roadkill."

"Cheers!"

"No offence, but she's right." Charl's deep voice rumbled around the space. "Level 25, no god and no Class. I should be able to one-shot you with my cock."

"Thanks for the visual. And 'you're welcome' for the lifesaving heals, by the way."

"But," Tenia chimed in, "your stats are all wrong. And I've never seen anyone with this Rank 2 bullshit, let alone a 'Title'. You're an odd little man. Don't take this wrong way," she looked over to Arebella, "but I presume he's telling the truth?"

The Veritas Assessor blushed and then nodded.

"Fuck. Okay." Hel started pacing. "From what the Temple Warder has said, you've basically got the Intelligence and Wisdom of a Level 50. 'Rank 2' attributes are effectively twice as strong as their Rank 1 equivalent. And no one will ever be able to tell that by looking at you. So, say your smart mouth and general air of punchability doesn't get you zeroed and you somehow make it to Level 50. You'll be, in real terms, a Level 100. That's absolutely insane. You won't need a Class by then. With your particular set of Skills - even if you can't add any more - you'll be pretty much unkillable by anything short of a god."

"Awesome. That is, of course, assuming I survive the next few hours."

"Who else knows about this Essence Transmutation Theory?" Arebella said, her arm being really quite distracting.

"I presume lots of people," he replied to her, "Latham told me about it."

"The more important question is, who knows about you being a walking, talking advertisement for taking the road less travelled?" Hel's eyes were filled with storm clouds.

"No one."

"You didn't tell - what did you call him - Mr. Law?"

"I didn't. I kept that under wraps." Mostly because he didn't ask, Lowe thought, but he sounded more stoic saying it this way.

There was a beat, and then Tenia smirked. "He didn't ask you about it, did he?"

No one needed Arebella's assistance to see the truth, as Lowe blushed a deep scarlet. "Maybe. Maybe not."

"Okay," Hel crossed to the office door and checked no one was in the corridor listening. "Well, I will tell you to keep it schtum around anyone else. In a previous life, I'd recommend you kill everyone you've already told, but I'm working on being a better person. I would advise getting Strength and Agility to Rank 2 and seeing what happens next. Maybe nothing. Maybe more spectacular bullshit. Do you need any gold to raise your latest Skill to Rare?"

Lowe shook his head. "I couldn't possibly . . . "

Tenia pulled a heavy bag from her inventory and threw it at him. He caught it, the money inside being instantly added to his balance. He blanched at the amount. "You broke me out of there. If anything, I owe you!"

"You saved Charl. And if there's one thing secret government hit squads are not short of, it's cash. Rank it up the expensive way. You hold on to your Progress Points." Hel's voice brooked no argument.

"Look," Arebella's face had grown increasingly pale throughout the discussion. "I cannot pretend to have followed most of this, but none of the danger has gone away, has it? Mr. Law is still out there, and you're no closer to solving d'Avec's murder. He's just going to keep coming for you!"

Lowe stood and brushed down his rumbled clothes. It was a bit of a losing effort. "I think we can do something better than hang around and wait for the inevitable."

Hel and Tenia exchanged a glance. "What are you thinking?"

"I'm going to go straight to him.

CHAPTER 41 – THE THIN STREAK WALKS TALL

"Straight" turned out to be somewhat of an exaggeration.

However, by the time Lowe had stopped off at home to refresh his clothes, clarified a few details about the Priestess's schedule with Mylaf and then stopped by Cuckoo House to make nice with Cenorth, the Celestial Temple was absolutely his next visit.

Things had started to slot into place sometime into his third bell of torture. It was funny how being repeatedly punched in the head seemed to help his deductive process. If he survived what was coming, he might need to try it out as part of his usual way of working. From the conversation he had just had with Cenorth, his boss appeared very open to putting together a team to help with a series of experiments of this nature.

Nevertheless, after first Mylaf and then his own detailed examination of *Grid View* had helped the jigsaw puzzle fill in, he was returning to the Temple with the first real moments of epiphany he'd had since the case began.

"I really don't think you should be coming with me," he whispered to his companion for the fifty-eight time.

Arebella smiled grimly and kept matching him stride for stride. "You are neither as brave as you pretend nor as smart as you think you are. At the very least, you need a good lawyer with you when you try this."

"And in the absence of a good one, you thought you'd step up?"

She kicked him in the shins. *Roll with the Punches* fixed the graze instantly, and his mana was returned to full even before her foot was back on the ground. Rank 2 was nothing to be sneezed at.

"Settle down, lovebirds," Hel said, her voice drifting across the spiralling tendril of wind she'd attached to their ears. "We're trying for covert infiltration. Enough people are already thinking the thin streak of piss in the cheap suit is spectacularly puncheable without anything happening to suggest this is a hostage situation."

"Fuck off, Hel." Lowe's irritation was more than slightly undercut by Arebella's giggling.

The towering height of the Celestial Temple loomed above them when they paused to reconfirm the plan of action. It seemed like the temporary block on sub-25 entry had been removed, and there were - literally - thousands of people flowing in and out of the entrance hall.

"I can't see Mr. Law anywhere," Lowe murmured.

"Of course you can't," Tenia was using the much more intrusive method of communication of having her words etched in dripping blood on the inside of Lowe's eyeballs. He was pretty sure that once this was all over and done with, he didn't want anything to do with a Nightmare Reaver ever again. "He doesn't need to be stood at the gate checking tickets like a wanker. He has people for that."

"Any chance Hel can do the talking? I'm in danger of looking like I have epic conjunctivitis, and, as she said, we're aiming for discrete here."

"How about we all start acting like we're on a covert mission and shut the fuck up. Lowe, look straight ahead. Four basic Hoodlums pretending to read newspapers. One of them is clearly the genius of the group, as he has it the right way up. There's another pair to the far left - again, common-or-garden muscle - and the same again about a dozen paces behind you. Don't look!" she hissed as his head almost instinctively jerked around.

"Someone really doesn't want you going in there," the words in blood dripped down his face, and Arebella handed him a handkerchief. "Makes a person wonder why."

"We can be sure to ask them - " Hel's voice was soft - "or at least one of them. Very briefly. Charl, clear the way for our sweethearts. Tenia, you go left. I'll take care of those at the back. Lowe, you understand that we will be of limited operational use once we get you in there. If your Temple Warder friend isn't on duty - or, more importantly, willing to help - it could get messy."

"Messy is where I live," Lowe said, the phrase sounding an awful lot cooler in his head than it did out loud.

"It's true. He has some shocking personal habits," Arebella noted helpfully.

"Children!" Hel buffeted them both with a quick pulse of wind.

"Just get me in there, Hel. I have a funny feeling Latham will be exactly where I need him."

***

Hoodlum was a fairly sucky Class.

There was a school of thought that being Classless was actually preferable as the demerits of selecting it were so significant. Sure, even a Level 15 Hoodlum had Strength enough to bend iron bars and enough Stamina to keep punching away long after more prestigious Classes had given up and gone home. However, there was such a commensurate drop in all other attributes that it was one of the few Classes that, once chosen, was unlikely to evolve. If this was not reason enough to steer clear, the gods of Soar were generally pretty unimpressed with worshippers who picked a Class with such limited scope for improvement. Only those right at the bottom of the Celestial Temple - the ones whose avatars tended to share offices and hang around the water cooler - would take an interest in them. This limited the range of patron-gifted Skills and upgrades, meaning that once the Class was locked in, it would pretty much become a dead end.

But not as much of a dead end as being a Hoodlum attempting to fight an elite 'Out of Bounds' squad. That pretty much redefined the term 'futile'.

Lowe didn't even see what happened to them, but suddenly those Hel had pointed out were no longer there, and he and Arebella were walking past a slightly bemused Temple Warder who was trying to brush blood off his coat.

"Where in Soar did that come from?" Lowe heard him murmur as they slipped past him inside the Temple proper.

"Good luck, guys," Hel whispered. "We'll do what we can to run interference."

"With the emphasis on 'run' if that fucking Advanced Class shows up," Tenia added, the words in some strange gothic font this time.

And then they were gone.

Arebella touched his arm. "Come on, Jana. No point in dragging this out."

And with that, they activated the portal stone to the Second Floor.

***

"I have no appointment for you, Mr. Lowe. And - as I am sure you can appreciate - the Speaker of Yolgorth is a very busy avatar."

"I think he will want to speak to my client." Lowe had never before had the opportunity to witness Arebella in full 'lawyer' mode, and it was doing a lot for him. "Please run along and let him know we are here."

Szana, an Executive Assistant, stared daggers back. As she appeared to have a number of unusual upgrades courtesy of Yolgorth, this was not a metaphor.

Lowe did the chivalric thing and stepped forward to tank them. They vanished as soon as they made contact with him, *Roll with the Punches* making the wounds vanish in a heartbeat.

"Assaulting a member of the Security Services during the course of his investigation is an interesting life choice. Interesting and somewhat devastatingly stupid. And not to mention," Arebella produced a thick book, flicked through it and found the statute she was looking for, "you are in breach of the Convention of Bugs, which forbids anyone in the employ of a post-Fourth Floor avatar from using offensive Skills against anyone sub-27. You are aware of the Convention of Bugs, I presume. It's an anti-paedophile law."

The Executive Assistant's perfectly manicured eyebrows shot upwards. "Anti-paedophile! He's at least twice my age!"

"I mean, I know I've had a rough couple of days, but that's a fairly harsh judgement."

"Hush, Jana. And half your level. The Convention noted that the power imbalance between those who work at the higher levels of the Celestial Temple and those below 27 was so significant that special circumstances apply. What you have just done should get you at least ten years in a very, very special prison. Unless . . . "

"Let me quickly contact the Speaker."

"Excellent choice."

Arebella and Lowe were left alone in the outer office. "Convention of Bugs?" Lowe asked.

"All those years of studying alone at night, waiting for my boyfriend to come home from whatever case he saw as more interesting than me counted for something."

"Interesting." Lowe took the book Arebella was quoting from off her. "And this had all that information in it, did it? The latest Hyran Fox romantic novel?"

Arebella blushed most pleasingly. "It worked, didn't it?"

"Why, Ms. Telut. I had no idea you were so sneaky."

She was spared answering further as the door to the inner chamber opened, and a rather white-faced Executive Assistant gestured for them to come inside. "You have until the next bell."

177

"Thank you, Szana. Your assistance has been noted."

"And the other matter?"

Arebella flashed her a wide smile. "I think, on this occasion, we can let it slide."

They pushed past her to begin their audience with Mdamic, Speaker of Yolgorth and pre-eminent challenger to Arkola's dominance over Soar.

CHAPTER 42 – DEATH BY PROXY

Lowe and Arebella found themselves in a massive room, at least half as big again as the one in which Gianna d'Avec had been discovered. In the centre of the chamber was a single, colossal throne made entirely of bone, on which sat the Speaker of Yolgorth.

Lowe knew - everyone knew - that the Speaker had been a Barbarian in his pre-evolved state. But knowing and seeing were two different things. Countless scars crisscrossed the avatar's weathered face, souvenirs from battles long past, yet his nose, absurdly, was as straight and pristine as a prince's, as if it had never seen the wrong end of a fist.

Most of the rest of Mdamic's face was covered by a tangled mass of hair: shaggy eyebrows, sprouting tufts from ears and nostrils and a beard cascading down his chest like a waterfall of iron-grey brambles. It was so unruly that it pretty much obscured the ceremonial dress he wore—robes that seemed to fit him as naturally as a bear in a tutu. The rich, deep purple fabric was embroidered with holy symbols and runes depicting Yolgorth in its various forms, which must have been quite the contrast to the coarse furs and rough leathers of his former life.

Despite the incongruity, Lowe thought he wore them with an air of begrudging dignity, like a wolf forced into a collar but still very much a wolf. He took a little half-step to put himself in front of Arebella.

"Come. Come," Mdamic beckoned to them.

As they drew closer, they both were very aware that the Speaker's massive frame dwarfed the macabre seat where he sat, which was audibly creaking under his weight.

Lowe couldn't help but notice that his hands were basically heavily calloused shovels. Each finger was adorned with rings of gold and bone, their designs clashing in a riot of barbaric splendour and ecclesiastical authority. This was a man who was used to hitting things and having the reasonable expectation that those things stayed hit. That he had also been granted the power to rain thunderbolts from the sky caused Lowe, not for the first time, to reflect that life really was not especially fair or kind.

The whole vibe in the greeting chamber would have been insanely intimidating if Mdamic was not currently sucking on a comically large, pink-striped lollipop.

"So, the Convention of Bugs, eh?" Mdamic's voice was only slightly muffled by the confectionary he was licking. "You have my assistant's knickers in quite the bunch."

Arebella made to answer, but the Speaker held up a finger. "No harm, no foul. I will enjoy unbunching them for her shortly." He gave a little giggle, which, when given context by his words, the room, his size and the lollipop, made Lowe determine the two of them were not going to be best friends.

"But -" the temperature in the room dropped through the floor as storm clouds covered the entire ceiling -"that is your one and only free pass. Should this audience displease me for a moment, should you lie to me, should you prevaricate, should I merely grow bored, then . . . "

A lightning bolt crashed down and struck the floor to Lowe's left. It left a little scorch mark in the tile, which - by the look of hundreds of fellow marks the length and breadth of the room - was not an uncommon occurrence. "Well, you will not be able to say you were not warned."

Satisfied he had been sufficiently clear, Mdamic sat back and gesticulated with his lollipop in a 'get the fuck on with it' gesture.

Lowe took a moment to reconsider the advisability of his plan: they were hazarding an awful lot on this play. While confronting the Speaker of Yolgorth in his own receiving chamber was a solid plan in theory, the reality of standing in front of the avatar was a deal. He had just enough time to experience a brief sinking feeling of dread before his mouth decided to take over. This, in his experience, rarely led to ideal outcomes.

"It looks as if you tried to have me killed."

Mdamic raised a bushy eyebrow. "I have to tell you, that seems spectacularly unlikely. You are, after all, still alive."

"You altered the Temple Warder rota to remove my protection detail and then sent four Security Squires to murder me in my home."

"Doesn't sound like me. I'm not known for my administrative capabilities. Rotas and suchlike hold little interest. Likewise, if you think I need to use others to do my smiting, then you really do not know very much about me at all. But I assume you have evidence to back up your outrageous assertion? My signature on a requisition form, for example?"

"You used another avatar's name on the paperwork. I have to say, I am disappointed to learn that identity fraud is still a thing, even at your level. I would expect a better class of fraud."

Arebella's breath caught as a torrent of lightning strikes exploded around them. Lowe held the Speaker's gaze throughout the storm, mainly because he was sure if he broke eye contact, he'd run.

"If you've quite finished? Not for nothing, but if you're going to try to pull off this sort of thing, I'd suggest you consider some sort of disguise. Cuckoo House had a series of very clear visuals of a rangy motherfucker with one eye, a spear and a giant thundercloud above his head, filing the appropriate paperwork. Maybe a hat next time? Honestly, it almost looks to me like you were hoping to be seen."

When he popped into Security Service HQ earlier, Cenorth explicitly did not give Lowe permission to view that particular file. Still, coincidentally, he had needed the toilet almost immediately after opening the recording stone on his desk and loudly forbidding Lowe to view it. He'd even knocked politely when coming back in to make absolutely sure Lowe wasn't looking at it.

Mdamic shrugged. "So? You think there's anyone who is going to care about what happens to some no-mark investigator without a Class?"

Arebella stepped forward. "Not at all, Speaker. You are, after all, quite within your rights to smite whoever you wish. While you occupy this floor, the Mayor is clear that there is no oversight that either Cuckoo House or the Tower of Law has over you or your actions. No, we are happy to leave such checks and balances to Arkola."

At the mention of the dweller of the First Floor, Mdamic glanced upwards and shuffled uneasily. "Quite right. It is not for you to question my motives. I am empowered to enact Yolgorth's will. So why are you here?"

"There have been suggestions that the recent death of Gianna d'Avec might have been at your hands."

"Have there?" Mdamic's voice had become dangerously low.

Arebella did her best not to shiver as the temperature continued to plummet. Instead, she attempted a little careless shrug. "You know what rumour is like, sir. From what I have heard, the High Priestess was all but measuring this room for curtains. That must have been rather humiliating. To drop down to the Third Floor after all this time? But that wouldn't be the end of it, would it? Whenever this has happened before, the displaced avatar did not just drop one place. The other gods scent blood and descend like vultures. It's a long and quick descent to the basement, is it not?"

"I rise and fall at Yolgorth's will."

Lowe decided he wasn't going to let Arebella have all the fun. "And if Yolgorth had wanted Gravalk's avatar to have an unfortunate accident, you would have acted?"

Mdamic moved his one-eyed gaze from Lowe to Arebella and then back to Lowe. Neither of them could quite shake the impression he was range-finding. However, when he finally spoke, his voice had transformed. Gone was the hectoring, belligerent sneer. In its place was something far more wry.

"What Yolgorth wants, Yolgorth gets. I can assure you that if I had been instructed to kill d'Avec, I would not have been able to rest whilst she still lived. I am comfortable to share with you that I received no such order."

"Yolgorth did not want her dead?" Arebella asked

Mdamic laughed humourlessly. "Yolgorth wants everyone dead, my dear. It's kind of his thing. However, in the specific rather than the general, there was no particular animosity to the Fire Demon's avatar. I had thought my, and Yolgorth's, impending drop down the Temple's floors would have been displeasing to my god. However - " he paused, as if considering his words, before shrugging and continuing - "Yolgorth rather enjoys the thrill of the chase, as it were. My god finds stasis boring. To tell the truth, I have sensed more pleasure emanating down our link at the prospect of hacking a bloody path back up the Temple than I have since reaching the Second Floor."

Arebella glanced at Lowe and then stepped forward again. "My client believes that you sent those men - extremely low Level grunts for someone of your reach - to ensure he kept looking into Gianna d'Avec's murder."

Mdamic didn't answer.

"That the attack was meant to fail and that your intention was to provoke him to continue, with greater focus, in his investigation."

Mdamic still didn't answer.

Lowe took over. "To be clear, I am working under the assumption that when I take things to the next step and bring matters to a close, I am not going to be making you into my enemy. That you actually *do* want this case solved. But you know what they say. Assumption is the mother of all fuckups. So here we are. Two beings standing in front of an avatar, politely checking that he doesn't want to kill them."

Lightning crashed down from the ceiling. Arebella and Lowe both closed their eyes, but crucially, they were not reduced to cinders.

The Speaker of Yolgorth laughed, a long, booming noise which was peculiarly unsettling.

"I have nothing more to say to either of you."

The door behind them opened and Szana was there, tapping her foot on the floor in a gesture of profound impatience. They were just exiting when Mdamic's voice echoed around the chamber once more.

"Yolgorth is looking forward to what happens next."

Lowe couldn't help but feel that statement could be taken any number of ways.

CHAPTER 43 – THROUGH THE GATES OF PANIC

Lowe and Arebella were portalled back to the ground floor of the Celestial Temple and took a moment to let the cold dread leak from their bones.

He had been pretty sure he'd been right about Mdamic's intention in sending the muscle Hel had slaughtered outside Lowe's building, but it was good to have it confirmed. It was as he had suspected: the Speaker had wanted to motivate him to keep his attention focused on the case - and had figured an ineffective murder attempt would do just that.

Lowe couldn't help but feel there were less potentially lethal ways to achieve that. If it hadn't been for Hel lingering around that night . . . well, he wasn't as confident as the Speaker of Yolgorth had been that he could handle four Security Squires. The danger of being the avatar of a god is that you forgot that lesser beings were somewhat more squishy.

Without Hel, what had been intended as a little light motivational exercise would undoubtedly have been game over.

Speaking of Hel . . .

"Well, who would have believed it! You're still alive. Wonders will never cease. That's ten pieces of gold I owe Tenia that I won't be seeing again, I can tell you. Stage one is complete then, I guess?"

"You never mentioned you were betting on my likely demise when we were discussing this plan," he whispered to the Wind Tyrant.

"Well, you know, I didn't want to bum you out. You were all wide-eyed and enthusiastic about it. Delighted to see I was wrong, though. But, just so that you know, we've spotted your Mr. Law."

Lowe's blood ran cold. That was earlier than he had hoped. He needed the answers to a few more outstanding questions before that - potentially fatal - confrontation. "Where?"

"Don't piss yourself yet. He's on the other side of the Temple, watching the crowds coming in. He looks royally pissed, though. You know," Hel continued, "when this is all over and done with, you might want to think about what it is about your personality that makes people so keen to kill you. I mean, I've got decades of blood on my hands, and I can pop to the corner shop without the expectation of being jumped and murdered—just something to think about."

"Cheers. I'll get right on that. Do you think he's noticed the missing Hoodlums yet?"

"Doubt it. I imagine he's got other things on his mind. As Tenia's poisoned the coffee he's drinking, I suspect he's not feeling too fresh right about now. Nothing lethal - although, I doubt she could pull that off, anyway - but he's staying close to the washroom if you know what I'm saying. Ah, there she blows. Poor diddums is on another trip to the porcelain throne."

Lowe gripped Arebella's elbow and manoeuvred her away from the portal stones. "Okay, this is as far as you go, Bella. Mr. Law is here already, and I'm not prepared to risk you against him. I will have to get through the next bit on my own. You need to go home."

"No."

"What do you mean 'no'?"

"It's pretty self-explanatory, Jana. I mean, 'no, I'm not leaving.'"

"What makes you think you have a choice here? Do you not understand who is coming after me? He'll kill you!"

Arebella put a hand on her hip and glared up at him. "It's been a year, Jana. A year of not knowing whether you were alive or dead. A year of waiting to hear you'd been found in an alley somewhere. A year of hearing people laugh when they mentioned your name: of listening to the jokes about the 'mighty falling'. If you think I've gone through all of that and then not having your back, you have another thing coming. Stop worrying about me and get on with your ridiculous plan."

Lowe was about to answer when bloody writing started appearing before his eyes. "If you don't want her, I'll be fucking her every which way and twice on Moon's day. The little lady has got some fire in her!"

He blinked Tenia's words away and opened his mouth to speak. However, before Lowe had a chance to answer Arebella, she was striding back towards the portal stones, moving past the long queue that built up during their stop on the Second Floor.

Chin in the air, Arebella marched straight up to the front and addressed the Temple Warder who stood before it.

"We," she glanced behind her to make sure Lowe had followed, "have an urgent message from the Security Services." Arebella brandished a scroll emblazoned with the seal of Commander Cenorth - *No, you absolutely may not 'borrow' my seal, which I will leave in the top drawer of my unlocked desk as I pop to see the officer next door. I won't be using it until tomorrow, by which time I expect to see it there again* - please stand aside so that we can deliver it."

The Temple Warder looked down at the diminutive lawyer, clearly unsure how to play things. Most people did their best to avoid the notice of Temple Warders, so someone actively being rude to them was quite a new experience. Indeed, part of the reason that Arebella insisted on coming along was how unlikely a Temple Warder was to punch her in the face. "Whereas," she had said to Lowe, "history would suggest that people simply cannot resist the opportunity where you are concerned."

He couldn't deny she had a point.

"That will be all, Eva," A familiar voice came from over Lowe's shoulder, and Latham strode forward to release the woman guarding the portal stones. Looking mightily relieved at the problem becoming someone else's, the Temple Warder slipped away, allowing Latham to take her place.

"What the fuck are you two doing here?" If Latham was pleased to see them, his brain had forgotten to tell his face.

"I'm fine, thanks for asking," Lowe said. "Had a bit of trouble literally seconds after you fucked off from having my back, but nothing some heavy psychotherapy shouldn't fix. I hear all the cool people have PTSD from epic torture sessions nowadays."

Something flashed across Latham's face. "I heard you were taken," he said softly. "But no one had any idea who by or where you were being held. I did ask." There was a pause. "Pretty persuasively, actually. But it was like you'd vanished off the face of Soar. No one knew anything. As it is, I'm glad to discover you appear to have more friends than just me. Astonished, to be honest, having spent some time with you." There was a pause. "I'm very glad to see you made it through."

"Unfortunately, it appears I have developed quite the capacity to absorb physical punishment. I'm still not sure whether I should be thanking you for that, by the way."

Latham shrugged. "Any day you wake up alive is better than the alternative. It sounds like you're in danger of becoming a whiny little bitch after a few love taps. Speaking of which, I hear you've been throwing your weight around on the Second Floor?"

"I wouldn't put it quite like that, Mr. Latham," Arebella began.

But Lowe couldn't make out the rest of what she was saying because Hel was back in his ear. "Shit. Bad news, Lowe. Mr. Law has successfully wiped his arse and has just spotted you. He's coming your way. And quickly. We'll do what we can to slow him down, but your plan suddenly has a fairly tight deadline."

There was a frustrated shout from behind him, but Lowe didn't turn to look around. He was not sure his nerve would hold if he saw that bland, nondescript face closing in on him.

"Fuck, he's already gone through Charl. I thought that would hold him for longer. Okay, I'm going to have to step in and help Tenia. We'll do our best, but . . . I wish you good luck, Mr. Lowe."

The kerfuffle behind Lowe increased, and Hel's voice vanished from his head. In something approaching panic, Lowe stepped close to Latham, grabbing him by the front of his tunic.

"I need you to let us through and then lock this portal."

"I can't do that, little man. The standing orders for that particular Floor are very clear." Shouts of outrage and surprise increased behind him, and Lowe - once again - fought the urge to turn around.

"Latham, I think I know what's been going on. But if you don't let me through, I'm not going to get a chance to clear it all up. Please! I think you're as interested as I am in getting to the bottom of the High Priestess's murder. But if you don't let me through, right now, I'll never have the chance to solve it!"

A massive gust of wind blew through the ground floor, smashing windows and flinging doors open. Latham glanced up and over Lowe's shoulder at the commotion.

At that moment, Arebella darted forward and activated the portal stone, pulling Lowe through behind her. He just had the chance to meet the Temple Warder's outraged expression and yell, "Lock it behind us!" as the light closed around them.

CHAPTER 44 – WHEN THE TEMPLE DRAWS STEEL

Leoto Bright held a hand to his queasy stomach and pushed the small group of sightseers out of his way. Whenever he was in Soar, the way people flocked to this place never ceased to appal him. It was like they viewed it as a quaint tourist attraction rather than the home of terrifyingly powerful beings. Being this close to avatars that could wipe him from existence made his teeth itch. That they would only be able to do so after some difficulty did nothing to lessen his sense of vulnerability.

However, right now, he had even more pressing things on his mind than the power of those on the floors above him. He wasn't sure what had gone wrong with this operation, but things were not quite working out as he had anticipated. This was such an unusual experience that - in other circumstances - he might have found it all rather diverting.

However, on this occasion, he had a job to do, and, for whatever reason, it was proving ridiculously difficult to get his hands around the throat of a piddly little Level 25 without a Class.

Bright had spotted Lowe from across the crowded concourse of the Celestial Temple, chatting with a Temple Warder. His little lawyer friend was with him, which - in theory - made everything rather straightforward. It saved him from having to hunt her down later. His employer had given him reasonable latitude in this operation, but he was willing to bet a stack of gold that the words 'no loose ends' would be coming to him soon.

Ideally, though, he wouldn't have to tangle with a Temple Warder on their own turf. Bright had no concerns that he would not come out ahead in any fight there, but there were political ramifications in such a skirmish that were always worth avoiding if possible. Nevertheless, as he had managed to bribe the Justicars to look the other way when he brutalised Lowe inside the Tower of Law, he felt reasonably confident he could find the price of the big man talking to the investigator.

Everyone had one, after all—even him.

Bright burped, and his stomach gurgled horribly. What in Soar was wrong with him? There were no known ailments that could even give his immune system a moment's concern. It must have been something he had eaten . . .

He was just recalling being given a coffee by an attractive, dark-haired Barista who, now he thought about it, was somewhat familiar when he was shoved roughly in the back.

Bright lost his footing momentarily, turning to growl menacingly at the oaf who had pushed into him. Doing so, he met the eyes of another familiar face - it was that Berserker Balloon he had been seconds from killing the day before! However, before he could react, the disturbance in his stomach magnified a hundredfold, and he felt his knees go weak.

The Berserker dived on top of him, the man doubling in size and bringing them both to the floor. There was a brief tussle - not as brief as Bright would have liked, but things seemed to be conspiring against him doing his best work that day - and the giant grunted in pain and deflated down to normal size, eyes rolling back in his head.

As he stood, Bright had a second when he considered stamping down on the unconscious form, caving in the man's head to ensure he never had to bother with him again, but then the pain in his stomach increased by a further magnitude, and he completely lost interest in the Berserker Balloon.

This was all starting to become a touch embarrassing. Although it was not unknown for Bright to give his quarry a sporting chance - sometimes, you had to add the odd handicap to make the whole thing interesting - there was a difference between artificially levelling the playing field and then actually being thwarted. He did not know what was happening, but he was done playing.

Closing his eyes, he traced the outline of the pain he was experiencing. As he had suspected, it was some minor curse which was inflicting an unusually high amount of damage over time. On another day, he might have been interested in recruiting whoever was capable of brewing up such a thing. Today was not that day.

In a moment, he had traced the curse's origin - a significant problem with D.o.T.s was that there were always mana echoes that led back to the caster - and took that attacker off the table with a quick mental squeeze.

In his peripheral vision, he saw the Barista drop bonelessly to the floor and grimaced. Yes, now he thought of it, she'd been there in the Peace District, too, hadn't she?

Lowe seemed to have allies, after all.

Speaking of Lowe . . . Bright turned back to face the Inspector and saw he was making his way towards the portal stones. Well, that would be wholly unacceptable. He restrained himself to an almost gentle stomp on the Berserker's chest - the crunch of ribs caused the growing crowd of rubber-neckers to wince in dismay and started to run towards Lowe.

And then he was in the air, carried away by a gust of wind, spinning arse over tit in a most undignified way. Fortunately, it wasn't a long journey. Although as that was because he impacted upon - and went straight through - the Temple's far wall, he was not sure 'fortunately' was quite the right word.

What on earth was going on!? In a blink, he exploded back through the Temple Wall and zeroed in on the Wind Tyrant that had diverted him. He had the satisfaction of seeing the look of dismay on her face as he punched out with his own stream of concentrated air, and then she was lost in the crowds of worshippers flung across the Temple floor.

Bright clicked his teeth in irritation at the devastation his strike had wrought: his employer would have his hide for that. You did not pay someone like Bright to undertake your business because you hoped for hundreds of casualties and newsworthy collateral damage. There were Out of Bounds Squads available for such destruction.

But he had to put that out of his mind. Bright's brief sojourn in the sky had been long enough for Lowe and the girl to have vanished through the portal. More disappointment there for his employer. Bright was going to be very lucky indeed to get paid at all here.

He blurred forward to stand before the Temple Warder.

"Let me through," he said, and then, because it was never a good idea to be unnecessarily belligerent with these people, he added, "Please."

Latham met the gaze of the nondescript man before him impassively. He had a pretty good idea who this was. Temple Warders were briefed on those in Soar who were to be treated with considerable caution, and if he was right, this guy was right at the top of the list. "I am afraid there is a queue, sir."

Bright looked over his shoulder and drained the life out of everyone who was waiting for the portal. *Life Leach* was a massively unnecessary Skill to use in the circumstances, but his frustration was getting the better of him. He could have achieved a similar effect with one of his hundreds of other Skills, but none of them would have been so visually impactful.

"It appears they have all suddenly decided to do something else. Please, Temple Warder, I do not want any further unpleasantness here."

Latham's eyes flitted to the ash that now lay in a neat line stretching away from the portal stones. He'd always known there would come a day when he'd have to make a choice between what was right and what was easy.

He just had hoped that he would be able to make more of a difference than the few minutes of time he assumed this would buy.

With his left hand, he reached out, gripped the portal stone, and crushed it, flaring every defensive Skill he had at his command.

Bright puffed out his cheeks. "Temple Warder, I would really rather not do his."

Latham drew his sword, settling into a guard position. "Okay, well, I guess you therefore have a choice. I am sure you have all sorts of exciting Skills and exotic abilities that can reconstruct a broken portal stone. I am also sure they probably need - even for someone like you - considerable concentration to enact. I can promise you that while I stand here, I'm not going to give you the opportunity to channel them. So, you can either walk away and chalk this one up to experience, or we can go round and round. Your call."

Bright glanced around to see a flurry of movement as other Temple Warders ran to support their colleague. Of course, they wouldn't be on time, but it was nice to see a little *esprit de corps* on display.

"Last chance," he said, returning to look at the Warder, "I am still willing to let you walk away from this."

Latham shrugged and sent a little prayer upwards. "Make this worth it, little man."

And then shit got real.

CHAPTER 45 – FAVOUR OF THE MONKEYS

Lowe had only once been on the First Floor of the Celestial Temple, and the memory of that encounter was not joyous.

It had been right at the start of his career when he was still bright-eyed and bushy-tailed. He'd caught some bullshit Fraud case, mainly because there was no one more senior around to pick it up, and it didn't look like the sort of thing that could be fucked up too badly.

On the face of it, it was a tale as old as time: rich bloke who wanted to get richer had found a way to persuade people with neither enough money nor enough sense to give him cash in exchange for fairy dust and magic beans.

And that wasn't a metaphor.

This wanker - Kyrian Green - had been boxing up crates of literal crud, slapping a fancy label on it and flogging it to the unwary, promising all sorts of healing properties.

In next to no time, Lowe had gathered enough evidence for the guy to be looking at - at least - two to three years in a dark cell. Even to get away with as little punishment as that, he'd need to get lucky, and it be that none of the suckers he'd fleeced had a powerful enough patron god to make waves. Some deities took such things personally.

Lowe was preparing to make his move - he favoured three o'clock raids with plenty of heavies to back him up - when a Courier had arrived at Cuckoo House with an urgent message that 'Arkola wants a word'.

At that stage, Lowe had been wet enough behind the ears to think this boded anything good. He had jogged along to the Temple, swaggered up to the portal stones, winking at the very unimpressed Temple Warder and activated the entry for Arkola's floor, fully expecting he was about to get a pat on the head for a job well done from the most powerful being in Soar.

Yeah, not so much.

Standing next to Arebella now, Lowe felt his pulse quicken at the memory and sweat flow down from his forehead.

"Are you okay?" she asked, gently taking his hand and pulling him down the long, thin corridor towards the closed door at the end.

"No worries," he managed, plastering on a sickly smile.

Arebella stopped and turned him around, pointing a finger up at her heart-shaped face. "Veritas Assessor, remember? And even if I wasn't, you were always the single worst liar in the whole city."

Lowe grimaced and rested a hand on the wall. His knees had gone weak, and there was the acrid tang of something metallic in his mouth. If he wasn't careful, he was going to pass out. "I'm just having flashbacks of the last time I was here. Not a nice memory."

She nodded sympathetically. "The Green case, right?"

He glanced at her in surprise. They had not been seeing each other for long when all of that had blown up. The cover-up had been so very thorough that he was astonished she remembered anything about it.

Arebella rolled her eyes at his bemused expression. "Jana, why do you always think that nothing that happens in your life will be of interest to those who care about you? Of course, I knew that you'd been personally warned off an investigation by Arkola. Even without it being the hottest gossip in the Tower, you barely spoke, ate or slept for the rest of the sevenday. I practically had to move in with you to be on suicide watch!"

Lowe thought he'd kept his fear and terror at the encounter under wraps rather better than that. And yet, now he thought of it, he had started to see much more of Arebella around that time. He'd thought it was his winning personality and witty banter...

But, standing here now, the full impact of that experience was on him again. It hadn't been anything as crude as being 'warned off' the case. He'd pranced down this corridor like a prizewinning pig, fully expecting to receive his latest ribbon - there were all sorts of positive noises coming out of Cuckoo House about the hotshot new detective blazing a trail through the criminal undercity - but instead of more kudos pouring down on him, when he'd pushed open that door at the end of the corridor . . .

Disappointment.

No, Lowe thought now, that didn't go quite far enough. The aura that had enveloped him the second he'd entered Arkola's receiving chamber had not been anything so mundane as 'disappointment.' His very soul had been picked up, examined and then put back on the shelf with the sort of disdain usually reserved for month-old egg mayonnaise.

The supreme being at the top of the Celestial Temple had been viscerally disgusted by his presence and wanted him to know that.

There'd been more to it, of course. But most of that experience, Lowe seemed to have buried under layer-upon-layer of critical self-protection against emotional trauma. Unfortunately, standing here right now had ripped off that scab, and mental puss was flying everywhere.

I would like you to drop your investigation into Kylian Green.

The strength of Arkola's suggestion had been so overwhelmingly potent that Lowe had turned around and was halfway back down the corridor towards the portal stone before his sense of professional pride had grabbed hold of his feet and dug his heels in.

"Why?" he had whispered back, not trusting himself to say anything much louder.

The worst thing was that his defiance seemed to cause the voice significant amusement. *'Why', Mr. Lowe? You would want to know 'why?'*

His body had suddenly twirled around, and he'd been marched - like a puppet whose strings were being worked by a malevolent toddler - back into the receiving chamber, the door slamming behind him.

There had been nothing to see in the pitch-black room, but the presence of Arkola was very . . . present. Lowe could not, even now, come up with a better way of describing it than that. The paucity of the quality of that description almost caused him more annoyance than anything.

Almost.

But as someone who had always prided himself on his powers of perception, not being able to recall anything more about the experience than an unlit room royally pissed him off.

"The 'why', Mr. Lowe, is because I ask it. That I ask it rather than order it shows you a measure of respect. For most, that would be enough. Please do not make me regret offering it to you."

Despite every survival instinct warning against it, Lowe had girded his loins and managed to bite back, "But he did it! Green conned those people out of their money. Why should he be able to get away with it?"

The pressure around Lowe had shifted slightly at that, the profound distaste and disappointment giving off tones of amused contempt.

"You are no neophyte, Mr. Lowe. There are wild currents in Soar that, even if you know nothing about them, you are nevertheless aware that they exist. That Mr. Green allowed himself to come to the notice of Cuckoo House is regrettable and he will be suitably punished for that misstep. But, to be clear, not by you. You will take this case no further."

"So you protect your friends, do you? That's how all this works, is it?"

Looking back, Lowe couldn't believe he had the balls to say that. Pre-Classtration Lowe had been a badass, apparently. He wondered why he'd forgotten that.

Amused contempt moved into just plain amused. "Not at all, Mr. Lowe. I had not heard of Kylian Green until this morning. But he has friends, and those friends have friends, and one of those friends knows someone who has reached out and asked me for a favour."

"And this 'favour' was to warn me off?"

"Actually, the favour was to lobotomise you and toss your gibbering body into a pen at Soar Zoo for it to be raped by monkeys. In that context, I rather feel you owe me a 'thank you' rather than whatever pathetic show of defiance this is."

Looking back, Lowe was sure there'd been further dialogue here, but his mind rebelled against recalling it. The next thing he had known, he was at Arebella's door, weeping uncontrollably and unable to explain why. Thinking about it now, it was hardly surprising it was an event she remembered.

Overnight, Cenorth burned all his notes on the Kylian Green case before Lowe could pull himself together enough to get back to his office. "Just looking out for you, Jana," he had said. "Sometimes, I don't think you always have your best interests at heart."

"Say that again, boss," Lowe muttered under his breath, looking down the corridor at the door to the receiving chamber.

"Jana?" Arebella asked, concerned.

"I'm all right," he said, taking a deep breath and - oddly - this time he meant it.

Giving her hand a reassuring pat, he strode forward and pushed open the door, Arebella hurrying behind to keep up with him.

"Arkola, I have a few questions concerning the death of Gianna d'Avec."

As the door shut behind them, they each pretended the portal stone behind them hadn't just flared into life.

CHAPTER 46 – GOD'S DON'T NEED ALIBIS

"Well, this seems all very official, Mr. Lowe. Nice to see you, by the way." If Lowe thought there was anything unusual in the supreme being of Soar being pleased to see him, too many panicked emotions were running through his head to process it properly.

The room they had entered was, as it had been when he had last been there, completely pitch-black.

Not dark.

Nothing as mundane as that. This was not the absence of light. Rather, they had stepped into the deepest black. It was as if they had moved beyond the boundaries of their universe and into another where such an unnecessary frippery as 'light' had long stopped being a consideration. Mind awash with questions, Lowe briefly wondered where that was true.

Whether, in entering this room, Arebella and he had left the world they knew behind and stepped into an alien realm.

"Before we start what I am sure will be an illuminating conversation for all of us, I think I will quickly switch off Ms. Telut's abilities."

Lowe heard a soft gasp from beside him and felt Arebella collapse to her knees. He reached out, groping in the blackness to find her, then helped her gently back to her feet. She was shaking.

"Are you okay?" he asked, almost scared to hear the answer.

"I don't know!" Arebella's voice was filled with distress. "It's like all my senses have been covered in a blanket. Everything is . . . greyed out. I don't know how else to explain it. Am I Classless?"

"Nothing permanent, I assure you. It's just that I like to maintain an air of mystery in all my conversations, and having a Veritas Assessor parse my words feels as if it would somewhat cramp my style. Not that I am planning to lie to you, you understand. But - well - it's more fun if you are unsure about that, isn't it?"

"Oh, it's a riot. Do you promise she'll be okay? Her Class will return once we leave this place?"

"Oh, Mr. Lowe. I rather feel that if you were genuinely concerned about Ms. Telut's wellbeing, you would not have embroiled her in a scheme that is the definition of a suicidal endeavour. To my understanding, you were informed - in no uncertain terms - that your investigation was likely to place her in significant danger. And yet you continued to meddle in matters that really should have been left well alone. And now, as if that recklessness with her life was not enough, here you are, dragging this poor girl into my overwhelming presence. Some knight in shining armour you have turned out to be, Mr. Lowe. And I had always found you to be so wonderfully chivalrous."

"Fuck you, you formless twat!"

Lowe had a moment of horrified regret that he had just sworn at the avatar who dwelt at the top of the Celestial Temple. But then he realised it wasn't him, but Arebella who was spitting the invective. He wasn't sure if this recognition made it better or worse.

"Jana hasn't dragged me anywhere. He's my friend, and he was in trouble. So, I'm here to help. That's what you do when you care for someone. Not that you'd know anything about that, you invisible wanker! And don't think I need my Skills to be active to know when someone is lying, either!"

Worse. Definitely worse.

Expecting them both to be immediately disintegrated, Lowe screwed up his eyes, before he realised the futility of doing so in the darkness of the empty space in which they were existing. Opening them back up again made no discernable difference.

"Mr. Lowe. You have quite the firecracker here, don't you! Maybe knights have no meaning in this game. Perhaps it is not a game for knights."

Wanting to take Arkola's attention away from the bristling ball of indignation next to him - he always did find Arebella to be at her cutest when she was angry - Lowe decided to crack on with his plan of putting his head in the lion's mouth.

"Look, let's get right down to it. Did you kill - or give orders that led to the killing of - Gianna d'Avec?"

"Oh, we're finished with the small talk, are we? Very well. What a shame. I get so few interesting visitors. The answer to your question is that it depends on your point of view."

Lowe shook his head in confusion, "How? You either did it or you didn't. Point of view has nothing to do with it!"

"Ah, I wish it were so simple as that, Mr. Lowe. You see, with great power comes great responsibility. For absolute clarity - for I see you require such a thing - I can confirm I did not personally descend two floors of the Celestial Temple and pull the High Priestess of Gravalk to pieces like the insignificant insect she was. Neither, for the removal of any doubt, did I make it known - tacitly or otherwise - that the removal of that turbulent priest would please me."

"So, you are saying you were not involved in her murder?" Lowe tried to keep the disappointment from his voice. This was his big play, and he couldn't believe he'd misread the situation so badly.

It all made sense for Arkola to be at the heart of things. It could only be the dweller of the First Floor that would have Mdamic stepping so carefully in his attempts to 'support' Lowe's investigation - and yes, Lowe did absolutely accept that the Speaker of Yolgorth would view motivational beatings as 'support'. Likewise, whoever was holding Mr. Law's leash and was pulling enough strings in the Council to bully Cuckoo House had to be a being of immense power. There really was not anyone else that fit the bill.

"You are not very effective at reading between the lines for a man who wishes to make his living as an investigator, are you? Would you like to help him, Ms. Telut?"

Muttering 'patronising dickhead' under her breath - Lowe did not think he'd ever heard Arebella swear so much during their whole relationship as she had in the short time they had been in this chamber - Arebella squeezed his hand tight. "I believe Arkola is hinting he was aware the murder would be taking place, was pleased when it did, but did not - actively - take part or agitate for it."

"Well done, my dear. Even without your abilities, you are simply delightful. Should I decide to let you both live following this audience, Mr. Lowe, I would recommend you seek to make amends for whatever stupidity has led to your estrangement."

Lowe pushed all of that to the back burner - pleased the darkness hid the deep blush that bloomed on his face. "You knew it was coming, you did not do anything to stop it and are happy it happened? You expect me to believe all that is true, and - powerful as you are - you didn't expedite proceedings?"

"I really could not care less what you believe, Mr. Lowe. However, I am - just about - finding this meeting to be diverting enough to waste a few more moments in elucidating you. Gianna d'Avec was an irritant. Not a major one, but bothersome enough to have reached my notice. Gravalk is an entirely unforgiving deity, and - across the broad branch of the unending realms - his rise to prominence is always accompanied by death, destruction and chaos. It may have escaped your notice, but those are not particularly enjoyable states in which to exist."

Lowe nodded, unsure of where this was going - or even if Arkola could see the gesture.

"Fortunately, such are the challenges of worshipping such an unstable being that it is rare for anyone of true power to remain sane enough to reach any real prominence. His cult blazes hot, extremely brightly and usually burns itself out with only minor collateral damage."

Thinking of his own experience in trying to commune with Gravalk, Lowe could believe it. "But that didn't happen with Gianna d'Avec, did it? Somehow, she was able to reach Level 67 and was all set to bring the Fire Demon to the Second Floor. If what you say is true, that gives you a clear motive to want her dead. You can even argue you did it for the good of Soar. So how can you prove to me you did not do it?"

Arkola's laugh was genuine. "Are you asking me for an alibi, Mr. Lowe? I am not sure how that would work for someone who - at least to your sense of time and space - is omnipresent. In any event, I do not need to 'prove' it to you. My word is more than enough."

Lowe felt a soft pressure in his mind, and he suddenly knew that to be true. Arkola was not his man, deity, avatar. Whatever.

"Was I concerned that Gravalk on the Second Floor would be destabilising to the common good? Yes. Was I delighted to learn such a thing would not come to pass due to her imminent murder? Also, yes. Since her death, have I been inclined to meddle in your investigation to ensure the person who alleviated my concern is not brought to justice? Again, a very loud 'yes'. Did I take the opportunity of your wrecking ball fumbling about to settle a few scores with those in Soar whose activities irritate my friends? Yes, yes, yes. But did I kill that blasted woman? That would be a resounding 'no'."

"And I suppose you are not going to tell me who it was that killed her, are you?"

"No, little man. Arkola is not."

Then light flooded the chamber, revealing an entirely empty room. One with a bloodied and battered Latham standing at the entrance of its open door.

CHAPTER 47 – KNIGHTS FALL, KING'S RISE

The Revive Crystal held tightly in Hel's hand shattered as she crashed into the Temple's back wall. As consciousness reasserted itself, she felt a momentary pang at the loss of such a priceless artefact, but - well - if you weren't going to play with all your toys when going toe-to-toe with an Advanced Class, then they should be given to another little girl who would appreciate them . . .

Ah, still a little concussion floating around here somewhere . . .

Shaking her head, then regretting it, Hel dragged herself to her feet and chugged down the strongest Health Potion she possessed. Lowe had given her a bunch of pasties that he swore were better Consumables than anything she had ever taken in battle, but, well, old habits die hard. A lifetime of assuming people were trying to poison you was the sort of instinct that became somewhat hard-wired.

Feeling a little more together, she had a quick glance around, which confirmed that Tenia and Charl were down. Not 'down down', but not 'give us a minute boss, we'll have your back shortly down'.

And that was fair enough.

The Nightmare Reaver had more than done her bit in slowing this fucking monster down, and Charl . . . well, he had earned a little shut eye. It was pretty much Tactics 101 that you didn't throw your meat shield at something that could eat him in one bite, and she had appreciated the loyalty the big man had shown in being up for running chin-first into Mr. Law again. Speaking of which . . .

It didn't take her long to spot her target; he was already at the Portal Stones and squaring up with a Temple Warder. With a smile, Hel noted that it was the one who seemed to have taken quite a shine to Lowe. She could dig that: for whatever reason, something about that human punching bag engendered protective instincts.

That smile swiftly fell away as Mr. Law straight-up murdered a bunch of people whose only crime was standing in an orderly queue, waiting their turn for the stones. Was that *Life Leach* that bastard had just used?

'Fucking hell', Hel breathed and started powering up a few of her own more exotic talents.

Their plan for Mr. Law had been predicated on the notion he was keen to fly under the radar. None of Hel's squad had any illusions they could take him down - not even Charl in full berserker-blindness - but they were operating under the assumption that if they were irritating enough, with enough people watching, Mr. Law might just decide to call it a day and wait for a more opportune moment. The dust of desiccated remains wafting across the floor of the Temple suggested that might have been a slightly erroneous idea.

Hel was just preparing to throw everything she had at the man when she realised something fairly interesting.

Despite the undoubted puissance of Mr. Law, the Temple Warder had not been reduced to a smear on the flagstones. In fact, as she watched the fastest fight she had ever seen, he appeared to be more than holding his own.

***

Sweating for the first time in years, Bright triggered *Kinetic Blast* and unleashed a torrent of energy to push the Warder backwards. The air around him crackled as invisible forces converged, launching a wave of raw power. The stone floor of the Temple tore up in a jagged line as the force travelled forward, but Latham stood his ground, simply raising his hand to form a shimmering barrier before him, absorbing the brunt of the attack. Bright's assault dissipated harmlessly, leaving Latham unscathed.

"Fuck's sake," Bright muttered, sending a whip of the same Skill around him in a wide arc, knocking the other Temple Warders converging on his position off their feet. They seemed susceptible enough to what he was throwing out, so what the fuck was this big guy bringing to the party?

As if he needed telling, every warning Skill Bright possessed was trilling loudly as Latham surged forward, his massive form moving with surprising speed, sword arcing down in a blow faster than anything a man of his Level should have been able to achieve.

Bright sidestepped, a blur of motion, and countered with a punch infused with *Heavy Hands*. Latham took the blow right on the chin, shaking his head as he absorbed the impact, the strike's power rippling harmlessly across his face like a gentle wave.

Bright danced back, eyes narrowing. The Temple Warder's Build was impressive, clearly designed to withstand and mitigate damage while having decent offensive capabilities. Bright rechecked the Warder's Level and frowned again: Level ?? covered a multitude of sins - especially within the grounds of the Celestial Temple - but there were limits to what those who were Rare Classed should be able to achieve. Even if this guy had min/maxed every possible option, he still shouldn't be able to show this sort of moxy.

Bright rolled his wrists, pinging out a few A.O.E attacks via *Kinetic Blast* to knock the other Warders staggering to their feet back to the floor. This wasn't going to be a quick one-and-done. It would require a bit more finesse and cunning, a chess game played with lethal pieces.

And all the time, Lowe was already on the First Floor.

That thought sparking him into haste, Bright summoned a field of *Temporal Distortion*: time slowed around the two combatants, the world becoming a sluggish tableau. Then, moving with all of his Class-empowered speed, he struck at the Temple Warder from multiple angles, hundreds of fists fracturing free from all manner of planes of existence, each thrown by an alternate version of Bright.

This was about as much of a 'finishing move' as Bright ever was required to use; however, although the majority of the blows hit their mark, leaving terrible damage visible on Latham's body and armour, the big man just tanked them and moved to launch his own attack.

Latham's sword blazed with *Divine Flame*, the swing creating a wave of purifying energy that was triply boosted by being activated within the aura of the Celestial

Temple. In something approaching alarm - when was the last time he had felt that emotion! - Bright conjured a shield of *Dark Matter*, absorbing the brunt of the assault and reflecting it at one of the alternate Brights, who burned up with a scream of indignation.

"Sorry! Survival of the fittest, right now," Bright thought to . . . himself, staggering as the force of Latham's attack pushed the core version of him backwards. His feet skidded across the ground, carving deep trenches in the Temple floor as he sought to find purchase.

As diverting as this was proving, this . . . scrap was not what Bright was here to do. His employers were already going to question the level of collateral damage he had brought to bear. At the very least, he needed to get on with completing his mission.

Draining a significant portion of his remaining Mana, Bright summoned a storm of *Spectral Blade*s. The ethereal weapons of those he had previously vanquished in battle converged on Latham, slicing through his armour, even as it flared with protective runes.

Bright gawped as the big man took the damage, then continued to move forward through the assault with grim determination, each step bringing him closer to Bright.

"What the fuck are you!" Bright shouted at the Warder, triggering *Elemental Fury*. Flames roared to life around him, the floor beneath them both turning to molten slag. Bright directed the inferno towards Latham.

In response, *Divine Light* shimmered around the Warder, the flames parting around him like water around a rock. He then charged forward through the inferno and swung his sword straight at Bright's head, who barely had time to raise a barrier of his own, the impact sending shockwaves through his body. He staggered back, his suit singed and smoking.

Breathing heavily, Bright's mind raced. He needed this to be over. Now. Crushing a Mana Stone, he felt his expended power reassert itself, eyes glowing as he tapped into the fabric of reality itself. The air around Latham solidified, bending to Bright's will as he prepared an attack that would, at the very least, cause all sorts of uncomfortable questions about the legality of such methods.

But, right now, Bright could not have cared less.

Latham winced, planting his feet and raising his sword high. The blade blazed as Bright unleashed his attack, a concentrated beam of *Reality Rend* that would tear the Warder out of existence. Should the technique hit, everything Latham had ever said or done would no longer have occurred. Every aspect of his being would be ripped free, leaving threads of Fate hanging across the reality gap, which would become the man's life.

It was a staggeringly overpowered Skill to use on this plane of reality, but Bright was pissed.

The attack collided with Latham's sword, the two forces clashing in a blinding explosion of light and sound. The ground shook, the air vibrating with the intensity of their struggle. Bright's eyes widened at the resistance and pushed harder, his mind straining, every ounce of his will focused on breaking through. The Warder's face was a mask of concentration, resisting the colossal impulse to blink out of existence.

Moments felt like hours as they remained locked in their struggle. The rip in reality crackled and sparked, tearing at the Temple's foundations, creating shockwaves radiating outwards throughout Soar.

Finally, with a final, desperate surge, Bright managed to break the stalemate. His beam of energy flared, pushing Latham out of time. It wasn't a permanent erasure, but it was enough. Into that space, Bright poured everything he had into Latham's soul.

In response, Latham . . . roared, a sound unlike anything Bright had ever heard in his life, and he swept his blade down to cleave Bright's beam in two, shattering the attack and sending a backlash of energy towards its creator.

Bright was thrown back, his body hitting the floor and sliding through a group of fallen Warders with bone-jarring force. He lay there, gasping for breath, his vision swimming.

For a moment, there was silence. Then, with a groan, Bright forced himself to his feet. Latham did the same, using his sword as a crutch. They stood there, facing each other, pieces of Portal Stone still pulsing behind Latham. And, crucially, still out of Bright's reach.

Bright adjusted his tie and straightened his suit; he couldn't help but offer a grudging nod of respect to Latham.

A card appeared in his hand, and he flicked it towards the big man. "I don't know what the fuck you are, but if you ever get tired of kissing godly arse, I can probably find you some work."

Latham watched the white square drop to the ground, then jutted his chin upwards. "We done here?"

Bright smiled broadly back. "For now." He started to vanish, his mouth being the last bit of him to disappear. "I look forward to Round Two on . . . shall we say, more neutral ground? Take care."

And then he was gone.

***

Hel rushed forward, literally dousing the Temple Warder in the strongest Health Potions she had in her inventory. She hadn't been able to follow the confrontation, which, in and of itself, was terrifying.

The fact the big man was still standing - albeit clearly one puff of wind away from collapse - was one of the most staggering things she had ever witnessed. And Hel had seen some shit.

Latham had activated some Heal Skill of his own and was chugging a veritable vat of Mana Potions of his own as she reached his side. "That was ... epic!" Hel said, awkwardly aware she sounded like the worst fan girl in the world.

Latham looked at her, eyes showing every sign of being within an inch of being zeroed and knowing it, and then turned and staggered for the portal. "You think that was impressive? Wait until you see what I've planned for an encore."

Hel moved to follow him, slipping one of his oozing, lacerated arms over her shoulder to provide some stability to his staggering. "Which is?"

"I'm going to persuade Lowe he's looking at all of this the wrong way."

CHAPTER 48 – CONNECTING THE DOTS, ONE DEAD PRIEST AT A TIME

"Mate! You look like shit. And trust me, when it comes to the aftermaths of a real shoeing, I know of what I speak! What in Soar happened to you?"

Lowe activated *Medic!* and pushed it towards Latham, who, he realised, was only standing because a red-faced and heavily breathing Hel was lodged under one of his armpits. Seeing that she also looked significantly worse for wear, he triggered a second instance of *Medic!* and cast it towards her, too.

"What do you think happened, you fucking idiot?" Latham put out a hand to lean against the doorframe of Arkola's chamber. "You kicked a hornet's nest and then ran away. The adult in the room then had to deal."

Lowe was so aghast at the amount of mana *Medic!* was sucking down to address the various injuries the Temple Warder and the Wind Tyrant were sporting that he had almost forgotten the reason both of his friends looked like shit. A vision of Mr. Law swam forward in his mind.

"And?"

Latham left a pregnant pause, straightening up slightly as Lowe's healing finally started to take effect. Once she was confident the big man could stand again under his own steam, Hel slipped free from under his arm and stretched out her back.

"What do you think happened? I took care of business."

Lowe's eyebrows shot up. He had a very clear memory of the capabilities of Mr. Law. He knew Latham was good, but . . . Lowe glanced Hel's way for confirmation.

She shrugged back. "To be fair, he's not lying. I've never seen anything like it. Tcnia, Charl and I were barely able to make the Big Bad miss a step, but then your man did his thing."

"So, we're safe?"

Latham laughed grimly. "Well, for now. But I wouldn't give much for any of our chances if we leave the Temple without having this all wrapped up. The two of us left things on somewhat of an 'I'll be seeing you soon' note . . ."

Lowe cursed and looked around the empty chamber, searching for . . . something. The imminent danger might have receded, but that didn't change the overall dynamic of the situation. It was clear their only path to survival was to solve the case and then hope they would no longer be worth bothering with.

That felt somewhat like a forlorn hope right now.

The moment Latham opened the door to let light flood in, Lowe had felt the presence of Arkola fade. Not that had had much more to say to Soar's supreme being. He had been so sure that the responsibility for all the week's events lay within this room: nothing else made sense of everything that had happened. But, to hear Arkola's version of events, they had simply taken advantage of someone else's throw of the dice.

And what was more, Lowe believed what he'd heard.

"So, what next?" Arebella said, tapping him softly on the arm. "If it wasn't Arkola who was responsible, who should we be looking at?"

Lowe's eyes glazed over as he activated *Grid View*. Thanks to all of his recent upgrades, he'd been able to leave it running more or less constantly after his Dungeon Dive. Moreover, he found that the speed at which he could review things had also increased exponentially. Being able to review everything that had happened in the last few days in an instant was quite a trip. On more than one occasion, Lowe had been close enough to death to experience his 'life flashing before his eyes.' This was like that.

With slightly less traumatic peril.

Latham cleared his throat, pulling Lowe out of his reverie. "Actually, whilst I was kicking Mr. Law's arse - "

"I mean, let's not get carried away here. You were damn impressive, but there was only one arse being kicked down there. The dude took off because he literally grew tired of whupping you."

"- as I was saying!" Latham continued, ignoring Hel's *sotto voce* commentary, "While fighting Mr. Law, I realised the problem with this case. We are looking at everything the wrong way around."

Lowe frowned, pausing his review of everything that he'd seen or heard recently. Even as he did so, he could feel there was something there that was waving its arms and shouting for his attention, but it wouldn't quite press forward. Ignoring that for a moment - often, it was concentrating on something else that let the hidden present itself - he looked up at the big man. "How do you mean?"

"From the very first moment this all occurred, we've been thinking too big."

"We have a dead Level 67 Pyromancer, ripped to pieces in the Celestial Temple under the full protection of her god. On top of that, we have an Advanced Class hitman floating around casually slaughtering people, a bunch of assassination attempts on the two of us, *another* dead Priest and then a heavy hitter from Jewel Town implicated. Dude, this is the definition of 'big'."

"All true. But we've become obsessed with looking for shadowy figures and massive conspiracies since the get-go. I just wonder if we've let ourselves be distracted by everything that happened after the murder."

"Post hoc, ergo propter hoc," Arebella exclaimed.

"What?"

Latham smiled slowly and nodded. "Exactly!"

"'Exactly' what?"

"Interesting," Hel's voice was soft, her expression thoughtful.

"What's 'interesting?' What the fuck are you all sagely agreeing about!" Lowe's sense of frustration was almost a distinct, separate person in the conversation. "Can I remind you there's only one investigator in this room? If anyone is going to have a moment of blinding epiphany, it is going to be me!"

"It was one of my Law Professor's favourite expressions. Post hoc, ergo propter hoc. Come on, you know this, Jana!"

"I'm going to go out on a limb here and suggest he's got no idea. From my very limited contact with your boyfriend, it strikes me that you're the brains, the beauty and *all* of the classical education. He's the . . . I actually don't know. At this stage, I have to assume he's an amazing lay, right?"

Arebella blushed at Hel's words and cleared her throat. "*After this, therefore, because of it*. It's a term in law for the logical fallacy of assuming one thing caused another merely because the first thing preceded the other. A whole host of things have occurred since the murder of Gianna d'Avec, but that does not mean they happened *because* of the murder. Or, at the very least, that the person who murdered the High Priestess was responsible for putting them in motion."

Lowe let that percolate in his mind for a moment. Both Arkola and Mr. Law had expressed something similar - that there had been 'opportunities' presented by the death of Gianna d'Avec, and they'd jumped all over them. But they'd each denied being responsible for firing the starting pistol, as it were. For all the sound and fury that had occurred since the discovery of the High Priestess's body, was there anything that couldn't be explained by powerful beings in Soar taking their chance to settle some private scores . . .

Lowe dived back into *Grid View*, trying to parse out anything that could be locked away in the file marked "Unrelated Shenanigans of the Rich and Powerful Being Wankers."

It left precious little.

Then it hit him. For the first time since Cenorth had arrived at his apartment and dangled the case before him, the pieces slotted together to reveal a coherent picture. When you faded out the noise and ignored the threat of violent death, what remained was actually pretty mundane.

It all came down to a piece of seaweed, a missing glove, and, of course, a second dead Priest.

Everything else was just the noise of Soar being Soar.

"You've figured it out, haven't you?" A massive grin was spreading over Arebella's face. "You always look that way when you've figured it all out. You know who's responsible!"

"Maybe," Lowe said, glancing at Latham and Hel. "You both feeling okay?"

"These things are relative. Could I stomp you like a bug? Sure. Do I have another entanglement with Mr. Law in me? Probably not."

Hel bumped Latham with her hip. "Don't listen to him, Lowe. He's more than fine. What have you got?"

Lowe took a deep breath and held it. If he was right - and he thought he was - then there was only one place left for them to go. "I think I might have it figured out. But proving it is going to be tricky. Where are your sisters?"

Hel frowned at the unexpected segue. "A friend is looking after them. Why?"

"Because I'm a drama queen, and it'd be good to pull all the players into one room when I talk through it."

"It's true. He is." Arebella affirmed, taking Lowe's hand in hers. "It's kind of his thing."

Hel looked between them, clearly baffled. "I mean, I can arrange for them to join us if you think it will help?"

"It will. It really will."

"Okay," Hel tugged on her connection with Irek, letting him know he should bring her sisters to her. "If you're sure this is necessary? But where is this big reveal going to take place?"

"Where else?" Lowe said, exiting Arkola's chamber and moving down the corridor towards the Portal Stone. "Let's go to where all this started: the High Priestess' Chamber." Lowe activated the portal to the Third Floor.

After the last of them vanished through it, the light in the First Floor corridor flicked off and - should anyone have listened carefully - an extremely satisfied sigh was heard from the now darkened chamber at the end.

CHAPTER 49 – THE GOD WORE CRIMSON

"Are we all sitting comfortably?"

Arebella did her best not to roll her eyes at Lowe's question. Sure, she recognised he probably deserved a little melodrama after what he had been through over the last few days, but perhaps now was not quite the time or place . . .

Neither were any of the people who had been - with various degrees of bad grace - gathered in Gianna d'Avec's receiving chamber sitting especially comfortably.

For some of them - namely Latham, Hel, Tenia and Charl - that was because they had just had seven shades kicked out of them, and there was no amount of healing nor tasty HP-restoring snacks that made you forget how it felt to be somewhat powerless in the face of overwhelming strength. Included in their little worse-for-wear group was Ortel Maybourne, but his cause of woe was self-inflicted rather than by nefarious, physical means: the smell of alcohol wafting off him was almost overwhelming to those sat next to him.

Then there were those who clearly believed that taking part in this sort of charade was significantly beneath their position in life, namely Mdamic, Khaled and the spidery figure of Cadi Velehim, the Senior Recorder. Indeed, the two avatars had only agreed to attend once they heard the distinct sound of Arkola clearing their throat behind them.

On the other side of the chamber, Aintra and Hiwalk were sitting, arms folded, peeved that so many non-believers had been allowed access to the inner sanctum of their High Priestess. They were making their displeasure at Gravalk's space being used for 'some sort of parlour game' abundantly clear. Little flame birds of prey kept appearing and disappearing above the head of the Hell Raiser.

To be fair, even without their personal reservations, it was understandable that everyone sat in the hastily arranged chairs was pretty unhappy to be in a room which, despite the best efforts of the Temple Cleaners, still bore all the hallmarks of an abattoir.

"Can we get on with this, please?" Mdamic said, storm clouds forming above his head. "Some of us have things to do."

"I'm sure," Lowe said, eyeing the flash of thunderbolts a touch nervously. "We just have a last few people to arrive, and then we can—"

Through the chamber's open door, the Portal Stone shimmer opened and closed twice in quick succession. " - ah, here are our last few guests."

The first person through the door was a wiry older man with a haggard expression. He looked around the chamber, nodded at Hel, and then turned back to beckon two heavily bundled-up figures into the room. Such was the volume of cloth covering them that it was impossible to tell if they were male, female, human or horse. The three of them moved to sit behind Hel's contingent, and - despite the strangeness of their appearance and the general mood of anxiety in the room - their arrival, or at least the man's, seemed to make everyone feel less tense.

Following close behind them came Lowe's boss, Cenorth, the Deathcaller Penarth Lant, and two uniformed Constables escorting a very sorry for himself looking, Markian Ulton. Seeing that arrogant man in chains - literally and metaphorically - put an extra spring in Lowe's step, and he felt a smile spread across his face.

"Excellent. I am so glad we were all able to find time in all our busy schedules to join this little soiree."

"Jana, cut the crap." Cenorth's voice was harsh. "The Council are pissing vinegar about this. By my reckoning, you have half a bell before I start receiving messages that I can't ignore any longer. Get the fuck on with it."

Lowe nodded. "Fair enough. Now, before we begin, I just want to set a few ground rules. You will notice my glamorous assistant here?" Lowe pointed at Arebella, who gave an embarrassed little wave. "Well, for those of you who do not know her, Ms. Telut is one of Soar's finest Veritas Assessors."

"And the possessor of a spectacular bosom," Lant added, slightly louder than was truly necessary. He met Cenorth's glare with a shrug. "It's not like I'm lying, is it? And that is the point you are making, Mr. Lowe, is it not? You have brought your own personal lie detector to proceedings?"

Lowe ignored the pot-bellied man and opened his arms wide. "I would also note that we have quite the collection of fell powers present here today. Thus, for the sake of all our survival, can I please ask that we think first, smite later should tempers run a little high?"

***

Cenorth looked around at the gathering and felt a little bead of sweat break out on his forehead. Lowe wasn't exaggerating. There was enough firepower in the room to sink a small continent - and that was just the people he recognised. He wasn't wholly sure what he would be able to do if things cut up rough. As a Sentinel of Justice, he had several Skills that had an Area of Effect mitigation to damage, but he'd never had to launch them against an angry fucking Avatar before. What in the name of Soar had Lowe talked him into here . . .

***

"I think," Khaled said, his entirely reasonable tone belying the blazing fury in his eyes, "it might be best if we were to get on with things. I am happy to confirm that I understand the delightful Ms. Telut will be able to identify lies and that it would be best if any retribution for the discourtesy shown here were saved for later." His reptilian eyes met Arebella's. "I can promise your Mr. Lowe that I will see him soon to discuss how the Chosen of Oh was dragooned into attending this . . . meeting."

Lowe didn't need to check with her if this was the truth or not.

"Okay. So, moving right along. We all know why you have been gathered here today."

After a few moments of no one answering and Lowe clearly pausing for effect, Verahalim coughed to clear his throat and supplied the response in his wheezy voice.

"The murder of Gianna d'Avec. Oh, and for the sake of transparency, I should note that I will be billing the Mayor for every contribution I am required to make to proceedings. On top of my per-bell rate, this delightful little distraction has cost the city 500 gold thus far."

Cenorth ground his teeth. He could already hear the Council making clear whose budget this was all coming out of. "For pity's sake, Jana, can you move this the fuck along!"

"Pity?" Lowe said, rolling the word around his mouth. "Pity. Yes, I think that's probably a good place to start. Because there's not anyone in this room who feels pity - any at all - for the death of the High Priestess. I am not wrong in saying that, am I?"

There were a few downcast eyes at that but also several shrugs and defiant glares. "No, Gianna d'Avec is not much mourned." Lowe started to pace around the room. "I don't think I have ever heard the word 'bitch' uttered so often about the recently deceased as I did in connection with the High Priestess. People were not quite lining up to shake the hand of whoever killed her, but neither was there much dismay. As I look around this room, I see person after person that danced a veritable jig at her passing."

Looking at each member of the group in turn, Lowe started to pace the chamber the opposite way around. "Maybe she was an upcoming rival, an uncaring employer, a murderer, a corrupt official, an *uncorrupt* official. A lover. Whatever. But a bitch. Pretty much everyone in the room was united on that score. Gianna d'Avec was a Level 67 Pyromancer and a Level 100 Bitch. And whoever killed her did Soar a favour. Am I right?"

Mindful of Arebella's presence, no one seemed interested in saying anything out loud, but Lowe saw few who disagreed with his assessment.

"But, and this is where things start to become interesting, as my investigation moved on, it became clear there was another side to d'Avec. One that does not seem compatible with the general, accepted view. For example, most of you will be aware that she chose not to live in the Celestial Temple, as would be her right. No. Instead, she would retire each evening to her modest childhood home. That strikes me as hardly the behaviour of someone so widely understood to be 'power-hungry.' A little thing, for sure, but I found that instructive. There are few more luxurious residences in Soar than the Celestial Temple, yet she chose home comforts."

Lowe's words made little impression on his audience. If any of them thought he had scored a point in d'Avec's favour there, they hid it well. Undeterred at the lack of reaction, the detective pressed on.

"And then there is the matter of her financial arrangements." Lowe spun to face the Senior Recorder. "To whom did she leave all her wealth, Mr. Verahalim?"

"As we discussed, Mr. Lowe, Gianna d'Avec dispersed the majority of her income in support of a large number of charities. They will each benefit significantly now that she has . . . died."

"When we spoke before, you mentioned that the charities she supported were all connected to," Lowe's eyes flashed as he pulled the words from his memory, *Orphans. War Veterans. Young Carers.* Is my memory of that accurate?"

Verahalim shrugged his agreement, adding, "760 gold if anyone is keeping count."

"So the bitch had a social conscience? Whoop-de-doo. Tell you what, I'll have a few bullocks slaughtered in her name, and my Vestal Virgins can have an hour of debauchery. How does that sound? We done yet?" The storm clouds above Mdamic's head were increasingly growing dark.

Lowe opened his palms to the Speaker of Yolgorth. "But don't you find it odd? Someone who, even in the event of her brutal murder, no one had a good word to say, being so keen to help others?"

"Not especially. No. People can be complex. Especially avatars."

"Ah. Maybe it's just me, then. How about you, Hel? Does hearing about d'Avec's philanthropy make you feel differently about her?"

All heads turned to the Wind Tyrant, who lifted her chin defiantly. "Not in the least. Why do you think it should?"

"I was just wondering. Because, as far as I understand it, your hatred for the High Priestess comes from her involvement in the murder of your families. *Orphans. War Veterans. Young Carers.* I could be wrong, but it sounds to me that most of that could apply to your little group."

Tenia snarled at that and made to stand, sickly-green Skills activating in the air around her. Hel hissed an order, gripped her wrist tightly and dragged her back to her seat. "Blood money, Lowe. She could throw as much cash around as she wanted, but that wouldn't wipe the slate clean."

"Interestingly liquid metaphor, there. The High Priestess herself said something similar to you, didn't she, Mr. Verahalim? 'When you have so much blood on your hands, every bit of mercy helps.' Weren't those her words?"

The Senior Recorder nodded. "Indeed."

"To wash away the guilt, I assume. Again with the water imagery, you will notice. Strange for the avatar of the Fire Demon. And instructive when we consider the manner of her death. Tell me," Lowe said, turning in a wide circle to face the people on the other side of the chamber, "what element are you most familiar with?"

All eyes were suddenly fixed on Khaled, the Chosen of Oh.

CHAPTER 50 – WHEN THE SKY SHATTERS

Khaled wet his suddenly parched lips. "As I am sure all in this room are aware, Mr. Lowe, those who worship Oh are granted some strength with the water element."

"Indeed, but - for the avoidance of doubt - you, as the Chosen of Oh, have a little more than just 'strength'. In fact, it might even be said that as Oh's avatar, you are amongst the foremost Water Mages in Soar?"

"Hardly." Khaled pointed upwards to where his Class and Level were on open display. "I am but a humble Level 60 dwelling on the Eighth Floor."

"The sixth." Latham's voice was suddenly thunderous in the chamber. "I hear on the grapevine your ascension was confirmed just this morning. Unusual to jump two floors in one go like that. Noteworthy, in fact. Someone must have made themselves very popular with the Council."

"Well, yes." Khaled's whole mouth had become very dry indeed. "I didn't think that news was common knowledge yet. But it is true. I have been granted a . . . small promotion in recognition of services rendered." Mdamic shifted in his seat to stare at Khaled, a small section of the thundercloud above him breaking free to hover over the other man's head. "But my wider point, after all, still holds. Someone of my situation can hardly be considered an appropriate antagonist for the High Priestess of Gravalk."

The silence in the chamber was only broken by the soft pitter-patter of rain falling on Khaled's head.

Lowe stared at him impassively. "I think we would all like to hear the nature of these 'services rendered.'"

"I don't think they're relevant to the matter under . . ."

Khaled blurred as a lightning bolt crashed to incinerate the chair where he sat, *Never Surprised* saving him once again.

Mdamic was up on his feet, face red. "I'll fucking decide if it's relevant! What did you do to earn the promotion? It's you that's been pouring venom in the Council's ears about me, isn't it? All that advice, all those cosy chats. You were fucking playing me!"

With as much dignity as he could manage, the Chosen of Oh returned to his feet, thoroughly soaked by the pulsating rain. He turned to face Arebella, enunciating his words with care. "Neither I nor any member of my cult were involved directly - or indirectly - in the murder of Gianna d'Avec. Any compensation that has come my way of late can be considered entirely tangential. Such rewards are connected to my work to support the Council's efforts in ensuring an appropriate balance of power in the Temple."

Lowe glanced her way, and Arebella nodded. "He's telling the truth."

"I don't give a fuck about whether he was involved in killing the bitch! Has he been specifically rewarded for working against me? That's the question I want asked. Fucking ask it!"

"That is indeed an interesting question, Mdamic. But perhaps we avatars can resolve the sudden popularity of the cult of Oh behind closed doors. It is, after all, never good for children to see Mummy and Daddy fight. Or, to put it more bluntly, your behaviour is scaring the cattle. Join me in my chamber. Now."

Everyone heard Arkola's voice, but not in so mundane a fashion as through their ears. And then Khaled and Mdamic vanished, and the chair was back in his reconstituted seat as if no lightning-based destruction had occurred.

Lowe glanced around at a sea of suddenly very nervous faces: no one liked to think they were under Arkola's notice. Bad things tend to happen when Soar's supreme being took a personal interest. Then the whole body of the wiry man sat behind Hel strained in effort, and the general sense of doom relented. Slightly.

As the tension lightened, Ortel cleared his throat. This took several attempts, eventually requiring him to lean to the side and spit out something darkly green. "As much of a fan as I am of all these courtroom theatrics, do you think we could try to get to the meat of the matter? If Oh isn't behind what happened to d'Avec, who is?"

Cenorth nodded his own frustration. "Time isn't your friend here, Lowe. If you have a case to build, do so. But it's now or never. I can sense a whole phalanx of Council flunkeys descending on Cuckoo House. They'll work out where we are in moments."

Lowe took a breath, then rubbed his chin. "Fair enough. So, let us see what we know, then." He held up a finger. "Two weeks before her death, Gianna d'Avec officiated in the trial of Trellen Ulton. He was accused of the murder of Lord Falyn, and, in short order, she summarily executed him. Was this a just act?" Lowe directed his question at Ortel, who shook his head emphatically.

"Trellen was innocent. He was guilty of nothing more than being in the wrong place at the wrong time." The lawyer glanced at the man wrapped in chains in the corner of the room. "And having the wrong brother."

"Quite." Lowe turned to Markian and cocked his head. "Trellen had found out you were responsible for Falyn's recent commercial losses, hadn't he? My understanding is that there was widespread corruption in the awarding of city contracts."

Markian, with some difficulty due to the weight of his chains, shrugged nonchalantly. "As I am under a Red Notice, my business dealings with Lord Falyn are a matter of public record. Am I guilty of, at best, sharp practice? Certainly. Are there those whom I represent who desired my brother to carry the can for Falyn's death? Again, I assume that to be the case. Was I personally involved in the murder of Falyn? No."

Noting the care with which he spoke, Lowe raised his eyebrows at Arebella. She frowned and shook her head. The chained man was not lying.

"Do you know who killed Falyn?"

"My brother was found guilty."

Lowe clicked his tongue and rephrased the question. "Do you believe he did it?"

"I accept the decision made by the High Priestess of Gravalk."

"That wasn't the question."

"Funny that."

Cenorth stepped forward and punched Markian in the face, breaking his nose. "Look, as much as you've tried to get your friends to wheedle you out from under it, you're still under a Red Notice. That means you have fewer rights than the shit beneath my shoe. We're all very impressed with your semantic gymnastics to avoid answering a direct question. Truly, you're the man. But if you keep fucking around, you're going to find out. And I will start breaking fingers next." He turned back to Lowe, giving him a thumbs up. "Your witness, Jana."

"Why did d'Avec execute your brother? Did you ask her to?"

"No." Blood ran down Markian's face, dying his teeth red. "I would have asked if it'd look likely he'd get off, but it wasn't going to come to that."

"Why not?"

Markian laughed grimly. "Do you have any idea how good the people you are blundering around against are? You've got a Temple Warder, an Out of Bounds Squad, and even fucking Arkola watching your back, and they've still managed to get to you whenever they wanted. Doesn't the fact you're still alive tell you anything?" He turned to look at the others in the room. "Doesn't it tell you *all* something? He's a useful fucking idiot. That's all. Nothing that is happening here isn't exactly as they want. He's a fucking Classless wrecking ball, and the minute he's not useful anymore, he'll be dealt with."

Lowe tried to let those words bounce off him, but he felt them leave their mark. But he'd worry about that later. "And what about Gianna d'Avec? Was she useful, too?"

"Of course she was! A High Priestess of Gravalk in my pocket? Made me into a fucking legend. She fried Trellen without even being asked to! And she did it because she thought she was protecting me! You should have seen the way she lost her shit when I tried to suggest there would be a reward in it for her. But that was always her problem, you know? All this bollocks about staying in the family house and keeping her old nanny around, and giving away her money to deserving causes. She was just a fucking pathetic orphan desperate for someone to love her and tell her it was all going to be okay. She killed her own parents, did you know that? Flash-fried them like last night's chicken when she lost her temper. It scared her so much she spent the rest of her life trying to make amends. The saddest of sad sacks. An open wound looking for anything to fill the void."

"And that's what you did for her?"

"It's what they wanted me to do, you better believe I fucking did! You saw what they did to that fucking priest who tried to back out of the deal he made with them! You don't have second thoughts with these guys. They employ fucking Leoto Bright, for Soar's sake!"

Hiwalk was up on his feet. "Who killed him? Who killed Setort?" Flaming falcons dipped and swirled above his head, diving to peck at Markian as the priest raged.

"Fuck's sake!" Markian hunched his shoulders, trying to protect his face. "What did he think was going to happen? You don't make a deal with these people and then try to stiff them for more. They paid him to get dirt on this Classless fuckwit, but that wasn't enough for him, was it? The way I heard it, he tried to blackmail them into making him into Gravalk's next High Priest. Threatened to go straight to Arkola with what he knew. Wanker's lucky Bright just ripped him to shreds for trying that.

And trust me, I've seen him do much worse! Like you'll fucking see when this is all over!"

A silence fell over the room, broken only by Lowe's slow footsteps as he continued to pace again. When he spoke, it was as if Markian's rant had never happened.

"But that's the interesting thing, do you see? What strikes me here - again - is the dichotomy in the way you describe the High Priestess's nature. Humble in her lifestyle, hugely generous with her money, and fiercely loyal to those she thought cared for her. And yet there is so much pleasure in this room at the woman's death."

Penarth snorted. "Fuck's sake, Temporary Reinstated Much-Maligned Inspector, we get it. She was a saint. A beloved woman snatched too quickly from this world. And anyone who thinks otherwise is just plain wrong. Put the smallest fucking violin in the world away and tell us what happened!"

"She fucking killed my family!"

As Hel stood, her sisters started wailing. Not just crying, but a full-on scream of heart-wrenching despair. Irek pushed out as many waves of soothing calm as he could, but it simply didn't touch the sides of the sorrow of the Wraiths. A widening circle of space appeared around them as everyone in the room backed away.

Hel pointed at Lowe, tears running down her face. "The Council was willing to let us go! We were finished as agents, we knew that. But there was no need for any further action. We'd have just slipped away. All of us. But she wouldn't let that happen. She persuaded them to make an example of us. She killed them. She killed them, Lowe! She killed them all!"

The plaintive note in that final repetition was heartbreaking to hear. For a moment, Lowe wanted to let it go. Wanted to throw his hands up in the air and be done with the whole thing. Who the fuck cared who had killed a High Priestess of Gravalk? The Fire God was a nightmare waiting to happen, and whoever curtailed his rise to power had done the whole of Soar a massive favour. What did it matter who was responsible for that?

Looking into Hel's pain-filled eyes, there was a part of him that wanted to let it go. But, just as he had a year before when all the pressure in the world was brought to bear upon him to look the other way, he just couldn't bring himself to do it.

He asked the question he'd been aching to ask the Wind Tyrant since his moment of epiphany on the First Floor.

"How do you know that, Hel?"

The Wind Tyrant opened her mouth to retort, her face twisted in anger. But then it stopped—confusion blossoming on her face.

"I . . . there was an official report. Highly confidential. I was able to get hold of a copy."

"A confidential written report. Think about it for a moment. From everything you've heard about the High Priestess, does it seem likely she'd have behaved that way? A woman haunted by what her power had done to her own parents? A woman who gave everything she earned to those making the world a better place. Why would she have advocated for the massacre of your family?"

Doubt was appearing all over Hel's face. "But . . . it was in the report. And it was almost impossible to get hold of. The hoops I had to go through to get it. There's no way it could have been faked."

"Why do you think that, Hel? How did you get it? Who gave it to you?"

Hel's eyes slipped to the right to where Cenorth had been standing.

But the Sentinel of Justice was already in motion, Skills triggering to slay Markian Ulton and the two Constables beside him in a mist of blood, and then he was taking hold of Arebella's hair and dragging her in front of him, hunching to cover himself behind her.

"For Soar's sake, Jana! You had one job. It comes to something when I can't even rely on you to fuck up an investigation properly."

CHAPTER 51 – THE LAST CANDLE BURNS

As he watched Cenorth drag Arebella out of the receiving chamber and into the hallway beyond, time froze for Lowe.

He was not sure what he had expected the Commander of Soar's Security Services to do once his role in misleading Hel's squad had been exposed, but this casual, violent slaughter complete with hostages certainly wasn't it. Lowe had banked on having enough firepower in the room to keep any such shenanigans under control. But he'd fumbled it.

Fucking Cenorth.

No, be fair. Fucking Jana Lowe. As if a Level 45 Sentinel of Justice was simply going to put his hands up, cop to all manner of misdeeds and then come along quietly. The bodies of Markian Ulton and the two headless Constables were testament to Lowe's spectacular misjudgement of the situation.

And now the bastard had Arebella.

Mechanically, shaking himself free from his stasis, Lowe charged after the pair, aware that Cenorth was flinging out all sorts of deadly, high-level Skills as he made good his escape.

"Fuck's sake, little man, take some cover!" Latham shouted, tackling him to the ground just as something metallic and fast-moving slashed through the space he had been about to enter. The aura of Cenorth's assaults had the sort of grim finality about them that suggested *Roll with the Punches* would likely have come up pretty short.

"You want to tell me what the fuck is going on here!" The Temple Warder bodily picked Lowe up and bundled him forward until they were pressed either side of the door leading towards the Third Floor Portal Stones. "Isn't this twat supposed to be on our side?"

Lowe looked back at the devastation Cenorth had wrought in d'Avec's former chamber. Apart from Markian and the two dead Constables from Cuckoo House - that he hadn't recognised either of them didn't improve the weight of guilt that was settling in Lowe's stomach - those who had gathered at his insistence had taken an absolute pounding in the wake of the escape.

Penarth was leaning over the Senior Recorder, Verahalim, pumping some manner of healing Skill into a spectacular chest wound. For a moment, Lowe found something incongruous about a Deathcaller being able to treat living patients, but then he realised he had bigger problems to ponder.

Ortel, despite missing an arm, had conjured up several Healing Totems, which were doing their best to mitigate some of the damage that Charl, Irek and Tenia were sporting. The Berserker Balloon had obviously tried to tank the worst of what Cenorth had flung out, but even so, the other two looked like someone had stuck them in a mangle and got cranking. And the two priests of Gravalk – Aintra and

Hiwalk — looked like shit, but neither seemed like they would be joining their ex-mistress in the afterlife in the imminent future.

The room stank of blood, mana and failure. Mostly failure.

Then, three shapes crashed against the wall next to Lowe. "I'm going to fucking kill him," Hel hissed, her sisters - free of their bulky clothing - screaming their agreement. Lowe did his best to keep his eyes off the writhing, sinuous forms of the two Wraiths.

That way, literal madness lay.

"I've turned off the Portal Stone, so the bastard's going nowhere," Latham chuntered, "but unless anyone gives me an update as to what the fuck is happening, I'm going to switch it back on and go for my tea break. This has been a fucking shitshow."

Lowe tried to still his racing heart. He didn't know if it was better that Cenorth's escape route was blocked or not. The man still had Arebella, after all, but then again, he wasn't getting her back without Latham's help—time to spill.

"Okay, so this is how I figure it went down . . . "

***

"Shut the fuck up!"

Cenorth viciously shook the small woman he had by the hair while trying, unsuccessfully, to get the Portal Stone to activate.

It wasn't supposed to happen like this.

Of course, he'd long planned out his steps if it all went to shit, but you never woke up and thought, 'Today's the day my life changes forever', did you?

He cursed as Arebella reached back and clawed at his arms, her nails digging into his skin. Cenorth released his grip on her hair and span her round to face him, squeezing her face between his hand as he lifted her a foot off the ground. "Listen, I'm having a bad day. Believe me when I say that if you keep this up, I will kill you. Now, tell me. Is what I'm saying the truth?"

Wide-eyed, she nodded back.

"Good." He spun her back around, trying to hide as much of his body behind her as possible. No one had yet come through the door at the other end of the corridor, but he doubted he'd wiped everyone in there with a few panicked strikes. He'd never been that lucky. Witness this fucking Portal Stone malfunctioning at just the wrong moment.

Fucking hell.

What made this shambles worse was that it had all been working like a dream. He hadn't believed it when Arebella and Lowe had appeared at his office door this morning outlining their fucking ridiculous plan to beard Arkola in their own den under the eyes of Leoto Bright! Cenorth couldn't have predicted that outcome even in his wildest fever dreams. Of course he'd given them all the information they needed to go down that particular road to destruction. It was such good news, it almost made up for Lowe slapping a fucking Red Notice on Markian Ulton.

Almost.

The whole point in reactivating Jana Lowe to investigate the death of Gianna d'Avec was that no one - literally no one - wanted that case solved. It had been a

213

running sore for Cenorth that his foolproof plan to remove the High Priestess - frame her for the slaughter of the families of an infamously effective Out of Bounds Squad - had never come to fruition. Those who ensured a steady stream of gold into his account had expressed their disappointment at her continued existence, but it hadn't been deemed a . . . fatal failure. He understood that Gravalk having access to the Second Floor might have changed that, but . . . well, with her death, he hadn't had to worry about that anymore, did he?

But then someone had actually managed to off her, and no one wanted anyone looking too hard at who had ripped that fucking bitch apart. But it would have looked suspect if they hadn't at least done a cursory investigation, and that's where Jana bloody Lowe came in.

Cenorth had argued to keep him alive after the shambles that led to his loss of Class last year for precisely this reason.

Sometimes, you need a useful idiot. Just in case.

The plan had formed in his head the moment he caught wind of the murder. Even as the body was cooling, Cenorth had lured one of those fucking Wraiths the Wind Tyrant thought she'd kept so carefully hidden to the Temple, nicked one of their gloves and left it somewhere even Lowe couldn't miss. He'd been looking at her head hanging from the chandelier as he activated the Sending Stone to wake the Classless man.

And it had, largely, gone as he'd expected. Right up to the moment, it hadn't. Cenorth still wasn't sure what had happened to have had Lowe pivot to suspecting him rather than revealing the existence of the Wraith's glove, but that was water under the bridge. For now, he needed to get out of here and then out of Soar.

And for that, he needed the Portal Stone to work.

"Okay," he said, pressing his mouth against Arebella's ear, "let's see how motivated your boyfriend is to negotiate."

***

Hel's fury ramped up as Lowe explained to Latham just how much of a colossal fool she had been.

At no stage had she ever questioned the veracity of what Commander Cenorth had told her about Gianna d'Avec's involvement in the death of her parents. He had been so manifestly conflicted about sharing the 'highly confidential' Council report with her. Hel had needed to work so hard - and over so long - to convince him it was the right thing to do. And he had been so horrified about the contents when he'd shared them with her.

It had never entered her head for a moment that he was playing her.

But that was always the case with the best of cons. The mark never even knew they were in a game. Cenorth had tried to use them to kill the High Priestess for him. For 'them'. Whatever. It didn't matter. She was going to kill them all.

Latham was nodding along to Lowe's explanation of the series of events that led them to be standing at the wrong end of a corridor, surrounded by casualties. The big man was keeping his face studiously neutral, but Hel could feel his judgement of her naivete.

Dammit, she was judging herself just as hard.

Latham's face had the bland indifference of a professional hearing how badly someone he had thought competent had fucked up.

"Are you sure he can't escape?" she asked, trying to focus on the matter at hand.

Latham shook his head. "No chance. Since the High Priestess's murder, this Floor has been effectively on lockdown. Even if he had previously had access, and we can obviously assume he did, it'll be locked for him now. Chances are, he'll have realised that by now. He's going to need someone to open it for him.

"And we're not going to do that, are we?"

Lowe and Latham's grim expressions were the only answer she needed.

"Hello? Is there anyone in there still alive?" Cenorth's voice echoed down the corridor.

Lowe peeked his head around the doorframe, and Hel summoned an *Air Shield to* drift in front of his face. She wasn't sure it would do much if a Sentinel of Justice truly wanted to blow a hole in Lowe's head, but it would give him a fighting chance to at least duck.

"Sorry, are we not supposed to be okay, boss? Because that was some weak ass shit you threw out there. I have to say I'm a bit disappointed: I always thought you had more game than that. The stories the boys tell about your performance in the field made me think you were quite the baller. "

"Tell that to Markian!" Cenorth snapped back.

"Tell him yourself, mate. Although he's pretty pissed off with you at the moment, so he might not be too receptive to a chat. I've got to tell you, we're hearing about all sorts of mischief the two of you have got up to together over the years."

Cenorth blinked at that.

He couldn't see how Ulton could possibly have survived a *Sword of Justice* cleaving through his head. But, then again, Earth Mages were famously hardy . . . Shit! Had he left that man alive? Those he worked for would not find that acceptable. Particularly with a Red Notice running and Cenorth no longer in place to 'lose' the data being gleaned . . .

He needed to clean that up if he wanted them to help him vanish.

"Tell you what," he said, keeping his voice level. "I'm feeling generous. Why don't I make you a deal? You send Markian out and switch this Portal Stone back on, and I will let you have the delightful Ms. Telut in, more or less, one piece. I can't say fairer than that, can I?"

"I don't know, boss. Ulton seems pretty unhappy with that idea. He appears to think you might kill him as soon as look at him. Not sure any of us back here want that on our conscience, to tell the truth."

"Well, I think you need to ask yourself this, Jana. Are you so committed to the pursuit of peace, justice and the Soar way that you are willing to have me throw chunks of Arebella back to you until you agree? Because that seems pretty pointless. Unlike my knife."

The Temple Warder's voice boomed in reply. "Commander Cenorth, as you will be requiring me to open the Portal for you, I might suggest you keep a civil tongue in your head. Mr. Lowe might be manipulatable with threats, but trust me, carving my initials into your colon feels much more attractive to me than letting you go. And you can ask Arebella to fact-check that for you."

Cenorth summoned a knife into his hand and ran it down Arebella's arm, causing blood to spurt to the floor. The Veritas Assessor tried to stifle her gasp, but Cenorth slashed again and again until she finally screamed.

"How long do we wish to continue this charade? Or, more importantly, how long do you wish me to continue to hurt Arebella? I like the girl, so this is pissing me off even more. Ironically, the only person I have to take it out on is her. Which is putting me in somewhat of a rage loop. But you can make this problem disappear: send Markian out and switch the stone back on. I haven't got anything else to add."

Silence greeted his ultimatum.

CHAPTER 52 – TWO GOBLINS IN A TRENCHCOAT

"What the fuck are you doing saying that? Markian's dead! We don't have anyone to offer in trade!"

Hel's frustration did little for the mood of her sisters, who were literally shimmering with barely restrained rage. Lowe thought it was a testament to their love for Hel that they hadn't just hulked out and eaten them all the moment the blades started flying. It also probably had something to do with a hero of an Empath Nullifier who, despite his own traumatic head wound, was maintaining the thickest of layers of *Calm* over the two monsters.

Mostly likely a little from Column A and a little from Column B, thought Lowe.

Latham looked at him and shrugged. "She has a point, little man. And I can't see it de-escalating this situation for us now to say, 'erm, sorry about that. Turns out the man you want is dead after all. Can we offer a smile and hand job instead?'"

Lowe risked another look around the corner of the door. All he could make out was a long, thin corridor - with no apparent options for cover - at the end of which was a clearly terrified Arebella, behind who was crouched the figure of Cenorth. "I don't suppose either of you is hoarding a secret Skill to take him out at this range without endangering Arebella?"

Hel and Latham shook their heads, the Wind Tyrant adding, "Not against someone of his Level and Class. If we were to rush him, I could probably deflect some of whatever crap he throws our way off us, but he'd have plenty of time to . . . well, to do whatever he wanted to her before bodying us."

Latham agreed. "I can take him if I can get close enough. I just don't see your girl surviving me running up there."

Lowe withdrew his head and looked back at the carnage in the room behind him. Those that could be stabilised had been, but the Senior Recorder hadn't made it. Lowe shuddered to think how much his estate would be billing the Mayor for that little mishap - but the rest of the group would pull through.

More or less. The headless corpse of Markian Ulton lay in a pool of blood next to the dead Constables, his body wrapped in thick chains. At least a Deathcaller was on hand to ensure this was all reported accurately.

Then, despite the morbid scene, a smile suddenly blossomed on Lowe's face. Apparently, all those Progress Points had been good for something, after all.

"It looks like you might have a plan, little man . . ."

"Maybe," Lowe replied. "Let's just say I think we'll need to play a little game of "Two Goblins in a Trenchcoat.""

***

Cenorth was getting antsy.

He hadn't been lying to Lowe when he'd said the Council had sent all manner of representations to Cuckoo House. As soon as the chaos at the Celestial Temple had been reported, the shit had well and truly hit the fan.

So much for Leoto Bright and his reputation for keeping things 'subtle' and 'in the shadows.' Cenorth gave a little tight smile at realising he wouldn't be the only one being hauled over the coals for today's succession of fuckups.

But, as soon as the grin appeared, it faded, and a snarl returned to his face. Time was running out if he wanted the opportunity to make it out alive.

"I'm getting bored here, Jana. Tell you what, to speed things up a touch, I'm going to count to three, and then Arebella loses a finger. Then, it'll be a finger every count of five until I run out, and I need to get more creative. You don't want me to get more creative."

There was no response from the other end of the hallway.

"Fine. Be like that. One. Two. Thr . . . "

A figure appeared in the doorway. Markian Ulton, blood covering his face, staggering forward under the weight of his chains. Fucking hell! Lowe hadn't been lying. The Earth Mage had survived a *Sword of Justice* to the head? That was pretty impressive. He'd have to be more thorough next time.

Markian took a few staggering steps forward and then stopped. Lowe stepped out from behind him to the one side, the Wind Tyrant taking up a similar position on the other.

"Fine. Let's trade, boss. You send Arebella down, and I'll send him up."

Cenorth shook his head. "No. That's not how this is going to work, Jana. You send me Markian, get your pet Temple Warder to activate the Portal Stone, and *then* I'll release the girl to you."

Lowe mirrored his dissent. "No can do. I'm not being funny here, boss, but you're not overburdened with credit on the 'honesty' front with me right now. This is the only card I have to play, and I'll be damned if I show you mine before you show me yours."

Cenorth growled in frustration. He hadn't got the time to waste bandying words here. "Fine. Be like that. Is there a particular finger you're not attached to?" He reached down and roughly pulled up Arebella's hand, pressing his knife into her palm. "Or, more to the point, that she's about not to be?"

"No need for that, boss. Look, how about this? On my word of honour, I promise this trade will happen. You send Arebella down, and I'll send your prize back up. None of us at this end will do anything to interfere. Get Arebella to confirm I'm telling the truth if you're worried."

Cenorth paused, grinding his teeth. In an ideal world, he'd like to slip out of here without any further bloodshed. He wasn't a psychopath, and he had no interest in torturing a girl he'd always quite liked. It wasn't her fault she'd ended up in the wrong place at the wrong time.

"Look at me," he ordered Arebella, pulling her head around to face him. "Is he lying?"

Arebella's eyes shimmered gold as she accessed her Skill. Trying not to look at the knife Cenorth was holding against her hand, she nodded. "He is."

"So, to confirm - " Cenorth called back down to the corridor, his gaze fixed on Arebella's eyes to ensure she kept her Skill active - "they'll both walk down the corridor simultaneously. You'll ensure the Portal Stone activates so I can get away, and neither you, your Temple Warder friend, nor that gullible bitch with the wind power tries to do anything to stop me. Straight swap, and then I'm off. Right?"

"Fuck you!" Hel shouted back, summoning a *Tempest* to swirl above her.

"No, thank you. If I were remotely interested, I'd have taken advantage of all the times you threw yourself at me to try to get hold of the file I was so anxious to keep confidential. So, so, so anxious. Look, Lowe, I'm getting old here, and I'm not hearing any agreement to my terms. Do I need to start cutting?"

"I agree with everything you say, boss. We swap them over, the portal opens, and none of the three of us will do a thing to stop you. I promise."

Cenorth watched Arebella's irises flair, and she nodded. "He's telling the truth."

"Well, it seems like it's your lucky day: matey boy cares more about you than he does catching the bad guy. Good for him." Cenorth gestured for Arebella to start walking back towards d'Avec's throne room. "Slowly now. No running. I can kill you just as easily at that end of the corridor as I can here."

Holding her chin high, Arebella started walking slowly but purposefully towards Lowe. The shambling figure of Markian Ulton did the same; the chains in which his body was wrapped made it difficult for him to do much more than awkwardly shuffle forwards.

Despite the pain and the blood dripping from her arms and the tears in her eyes, she beamed at Lowe, conscious as to how his eyes were glued on her, his expression haunted.

It wasn't too long before the two hostages crossed each other, at which stage Arebella felt a strange sensation, like a cold breeze, ripple across her skin. Nevertheless, she did her best to keep looking forward, not wanting to give Cenorth any excuse for making good on his threat.

***

At the far end of the hallway, Cenorth gestured impatiently for his co-conspirator to move a bit faster. "Come on, come on. We've got to go!" But in response, Markian just continued to stare straight ahead, his feet plodding ponderously forward. "Open the Portal now!"

The giant figure of Latham lumbered up behind Lowe and raised a glowing hand. Cenorth felt the Stone behind him turn from red to green, and he felt himself begin to relax. For the briefest of moments, he considered opening up with a barrage of *Blades of Prosecution* and simply cutting down everyone at that end of the hallway . . .

But no. It didn't do to get a reputation for being profligate. His backers had Leoto Bright for that sort of work. And then the moment was over, Arebella reached the far end of the corridor, Latham and Hel quickly pulled her back into safety in d'Avec's chamber.

Lowe, though, just stood there. Watching him.

Frowning, Cenorth beckoned towards Markian to hurry up, then stepped forward to grab him by the arm and drag him through the Portal Stone.

However, as he took hold of the sleeve of that man's expensive robe, two notable things happened.

Firstly, Markian's head fell off.

219

Cenorth gawped as he felt the threads of wind that had been ensuring it floated just above the thick wrappings of chains collapse into nothingness.

Secondly, and this was an equally surprising turn of events for Commander Cenorth, the chains around what he had assumed was Markian's body fell away to release two very angry, very frustrated, very motivated Wraiths.

Ignoring the shrieks and screams, Lowe watched his former friend's evisceration without blinking.

Some things needed to be witnessed.

<u>EPILOGUE</u>

Unsurprisingly, the fallout from the events on the Third Floor of the Celestial Temple had been pretty seismic.

After all, it wasn't every day that a Commander of the Security Services selflessly sacrificed himself to protect innocent members of the public from the predation of rampaging Wraiths. On reflection, all involved recognised that headline could have used some sub-editing.

Nevertheless, the story of Cenorth's doomed noble stand against two horrific monsters - holding the Portal Stone open so others could escape, even as the Constables at his side were cut down and slain - was surely destined to go down in Soar legend.

And it was not just the deaths of Commander Cenorth and his fellow officers that were to be mourned. No. Not at all. On top of that appalling tragedy, it also had become known that the renowned philanthropist Markian Ulton had also perished to those fiends, leaving a gaping hole in the social calendar of Jewel Town, the likes of which had never been seen before. At least, not that week. And horror upon horror, Cadi Verahalim, lawyer to the rich and famous, would likewise see the morrow no more.

Stop all the clocks, etc etc.

If anyone had questions as to why such an eclectic collection of people had been gathered together at the scene of another high-profile murder, then they were sensible enough to hold their tongues.

There were cover-ups, and then there were Soar cover-ups. And enough people had lost their lives during the d'Avec investigation for there to be somewhat of an interest fatigue.

Lowe wished that surprised him. He wished for a lot of things.

"You okay, little man?"

Lowe looked up over the rim of his cup of coffee at the concerned face of Latham. The Temple Warder had done as much as any of them to try to leak the true story of what had happened that day on the Third Floor, but you couldn't sell what no one was buying.

There was a rumour that Arkola themselves had had 'a quiet word' to get him to drop it, but Lowe hadn't had the heart to ask him about it, and Latham wasn't sharing.

"Sure. Fine and dandy. You?"

Latham shrugged. "Same old, same old. How's your girl holding up?"

That did bring a genuine smile to Lowe's face. Because, at least for now, Arebella was very much 'his girl'. Nursing her back to health after what had happened had seemed the very least he could do. Of course, for him to keep up a regular stream of applications of *Medic!,* he had insisted that she move in with him. And once she'd

221

tasted Mylaf's food, he didn't think he was ever going to get rid of her. Also, fun fact: you could do all sorts of athletic things, even with some rather nasty injuries.

"She's good, thank you. How about yours?"

Latham blushed. A rather odd thing to see appear on his massive, blunt face. "All good. But we're taking it slow. I think Hel's going to have some significant trust issues for the near future."

Lowe nodded. That sounded like a bit of an understatement. "And erm, her family? They're all okay?"

"They're fine. If anyone asks, they're taking an extended tour of the countryside alongside some friends of hers. You know. Just until the heat dies down a bit."

That seemed sensible. If there was one thing an Out of Bounds squad - even a retired one - was good at, it was going missing until those looking for them lost interest. Lowe was sure they'd be back.

Especially as no one showed any interest in uncovering what had really happened in the Celestial Temple.

"Shut the fuck up and listen to me. This is the Council's final offer," Acting Commander Pernille Staffen had said, dark shadows under her eyes suggesting she wasn't loving the promotion yet, "you get to come back on full pay, a backdated pension, corner office and a fucking partridge in a pear tree. It's a moonshot, Jana. There's never been a Classless Inspector in the history of Cuckoo House. You need to bite their hands off. I can't get any more from them for you."

"But?" Lowe had asked, already knowing the rotting tooth in this particular gift horse's mouth.

"But they don't want to hear another word about Gianna fucking d'Avec. As far as that is concerned, the case is closed. Wraiths in the city and all that."

He'd wanted to tell her where to stick it. That, until he was satisfied that he knew what had happened in the High Priestess's chamber, there wasn't any bribe in the world that would stick.

But then he remembered the look on Arebella's face as she'd walked down that corridor towards him, blood oozing from the wounds from Cenorth's knife, and he'd decided to get over himself.

For once, he could let sleeping dogs lie.

"Are you sure you don't want me to come with you?" Latham asked. "You might need backup? For old time's sake?"

Okay, so that homily about the slumbering canines might have been the sweatiest of bollocks.

Lowe stood, brushing crumbs off his best, Mylaf-ironed suit and flashed Latham a smile. "Thanks for the offer, mate. But I've got this."

***

Aintra Weber paused at the junction of Beldam and Caprice and took a deep, cleansing breath.

Life had been extremely busy of late.

For most of those in Gravalk's cult, the inevitable drop down the Temple hierarchy that had accompanied losing their High Priestess had been humiliating. But, unlike his fellows, that wasn't how he saw things.

As his father, and his grandfather, had always said 'it wasn't the intensity of the flame that mattered. It was how long it burned.'

And the Coal Stirrer intended to keep burning for a long time yet, thank you very much.

He was just preparing to cross the street and make his way towards the Fountain of Youth when a shadow fell over his path. Looking up, he saw the solemn face of the last man he expected to see in the Quarter of Ash.

"Mr. Lowe. What brings you all the way out here?"

Lowe gave a tight little smile. "It's Inspector Lowe."

"Ah, then your heroics in the Temple have not gone unrewarded? I am very pleased to hear it. I sang your praises in my debrief, I'll have you know."

"I rather think my reinstatement has more to do with political expediency than any recognition of 'heroics', but thank you very much, all the same. Do you have a moment, sir?"

Aintra looked up and down the street, unsure what was expected of him. "I do. Until a new High Priest - or High Priestess, of course - is named, I doubt anyone will look askance at me being a little late. What is it you wanted to talk about?"

"I know you killed her."

The statement was so unexpected that the Coal Stirrer found himself laughing in genuine surprise. "You know what?"

"Gianna d'Avec. It was you who killed her."

Aintra ran his tongue across his lips and frowned. "I think that joke is in very poor taste, Mr. Lowe."

"Inspector."

"Yes, of course. You said. In any event, that is not something you should jest about. The Cult of Gravalk is still in mourning for the loss of our great leader. It hardly seems appropriate for you to accost me in the street and make light of that fact."

"I'm not making light of it." Lowe dipped a hand into his pocket and withdrew a bulky black glove. "This was hidden in the cupboard under your stairs."

"The cupboard under my . . . What were you doing in my house? You had no right to break in and remove my property!"

"Ah, that's a shame. You were doing so well. You were hitting just the right note of confused, injured injustice. But that's your first mistake, right there. I think you will find that the correct response would have been, 'I've never seen that before in my life.'"

Aintra stepped back, trying to get some distance between them. Trying to think. "I haven't seen it before. What is it? A glove? I must have hundreds of gloves."

"Come on, Mr. Weber. You need to be quicker than this. Pick a lane. You either haven't seen it before or have loads like it. Although, I should point out that if you have 'hundreds' of gloves that are carrying traces of Wraith skin cells, then you are one freaky son of a bitch."

The Coal Stirrer found himself pressing back against a wall, Lowe remorsefully pressing forward. "Let me level with you, mate. At the moment, you having this glove is the only thing you have going for you. Because it suggests that you have a conscience. That you weren't willing to have someone else take the blame for a crime you know you'd committed. I'd grab hold of that life jacket if I were you."

As Lowe spoke, Aintra was transported back to d'Avec's chamber that night. Seeing, through the open door, the first member of the Security Services on scene carefully place a glove he had taken from his pocket onto the floor near one of the High Priestess' legs. As soon as that man had left, locking up the active crime scene behind him, Weber had swooped back in - utilising his *Secret Keeper* Skill to get access to the chamber - and retrieved the evidence.

"How did you find out?"

"Ah, that's better. I'm always more comfortable once we move out of the Denial stage of proceedings. Full disclosure, though, if you get to Anger and feel the need to lash out, I'm going to kick your arse. I've got some frustrations that need to be worked out."

"How did you know it was me?" Aintra's voice was faint.

"Poisoning my coffee. That was just fucking stupid."

"Your coffee?"

"Yeah. And there's a dead Junior Server I'm adding to your side of the ledger, too. It's one thing trying to kill me - it's an occupational hazard, and more often than not, I'd overlook it - but you got that poor kid involved, and that was only going to end one way. I tend to take that sort of shit personally. Now I think of it, that probably cancels out you taking the glove."

"I am afraid, Mr. Lowe - "

"Inspector."

"- Inspector Lowe that you are not making any sense. First, you show me a glove you have illegally obtained from my house and suggest this is evidence of my guilt. Then you segue into some nonsense about poisoning your coffee. I must confess, I have no idea where you are going with this. What is it you are accusing me of?"

"Fair enough. Let's make it plain then, shall we? Unfortunately for you, the proprietor of 'Drink U Like' who - would you believe it, is selling a very different product than coffee - has been experiencing a number of robberies of late. I know! I know! It's getting like you can't run an entirely clandestine drug business in Soar without someone trying to rip you off. Whatever next, eh? Where was I?"

"I really could not begin to tell you."

"Ah, yes. 'Drink U Like'. Well, in response to his third shakedown of the week, the owner decided to install a pretty snazzy Observation Hub in the street outside his shop. And what do you think I found on there?"

"I have absolutely no idea."

"Really? Okay, then let me tell you. On the day in question, I see me and my esteemed Temple Warder friend enter for a refreshing cup of joe and - what do you know? - just a moment later, a shady-looking motherfucker sneaks around the back and has a very animated conversation with a poor Junior Server, after which a small packet is handed over and said shady dude slinks off. And do you know what?"

"What?" Aintra said faintly.

"That was actually your big mistake. Because if you'd hung around for just a few more moments, to actually watch the deed being done, you'd have seen the poor lad throw the empty packet you'd given him in the recycling bin. Good habits die hard, apparently."

"And I suppose you have retrieved that packet?"

"Of course. Complete with all sorts of fingerprint goodies. Well, not me, obviously. But Soar's Deathcaller - a complete wanker, but pretty good at his job when all is said and done - has it, and he has lots of interesting things to say. Did you know, for example, that there are certain types of seaweed . . . no, sorry. Penarth tells me I should call them *microalgae*. But that sounds rather poncy. But hey, whatever they are, if you mix them with certain other substances, they are really appallingly toxic. I can testify to that. Yet another shirt down the drain. Tell me, was that something of which you were aware?"

"I am not sure it would be wise for me to answer."

"Oh dear. I hoped to get a bit further through things before we reached the 'no comment' stage of proceedings. Never mind, I'm sure I can do a monologue. Feel free to chip in when you know the words. Because it turns out you are very aware of that because, and this strikes me as some pretty specialised knowledge, Coal Stirrers are encouraged to experiment with the use of microalgae in the creation of scented candles. Your father was quite an expert in that craft, I understand? I imagine there are all sorts of samples lying around that house of yours."

"No comment."

"Ah, thought I could trick you there. No worries. As I'm sure you've guessed, I've already searched it and have quite the haul of potential murder weapons. So here I am, with a packet of pretty nasty poison, a Coal Stirrer with no motive I could think of to want me dead, a High Priestess who, literally, blew her top with a fucking seaweed candle lit in her room. Where do you think all of that should take me?"

"You can't prove anything."

"Maybe not. I'd like to know what happened, though."

Aintra sighed. A deep, weary sigh, and Lowe had the impression of a great weight being lifted from his shoulders as he spoke. "The powerful think they are better than the rest of us. Have you noticed that?" The Coal Stirrer glanced up at Lowe's Classless state and nodded to himself. "I'm sure you have—more than the rest of us. Once upon a time, we were the same level, Gianna and I. Did you know that? We entered the Temple at exactly the same time. Of course, there was no question that she was destined to be the star. And I was more than content to serve. But then she didn't want me anymore."

"You killed her because she fired you?"

"I killed her because she discarded me. A woman who never threw a thing away in her life. Who lived in a rundown house, who employed her parents' Drudge, who gave away every penny she earned to the 'poor'. But when it came to me, the person who knew her best, the person who had sacrificed his own ambitions for her? Well, for me it was 'thank you and goodbye'. 'You've been found wanting.' Damn right, I killed her."

Lowe rolled his shoulders, trying to ease the tension he could feel building.

"You poisoned her?"

"Seaweed is an amazing thing, you know? With the right encouragement and skill set, microalgae induces oxygen depletion and then releases toxic compounds. My father was quite an expert at magnifying that effect. I lit one of his candles for her after she dismissed me and watched as she slowly drifted off into a peaceful sleep. All that power, all that belligerence, and she had no protection to simple smoke. I doubt she even felt the moment when her mana transformed into water. It strikes me there are worse ways to go."

Lowe looked at the old man, trying not to let the disappointment on his face show. After everything that had happened, he had hoped for something . . . more. For the murder that had started so many tumultuous events to have been more noteworthy than petty revenge.

"And you specifically asked for me when you found the body because?"

"You hardly have a sterling reputation, Inspector Lowe. And I'm sure there's no way you can prove it," Weber said, the colour returning to his cheeks.

"No," Lowe sighed. "I suppose not. Tell you what, I'll just stop being an 'Inspector' momentarily and go back to being plain old Jana Lowe." As he spoke, he took his other hand out of his pocket to show Aintra a burning incense stick. "And Mr. Lowe knows one thing for certain."

Aintra frowned at the incense stick. "Which is?"

Lowe smiled. "That your god is sounding pretty pissed off about the whole thing right now . . ."

The Coal Stirrer's eyes widened in the moment before Gravalk's fire took him. He burned for far longer than Lowe would have thought it was possible for a human being to be alight.

Eventually, though, Aintra Weber collapsed into ash, and the breeze swept up his remains, leaving Lowe standing in quiet contemplation.

For a fanciful moment, he wondered whether Gianna d'Avec would rest a little easier now her murderer had been brought to . . . well, not justice, but something justice adjacent. But what did such things matter once you were dead? When you were sleeping the big sleep, he assumed you were not too bothered by things like that.

He guessed it was just the way things were in Soar.

With a nod of his head, watching specks of Aintra float in the air, Jana Lowe began the walk home.

***

Inspector Lowe will return in Death of a Curator is Missing'.

THANK YOU

I hope you have all enjoyed this first instalment of my Soar Chronicles.

I have always had a fascination with all things to do with hardboiled detective fiction – in particular, the works of Raymond Chandler and Dashiell Hammett. Across this trilogy I wanted to see what would happen if we took that energy and put it into a LitRPG universe. On Royal Road, someone described this as Grimdark Discworld and I think I just nearly died and went to heaven.

A huge thank you to everyone at Legion Publishers for helping to bring this series into existence. I could not have found a more secure place for my work. If Jana has Latham having his back, then I have you guys.

Hopefully, there's plenty more where this comes from.

Cheers,

Malory

27/3/2025

DEATH OF A CURATOR

Book 2 Soar Chronicles

By Malory

When a series of gruesome murders at the Soar Museum leaves victims dissolved into necrotic slime, Lowe is the man on the spot.

In the shadow-drenched alleys of Soar, Inspector Jana Lowe is walking a treacherous line. His badge restored but his Class still stripped, he's a man with precious little to lose and a desire to reclaim his former glory.

Delving into the city's underbelly, Lowe confronts Grackle Nuroon over a conspiracy with more twists than the labyrinthine Dungeons lurking beneath their feet. With each clue uncovered, Lowe begins unlocking Skills the Council would rather remain buried.

But progression comes at a price. As godly forces transform parts of the city into a Dungeon, Lowe must navigate deadly traps, battle monstrous entities, and outwit adversaries who are not at all what they seem. With his Level steadily rising, the stakes raise even higher. Can Lowe grind his way?

Because remember; in Soar, the past isn't just a memory—it's the endgame boss

Coming Soon!

JOURNEY TO THE DARK TOWER

By Malory

Nothing ruins your day like a quest with a ransom note.

Especially when you're a fake wizard with real problems.
I was supposed to be dead. Instead, I'm stumbling through medieval Britain
with Merlin's ghost backseat-driving my magical education.
And now? Princess Guinevere's gone missing, and everyone's looking at me like
I'm supposed to know what to do about it.

Fantastic.

Nothing says "qualified wizard" like leading a rescue party of misfits—a prince
with anger issues, a berserker who thinks diplomacy means hitting people slightly
less hard, and me, still trying to figure out which end of my sword shoots fire.

Between dodging Saxon war parties, navigating the Enchanted Forest, and
searching for a Dark Tower that's playing hard to get, I'm starting to think death
might have been the easier option.

**Welcome to the Dark Tower, where the quests are impossible, the magic
is unreliable, and historical accuracy is someone else's problem.**

Order Now!

RISE OF MANKIND 6 : AGE OF GLASS

By Jez Cajiao

The Age of Glass dawns, a fragile era balanced on the edge of oblivion. Will it shatter beneath the relentless hammer of fate?

From the depths of despair to the pinnacle of power, Matt's ascension to Dungeon Lord has been a crucible of blood and terror. But the higher he climbs, the more precarious his perch becomes. As winter's icy fingers close around his hard-won domain, Matt and his beleaguered allies yearn for respite. Instead, they face a nightmare beyond imagining.
The Coronaught infection sweeps through the land like wildfire, twisting human flesh into abominations that defy sanity. Grotesque mutations stalk the shadows, their hunger insatiable. In this maelstrom of horror, Matt must be more than a leader – he must become a legend.

With each agonizing decision, the weight of command threatens to crush his spirit. Can he salvage the humanity of the infected, or will the price of compassion be too steep? Nuclear fire looms on the horizon, a cleansing inferno that promises annihilation. How much of his soul will Matt sacrifice to shield his people from the coming storm?

In the bowels of the earth, Matt labors to transform his dungeon into an impregnable fortress. But in a world where loyalty shatters like spun sugar, yesterday's allies may become tomorrow's executioners. Survival exacts a terrible toll, paid in blood and betrayal.

Step carefully into the Age of Glass, where every triumph balances on a knife's edge, and a single misstep can leave you bleeding in the dark.

Preorder Now!

<u>THEFT OF DECKS</u>

By Lars Machmuller

When the deck is stacked against you? Change the game!

In the frontier town of Isarn, Chase will never be more than the lowly Darkborn thief he is. Banned from training, banned from acquiring better cards, if the Lightborn had their way, he'd be banned from life itself.

He's not alone though, and the one thing he and his friends have is determination. Losing a hand to a brutal punishment only fueled his obsession to get access to his own amazing, reality-bending cards.

That is the path to power and a future for them all. Nobody cares where you came from when you're rich enough. For now, though, they're facing both established powers, churches and age-old prejudices. It's time to get to work, and if the Lightborn won't share and play nice?

Sometimes the only way to get dealt a better hand is to steal the whole damn deck!

<u>Buy on Amazon</u>

<u>QUEST ACADEMY</u>

By Brian J. Nordon

A world infested by demons.
An Academy designed to train Heroes to save humanity from annihilation.
A new student's power could make all the difference.

Humans have been pushed to the brink of extinction by an ever-evolving demonic threat. Portals are opening faster than ever, Towers bursting into the skies and Dungeons being mined below the last safe havens of society. The demons are winning.

Quest Academy stands defiantly against them, as a place to train the next generation of Heroes. The Guild Association is holding the line, but are in dire need of new blood and the powerful abilities they could bring to the battlefront. To be the saviors that humanity needs, they need to surpass the limits of those that came before them.

In a war with everything on the line, every power matters. With an adaptive enemy, comes the need for a constant shift in tactics. A new age of strategy is emerging, with even the unlikeliest of Heroes making an impact.

Salvatore Argento has never seen a demon.
He has never aspired to become a Hero.
Yet his power might be the one to tip the odds in humanity's favor.

<u>Buy on Amazon</u>

WANDERING WARRIOR

By Michael Head

A divine quest to deliver justice.
One year to accomplish his mission.
After nineteen planets, there's something different about this one.

James Holden has reached the maximum level there is for a human. That's perfect, since he's the only one of his kind. A wandering warrior, without control of his destination, tossed between universes by gods who've failed to tell him why. James is the lone Judge on a new world in need of someone to balance the scales. He isn't afraid to do so with extreme prejudice. As the Chief Justice, he has to right the wrongs the innocent can't fix themselves.

As James quickly discovers, the roots of corruption run deep. Guilds choose to protect themselves rather than the people. Monsters roam the wilderness unchecked. Judgment is usually a decision between right and wrong, but nothing is ever that simple. This time, being the strongest human won't be enough to punish the guilty. James might have to recruit some new blood, even if he prefers to work alone.

On his twentieth world, he is going to win, no matter the cost. James will have to find a way to break past the limits of the system if he's going to have a chance at making a difference.

Buy on Amazon

KNIGHTS OF ETERNITY

By Rachel Ní Chuirc

When Zara awoke in chains she thought she'd gone mad.

She was Zara the Fury - mistress of flame and fear. Her name was whispered across the land, from ramshackle taverns to the royal court. Even the heroic Gilded Knights thought twice before crossing her path.
She was feared—*respected.*
Now she was curled up on a dirt floor on her fiancé's orders. Valerius, leader of the Gilded, mocks her cries for help. And the kingdom is on the brink of war over the missing Lady Eternity…
But that wasn't why Zara thought she had gone mad.
The reason why is that the last thing she remembered was blood, an arcade screen, and the gun that changed everything.

But no chains can hold the Fury, and when she gets out?
The world is going to *burn.*

<u>Buy on Amazon</u>

SCARLET CITADEL

By Jack Fields

Gormon Hughes is 19, thin as a broom, and has—not for the first time in his life—been swept into the path of trouble. Poor, recently heartbroken, and indebted to the sort of people who file their teeth into needle points and devour wriggling bloated spiders for fun, Hughes sets his sights on salvation.

That salvation is the Scarlet Citadel, a wealthy organization of pageant fighters, monster hunters, and secret keepers. With the aid of strange oracles, rare good fortune, and a unique power that bubbles like champagne in the core of Hughes' being, he must join the Citadel and advance himself.

But the ladder of progression is harsh and dark. The rungs are slippery.

And falling means disaster…

Buy on Amazon

<u>LITRPG!</u>

To learn more about LitRPG, talk to other authors including myself, and to just have an awesome time, please join the LitRPG Group

<u>www.facebook.com/groups/LitRPGGroup</u>

FACEBOOK

There's also a few really active Facebook groups I'd recommend you join, as you'll get to hear about great new books, new releases and interact with all your (new) favorite authors! (I may also be there, skulking at the back and enjoying the memes…)

https://www.facebook.com/groups/LitRPGlegion/

https://www.facebook.com/groups/GamelitSociety

https://www.facebook.com/groups/LitRPG.books

https://www.facebook.com/groups/LitRPGforum/

MALORY